IMPLACABLE

THE LOST FLEET ◇ OUTLANDS

Ace Books by Jack Campbell

The Lost Fleet

DAUNTLESS
FEARLESS
COURAGEOUS
VALIANT
RELENTLESS
VICTORIOUS

The Lost Fleet: Beyond the Frontier

DREADNAUGHT
INVINCIBLE
GUARDIAN
STEADFAST
LEVIATHAN

The Lost Fleet: Outlands

BOUNDLESS
RESOLUTE
IMPLACABLE

The Lost Stars

TARNISHED KNIGHT
PERILOUS SHIELD
IMPERFECT SWORD
SHATTERED SPEAR

The Genesis Fleet

VANGUARD
ASCENDANT
TRIUMPHANT

Written as John G. Hemry

Stark's War

STARK'S WAR
STARK'S COMMAND
STARK'S CRUSADE

Paul Sinclair

A JUST DETERMINATION
BURDEN OF PROOF
RULE OF EVIDENCE
AGAINST ALL ENEMIES

IMPLACABLE

THE LOST FLEET ◊ OUTLANDS

JACK CAMPBELL

ACE

New York

ACE
Published by Berkley
An imprint of Penguin Random House LLC
penguinrandomhouse.com

Library of Congress Cataloging-in-Publication Data

Names: Campbell, Jack (Naval officer), author.
Title: Implacable / Jack Campbell.
Description: New York: Ace, [2023] | Series: The lost fleet: Outlands
Identifiers: LCCN 2022043356 (print) | LCCN 2022043357 (ebook) |
ISBN 9780593199022 (hardcover) | ISBN 9780593199046 (ebook)
Subjects: LCGFT: Novels.
Classification: LCC PS3553.A4637 I47 2023 (print) | LCC PS3553.A4637 (ebook) |
DDC 813/.54—dc23/eng/20220928
LC record available at https://lccn.loc.gov/2022043356
LC ebook record available at https://lccn.loc.gov/2022043357

Printed in the United States of America
1st Printing

Book design by Laura K. Corless

To Simcha Kuritzky

"To be a mensch is to be supportive. To be a friend,
to be calm in troubled times. To support others."
—THE HONORABLE MICHAEL KIRBY AC CMG,
FORMER JUSTICE OF THE HIGH COURT OF AUSTRALIA

◊

For S., as always

THE FIRST FLEET OF THE ALLIANCE

ADMIRAL JOHN GEARY, COMMANDING

FIRST BATTLESHIP DIVISION
Gallant
Indomitable
Glorious
Magnificent

SECOND BATTLESHIP DIVISION
Dreadnaught
Fearless
Dependable
Conqueror

THIRD BATTLESHIP DIVISION
Warspite
Vengeance
Resolution
Guardian

FOURTH BATTLESHIP DIVISION
Colossus
Encroach
Redoubtable
Spartan

FIFTH BATTLESHIP DIVISION
Relentless
Reprisal
Superb
Splendid

FIRST BATTLE CRUISER DIVISION
Inspire
Formidable
Dragon
Steadfast

SECOND BATTLE CRUISER DIVISION
Dauntless
Daring
Victorious
Intemperate

THIRD BATTLE CRUISER DIVISION
Illustrious
Incredible
Valiant

FIFTH ASSAULT TRANSPORT DIVISION
Tsunami
Typhoon
Mistral
Haboob

FIRST AUXILIARIES DIVISION
Titan
Tanuki
Kupua
Domovoi

SECOND AUXILIARIES DIVISION
Witch
Jinn
Alchemist
Cyclops

TWENTY-SIX HEAVY CRUISERS IN FIVE DIVISIONS

First Heavy Cruiser Division
Fourth Heavy Cruiser Division
Eighth Heavy Cruiser Division

Third Heavy Cruiser Division
Fifth Heavy Cruiser Division

FIFTY-ONE LIGHT CRUISERS IN TEN SQUADRONS

First Light Cruiser Squadron
Third Light Cruiser Squadron
Sixth Light Cruiser Squadron
Ninth Light Cruiser Squadron
Eleventh Light Cruiser Squadron

Second Light Cruiser Squadron
Fifth Light Cruiser Squadron
Eighth Light Cruiser Squadron
Tenth Light Cruiser Squadron
Fourteenth Light Cruiser Squadron

ONE HUNDRED FORTY-ONE DESTROYERS IN EIGHTEEN SQUADRONS

First Destroyer Squadron
Third Destroyer Squadron
Sixth Destroyer Squadron
Ninth Destroyer Squadron
Twelfth Destroyer Squadron
Sixteenth Destroyer Squadron
Twentieth Destroyer Squadron
Twenty-third Destroyer Squadron
Twenty-eighth Destroyer Squadron

Second Destroyer Squadron
Fourth Destroyer Squadron
Seventh Destroyer Squadron
Tenth Destroyer Squadron
Fourteenth Destroyer Squadron
Seventeenth Destroyer Squadron
Twenty-first Destroyer Squadron
Twenty-seventh Destroyer Squadron
Thirty-second Destroyer Squadron

FIRST FLEET MARINE FORCE
Major General Carabali, commanding

3,000 Marines on assault transports and divided into detachments on battle cruisers and battleships

IMPLACABLE

THE LOST FLEET ◇ OUTLANDS

ONE

EVERYTHING had gone very smoothly for the last week.

As urgent alerts sounded throughout the Alliance battle cruiser *Dauntless*, Admiral John "Black Jack" Geary belatedly realized that should have worried him.

The Alliance fleet he commanded was, after all, orbiting in a star system controlled by an alien species, and was as far from human-controlled space as anyone had ever been. At least, as far as was known any humans had ever been. The aliens humanity called Dancers (because of the graceful maneuvers of their spacecraft) had finally provided a copy of a star chart showing how many other intelligent species the Dancers had made contact with, and the star systems they controlled. Humanity while pushing down the galactic arm had unknowingly been bumping up against space already claimed by other species. The Dancers seemed friendly, though their motives and much else about them remained unknown. But other alien species, such as the mysterious enigmas and the ruthless Kicks, had responded to human contact with murderous violence.

Which was why the Alliance had sent Geary and the fleet he commanded to escort a diplomatic mission to the Dancers. And why, even though the fleet was in a supposedly safe Dancer-controlled star system, alarms warning of danger shouldn't be a surprise.

But as Geary walked quickly onto the bridge (because seeing the admiral running could create panic in even the steadiest sailors) and dropped down into the fleet commander's seat, he still stared in disbelief for a moment before he could speak. "Syndics? Here?"

"Syndics. Here," Captain Tanya Desjani confirmed. She was in the ship commander's seat next to Geary's, studying her display as she sized up the new arrivals. "And they have Dancer escorts."

"The Syndics couldn't have gotten here without Dancer escorts. But why did the Dancers bring them here instead of telling them to go home? The Dancers know what Syndics are like." The Syndicate Worlds, a corporate-run human empire, had been falling apart in rebellion and revolt since finally losing a century-long war with the Alliance. The Syndics could still muster the resources of scores of star systems, but with so much of those engaged in internal warfare, the Syndicate Worlds no longer had the ability to field a fleet to match that of the Alliance.

Desjani sat back in her seat, frowning. "A half-dozen battle cruisers, ten heavy cruisers, and twenty-three Hunter-Killers. It's impressive that the Syndics managed to commit a force like that to coming here, but that's a very light force to fight your way through enigma space with. I'm surprised they made it. Maybe they took serious losses while crossing enigma-controlled star systems."

Geary shook his head, frowning as well. The enigmas, obsessed with their privacy, assaulted every human force that tried to enter space controlled by them, and had attacked human-controlled star systems as well. Most recently they had wiped out an attempt by a small group of ships from the Rift Federation to reach Dancer space without Alliance help. "I could believe serious losses, but I'm not seeing any signs of battle damage on any of the Syndic ships that made it here."

"Lieutenant Yuon?" Captain Desjani called to one of the bridge watch standers.

"Yes, Captain," Yuon responded as he studied the display before his watch station. "The fleet's sensors see some hull repairs on two of the battle cruisers, but it's the sort of work that the Syndics only do in space docks. There are no other external signs of combat damage on any of the Syndic warships."

"They got through enigma space without sustaining any combat damage? That rules out a big fight with the enigmas. How did they manage getting through unscathed with so small a force?" Geary wondered.

"Maybe they just got lucky," Desjani said. "We did inflict a lot of losses on the enigmas on our way here. It's possible at the moment the enigmas couldn't muster enough ships to deal with a Syndic force even that small."

"We have an incoming message from the Syndics, Admiral," the communications watch reported.

"Maybe they'll tell us how they did it," Geary said. Not that he was looking forward to discussions with a Syndic CEO. "Accept the message. We might as well get this over with."

The hypernet gate that the Syndic warships and their Dancer escorts had arrived at was four and a half light hours from the star, a distance of nearly five billion kilometers. That meant it had taken nearly four and a half hours for the light showing their arrival to reach Geary's fleet where it orbited near a Dancer-inhabited planet. A message sent by the Syndics when they arrived required the same amount of time to cross that immense distance. When measured against the size of space, even light itself felt slow, but at least the Syndics had sent a message almost as soon as they arrived here, rather than arrogantly waiting for the Alliance ships to acknowledge them first.

An image appeared on the bridge displays, showing a woman wearing the immaculately tailored suit of a Syndicate Worlds CEO. Her hair wasn't simply finely styled as usual, though, but looked as if it had been obsessively worked into rigidity. And the CEO's face . . .

"What's wrong with her eyes?" Captain Desjani wondered. "Is it just me that thinks something isn't right there?"

"Something's wrong, and not just with her eyes," Geary said. The eyes were too bright, held wide open, in a face drawn tight with either tension or excitement. "Is she an avatar rather than a real human?"

"It doesn't feel like an avatar," Desjani said. To hide their real appearance, the enigmas always used human-appearing avatars when communicating with humans. But humans could sense the so-called uncanny valley in such avatars, the feeling that something was fundamentally wrong with the "person" they were seeing even if they couldn't pinpoint just what that was. "And the Syndics don't use avatars. Their CEOs always want to put their faces out there."

The woman had begun speaking, her voice as tight as her expression, her words coming very quickly. "This is CEO Sara Okimoto Gardonyi of the Syndicate Worlds. We are here to negotiate exclusive deals with the ArachnoLupin species. Any interference or attempts to negotiate your own deals are forbidden and will be met with all the force at my command. You are ordered to depart this star system and ArachnoLupin-controlled space. ForthepeopleGardonyiout." The ending words, often rushed by Syndic executives who didn't really believe the phrase "for the people," were this time spoken so fast they seemed to form a single word.

Desjani gazed at her display in disbelief. "All the force at her command? She's got six battle cruisers. We've got eleven, plus twenty battleships. Why would she make a threat like that against those odds?"

"It doesn't make sense," Geary agreed. "What's wrong with her?"

"Maybe she's riding on Up patches," Desjani suggested, referring to the drugs that could keep people awake and alert for long periods, though at an eventual price. "For about a week from how quickly she was talking."

"The snakes wouldn't allow that."

Geary looked toward the back of the bridge. Kommodor Bradamont had arrived and was standing by the observer's seat, gazing in bafflement at the lingering image of the Syndic CEO. "Syndicate Worlds Internal Security?" he asked her.

"Yes, Admiral." Bradamont shook her head. "That CEO is clearly not thinking straight. The Syndicate allows some eccentricity in the highest ranks, but not something like that. The snakes aboard her flagship should have already taken her out, either temporarily or permanently. That's how the Syndicate does business."

Bradamont would know. Originally an Alliance fleet officer, she'd joined the fleet of Midway, a star system that had rebelled from the Syndicate Worlds and retained plenty of knowledge of how the Syndics worked.

But someone else aboard this ship had even better inside knowledge, borne of having survived that system on the inside. "Could you get Colonel Rogero's take on this?" Geary asked.

"Certainly, Admiral," Bradamont said. She and Rogero had both been sent along on this mission by Midway, and while Midway was technically only "associated" with the Alliance, it was in everyone's interest for the mission to do as well as possible.

Captain Desjani glanced at Geary. "Since I made an untrained medical assessment of that CEO, maybe we should ask for a trained opinion."

"We should," Geary agreed. "I'll be interested to see what Dr. Nasr thinks of her." He tapped a command to forward the message to *Dauntless*'s chief medical officer.

Colonel Rogero (formerly Executive Rogero of the Syndicate Worlds ground forces) arrived on the bridge a minute later, frowning. "Syndicate CEO protocol demands a calm demeanor and a superior attitude. I've seen CEOs on the verge of breakdowns whose behavior resembled this, because they knew it was only a matter of time before the hammer fell on them. But CEOs with that kind of short future are not tasked with missions of this nature. The Syndicate takes care to choose people they believe they can count on in command of such missions."

"Then why haven't the snakes taken her out?" Bradamont asked.

"I have no idea." Rogero shook his head. "Something this obvious should have caused the snakes aboard that ship to intervene already and remove her from command. They would arrest and execute someone on far less serious grounds than that. The sub-CEOs and executives in that Syndicate force might be reluctant to act against their CEO, but the snakes would be merciless."

An urgent tone alerted Geary to an incoming call. Seeing it was from Dr. Nasr, he accepted it immediately, causing the doctor's image to appear before him.

"The Syndic CEO's appearance is not typical. I believe I have identified the reason for this," Dr. Nasr said, plainly unhappy. "I ran a copy of the CEO's message through our diagnostic system and to my surprise the diagnosis referenced old records of early experiments on the impact of prolonged time in jump space on humans. Our medical systems say this Syndic CEO's appearance and behavior match a number of mental and emotional afflictions. Given the circumstances that she has just arrived at this star, the medical analysis systems suggest we consider what was known as Severe Jump Space Syndrome."

"The Syndics were in jump space for a prolonged time?" Geary asked, startled. Stories still circulated through the fleet about those early experiments, which had discovered in sometimes horrific ways that prolonged time in jump space had increasingly severe impacts on the human mind. Even though the much newer hypernet gates offered faster-than-light travel between stars without the discomfort and dangers of jump space, many star systems still lacked the expensive gates and could only be reached through the old-fashioned jump drives. "But the route to Dancer-controlled space only requires jumps well within human tolerance. Why would the Syndics have needed prolonged jumps to reach here?"

"I do not know, Admiral. I'm a doctor, not a fleet navigator."

"True enough," Geary said. "Captain Desjani, see if your people can figure out how the Syndics could have reached Dancer space in a way that required prolonged time in jump space. All right, Doctor, here's something you should be able to tell me. How badly does this Severe Jump Space Syndrome affect individuals? I know what horror stories say. What did the experiments show?"

"They did not show Jump Zombies or Jump Vampires or Jump Demons," Dr. Nasr said, nearly rolling his eyes at the most common of the jump monster stereotypes. "What they did show was an increase in the mental and physical discomfort that grew with every additional day in jump." He gazed over at something he was reading. "Not a linear increase. An exponential increase."

"You're talking about things like that feeling your skin doesn't fit right anymore?" Geary asked.

"Worse," Nasr replied. "Mental and emotional instability, described as detachment from a typical sense of normality. To put it another way, the test subjects showed a tendency to lose their grip on what we call reality, resulting in decisions and actions divorced from any sense of real consequences."

"I've known people like that who'd never been in jump space," Desjani said.

"Typically," Dr. Nasr added, "the syndrome impacted individuals for anywhere from one to six standard months."

"Ancestors save us," Geary said. "So what you're telling me, Doctor, is that if this is Severe Jump Space Syndrome, then that Syndic CEO we're dealing with isn't just the usual cynical, truth-challenged, and untrustworthy Syndic. They're also, for want of better words, temporarily insane."

"For one to six standard months following their latest exit from jump space," Dr. Nasr said, nodding. "The old testing never identified a way of determining why some individuals recovered sooner and others required more time. That means we cannot predict how many weeks that Syndic CEO, in particular, will require to recover."

"In particular?"

"Every Syndic on those ships would have also been exposed to jump space for a longer-than-safe period," Nasr pointed out.

"Great." Geary rubbed his face for a moment as he thought. "Give me the worst case. What were the worst outcomes of those old experiments?"

For a moment, even normally unflappable Dr. Nasr showed a flash of revulsion. "Mutilation. Murder. Cannibalism. If you wish me to send you detailed files—"

"No. Thank you. Obviously the Syndics weren't in jump space that long." Geary realized he was developing a headache. "Then and now, is there any treatment?"

Dr. Nasr shrugged. "Time. One, um, interesting discovery from the old experiments was that sedating the subject caused the syndrome to last longer. Apparently the mind has to be fully functioning and aware in order to repair the damage caused by the time in jump space."

"Wonderful. Thank you, Doctor." Geary suppressed a sigh, wondering why Ambassador Rycerz, the Alliance's primary representative for this mission, hadn't already called him demanding to know why the Syndics had sent their message to him instead of to her. But as much as he'd like to pass this problem off to the diplomatic side, it was clearly a matter falling under his responsibility for the safety of the mission.

He looked around, seeing Kommodor Bradamont huddled with Lieutenants Castries and Yuon near their watch stations, Desjani monitoring their discussion from a slight distance.

Castries ran both hands through her hair in exasperation. "It doesn't make sense. Unless . . . maybe it has something to do with how the Syndics made it past the enigmas without a fight?"

"What?" Kommodor Bradamont said, an expression of growing shock on her face. "Ancestors. That might be it. Is there a way to reach Dancer space through jump space avoiding enigma-controlled stars if the Syndics used longer jumps?"

Lieutenant Yuon was already running the courses, nodding quickly. "Yes. In theory. But it would require jumps longer than Syndic jump drives, or Alliance jump drives, are capable of safely making."

Lieutenant Castries studied Yuon's work. "Kommodor, didn't the enigmas make longer jumps to attack Iwa Star System?"

"Yes," Bradamont said. "They—" She broke off speaking, turning a bleak face toward Geary as she addressed Yuon. "Lieutenant, are your theoretical jumps within the range the enigmas must have developed to reach Iwa?"

"Uh . . . yes, Kommodor." Yuon blinked in amazement. "The Syndics got that technology from the enigmas? How?"

"We haven't been able to recover anything from them," Captain Desjani said. "How would the Syndics . . . Oh, hell." She looked at Geary. "We've guessed that during the war between the Alliance and the Syndics the enigmas leaked hypernet technology to both sides in order to keep the war going."

He got it. "So maybe the enigmas have leaked their new jump capabilities to the Syndics. They knew some humans, at least, could fight their way through to the Dancers. So they're trying to mess with our attempts to represent humanity by giving the Syndics a way to get here, too. A way that keeps humans from passing through enigma-occupied star systems."

"I'm willing to bet it's not just the Syndics," Desjani said. "Hypernet tech was 'independently' discovered essentially simultaneously all through human-occupied space. The enigmas probably didn't want to give any human faction any advantage over any other."

Geary knew where she was driving with that. "Which means that longer jump drive capability, offering an apparently much safer route to Dancer space, may have become widely available after we left."

"Everyone also has access to the results of those early jump experiments," Kommodor Bradamont protested. "They'd know what those long jumps would do to those who undertook them."

"That didn't stop the Syndics," Desjani said.

Colonel Rogero, quiet for some time, spoke up again. "The Syndicate always officially claimed that its leaders were literally superior humans. They were leaders because they were superior. And since every citizen of the Syndicate had grown up under the Syndicate's rules, all of them were automatically stronger and better than anyone from a weak, disorganized culture like that of the worlds of the Alliance."

Bradamont nodded slowly. "The Syndicate's leaders would have told themselves that their people could endure things the people in the early experiments couldn't."

"Just so."

"The snakes must be crazy, too. I mean, even crazier than usual. Why haven't they killed everyone?"

Rogero paused to think. "Habit," he finally said. "Syndicate rules and regulations are rigid for all but CEOs. Even the snakes are only supposed to execute offenders using certain procedures when possible. Would this severe syndrome exaggerate fears? If so, anyone thinking they should do something different might be paralyzed with worry." His lips twisted in a dark sort of smile. "If I had the actions on my conscience that the average snake does, I would certainly be afraid to be called to account for any of them."

Desjani shook her head at Geary. "This looks like a real mess. When do we answer Crazy Syndic CEO? Even if the Syndics ramp up their speed we've got at least a couple of days before they can get within weapons range of us."

"I'll talk to the ambassador," Geary said. "And one other person."

He touched an internal communications command. "General Charban? We have another problem. The Dancers just escorted a Syndic flotilla here. According to our doctors, the Syndics are likely all temporarily insane. Could you and your people please ask the Dancers why they escorted an armed force of insane Syndics here?"

Charban's image gazed back at Geary, his expression that of someone who could no longer be surprised by whatever absurdity the universe decided to produce next. "I'll see what I can do, Admiral. You know the Dancers aren't always forthcoming about their reasons for doing things. May I ask why the Syndics are temporarily insane?"

"Extended-length jumps to reach Dancer space while avoiding the enigmas," Geary said. "They may be the first of many temporarily insane human visitors to Dancer space."

"Of course. I thought things were going too well." Charban offered a half-serious thumbs-up. "We'll get right on it, Admiral."

"Thanks." That call ended, Geary stood up. "I need to call the ambassador. I probably ought to do that from my stateroom."

"Good idea," Captain Desjani said.

HIS stateroom wasn't huge or luxurious, but it was private. Geary activated the security features before sitting at his desk to make his call.

Ambassador Rycerz was aboard the converted cruise liner *Boundless* orbiting less than a light second from *Dauntless*, where it was serving as the diplomatic base for this mission to the Dancers. Since Rycerz answered immediately she must have already been informed of the arrival of the Syndics and been awaiting Geary's call. "What's going on, Admiral? Why did the Syndics direct their message to you instead of to me?"

Something about her attitude made him want to start with *it's not my fault*, but Geary instead explained what had been learned and guessed about the new arrivals. Not happy himself with the situation, he got some satisfaction from seeing the growing distress on the ambassador's face. "That's what we have so far," he finished. "I have not yet replied to the Syndic ultimatum."

"There's only one possible reply," Rycerz said. "We're here at the invitation of the Dancers. Only the Dancers can tell us to leave. And the Syndics have absolutely no authority or legal standing to demand that we make no arrangements or agreements with the Dancers. But there are different ways to phrase that reply. I'll consult with my staff on the best wording." She paused. "I know this is a security matter, and under your responsibilities, but I'm sure you understand there's a strong diplomatic element as well."

"I do," Geary said. "The Syndics were still accelerating in the latest light to reach us from them, but if they are constrained by the velocity of their Dancer escorts it will take them close to two days to reach us. We need to try to defuse the situation before then."

Ambassador Rycerz nodded wearily. "Defusing an unstable explosive is more challenging than the usual crisis."

"I need to emphasize that while a rational opponent would not attack us given our large superiority in numbers and firepower, the Syndic flotilla's leaders are not currently rational. I can't rule out an attack on us if we don't do as they say."

"We cannot do what they say!"

"I agree. But that may mean a nasty fight inside a Dancer-inhabited star system," Geary said. "Knowing that everyone on their ships is likely irrational, if the Syndics attack I'll have to do my best to completely destroy their flotilla."

"Oh, that'll look good to the Dancers." Rycerz sat back, grimacing. "But you're certain of victory if it comes to that?"

"As certain as such things can be," Geary said, remembering all the things that could go wrong in any battle. "What I don't know is what the cost of victory would be. How many ships damaged, whether we'd lose some ships, including potentially battle cruisers, and how many of our sailors might die fighting a completely senseless battle."

"Fair enough," Rycerz said in a low voice, avoiding Geary's gaze. "We have no wish to pay such a price in a battle we don't want." She clenched a fist and thumped it on her desk. "Why did the Dancers set this up to happen?"

"Maybe they consider it a human problem."

"Or maybe they want to have front-row seats to a human battle, as if we were gladiators. There are people all too willing to believe that sort of thing of the Dancers." Rycerz didn't continue for a moment, covering her face with one hand. Finally, she lowered the hand, giving Geary a frank look. "This moment was bound to come, though we hoped it wouldn't be for a long time. Not everyone in human space wants the Alliance government to be the sole point of contact with any alien species. My instructions are to make a deal as soon as possible." She sighed heavily. "Unfortunately, the Dancers haven't been willing to act quickly."

Geary nodded in sympathy. He was all-too-well acquainted with situations where the best intentions were sabotaged by reality. He and the ambassador had different responsibilities but dealt with the same sort of uncertainties and problems. "What are your instructions from the government if another human faction showed up before we completed any deals with the Dancers?"

Ambassador Rycerz smiled. "I reviewed them while I was waiting for your call. Stripped of diplomatic phrasing, my instructions come down to 'let's hope that doesn't happen, and if it does, get your job done anyway.'"

"Your superiors and mine sometimes seem to have a lot in common," Geary said. "Is there anything new from the Dancer side?"

"No." Rycerz let her exasperation show. "After they provided us with that star chart we thought there'd been a breakthrough. But since then we seem back to the old delay and noncommittal situation. If we could only figure out what the Dancers want we might finally make some progress, but we can still only guess why they offered us the star chart."

"That gesture came right after my portion of the fleet returned from the Taon star," Geary said. "Maybe the fact that we avoided getting involved in the Taon internal wars pleased the Dancers."

"Maybe." Rycerz waved off the possibility. "Right now I need to focus on convincing a crazy Syndic CEO not to commit ugly suicide in front of the Dancers by attacking us."

"Do you want me to respond in any way to the Syndic message to me?"

"No. I'll handle that. We don't want anyone back in human-controlled space claiming the Alliance fleet engineered an unnecessary fight for the glory of an easy victory." She looked down at her desk, her expression growing thoughtful. "Is this a test? Are the Dancers deliberately trying to see how we handle a mess like this?"

"Maybe General Charban will get an answer out of the Dancers that explains something."

"I won't be holding my breath on that."

TWO

GEARY sat in his stateroom, frowning at his display. There were a lot of things to do, a lot of orders to give and decisions to make, as always, even when not facing a potential battle within the next two days. One lingering problem was what to do with Captains Pelleas and Burdock and Commander Cui, former commanding officers of, respectively, the battleships *Gallant*, *Encroach*, and *Magnificent*. That was technically an easy problem since the penalty for mutiny was death by firing squad. But both Pelleas and Cui had served valiantly and were popular among the fleet, and much of the evidence was indirect. Until he could prove their connection to the murder of one of *Dauntless*'s sailors and the attempted murder of himself, he wanted to hold off on the firing squads.

So Geary stayed quiet, gazing at the three-dimensional depiction of the Alliance fleet that floated over his desk. Over three hundred warships, ranging from the small and sleek barracuda-like destroyers to the massive, swift sharks of the battle cruisers, and the even more massive and deadly killer whale shapes of the battleships. None of the ships were designed to go into atmospheres so their shapes had nothing to do with streamlining. Instead they reflected engineering realities, that sharp edges and corners attracted stress and cracked, whereas curves distributed that stress, and secondarily that curved shapes were more likely to deflect a hit than a flat one or corners aptly called "shot traps" by ship designers.

Even with this many ships, the fleet was much diminished from what it had been near the end of the century-long war with the Syndicate Worlds. It had taken terrible losses just before Geary found himself thrust into command, and smaller but painful losses in every battle since then as he brought the fleet home against all odds and finally forced the apparently endless war to an end.

But the formation of warships, arranged in a lattice resembling a huge box as it orbited, was still significantly larger than Geary had known a century ago.

His eyes went to one of the heavy cruisers, the display detecting his focus and automatically zooming in on the ship as detailed information popped up. Sapphire. Commanding Officer Commander Sean Eric Boudreaux. All systems operational. Crew status ninety-six percent, all critical skill requirements met.

He'd been in command of a heavy cruiser on that day now more than a hundred years gone. *Merlon.* Caught in a one-sided fight, buying time for other Alliance ships to escape the Syndic surprise attack that started the war. To everyone else in the fleet that fight was long-ago history. To him, presumed dead, frozen in survival sleep in a damaged escape pod for more than ninety-nine years, it still felt like yesterday. And to nearly everyone else in the fleet, born and raised during the war, Geary was a legendary commander, the greatest commander ever, his reputation elevated to suit the needs of a wartime government desperate for heroes to inspire its people as the war dragged on for decade after decade. He knew none of the legends about him were true, but these people who were the descendants of those he'd grown up with had needed their hero, so he'd done his best.

Fortunately, some of them knew he was human. Without that, the burden would have long ago overwhelmed him.

"Admiral?"

Geary looked over to see Captain Tanya Desjani at the door to his stateroom. "Captain?"

"I just dropped by to see if you needed to discuss anything," she said, coming inside the stateroom but leaving the door open as usual.

He weighed talking about his moody thoughts but decided against it. "How do you recommend we handle the Syndics if they come at us?"

She made a face. "We want it to be obvious they attacked and we defended, right? And we have an overpowering advantage that we should use. You know that Syndic CEO is going to target this ship, right?"

"Because?" Geary said, already knowing the answer. "It'd make more sense to go after *Boundless*, to cripple our diplomatic mission, or the fast fleet auxiliaries to force this fleet to head home sooner than planned when our supplies got low."

"It would," Desjani agreed. "Under normal circumstances, I'd list both as primary targets. But this isn't normal because that Syndic CEO isn't rational. She's going to be thinking what a huge hero she'd be if she was the one to finally kill the legendary Black Jack Geary, about the rewards and honors that would shower on her when she returned to Syndic space." She laughed. "Of course, there's as close to a hundred percent chance as it gets that the CEO will die before her ship gets within range of *Dauntless*, but that's what a rational person would worry about.

"Rearrange our current box with *Dauntless* near the back, the auxiliaries and *Boundless* behind her. Arrange all of the battleships in a matrix the Syndics will have to face, with the rest of the fleet arrayed to hit the Syndics from all sides as they make their approach." Desjani shook her head. "Nothing living will get through that."

"I was thinking the same thing," Geary said. "If the Syndics veer onto another vector to hit us from a different angle we can pivot the box to keep the kill zone centered on their approach. But I was also thinking it'd be a good idea to form the battle cruisers, except for *Dauntless*, into two separate formations that can react to anything else the Syndics do."

Desjani nodded. "I concur. This could be a one-pass, total-annihilation battle if the Syndics do what's expected. If they don't, those two battle cruiser formations will be insurance to keep the Syndics from running amok."

Geary raised one eyebrow at her. "You're unusually calm about proposing a battle in which *Dauntless* will likely not strike a blow, let alone get any Syndic ship kills."

This time she shook her head. "You know I like blowing up stuff, the bigger the better. And I like a good fight. This, though, is going to be a one-sided slaughter over nothing. There's no joy in that. My ancestors will understand why I have to participate, but I doubt they'd be pleased if I was gleeful about it."

"No. I don't think they would be."

Desjani tilted her head slightly as she studied him, one hand reaching across to touch the wedding ring on her other hand. It was their way of communicating when discussions could get personal. "Are you okay, Jack?"

"I think so." He managed a smile. "I could use a miracle or two, but there's nothing unusual about that."

"I'm all out of miracles today. Do you need to see Dr. Nasr to check if your happy meds need adjusting?"

"I probably should," Geary said. "Happy meds," the fleet term for various ways of treating stress and depression, had been rarely used a century ago. After a hundred years of war marked by massive losses of human life, their use had become routine to keep sailors and officers going. "It's stupid to wish there was something else I could do to deal with this situation, but I can't help it."

"Maybe the Dancers could do something," she said.

"They created this mess by bringing the Syndics here!"

"And maybe they want to see if we handle it by killing the other guys or asking for help in preventing that."

He gave her a long look. "That's an excellent idea. What would I do without you?"

"Hopefully you'll never know." Desjani lowered the hand touching her wedding ring. "You good, Admiral?"

"Yes, Captain. Thank you. I'm going to see General Charban."

She left, but he spent a moment longer looking after her. Tanya Desjani and he had married during a short period when she wasn't under his command. Since then, they'd maintained strictly professional attitudes on duty, and whenever they were aboard *Dauntless* they were both on duty. He'd kept waiting for higher-ups to complain or order the arrangement to end, but apparently his enemies were still hoping that he and Desjani would act unprofessionally and give them another avenue to attack the almost untouchable hero.

Because the ugly truth was that the legendary Black Jack could get away with almost anything if he wanted to. John Geary was determined never to give in to that temptation.

But it was always there.

GENERAL Charban was retired but had consented to continue serving as a liaison of sorts to the Dancers and other alien species, a task at which Geary thought Charban had proven invaluable.

When Geary reached the compartment where Charban worked, he found it occupied by every one of Charban's motley assemblage of assistants. Lieutenant Iger, a fleet intelligence officer, had proven himself capable of crafting communications with the Dancers in the poetic formats the Dancers preferred. Lieutenant Jamenson, her naturally bright green hair a genetic-engineered legacy of proud ancestors on her home world of Eire, had a unique ability to hide information in confusing formats, which also allowed her to spot patterns in otherwise baffling collections of data. John Senn was an historian, one who had been ostracized for his entire career for seriously investigating indications of alien species having visited Old Earth or other worlds humans had settled. After the recent discovery of actual alien species, he had suddenly become the only reliable expert on such matters, which hadn't stopped the scientists aboard *Boundless* from disdaining any possible input from a mere historian. He had found a home here with Charban's group, though.

The last member of the ad hoc group was Dr. Jasmine Cresida, a brilliant physicist who had proven capable of unique insights into Dancer thinking. Geary wasn't sure why she'd chosen to continue assisting Charban instead of returning to *Boundless*, where the other scientists attached to the mission resided. He was grateful for her decision, but Dr. Cresida had never hidden her dislike for Geary himself. He doubted she would ever forgive him for the death of her equally brilliant sister, Jaylen, who had been killed while under Geary's command, while carrying out orders that Geary had given.

The two lieutenants sprang to their feet as Geary entered the compartment, the historian eyeing them as if studying the customs of an ancient society, while Dr. Cresida ignored Geary's arrival, her eyes staying on her pad as she worked on something that would probably be incomprehensible to all but perhaps a dozen other people in all of human-occupied space.

Geary waved Iger and Jamenson back to their seats as General Charban smiled briefly in welcome. "Any word from the Dancers?"

Charban's smile slipped. "Surprisingly, yes." He hesitated, glancing at his assistants. "We were just debating possible alternate meanings to their answer, but it seems only one interpretation makes sense."

"And that would be?" Geary asked.

"Stripped of poetry and rhyme, the Dancer reply comes down to saying they brought the irrational Syndics here because the behavior of the Syndics appeared to the Dancers to fall within normal parameters for human behavior."

Geary heard someone bark a sardonic laugh and realized it was him. "The Dancers couldn't tell the difference between humans acting crazy and humans acting human?"

General Charban shrugged. "In all fairness, even among ourselves humans often have trouble identifying the differences."

John Senn the historian shook his head, his gaze on the table. "One of the reasons humanity looked forward to meeting intelligent aliens was because they could hold up a mirror for us, let us see how humanity was perceived by nonhumans. I guess there never was any reason to think that mirror would show us things we liked."

"If that's true," Lieutenant Jamenson said, her voice sharp, "then the Dancers are looking at all of us, Alliance or Syndic or whatever, and just seeing 'human.' Not individuals. That's no way to deal with any species. We're not ants with identical behavior patterns."

"True enough," General Charban said. "We need to get the Dancers to see the individuals, not the species. But, for now, they've dumped these crazy Syndics in our laps."

"I need you to follow up," Geary said. "It's too late to tell the Dancers not to bring the Syndics here, but we can try to explain to the Dancers that these Syndics are temporarily capable of actions that could harm anyone and everyone in this star system. It's to the Dancers' own best interests to help us prevent the Syndics from flying off the handle. If they can do anything to limit the actions of the Syndics, it will be to everyone's advantage."

Charban nodded. "Including the Syndics'. Do I read the odds right?"

"Yes. If it comes to a fight, we'll annihilate them," Geary said. "We need to convince the Dancers that we'd be extremely grateful if they help us avoid that."

Lieutenant Iger spoke up in a low voice. "Wiping out the Syndics would . . . simplify things."

Lieutenant Jamenson nodded but didn't say anything. John Senn gave Iger a distressed look but also remained quiet. Dr. Cresida acted as if she'd heard nothing.

General Charban glanced at Geary.

Geary nodded to Charban, accepting the offered chance to respond first. Fortunately for him, he'd already been trying to imagine what advice Victoria Rione would be offering if she were still alive, and had realized how she'd probably try to make the most of the situation by using her opponent's weaknesses against them.

"It might simplify things in the short run," Geary said. "*If* seeing us wipe out the Syndics instead of working out an accommodation with them didn't backfire by making the Dancers less willing to deal with us. But, in the long term, you've probably all heard that we expect more ships to show up from other human factions, worlds, businesses, governments, and who knows what else. They'll all want to make deals. We need to show the Dancers that the Alliance is who they should deal with. If we're in that kind of contest, trying to convince aliens who can be trusted to keep their word, who will offer the fairest deals, and who will play straight with them, I can't think of anyone I'd rather be competing against than Syndics."

Charban nodded, smiling. "It's to our advantage to have the Syndics as the alternative. And once the Dancers choose us over the Syndics, we'll have a built-in advantage against every subsequent competitor."

"Right. We have to think long term, and outside the military box."

Lieutenant Iger looked embarrassed. "Of course, Admiral. I should have realized that."

"When you're more than a century old, you'll think of things like that," General Charban assured him.

"I'm only a century old chronologically," Geary said. "Listen, there's one other thing we need from the Dancers. See if they'll tell us how long it's been since those Syndic ships left jump on arrival in a Dancer star system. That will tell us whether we have any hope of any of the Syndics starting to recover soon."

"Of course," Charban said. "We'll do our best, and stress the urgency of our requests to the Dancers."

"Perhaps I can help with that," Dr. Cresida said, speaking up for the first time.

"Your assistance would be very welcome," Charban assured her.

"I need you all to understand," Geary said, "that there's a strong chance we won't be able to dissuade that irrational Syndic CEO from attacking us. We may be forced to fight. Dr. Cresida, if you would rather not be aboard a warship during such a battle, I can get you back to *Boundless* in plenty of time."

"I'm comfortable here," Cresida said, not looking at Geary.

"How about you, Citizen Senn?" Geary asked the historian. "Do you want to return to *Boundless*?"

John Senn shook his head firmly. "No way. From what I've seen, there's no safer place in this fleet than right here."

"Thank you, but a battleship has a number of advantages when it comes to safety," Geary said.

"And I'd like to observe the, um, activity from this ship. If I may," Senn added hastily.

"I'm sure General Charban can help with that."

"Are you going to ask the duck whether he wants to remain on the ship?" Dr. Cresida asked, her eyes still on her work pad.

Everyone else smiled, but Geary kept his face and tone serious. "Ensign Duck is officially a member of the crew. He has to stay aboard unless Captain Desjani chooses to temporarily transfer him to another ship."

"I've been meaning to ask," General Charban said. "What are Ensign Duck's official duties?"

"He conducts security patrols of the ship," Geary said, still serious.

Lieutenant Iger nodded. "The duck spotted that intruder in a stealth suit that was invisible to the ship's interior sensors."

"Exactly," Geary said, not adding that the duck's ability to do that had probably saved his own life. "Speaking of threats, do you have anything new on the Syndics, Lieutenant Iger?"

Iger replied, his voice automatically taking on the formal tones of a briefer. "We still haven't received any useful intelligence from the Syndic flotilla, Admiral. The only thing my analysts have noted is that the Syndics are maintaining their formation more precisely than they usually do."

"They are?" Geary ran that through his mind before nodding. "Colonel Rogero and Kommodor Bradamont speculated that the Syndics have kept going despite the jump space syndrome because they're sticking obsessively to their rules and procedures, any natural paranoia exacerbated by the syndrome. It makes sense they'd be more attentive to keeping station in their formation. Any deviation from anything might cause all hell to break loose on those ships. Lieutenant, share anything you can with Kommodor Bradamont. Her experience with Syndics might help her spot things we can't."

"Yes, Admiral."

"Exactly how much time do we have?" General Charban asked.

Geary checked the time. "The Syndics have been pushing their Dancer escorts, but the Dancers have been holding firm at point one light speed. At that rate, the Syndics will reach us in another forty-one hours. If the Syndics are showing evidence of hostile intent when they reach ten light minutes from us, I'll bring the fleet to full combat readiness at that time. If the Dancers are going to help, they need to do so within the next forty hours."

John Senn stared at Geary. "What would be evidence of hostile intent?"

"Strengthening their shields, powering up weapons, activating fire control systems, that kind of thing," Geary said. "Signs they're getting ready to fight. I don't want to take similar measures until I have to, because I don't want the Syndics thinking I'm getting ready to hit them, but if I see them getting ready, I'm going to have to prepare my ships. And I repeat my offer to transfer you to another ship. There's a good chance that if the Syndics come at us they will target this ship in an attempt to kill me."

Senn looked a bit nervous, licking his lips before replying. "Well, Admiral, they say you're on the good side of the living stars, so this should still be a safe place, right?"

Geary found himself unable to find words to answer that.

But as he struggled with a reply, General Charban spoke slowly. "I can assure you, having myself miraculously lived through too many bloody battles, that virtue or being on the right side has little or nothing to do with surviving. That all too often seemed merely a matter of chance. The righteousness of our cause was no armor at all against any weapon. I don't know where the gaze of the living stars rests when battles are fought, but most often it seemed to be elsewhere when most needed."

Dr. Cresida spoke in the silence that followed, her eyes fixed on Charban. "And yet you continued to fight."

"Yes," Charban said. "Because I had friends and soldiers under my command who I did not want to let down. I have seen too many die in battles that seemed to have had little purpose or meaningful results, which has reinforced my belief that such sacrifices should be demanded only when absolutely necessary. When I was in a position of command, I could try to make a difference, because as much as I hate it, sometimes those sacrifices have to be asked of those we are given responsibility over. But I reached the point where I simply couldn't do it anymore. That's when I retired."

"General," Lieutenant Jamenson said earnestly, "you earned that. No one can say you didn't do your duty for longer than many could have."

"Thank you, Lieutenant." Charban shrugged. "But the fact remains that now the responsibility to only spend the lives entrusted to us wisely lies in the hands of officers such as the admiral here. I am on this ship because I believe the admiral feels that responsibility as keenly as I did.

And that is why he warned that no one should feel safe because of his presence."

"I understand," John Senn said, now looking abashed. "There's a saying about there being no atheists in battles, but I guess that's not true."

"Of course not," Charban said. "As Lieutenant Jamenson pointed out, every individual is different. Many do become stronger believers. Others, seeing the apparent arbitrariness with which some die and others live, conclude there is nothing overseeing the messy universe we live in. Both perspectives are within what the Dancers call normal human parameters."

Geary nodded. "So let's see if we can minimize how many die this time around. Let me know if you learn anything or need anything."

"We're not required to run any more messages past the ambassador for approval before transmitting them to the Dancers?"

"Not today, General."

EVEN for veterans of many space battles, the times involved were hard to get used to. Human instincts, developed on the surface of a planet with limited lines of sight, went on alert when enemies were in view. But in space an enemy force could be clearly seen even if billions of kilometers distant and days away from contact. Instinct urged humans to remain alert against the enemy that could be seen even though remaining in full combat readiness for days would seriously degrade a crew's ability to fight when the battle finally got to them.

After updating his fleet on the current situation and his intent to go to full combat status when the Dancers were ten light minutes away, Geary ordered his ships' commanding officers to ensure their crews got rest and carried out any important maintenance or repair work. Because the upside of being able to see enemies approaching from so far away was that surprise was very hard to achieve unless ships were close to something like a star or large planet behind which enemies could hide.

Ambassador Rycerz's reply to the Syndic CEO went out six hours after the CEO's message had been received. Rycerz had plainly involved the medical staff aboard *Boundless* in drafting the message. At no point did it directly say no to the Syndic demands, instead trying different means of diverting the discussion into other, safer areas. The tone of the message was calm, soothing, rational.

Because of the distance remaining between the Syndic flotilla and the Alliance fleet, it would be at least eight hours until any reply from CEO Sara Okimoto Gardonyi was received.

Maybe, if the Dancers had kept the Syndics waiting for a few weeks before they brought them to this star, and if CEO Okimoto Gardonyi was one of those who recovered faster, the reply would be more measured, more rational, and less threatening.

A little over eight hours later, Geary was awakened from restless attempts at sleep by the communications watch. "Admiral, we've received another message from the Syndics."

"A message addressed to us?" Geary asked, sitting up in his bunk.

"Addressed to *you*, Admiral."

Great. "Before we accept, get Captain Desjani and Dr. Nasr linked in. I want them to view the message, too."

"Yes, Admiral." A slight pause. "All ready, sir."

Geary dropped down into the seat at his desk, activating the display there as he stifled a tired yawn. "Go ahead."

If anything, CEO Sara Okimoto Gardonyi seemed even more hyper and compulsive than in the first message, her eyes so wide they seemed to fill her face. "You cannot fool us, Black Jack! The message from your lackey is insulting and weak, betraying your fear. Citizens of the Syndicate are not so easily bluffed! Nor are we so easily subverted. My chief security officer has warned me of the otherwise undetectable transmissions from your ships that seek to gain mental control over my workers.

A dozen workers so weak-minded as to fall under your control have already been executed before they could do damage. You thought your subversion would be concealed from us until too late by not giving your puppets orders to immediately commit sabotage, but I know the fact sabotage had not been carried out was proof it was being planned by them! I will no longer accept your mere departure from this star system. You must be stopped! You are ordered to surrender your ships immediately! Your workers will be interrogated and if found to be misled minions will be permitted to live and serve the Syndicate Worlds in one of our job-training facilities. You will see no such mercy, Black Jack! ForthepeopleGardonyiout."

The image of the Syndic CEO froze, looking even more disturbing without any movement or words to distract from her appearance.

Captain Desjani's image appeared next to it. "Looks like we're going to be fighting a battle."

"Looks like it," Geary agreed. "Doctor? That CEO doesn't seem to be getting any better."

"No," Dr. Nasr agreed, his own image appearing next to that of Desjani. He looked not just physically tired but also dejected at the knowledge that his skills offered no good answers. "I will consult with my colleagues, but my initial impression is that the stress of facing battle with us is making her symptoms worse."

"She seems pretty certain of victory," Desjani pointed out. "I mean, that's total delusion, but if she's that sure, why should she be stressed?"

"Because buried in her mind is a rational thinker," Dr. Nasr said. "Observing, unable to exert control, knowing what will happen if it cannot regain control soon. The CEO is confident, and terrified."

"Captain Desjani, please have this message forwarded to Ambassador Rycerz," Geary said, "and to Lieutenant Iger, Kommodor Bradamont, and Colonel Rogero. Doctor, any idea why that CEO thinks I'm using undetectable mind-control transmissions?"

Dr. Nasr sighed. "She is seeing enemies everywhere. You heard her.

Not being able to detect your mind-control transmissions is proof they exist. It is mental illness, not something you can logically debate."

Geary nodded, wondering why he felt guilty about the deaths of a dozen Syndics who had been suspected of helping him. Their deaths weren't his fault. But they still stung. "I'm wondering how many crew members have already been killed on those ships. Even with automated controls, that's going to hurt their ability to fight."

"If they kill too many of their own," Desjani observed, "they may not even make it to the fight."

Geary was on the bridge of *Dauntless* five hours and twenty minutes after Tanya Desjani made that prediction, gazing at his display as he pondered possible outcomes when the Syndics got closer. His thoughts were interrupted by the sounding of a sudden alert as the display highlighted a red marker that had appeared.

"Captain," Lieutenant Yuon called out, "one of the Syndic heavy cruisers exploded."

"I can see that, Lieutenant," Desjani said, her eyes fixed on her own display. "There weren't any signs of problems before that happened?"

"No, Captain. No indications of any problems. Comms in the Syndic formation appeared normal, and sensor readings from the heavy cruiser's power core didn't show any signs of trouble."

Geary looked at the red marker on his display that highlighted the expanding cloud of dust and debris that had once been a Syndicate Worlds heavy cruiser and its crew. It was odd how immediate it felt even though the explosion had happened over three hours ago. His gaze shifted as another marker sprang to life on one of the Syndic Hunter-Killers that had been closest to the destroyed heavy cruiser.

"One of the Syndic HuKs seems to have taken damage from the debris from the heavy cruiser," Lieutenant Castries announced. "Sensors can see hull damage, and the shields on the HuK have collapsed."

"No surprise there," Desjani said, her voice grim.

Geary nodded in agreement. Syndic Hunter-Killers were smaller than Alliance destroyers, with weaker shields and less armament. Such small warships were well suited to some tasks, but they were also expendable, easily destroyed by hits that larger warships could shrug off.

He watched the stricken HuK sliding slowly away from its position in the Syndic formation, a sign that the ship's maneuvering systems must be out of action.

Two of the surviving heavy cruisers leapt away from their positions in the Syndic formation, closing rapidly on the damaged HuK.

"It appears that the Syndics are sending heavy cruisers to assist the damaged ship," Lieutenant Yuon reported.

More alerts sounded as the Alliance fleet's sensors received the light of events that had occurred more than three hours ago.

Hell lance beams, concentrated streams of charged particles, shot from the two heavy cruisers, riddling the helpless Hunter-Killer. Coming closer, the Syndic heavy cruisers unleashed grapeshot, swarms of metal ball bearings that vaporized the HuK's hull when they struck, breaking the ship into several larger pieces and a field of smaller debris.

Their task done, the heavy cruisers swung back into their positions in the Syndic formation.

"Our sensors can't spot any escape pods amid the wreckage of the Syndic HuK," Lieutenant Yuon reported, his voice tighter than usual.

"Damn," Desjani muttered.

"Why?" Geary asked out loud.

Kommodor Bradamont had reached the bridge and answered him. "At a guess, Admiral, the Hunter-Killer was ordered to return to its place in the formation. It didn't. The ship was declared mutinous and ordered destroyed as an example to the rest of the crews in the flotilla."

"Even though the ship physically couldn't comply with the order?" Geary said.

Colonel Rogero had just arrived on the bridge as well, and nodded quickly in reply to Geary's question. "I have seen Syndicate citizens killed for their inability to carry out orders that could not be obeyed," he said, his voice grim. "In this case, destroying one of their ships was an extreme measure, but that would reflect the irrational impulses driving the Syndicate commanders."

"Admiral, we have an incoming message from the Syndic flotilla!"

The smile displayed by CEO Sara Okimoto Gardonyi felt terrifying even from a distance of billions of kilometers. "Your unprovoked and underhanded attack on this flotilla has failed, Black Jack. Despite the loss of one of our mobile forces units, and the need to deal with mutinous workers on another unit, this flotilla remains ready to force you to pay for your crimes! Even your attempt to replace the Internal Security Service agents aboard my own unit with your own look-alike minions has failed, as loyal agents valiantly sacrificed themselves to kill every traitorous doppelganger. You cannot escape your fate! Forthe-peopleGardonyiout."

Kommodor Bradamont, aghast, was staring at the image of the Syndic CEO. "Does what she said mean what I think it does?"

Colonel Rogero, by contrast, was smiling broadly. "The snakes aboard her ship wiped themselves out, turning their own paranoia and extremism against each other. If only that would happen everywhere in what remains of the Syndicate."

Geary's communications alert buzzed urgently. He accepted the call, seeing Ambassador Rycerz gazing worriedly at him.

"Did you cause the Syndic ship to explode?" the ambassador asked.

"No," Geary said, trying to see the humor in the question. "We have no way of doing that from this distance. We didn't destroy the other Syndic ship, either," he added.

"I could see that." Ambassador Rycerz clenched both fists. "One of the doctors aboard this ship tells me there's a form of mental illness where someone thinks those close to them have been replaced by exact duplicates. That must be what caused these latest deaths on the CEO's ship, though the doctor couldn't tell what specific thing might have triggered the delusion. The Syndics on those ships will blame every stubbed toe on us right now, won't they? There's no way to negotiate with people in that condition. Will you be ready for them?"

"We'll be ready for them," Geary said.

A bit over a day later, he was back on the bridge of *Dauntless*, looking over his display at the data on his ships. Every single destroyer, light cruiser, heavy cruiser, battle cruiser, battleship, assault transport, and fast fleet auxiliary was at maximum readiness, awaiting only his command to come to full combat posture. *Boundless*, boasting nothing in the way of weapons but a couple of close-in protection systems, was also as ready as that ship could be. The Alliance ships were already in battle formation, the former box realigned into almost a cube, *Dauntless* centered near the back of the cube, the auxiliaries, the fast assault transports loaded with most of the Marines, and *Boundless* behind *Dauntless*. In front of *Dauntless*, twenty battleships were arrayed, most of the remaining Alliance warships spreading out from there to help form a deadly three-dimensional lattice. The four ships of the First Battle Cruiser Division under Captain Duellos aboard *Inspire*, along with a squadron of light cruisers and two squadrons of destroyers, formed a separate, small formation above and to one side of the main formation. The battle cruisers of the Third Division and the remaining ones from *Dauntless*'s Second Division under Captain Badaya on *Illustrious*, along with more squadrons of light cruisers and destroyers, were stationed below and slightly behind the main formation.

"The Syndic flotilla is fifteen light minutes distant," Lieutenant Yuon announced. "They are maintaining point one light speed but have moved very close to their Dancer escort ships and appear prepared to accelerate past them."

"You tried," Captain Desjani said to Geary. "But it only takes one to start a fight."

Before he could reply, General Charban called. "The Dancers have finally sent us a reply, after Dr. Cresida sang an aria at them emphasizing the urgency of our requests." He paused, looking crestfallen. "The important thing about the Dancer reply is summarized by four words of it. 'Human problem. Humans fix.'"

"Human problem?" Geary said, not sure whether or not to be angry. "Didn't the Dancers themselves bring the Syndics here?"

"John Senn has a theory about that," Charban said. "A bunch of Syndic warships showed up in a Dancer star system. They probably refused to leave. So the Dancers brought them here, expecting us to do what they've seen Alliance warships do to Syndic warships many, many times over the last century."

That made far too much sense to disregard. "The problem is crazy humans, so other humans need to solve it instead of expecting the Dancers to fix things."

"Pretty much," General Charban said. "It's . . . not an unreasonable position for them to take."

Further discussion was interrupted by alerts on everyone's displays.

"Fifteen minutes ago the Syndic flotilla increased their shield strengths to maximum and powered up weapons," Lieutenant Castries reported.

"They're more than two hours out from reaching us," Captain Desjani said. "I guess they're really eager to fight. But there's nothing close enough for them to fight except their Dancer escorts."

On the heels of her words an awful thought struck Geary, but before he could speak it a strident alert sounded as threat symbols multiplied on his display.

"The Syndics opened fire on their Dancer escorts!" Lieutenant Castries called out, sounding as shocked as Geary felt.

THREE

"ALL units come to full combat readiness," Geary ordered on the main command circuit before looking around the bridge. "Give me an intercept on the Syndic flotilla!"

Desjani's hand was already flying over her display, working up the maneuver. "Got it."

He ran his eyes over the solution she sent. It looked good, as anything from Desjani always did. "All units in Formation Alpha," he ordered. "Immediate execute. Come port zero three one degrees, down zero zero six degrees, accelerate to point one light speed. Rotate formation around guide ship *Dauntless*. Formations Bravo One and Bravo Two maneuver independently to expeditiously intercept and assist Dancer spacecraft under attack."

Space didn't have lefts or rights, ups or downs, but human ships were always near stars, so humanity used them as a common reference for maneuvers. Port was a turn away from the star, starboard (or starward) was a turn toward the star, while up and down were established relative to the plane in which planets orbited the star.

Thrusters fired on every hull to push ships onto new headings, followed by main propulsion units lighting off aft, the bulk of the Alliance fleet veering away from the star, aiming slightly down, accelerating onto a vector that would rush to meet the oncoming Syndics and the Dancer ships under attack.

The two smaller formations built around battle cruisers bolted ahead, accelerating faster than the main body could manage, with its battleships, auxiliaries, and *Boundless* unable to match the agility of the other ships.

Only then did Geary call General Charban. "General, inform the Dancers that we are proceeding to offer aid to their ships that are under attack." He made another call, this time to *Boundless*. "Ambassador Rycerz, the fleet is moving to assist the Dancer escorts to the Syndic formation which are being attacked by the Syndics."

Rycerz gazed back at Geary anxiously. "They're still a long distance from us."

"Yes," Geary said. "Fourteen light minutes now. We're still accelerating, but at a combined closing rate of point two light speed we'll require a little over an hour to cover the distance between us. I've sent most of my battle cruisers ahead to reach the Dancers faster, but even they will require at least forty-five minutes given the need to brake their velocity prior to intercept."

"Can the Dancer ships survive that long?"

"We'll have to hope they can."

Ending that call, Geary sat back, trying to think of anything he'd forgotten.

"Admiral."

Desjani's voice was deceptively calm. He looked at her, seeing her expression tight from having to sit among the slower-moving formation while the other battle cruisers raced to the rescue of the Dancers. "Tanya, the other battle cruisers can handle those Syndics."

"If the Dancers can survive that long." Captain Desjani eyed him.

"But if the Syndics see a target they really want to destroy, they'll leave off chasing those Dancers and come after it."

It only took him a moment to see what she was driving at. "We pull *Dauntless* out of the formation, charging out alone ahead of the rest of the ships. When the Syndics see us on our own, they'll leave off engaging the Dancers and head on an intercept to destroy *Dauntless* while the ship is exposed."

"That sounds like a great plan, Admiral," Desjani said, just as if she hadn't prompted him on it. "We should do that."

"*Dauntless* can't tangle with six enemy battle cruisers."

"The hell she can't. Sir." Desjani smiled, flexing her fingers. "I can keep those Syndics chasing their own tails until the rest of the fleet arrives and sends them all to greet their ancestors."

She wasn't boasting. Geary knew that Tanya Desjani was one of the best ship drivers in the Alliance fleet.

It would be a big risk, though. Six-to-one odds were nothing to laugh at, even if Captain Desjani was commanding the one.

If the Dancers saw their own people getting killed by humans while Geary's fleet took its time getting there to save them, any hope of future agreements might disappear. The entire purpose of this mission might be sabotaged, along with humanity's hope of close relations with the first alien species willing to talk with humans.

Hell. He didn't really have any choice, not if he kept the big picture in view.

He touched his comm controls to speak with Captain Armus, commanding officer of the battleship *Colossus*. "Captain Armus, I'm going to transfer command of the main body to you while *Dauntless* tries to draw off the Syndics attacking the Dancers. Keep moving to intercept and engage the Syndics."

"I understand," Captain Armus said, not displaying any surprise at the sudden change in plans or worry about Geary's maneuver. As stolid and ponderous as the ship he commanded, Armus would never be accused of going off half-cocked, but he was as reliable as any officer could be. "Good luck, Admiral."

The next call was to the fleet. "All units in Formation Alpha, this is Admiral Geary. Effective immediately, Formation Alpha is under the command of Captain Armus aboard *Colossus. Dauntless* is proceeding to lead the attack and draw the Syndics away from the Dancer ships they're attacking. To the honor of our ancestors, Geary, out."

That done, he nodded to Desjani. "Let's go, Captain."

Desjani grinned. "Yes, Admiral. On the bridge! This is Captain Desjani. I am assuming personal control of maneuvering."

The others on the bridge acknowledged Desjani's words with a chorus of ayes that was only slightly staggered by everyone's hasty moves to strap into their seats as well as they could. "All hands prepare for imminent heavy maneuvers," Lieutenant Castries broadcast through the ship. "Secure yourselves *now*."

Desjani's fingers played across her controls, *Dauntless* pivoting under her thrusters, then a mighty hand pinned Geary into his seat as the main propulsion lit off at nearly full, the acceleration so strong that some of it leaked past the inertial dampers that kept the stress from tearing apart the ship and squashing the crew.

Geary saw the projected vector for *Dauntless* spring to life on his display, a vast curve running outward to meet up with the projected track of the Syndic ships and the Dancers fleeing from them. This was what battle cruisers were for, sacrificing most of the armor and some of the firepower of battleships in favor of less mass and more main propulsion. Despite their size they were the most agile ships humanity had ever constructed, made to get where they needed to be as fast as possible, and catch anyone trying to outrun them.

His comm circuit came to life. "Admiral! What are you doing?" Ambassador Rycerz demanded.

"Trying to save those Dancer ships," Geary said, hearing his voice distorted slightly because of the strain of acceleration his body was under. "Don't worry. *Boundless* and everyone aboard her is safe."

"I do not want to lose *you*, Admiral."

"We are in agreement on that, Ambassador. I assure you the only people who are going to lose this day are the Syndics."

He couldn't really promise that, not when *Dauntless* was trying to draw off six Syndic battle cruisers single-handedly until more Alliance support could arrive.

As *Dauntless* shot away from the rest of Formation Alpha, Geary found himself wondering how Dr. Cresida and John Senn were feeling about their decisions to remain aboard the ship.

THE images of the fighting, now only ten minutes old, showed the three Dancer ships that had been escorting the Syndics maneuvering wildly to avoid a storm of hell lance shots. The Dancers were doing their usual amazing job of flying their ships, but against the odds and firepower they were facing, that wasn't good enough. Hits were being scored, the shields on the Dancer ships being worn down. No shots had penetrated the Dancer hulls yet, but that was only a matter of time.

"They should be seeing our maneuver about now," Lieutenant Yuon reported.

That meant that even if the Syndics immediately shifted vectors to aim for an intercept of *Dauntless*, it wouldn't be seen on *Dauntless* for at least another ten minutes. But it might immediately take pressure off the Dancers.

Desjani had chosen a vector that avoided joining up with either of the Alliance battle cruiser formations, and in fact was accelerating so quickly that *Dauntless* was drawing out ahead of both groups of battle cruisers. Geary realized that in terms of bait that was probably the best move to make, even though under other circumstances as a tactic it was recklessly aggressive.

Geary saw a red warning pulsing on his display.

"Captain," engineering called, "we're getting hull stress warnings. Recommend reducing acceleration to a safe level."

"How long can she handle this?" Desjani asked, her voice calm.

"I . . . don't know, Captain. We're not supposed to *do* this."

"*Dauntless* can take it a little longer," Desjani said.

Geary gave Desjani a side-eyed look, sure that his worry showed. She winked in reply, smiling. "She can take it," Desjani repeated.

Geary was trying to focus on his display when a prolonged groan came from the ship's structure somewhere deep inside *Dauntless*. The whine of the overloaded inertial dampers, usually far below the level of human hearing, had risen to a low buzz like that of an approaching hornet.

Desjani's hand finally moved again, *Dauntless*'s acceleration slackening, the whine of the inertial dampers subsiding, the ship seeming to sigh with relief as the strain on her structure fell back within normal parameters. "We needed to get out in front. Alone," she said.

"That's a good plan," Geary agreed, glad to no longer feel pinned in his seat by acceleration forces leaking past the dampers. "Have you ever actually destroyed a ship that way?" he added in a low voice.

She pretended to ponder the question. "Do you mean by accident or on purpose?"

"Never mind."

Calls were coming in from Captain Duellos and Captain Badaya, the commanders of the two battle cruiser groups, so Geary linked them and answered both together. The ships were still only several light seconds apart, making real-time conversation possible. "You probably wonder what we're doing."

Captain Duellos smiled, hoisting an imaginary glass in a toast. "It's obvious that Tanya is driving. No one else could get that sort of performance out of a battle cruiser."

Badaya, far less diplomatically, shook his head. "You need to fall back so we can join up."

"No," Geary said. "The whole point of this is to give the Syndics a target so attractive they forget about attacking those Dancers and come charging in to try to destroy *Dauntless* before any other Alliance ships can catch up."

"Isn't it obvious that you're doing just that? Trying to bait them?" Badaya's expression cleared as he realized the answer to his own question. "The Syndics aren't thinking straight. All they'll see is the opportunity they want."

"I'm still a bit worried by how far ahead of us you'll likely be when the Syndics intercept you," Duellos said.

"We have to make the bait look attractive," Geary said. "Do not try to close the distance until we engage the Syndics."

"Yes, Admiral."

That call ended, Geary pondered for a moment before turning toward the comms watch. "I want to send a message to the Syndic CEO."

"Yes, Admiral. It's ready, sir. Circuit four."

Geary straightened in his seat before touching the command. "CEO . . . Gordini is it?" If he wanted to get the Syndics chasing him, he might as well enrage the ego of the CEO a little more. And this message would confirm for the Syndics that he was still aboard *Dauntless*. "You are ordered to cease all offensive action and depart not only this star system but all of Dancer-controlled space. The Alliance will not stand by while you attack our friends." The Dancers would surely pick up the transmission. He might as well say things the Dancers would like. "To the honor of our ancestors, Geary, out."

After ending the message he heard a chuckle from the back of the bridge. Colonel Rogero had strapped into a pullout seat near the observer seat occupied by Kommodor Bradamont. Now he was smiling.

"Admiral, even if that CEO was completely sane she'd be enraged by that message. Their pride is very important to them."

Desjani turned to smile at Bradamont. "How was that driving?"

"Not bad," Bradamont said, acting unimpressed. She had once commanded the Alliance battle cruiser *Dragon*. "I see you've learned a few things from watching me."

"From watching you?" Desjani laughed. "Do you really think you could teach me anything about driving a battle cruiser?"

"Anytime you want to give it a test," Bradamont said. "If you're not worried about going head-to-head with me."

"It's on. Next time we're at Midway," Desjani said, while Colonel Rogero eyed Bradamont with open worry.

"You're not going to race Bradamont once we're back at Midway," Geary muttered to Desjani. "That's not authorized use of a battle cruiser. And I have a feeling that President Iceni will feel the same way about Bradamont borrowing Midway's battle cruiser to race you."

"Hey," Desjani said, "before you returned from the dead I was sure I'd be with my ancestors sooner rather than later. I'm getting my love of life back. And I do love driving a battle cruiser."

"We're seeing the Syndics break off from the Dancers," Lieutenant Yuon reported.

Geary studied his display, watching the aspects of the Syndic warships change as they altered vectors. The once unusually rigid Syndic formation had nearly fallen apart while the Syndics pursued the Dancers, and completely dissolved as Geary watched. Ten minutes ago, the Syndics had abandoned any other task and hurled their ships on intercepts with *Dauntless*.

But as the Syndics left off pursuit of the Dancers, missiles shot out from the Syndic battle cruisers, arcing around to chase the Dancer ships. The Dancers, freed from dodging hell lances, were accelerating straight out at rates human ships couldn't match, walking away from the Syndic missiles.

Geary blinked, trying to resolve blurs that were appearing on his display's images of the Syndics. "What's happening to the displays?"

"Admiral, we're passing point two light speed," Lieutenant Castries replied. "The Syndics are coming up past point one light. That's a combined velocity of more than point three light speed, and at point three light speed and above, our sensors can't precisely compensate for distortion of space-time caused by relativity. They can't show us exactly where the Syndics are or exactly what they look like. The blurs will grow larger if we keep accelerating."

"That's what lieutenants are for," Captain Desjani murmured to Geary. "To remind admirals of things they should already know."

"I was focused too much on the Dancer problem," Geary grumbled in reply.

"As you should be," she said. "I can handle *Dauntless*'s engagement with these guys. Armus, Duellos, and Badaya can handle vectoring their formations to hit the Syndics. You taught them how to do that well. Which means you can and should focus on other things."

He took a deep breath before nodding. "Right. I don't have to call all of the shots anymore. Not in this kind of situation. I have to trust my people to do their jobs. But I want to ensure those Syndics stay focused on hitting *Dauntless*. We have to make sure they have a target they think they can hit."

"And chances of a hit at our current combined velocities are effectively zero," she agreed. "They'll have a decent target, Admiral. We'll brake in plenty of time for that. I'm going to stop acceleration when we hit point two five light."

Geary sighed. "Hard braking?"

"Not *that* hard." Desjani grinned. "We have to look like we want a fight."

"You do want a fight, Captain."

"Yes. Yes, I do." Her expression shifted to serious. "Since it's been forced on us, I am going to fight this one and win it."

Only two minutes later Desjani cut off the main propulsion as *Dauntless* reached point two five light speed. They could have kept accelerating, limited only by their amount of fuel and by relativity, which would cause the mass of *Dauntless* to increase the closer they got to the speed of light. But slowing down required the same amount of fuel to brake velocity as accelerating did. No one wanted to be caught in a ship traveling at point four or point five light speed without enough fuel to slow down again.

Desjani's fingers moved on her controls and moments later thrusters fired on *Dauntless*, pitching the battle cruiser over and around so her main propulsion was aimed in the direction the ship was going, her bow now facing back the way they'd come. As soon as the ship lined up, the main propulsion thundered back to life, now working to slow the ship it had been accelerating.

Fortunately, already out ahead of the other Alliance ships, they had more time to slow down and didn't have to brake as hard as they'd accelerated. Even though the engineering watch had their eyes glued to the stress readouts, the readings only veered to the edge of the red danger zone without going into unsafe levels.

"Fifteen minutes until intercept," Lieutenant Yuon reported.

The Dancer ships that the Syndics had been attacking had avoided the Syndic missiles and were coming back around. Were they going to assist in the attack on the Syndics? Probably not, since they weren't accelerating all out anymore. In fact, there wasn't any indication the Dancers were going to help with a "human problem."

A sudden thought hit him, prompting another call to Charban. "General, that last Dancer message where they told us this was a human problem for humans to solve. Did you get any sense of emotion in that message?"

"It's odd you should ask," Charban replied. "We were discussing that. Dr. Cresida and Lieutenant Jamenson both noted that the lines in the reply were briefer, ending in ways that felt abrupt, and the words used also shorter. Lieutenant Jamenson says the Dancer reply feels angry to her."

"I was afraid of that," Geary said. "This isn't just the Dancers telling us to fix a human problem. They're upset that our human problems are spilling over into their area of space."

"I can understand that," Charban said. "But surely the Dancers understand that we're not the sheriffs of humanity. We can't . . . what's the old expression . . . ride herd on every other human who wants to contact them."

"But the Dancers may want us to do just that," Geary said. "And the enigmas may have known that when they threw open the gates for humanity to get to Dancer space more easily than before."

"Even after this battle is over, this whole thing is going to be even more difficult than we expected, isn't it?"

"I'm afraid so." Geary checked his display. "We're ten minutes from intercept. Excuse me while I oversee a battle."

The oncoming Syndics were slightly below and to the left of *Dauntless*, their relative bearing unchanging since they were headed straight for an intercept of the Alliance battle cruiser. What had begun as a formation with interlocking fields of fire had become one big blob of ships led by the Syndic battle cruisers followed by some of the heavy cruisers and Hunter-Killers, another blob extending back and upward with the rest of the heavy cruisers, and a smaller, extended blob holding four Hunter-Killers. With the battle cruisers and heavy cruisers accelerating all out, the small HuKs were unable to keep up and were slowly sliding farther behind the other Syndic warships.

Almost directly behind *Dauntless* was Formation Alpha, the main body of the Alliance fleet. Accelerating much more slowly, they probably wouldn't reach the fight in time to make a difference. But since their primary task remained defending *Boundless*, the auxiliaries, and the assault transports, that wasn't critical.

Behind, to the right of, and above *Dauntless* were the battle cruisers of Formation Bravo One under the command of Captain Duellos, racing to join the fight. Behind, slightly below, and to the left of *Dauntless* were the battle cruisers of Formation Bravo Two, commanded by Captain Badaya, also charging toward the fight. The relative positions of both of those formations were slowly shifting, because they were aiming not to intercept *Dauntless* but for the area they thought the Syndics would be in when their ships reached the battle somewhere between fifteen and twenty minutes after *Dauntless* and the Syndics met up.

Desjani was braking *Dauntless* at a rate that would have the battle cruiser traveling at point one light speed at the projected time to intercept the Syndics. The Syndics were braking velocity now as well, coming down toward point one light speed themselves. *Dauntless* would meet the Syndics at a combined velocity of point two light speed, the maximum at which human fire control systems could compensate for relativistic distortion and achieve hits on enemy ships tearing past at incredible velocities.

"What's your plan, Captain?" Geary asked Desjani.

She pointed at her display. "The Syndic battle cruisers are still close enough to each other that I can't make a firing pass on one without risking getting hit by fire from two or three others as well. There's no need to run that risk. We want the Syndics to continue coming at us, right?"

"Absolutely," Geary said.

"Then I was thinking of appearing to be lining up for a firing run on this Syndic battle cruiser," Desjani said, highlighting one, "but making a last-moment minor change in vector to bypass him and instead run through this group of four Hunter-Killers." She indicated the four HuKs struggling to keep up with the heavier ships, but slightly down and behind the rest of the Syndic warships. "We should be able to knock out at least three of them. That should seriously upset the Syndics and motivate them to come around to try to hit us and even the score."

"Good plan," Geary said, nodding. "The Syndics are likely to come around after you independently, scattering even more, so you can aim for whichever of them is most isolated."

"You want me to keep engaging with them, right? Even for a third pass?"

"Even for a third pass," Geary said. "By then Duellos and Badaya should have caught up."

Desjani paused, giving him a sidelong look. "None of this negates the chance that the Syndics get some lucky hits on us, or one of them blunders into our exact path and we become an instant dust cloud. We'll be facing bad enough odds on the first two passes that those possibilities have to be taken into account."

"Understood," Geary said. "Every ship in the fleet faces those possibilities every time we engage with an enemy."

"Every ship in the fleet doesn't have a certain admiral aboard."

"My life isn't more valuable than anyone else's."

Desjani blew out a derisory laugh. "I'm going to do what I hate to do, saying what I think Victoria Rione would have said to you about that. Ready?"

"No."

"*You* are important. Failing to recognize that is not a virtue." Desjani sat back, eyes on her display. "That said, let's get this done." She tapped her controls. The main propulsion units shut off, thrusters firing immediately afterwards to swing *Dauntless* around again so she faced the approaching enemy bow on, where (as on all warships) the battle cruiser's strongest shields, strongest armor, and heaviest weapons were concentrated.

"Two minutes to intercept," Lieutenant Yuon said. "All weapons ready."

"Primary target is this battle cruiser," Desjani announced to her crew as she tagged the ship on her display. "We will not engage it, instead sidestepping to hit these four HuKs as secondary targets. I want all four of them out of the fight. Understood?"

"Yes, Captain!" the bridge watch standers chorused.

"One minute to intercept," Lieutenant Yuon added.

Desjani entered the last-moment change of vector into the automated maneuvering controls, which would (hopefully) avoid any collisions while getting close enough to the intended targets for weapons to get hits.

Geary felt thrusters and main propulsion jerk the ship slightly as it entered the final approach, making a minor change to *Dauntless*'s vector that translated into enough difference over thousands of kilometers. Moments later two specter missiles leapt from *Dauntless* toward the Syndics.

Alerts sounded as every Syndic battle cruiser pumped out missiles targeted on *Dauntless*, followed less than a second later by missiles from the Syndic heavy cruisers.

He had just an instant to take in that information, to see the enemy missiles launched, to know that if the Syndics had properly guessed where *Dauntless* would be in the next instant, then the battle cruiser would be badly hurt at best, or destroyed so quickly he'd never have time to know it was happening. Not enough time for his body to respond to the fear. Just enough time for him to accept that this instant might be his last.

At the velocities the Syndics and *Dauntless* were traveling, the two groups of ships went from thousands of kilometers away to *there* to thousands of kilometers past in the blink of an eye. Human reflexes were far too slow to use when firing opportunities were measured in tiny fractions of a second, but human ingenuity had managed to produce automated systems that were up to the task.

Geary didn't feel the shock of weapons firing aboard *Dauntless*, didn't have time to realize that he was still alive, until after the enemy was well past. He also registered tremors in the ship from hits, his eyes going to his display to see what had happened in that moment when the opposing ships had unleashed hell lances and grapeshot at each other.

"Three hits on our shields," Lieutenant Castries announced. "One near miss from a Syndic missile detonation. No shield penetrations or hull damage."

On the displays, the remaining Syndic missiles were still curving back and around, trying to manage new intercepts on *Dauntless*.

The Syndic battle cruisers, aiming their missile intercepts, hell lances, and grapeshot fire at where *Dauntless* would have been if she hadn't made that tiny change in vector, had wasted most of their shots. A heavy cruiser had almost managed a missile hit on her, and even three of the hapless Hunter-Killers had scored hell lance hits as *Dauntless* ripped through them. But the HuKs, faced with the firepower of a battle cruiser, had taken far worse punishment.

Two had blown up, their power cores exploding under the stress of multiple hits. A third had broken in half, the pieces tumbling away. The fourth appeared still intact but was sliding silently off into space, all systems apparently knocked out.

"Nice job," Geary said against the strain of *Dauntless*'s latest maneuver.

Desjani was bringing the battle cruiser up and around to the left of the initial engagement, not yet having chosen a target or final vector, her eyes on the Syndic missiles still trying to catch their target, but running out of fuel to maneuver and self-destructing.

The remaining Syndic warships had lost all pretense of being an organized force, every ship moving by itself as they looped up, down, or to either side to try to hit *Dauntless* again.

One of the heavy cruisers hadn't come about, instead angling slightly to aim for the center of the Alliance Formation Alpha in an insane single-handed attack. "Crazy," Lieutenant Yuon muttered loud enough to be heard, an assessment which was literally true.

"There," Geary said, indicating one of the other Syndic heavy cruisers that had made the mistake of swinging up and to one side in a way that left it out of supporting range of every other Syndic ship.

"I see him," Desjani said, tagging the heavy cruiser as primary target.

Dauntless swung about, steadying on her vector as the Syndic heavy cruiser tried to evade.

The cruiser's efforts weren't enough. *Dauntless* flashed by, hammering the isolated ship.

"The heavy cruiser's bow shields have collapsed. He took heavy damage forward," Lieutenant Castries reported. "He still has some maneuvering control but is assessed to have lost all of his weapons."

Desjani was bringing *Dauntless* down and around again, forming an immense loop through space. But the six Syndic battle cruisers and surviving heavy cruisers by chance or design were coming around again as well, in maneuvers that would box in the single Alliance battle cruiser and ensure she was hit by several ships.

"This will be challenging," Desjani muttered, her eyes fixed on her display that showed the closest ships.

Geary gazed at the Syndics closing in, his mind running through possible maneuvers faster than he could have tested them on the display, seeing no way to avoid intercepts by multiple enemy warships. He saw Desjani angling *Dauntless* up and to the right, aiming for the one vector that might get them through the gauntlet with the least amount of damage.

Which might still be a whole lot of damage.

Everyone else on the bridge could see the situation and knew what was coming, but in a testament to their training by and confidence in Captain Desjani they were all waiting stoically to do what they could during the looming lopsided fight.

"Primary target," Desjani said, highlighting the Syndic battle cruiser that would, by a fraction of a second, be the first to come into range of *Dauntless*'s weapons.

"Primary target locked on," Lieutenant Castries said. "All weapons ready to fire when we enter range."

Geary tore his eyes from the closest ships, which were all enemy, looking around his own display showing a much wider region of space. He saw projected course vectors reaching through space, and smiled. "We're okay."

Duellos and Badaya had reached the fight, and the odds had suddenly flipped.

Captain Duellos led his formation diving down through one side of the disorganized tangle of Syndic warships. The battle cruisers *Inspire*, *Formidable*, *Dragon*, and *Steadfast*, along with their escorting cruisers and destroyers, hammered at the nearest Syndic battle cruiser, the one *Dauntless* had designated a primary target, and other warships within reach. In their wake the Syndic battle cruiser shattered into dozens of pieces, one heavy cruiser exploded, and another remained intact but with nearly every system shot out. Seven Hunter-Killers were also destroyed or knocked out.

Moments later Captain Badaya's formation shot upward through the bottom edge of the Syndics. *Daring*, *Victorious*, and *Intemperate* targeted one Syndic battle cruiser, while *Illustrious*, *Incredible*, and *Valiant* went after another, their escorting cruisers and destroyers hitting anything within their range.

Both of the targeted Syndic battle cruisers came apart, as well as three more heavy cruisers, and nine more HuKs.

But the three surviving Syndic battle cruisers and two of the surviving heavy cruisers along with the last two Hunter-Killers remained fixated on *Dauntless*, coming in from multiple angles while Duellos and Badaya brought their formations back around through the vast distances such vector changes required at these velocities. Even though their destruction in the near future was certain, the remaining Syndics appeared to be determined to take *Dauntless* along with them.

"This might still be a bad one," Desjani murmured.

FOUR

"THEY'RE going to expect us to dodge again," Desjani said. "We've done it twice and now there's help close at hand there's no reason to risk a close firing run."

"Probably," Geary said.

"But even if we dodge, they've got us boxed in along any feasible vectors. We're going to get hit this time."

"Probably," Geary said once more.

Desjani glanced at him. "So this time let's target their flagship and mean it."

"What happened to me being so important?"

"Do you concur or not, Admiral?"

Geary gave her a twisted half smile. "I concur, Captain."

Dauntless slewed about under the push of her thrusters, main propulsion kicking in to shove the battle cruiser onto a vector slightly higher and to the right. A vector aimed at intercepting the current track of the Syndic flagship. "Let's make sure that CEO feels this!" Desjani called to her bridge watch. "We're going to try getting close enough to trigger the null field."

Geary suppressed a shudder. Null fields were one of the only weapon advantages the Alliance had over opponents, a device that generated a field in which molecular bonds failed, turning anything inside into component atoms. Metal, atmosphere, people. It was a highly effective weapon, limited by its very short range, its inability to function too close to large gravity wells such as planets and moons, and size and power requirements that limited its use to Alliance battle cruisers. Highly effective, and to Geary's mind a horrible weapon, but one that had to be used at times. To the rest of the Alliance fleet, hardened by a century of war, it was just another weapon.

As *Dauntless* and every Syndic ship settled on the vectors for their firing runs, four more specter missiles jumped away from *Dauntless*, aimed at the targeted battle cruiser.

The Syndics unleashed their own barrage of missiles in the moment before intercept. There was no way to tell, on the final approach, whether the Syndics were all targeting *Dauntless*'s current vector, or if they were hedging their bets that she'd dodge again and planning a wider net of attacks.

The far distant Syndic warships were suddenly there, all around *Dauntless*, and just as suddenly gone, far behind. *Dauntless* shuddered both from unleashing every weapon she had at the Syndic flagship and as a result of numerous hits.

Desjani's hand hovered over her maneuvering controls, but she waited, watching for damage results to come in to ensure she didn't overstress any part of *Dauntless* that had taken hits.

"Multiple hell lance hits along bow and side shields," Lieutenant Castries announced, her voice steady. "Grapeshot impacts along bow and port side. Estimate three hell lance penetrations of shields. Several compartments holed. Inner bulkheads holding. Bow and port shields rebuilding but damage to shield generators near bow will limit strength to sixty percent of maximum. Hell lance battery Two Alpha out of commission. Initial casualty reports show a dozen wounded."

Captain Desjani finally entered new commands, *Dauntless* coming up and around once more. "We got lucky. A lot of their shots were aimed assuming we'd dodge another time."

"That wasn't luck," Geary said. "That was tactics."

"Targeted battle cruiser lost its forward shields," Lieutenant Castries continued. "Major damage in bow area. Null field impacted starboard bow area of the Syndic battle cruiser, wiping out defenses and weapons in that part of the ship. The battle cruiser retains full main propulsion but has lost substantial maneuvering capability."

"Here come Duellos and Badaya again," Desjani said.

Odds were the Syndic CEO was still alive. On Syndic warships, as on Alliance warships, the command bridges were buried deep inside the ship, as well protected as possible. Geary wondered if any flashes of sanity were coming to her at this moment, or if she was still consumed with irrational anger and ambition.

The crippled Syndic flagship tried to alter vector, coming about awkwardly in what seemed another attempt to engage *Dauntless*. "They're coming onto a direct intercept," Lieutenant Castries reported, her voice calm. "Estimate they intend ramming."

At the velocities the ships were moving, such a collision would instantly shatter both ships and everything and everyone on them into dust.

It was a move of desperation, and a futile one.

Duellos's battle cruisers had come around and tore past the Syndic flagship, hurling out hell lances and grapeshot, two more null field hits gouging huge hunks out of the hull of the Syndic battle cruiser.

The Syndic flagship broke apart under the stress, the bow section tumbling away from part of the midsection. The largest portion, midsection and stern, suddenly vanished as the Syndic ship's power core overloaded.

A brief cheer arose on the bridge of *Dauntless*.

"Don't cheer," Geary said. "The poor devils are dying. They never stood a chance."

Desjani shrugged. "We gave them a shot at us."

"Yes." There weren't any escape pods coming off the remaining sections of the former Syndic flagship. "Looks like the whole crew died."

"Those that were left," she reminded him. "We know there was a lot of infighting aboard those ships before we engaged them."

Badaya's formation swept through the disorganized remnants of the Syndics, destroying another of the remaining battle cruisers and both of the heavy cruisers there. The last two Hunter-Killers had hurled themselves at *Illustrious* in other possible ramming attempts but had been wiped out before reaching their target.

The last remaining Syndic battle cruiser swung off an intercept vector with *Dauntless*, instead pointing his bow straight up, his main propulsion flaring.

"He's at maximum acceleration," Lieutenant Yuon reported.

"He's accelerating beyond safe limits," Kommodor Bradamont added, her face stricken. "He can't keep that up."

"Escape pods leaving the last Syndic," Lieutenant Castries said.

Pods were leaping away from the battle cruiser, which continued to climb at maximum.

"How many?" Geary asked.

"It depends how many are in each pod," Bradamont said. "At a guess, that's anywhere from one half to one quarter of the crew. Ease off, you idiot!" she cried as if whoever was driving that Syndic battle cruiser could hear her.

Instead, the battle cruiser's main propulsion flared a little brighter, as if safety limiters had been bypassed.

The Syndic warship didn't explode as its inertial dampers failed. It shattered into thousands of pieces. Any humans still aboard would have died instantly. The myriad fragments of ship and crew continued on their last vectors, a swiftly moving, slowly expanding field of wreckage heading out of the star system toward the infinite dark beyond.

"Damn," Desjani muttered.

It was one thing to see ships destroyed in combat. They'd seen far too much of that. But watching any ship destroy itself, even an enemy, was far harder.

"Captain," Lieutenant Yuon said, his voice a little shaky. "The last Syndic heavy cruiser reached Formation Alpha."

Geary checked his display. Minutes before, the Syndic cruiser had charged straight into the center of the major Alliance formation. Fire from multiple destroyers and light and heavy cruisers knocked down its shields and riddled its hull. By the time the wreck came in range of the Alliance battleships, there probably wasn't anyone left alive aboard. But shattering the heavy cruiser by fire from the battleships might produce large chunks of debris that could collide with Alliance ships in the rear of the formation. Geary wasn't surprised that Captain Armus had told his battleships to hold fire to avoid that. Instead, some of the battleships and two of the auxiliaries altered vectors slightly to ensure the hulk wouldn't collide with them as it shot heedlessly the rest of the way through and past the Alliance formation.

"Destroyer Squadrons Four, Nine, Fourteen, and Sixteen, detach from your formations to recover escape pods," Geary ordered. "Fifth Assault Transport Division, assign one transport to each destroyer squadron to assist in removing Syndic personnel from the escape pods. General Carabali, I want Marines in riot control gear standing by as each escape pod is opened. Use any necessary means to subdue and sedate any Syndic personnel who pose a danger." He paused. "Well done, everyone. To the honor of our ancestors, Geary, out."

His gaze lingered on his display. In addition to the hundreds of Alliance warships in or approaching this region of space, the three Dancer ships that had been escorting the now-vanished Syndicate Worlds flotilla were still orbiting well off from the area of fighting. Despite *Dauntless* dashing to their rescue, they had stood off during the fight instead of coming to the assistance of the Alliance battle cruiser. Now they were probably awaiting orders from their Dancer superiors on what to do next.

Geary touched another comm control. "General Charban, please inform the Dancers that we have dealt with the 'human problem.'" He felt like adding something that would be either bitter or angry, but decided to leave it at that.

A week later, the Alliance fleet was back orbiting near the primary Dancer-occupied world in this star system. And Geary was back in a conference room, overseeing a virtual gathering of senior captains in the fleet as well as others who could contribute to the discussion. In addition to Captain Desjani, Captain Duellos from *Inspire*, and Captain Badaya from *Illustrious*, there were battleship Captains Armus of *Colossus*, Plant of *Warspite*, Hiyen of *Reprisal*, Casia of *Conqueror*, and Jane Geary (Geary's grandniece) of *Dreadnaught*. Captain Smythe, the fleet's chief engineer, was here from the fast fleet auxiliary *Tanuki*. Also attending were Dr. Nasr, and General Carabali of the Marines. Fleet intelligence was represented by Lieutenant Commander Christopher George, who was aboard *Tsunami* along with General Carabali, and Lieutenant Iger. General Charban sat near Geary, as did Kommodor Bradamont and Colonel Rogero.

"Let's start with Lieutenant Commander George and Lieutenant Iger on what we've learned from the Syndic prisoners," Geary said.

Lieutenant Commander George stood up and began speaking like someone who had given countless briefings. Which he very likely had. "Most of the Syndics rescued from escape pods are still affected by Severe Jump Space Syndrome and could not provide reliable information. Fortunately, a few are recovering. One of them is a Syndic officer, a sub-executive, who was able to confirm for us that our speculations were accurate. The Syndic flotilla did get to Dancer space using new modifications to their jump drives, one of the jumps being nearly a month in duration."

"A *month*?" Captain Casia blurted out. "Continuously in jump space?"

"Yes, Captain."

"Ancestors preserve us all," Casia said, shaking his head. "No wonder they went crazy."

"The sub-executive," George continued, "said the Syndic officers were told that the new modifications to the jump drives were the result of breakthroughs by Syndicate Worlds' technicians. Since his job responsibilities were in weapons control, he knew nothing more about them."

"There wasn't any discussion or gossip among the officers about the modifications?" Captain Smythe asked.

Colonel Rogero shook his head. "It's very dangerous in the Syndicate to discuss job details with anyone outside of your work group. Anyone overheard doing that would face serious questioning from the snakes."

Lieutenant Commander George nodded. "That's what the sub-executive told us. Everyone assumed any questions about the jump drive modifications would result in unwelcome attention from Syndicate Worlds' Internal Security agents."

"What about the jump space syndrome? How did that manifest among their crews?" Captain Jane Geary asked.

George hesitated, glancing at Lieutenant Iger, before replying. "It was . . . bad. The sub-executive said at first things 'just seemed more so.' That's how he explained it. Everyone was told nothing had changed and no one was suffering any significant symptoms, but everything became strenuous. And as things went more and more off the rails it all still felt natural. Even when . . ." Lieutenant Commander George grimaced. "People started dying. Our source estimates at least one-third of the crew aboard his ship died in the last part of the journey here or before the battle. Fights, executions by security agents, accidents, suicides, attacks on officers, and other causes. His stories, confirmed by three other Syndics who have mostly regained rationality, are . . . very difficult to repeat."

"We have records of all of them," Dr. Nasr said, his voice quiet but authoritative. "For anyone who wishes details and has a strong stomach."

"What ship was your sub-executive aboard?" Captain Plant asked, apparently unaffected by the most recent topic.

"The last battle cruiser to survive," Lieutenant Iger said. "Most of our prisoners came from that ship."

"Did he have any idea why that ship took off for deep space like it did?"

"No, Captain," Lieutenant Commander George said. "He said acceleration suddenly hit them hard. Nothing from the captain, just sudden acceleration. He said he was trying to contact someone he knew on the bridge of the Syndic ship when word went racing through the crew that orders had been given to abandon ship, and the surviving crew stampeded for the escape pods. He has no idea who ordered abandon ship, or even if it really had been ordered. The crew fell apart, total panic. There were fights to get aboard the escape pods in which a number of the remaining crew died or were seriously injured and left behind."

Dr. Nasr nodded, his expression grim. "The doctors aboard the assault transports have treated many injuries among the prisoners consistent with brutal fighting hand to hand."

"Some of it continued in the escape pods," General Carabali said. "My Marines had to deal with some ugly scenes when those Syndic escape pods were cracked open."

Captain Hiyen shook his head in despair. "Is that the fate awaiting anyone else who rushes to use those new jump drive modifications despite the worries about jump drive syndrome? Will the next arrivals be from my Callas Republic, or the Alliance, and also be such hellholes for their crews?"

"It may not be as bad," Colonel Rogero said. "You heard what the sub-executive said. Things on the ships became 'more so.' In a Syndicate unit, the workers are usually treated as wage slaves. Even the executives, the officers, are in constant fear of the snakes and of each other. The workers, what you call sailors, are kept on an extremely tight leash. Even under what the Syndicate considers 'normal conditions' worker riots can take place, and be suppressed with lethal munitions."

Rogero sounded matter-of-fact. This was the system he'd grown up with. Geary saw some hostile side-glances at Rogero and spoke up. "I'll remind everyone that Colonel Rogero, and all of those we deal with on Midway, revolted against that system. They put their lives on the line to change things."

"But that Syndic system was in full force on those ships," Desjani said. "They were already hellholes, in a way."

"Yes," Rogero said. "The jump space syndrome aggravated those things. I have seen how your units operate. They are not always happy, friendly groups, but you have nothing like the snakes watching and listening to your every move, with the power to execute on suspicion or on a whim. Your officers do not inform on each other to get ahead, or plot assassinations of superiors to gain a promotion opportunity. I'm not saying there would not be problems on your ships, some fights, suicides most likely I would think as a veteran of much combat myself, but it shouldn't be as horrendous."

"I believe he is right," Dr. Nasr said. "Not to minimize how much pain and death might result on one of our ships."

"So still not something we should willingly expose our crews to," Captain Duellos emphasized. "We could not consider providing solid warning to those back in the Alliance before this, because we could only guess what had happened. Now we have proof."

"How do we warn them?" Captain Armus asked. "To get a warning back through enigma-controlled space would require a substantial force."

"Leaving us with that much less of a force here," Captain Desjani said.

"What about using the new path using longer jumps?" Captain Badaya said. "Take the crew off a destroyer, give its navigation system all the information it needs, and send it home with the warning."

"If it ran into trouble and never made it, we wouldn't know," Captain Plant objected.

"More importantly," Captain Smythe observed, "we can't use that route because we don't have the jump drive modifications that everyone else in human space may now have. Every Syndic ship was destroyed, so we couldn't learn anything from their jump drives."

"Oh, blazes," Badaya grumbled. "That's just like an engineer. We come up with a brilliant idea and you have to bring up all the ways it's impossible."

"That is one of the functions of an engineer," Smythe said with a smile. "But I think there's another less ironclad reason why that wouldn't work. Who'd believe the warning?"

"We have interviews, firsthand accounts," Dr. Nasr said, surprised at the question.

"Those can be faked," Smythe said, leaning back. "Look, from what we were told, all the information anyone needed about the danger posed by those long jumps is already available to anyone who looks. We had no trouble looking it up in our medical files, correct, Doctor? The Syndics came anyway, doubtless convincing themselves, as I have heard our friends from Midway argue, that their people now are much stronger or accustomed to jump space or whatever." Captain Smythe let out a long sigh. "Everyone else is going to do the same. Even if we send them all of those records and swear it's all true. They won't want to believe they can't do it, and they will want to believe that we're just trying to monopolize access to the Dancers."

A long silence followed Smythe's words. Finally, Captain Duellos cast a resigned glance toward Geary. "He's right, Admiral. Nothing is going to stop them from coming here, and learning their own lesson the hard way."

"Oh," Captain Smythe said, "they might keep doing it even after the warnings prove accurate. People are like that. Believe me, engineers encounter that problem all the time."

"There must be something we can do," Captain Badaya said, sounding partly plaintive and partly angry. "I have no love for Syndics, but I shudder to think what those crews experienced."

"We could send some of the Syndic prisoners along with the warning. As many as possible," Dr. Nasr suddenly suggested. "They have no reason to lie for the Alliance. Some of them will not have recovered by the time they reach the Alliance. They are living proof, and personal eyewitnesses."

"You're talking about sending one of the assault transports back the way we came through enigma space to Midway," Geary said. Using that route would avoid the dangers of the extended-length jumps, and getting rid of those prisoners would be welcome, but it would cut his assault transport force from four to three.

"If necessary, yes."

"Is anyone going to believe Syndics?" Captain Plant asked, her voice arch with skepticism.

"That is a problem," Jane Geary agreed. "But what is our alternative? Does anyone think we shouldn't try, that we should just let everyone learn their lesson the hard way?"

"That's a tempting idea," Duellos said dryly.

"They'll listen to a message from the admiral," Badaya said, pointing to Geary. "A lot of them, anyway. And those who don't might listen to the doctors, or to the Syndics. All of you know I'm a practical person. I don't have a lot of room for idealism. But I firmly believe that our ancestors expect us to *try* rather than simply accept we can't do anything."

Even Badaya could hit the target at times, Geary thought. He looked at Desjani.

She nodded. "Captain Badaya is right. It's our duty to try."

"That assault transport would need a strong escort," Captain Armus said. "Not battle cruisers. Battleships that can fend off attacks. At least one division. And two divisions of heavy cruisers."

"Would one division be enough?" Jane Geary asked. "We've seen the sort of forces the enigmas can bring together."

"We wouldn't be lingering, just passing through," Armus said. "But, yes, two divisions of battleships would probably be the minimum."

"You'd be sending a lot of Marines with it," General Carabali cautioned. "Even if I redistribute some of those aboard, you're still talking about four hundred Marines no longer available to this fleet."

"We'll be temporarily sacrificing a lot of capability," Geary said. "I want recommendations on which ships to send."

"*Dreadnaught* needs to be one of them," Badaya insisted. "Jane is a Geary. There'll be no doubt that she's speaking for you."

"That's true," Jane Geary said, sounding resigned. "My Second Battleship Division should go."

"I volunteer the Third Battleship Division," Captain Plant said.

"All right," Geary said. "I'll designate two divisions of heavy cruisers, three squadrons of light cruisers, and six squadrons of destroyers as escorts. Are there any recommendations as to which assault transport to send?"

"*Mistral*," General Carabali said. "She already has most of the Syndic prisoners aboard. If you agree I can notify Commander Young that she's volunteered for the mission."

"*Mistral* would be a good choice," Geary said. Young had proven her reliability at Unity Alternate.

Unity Alternate. Prisoners. Something that had been prowling around the back of his mind ever since Dr. Nasr proposed sending the Syndic prisoners back finally showed itself.

"We'll put all the Syndic prisoners aboard *Mistral*. There's room for them, isn't there?"

"The assault transports have troop compartments that can be modified into cells for large numbers of prisoners," Carabali said. "There'd be plenty of room."

"I want to add on the other prisoners," Geary said, drawing surprised looks as the rest tried to figure out who he was referring to. "Captains Pelleas and Burdock and Commander Cui, and all of the lower-ranking mutineers. As well as that agent who's been sitting in the brig aboard *Dauntless* ever since he tried to kill me."

A brief silence followed Geary's words.

"They should be shot," Captain Badaya finally said. "Firing squads. Why send them home to suffer the same fates?"

"Two reasons," Geary said. "The first is that regulations require that the executions of mutineers be transmitted live throughout the fleet. We have to assume those transmissions would be monitored by the Dancers. I don't know what their reaction would be to watching us kill so many of our own. It might be very negative, though. I don't want the deaths of those mutineers to achieve what the mutineers sought, destroying our chances of successful negotiations with the Dancers."

Another short silence before everyone began showing agreement. "If carrying out the firing squads here would serve their purposes, everyone will understand why their executions are going to take place elsewhere," Captain Armus said. "Or do you hope some of them, seeking to save themselves, might provide authorities back in the Alliance with information about their supporters and superiors?"

"That's the other reason," Geary said. "Dead, they can tell us nothing more. Alive, having had time to anticipate the firing squads, and knowing their deaths will not further their aims, some might talk. At the least, back home there will be the resources to find out exactly who the agent who tried to kill me is, and that may lead to whoever sent him here."

"We need to learn more, if possible," General Carabali said. "I'm not picking up any indications of other threats within this fleet, but I think it would be wise to assume whoever is setting these things in motion has not yet fired their last shot."

"Agreed," Armus said.

"I'll issue orders to transfer all prisoners, Syndic and mutineers, to *Mistral*," Geary said. "We'll get *Mistral* to Midway. *Mistral* can probably drop off some of the Syndic prisoners there, and then use Midway's hypernet gate to get directly to Alliance territory. To make this work, we're going to need the Dancers to escort our warning force to the Dancer border star system where we arrived, and then escort the force back here when it returns from Midway. General Charban, please have your people start on a message telling the Dancers what we want to do, emphasizing that the sooner they agree the sooner we can limit how many humans try to use the extended jumps to reach Dancer space."

"Hopefully," Charban said, "the Dancers won't consider this also to be a human problem."

"Hopefully," Geary agreed. "Speaking of which, I have one other thing to toss around before I go to the ambassador and explain what we're doing to try to warn everyone back home. The Dancers. In the past, they've been actively helpful. This time, dealing with the Syndic flotilla, the Dancers didn't try to assist or even offer to assist, even though the Syndics attacked some of their ships. What made this time different?"

Kommodor Bradamont spoke up. "As a somewhat outsider now, I think I can answer that. The Dancers helped the Alliance when it fought the Kicks, and the enigmas, and the artificial intelligences controlling the Defender Fleet. None of those battles involved humans fighting humans."

"'Human problem, humans fix,'" General Charban said, nodding in agreement. "The Dancer messages we received about the Syndics felt increasingly angry to me and my staff. As if they were upset that *we'd* allowed the Syndics to come here and hadn't already taken care of everything ourselves."

"Do they expect us to police *their* star systems?" General Carabali asked, making it clear how little she liked the thought of that.

"I don't know," Geary said. "Just what it is the Dancers expect of us remains unclear. But we're going to do our best to nail down this particular thing as fast as we can."

LATELY, Ambassador Rycerz always seemed to have a headache whenever Geary called her. "You have to send that much of your force away? For all we know, an even bigger Syndic flotilla might show up while that part of your fleet isn't here."

"The only way we have a hope of preventing more Syndic flotillas from showing up like that is to get our warning to them," Geary pointed out. "Not to mention anyone else who might be preparing similar missions as we speak. Colonel Rogero pointed out that Syndic CEOs aren't going to care about the human costs of more attempts, but they'll be aghast at the amount of expensive equipment destroyed, and at discovering the flotilla was tearing itself apart before we even came in contact with any part of it. He thinks a warning might work as a necessary deterrent even for them. Detaching a large part of my fleet for a while is a risk, but I think that risk is more than justified on both humanitarian and practical grounds."

Ambassador Rycerz grimaced. "I can easily imagine the condemnation we'd receive if we didn't try to send a warning. Or if we limited our warning to only the Alliance, even though we'll certainly catch heat for passing on the warning to the Syndicate Worlds. How certain are you of the reliability of the forces you're sending? You had that attempted mutiny while you were at the Taon star system."

She had every right to ask that, Geary told himself. He had no right to get upset at the question. But it still stung. "The overall commander of the task force will be Captain Jane Geary on *Dreadnaught*. She is absolutely reliable. Backing her up will be Captain Nanami Plant on *Warspite*, also a commander in whom I have complete confidence."

"What about the transport? That's a critical part of things. Are you sure the mutineers won't try to take over that ship? How reliable is its commanding officer?"

"Commander Young played a major role in evacuating the facilities at Unity Alternate," Geary said. "Colonel Rico will be the senior Marine aboard. Both are as steady as a red dwarf star. I have no concerns regarding *Mistral*."

"I suppose we have no alternative," Rycerz said. "When is this going to happen?"

"As soon as we can get the Dancers to agree to escort the task force through their hypernet back to their border star system so our ships can make the necessary jumps through enigma space and on to Midway. Only *Mistral* will continue on to Alliance space. The other ships will return here."

"The Dancers." One of Ambassador Rycerz's eyes twitched. "Why are our messages with them going in circles? Why did the apparent breakthrough after you returned from the star system controlled by those other aliens, the Taon, not lead to continued agreements?"

Since Rycerz already seemed unhappy, Geary decided to go ahead and press a point he thought needed more attention. "What about that theory my people came up with? That information about other intelligent species is a form of currency between different species."

The ambassador made a tossing gesture with one hand. "My experts on *Boundless*, economists, sociologists, anthropologists, thought that idea was . . . interesting."

"I see." That sounded like the idea had been dismissed out of hand. "Who is in charge of the scientists with Dr. Macadams still confined to his stateroom?"

Rycerz smiled. "Sadly, yes, Dr. Macadams remains confined to his stateroom. Colonel Webb believes that Macadams constitutes a security threat, and until his investigations are concluded, he feels Macadams must remain confined. I cannot overrule Colonel Webb on security issues."

The last part of that was certainly true enough. Webb and his "security force" (who despite their public image as ordinary ground forces soldiers meant to serve as an honor guard had been outed as elite special forces) were supposed to protect the ambassador and *Boundless*, the ship she was aboard. In fact, Webb had been given an unusual amount of authority by the Alliance government over anything concerning "security" when it came to the ambassador. But Geary hadn't asked about Colonel Webb, and had been around Victoria Rione enough to spot a deflection that didn't really answer the question. "So, who is in charge of the scientists?"

The ambassador kept her smile. "Leadership of individual projects is being assigned on an ad hoc basis consistent with specific project requirements."

Anybody who'd spent time working with bureaucrats knew that answer also wasn't really an answer. "Who would I talk to about that knowledge transaction theory?" He wasn't expecting a name on this third try, and he didn't get one.

"They're all aware of it. I'm sure if any of them have any questions they'll get in touch with you."

"Very well," Geary said, because that was what you said on a ship when there wasn't anything else you could do about it. "Are we still on the same team, Ambassador?"

"Of course we are," Rycerz said. "But you have your responsibilities and I have mine. There's a lot I need to get to," she added, at least having the grace to sound apologetic.

"Yes." He shouldn't. He really shouldn't. Oh, hell, why not? "I'll let you get back to your work, but I wanted to pass on something that concerns me. Your experts might be able to offer some ideas about it. The Dancers clearly told us they only wanted to 'deal with one' when the representatives of Midway Star System tried to speak with them. Why, then, did the Dancers bring the Syndic flotilla here? The only clear answer we've received on that is 'human problem, humans fix.' Which implies that what happened is the outcome the Dancers sought. We eliminated another human presence, leaving us as the sole human contacts they have to deal with. We all expect more human ships to show up, ships from places like the Rift Federation, the Old Colonies, worlds newly independent from the Syndics, maybe even Old Earth itself. Are the Dancers going to expect us to eliminate those voices, too?"

The ambassador stared at Geary, her smile gone. "They wouldn't . . ."

"I'll be interested in hearing what your experts think about that," Geary said. "Until later, Ambassador." He ended the call, imagining Victoria Rione applauding him. He probably had spent too much time around her.

He knew what had knocked the ambassador back on her heels wasn't the question itself, but rather the fact that it fit far too neatly with what had happened so far.

After all, they still knew next to nothing about Dancer society or politics or anything else. They didn't know what the Dancers considered appropriate ways to settle disputes among themselves. What if the pattern the Dancers sought to complete involved one single human government?

Because that wasn't going to happen. But an awful lot of people might die if anyone decided that was what the Dancers wanted.

FIVE

A week later, Geary sat on the bridge of *Dauntless*, watching as the task force sent to Midway vanished when it entered the Dancer hypernet four and a half hours ago.

That particular set of problems was out of his hands now. Captain Jane Geary would get *Mistral* to Midway, and once *Mistral* made it back to the Alliance, the mutineers would be turned over to a higher authority for interrogation. Having seen how brutal and unforgiving military justice had become over the hundred years of the war with the Syndicate Worlds (and military justice had never been lenient or understanding to begin with), Geary thought it possible someone like Captain Pelleas might try to work a plea deal in exchange for information.

Unless Pelleas thought he had patrons with enough power to get him pardoned. Captain Numos had held out for a long time thanks to that sort of calculation.

But even Numos had cracked eventually, when threatened not with death but with the prolonged agony of a discharge with dishonor.

Geary stood up, grateful for the chance to focus on other matters.

He hadn't yet made it off the bridge when an urgent alert sounded.

"A new ship has arrived," Lieutenant Yuon called out.

A new ship. In the seconds it took for Geary to reach his fleet command seat once more, a dozen thoughts cascaded through his mind.

Every arrival of a new ship brought a burst of tension and questions. Was it another Dancer ship, either jumping in or using their hypernet gate, and therefore nothing to be concerned about? Was it more human ships arriving, meaning more temporarily insane people, perhaps heavily armed temporarily insane people, who would have to be dealt with somehow? Or was it a ship belonging to another known, or unknown, alien species, creating a new and different set of challenges while the humans here were still trying to work out relations with the Dancers?

"It arrived at the Taon jump point," Lieutenant Yuon added. The place where space-time was stretched thin enough by the star's gravity well to allow entry to and exit from jump space was the same used to reach the star system where Lokaa the Taon maintained their fleet. "But it's . . . not Taon."

Geary stared at the image on his display. Despite the billions of kilometers separating them from the new ship, the fleet's sensors produced a crystal-clear image of it.

"What the hell is that?" Desjani blurted out in surprise.

Geary couldn't blame her, having nearly expressed the same shock.

So far, the spaceships of every species they'd encountered all followed roughly the same rules in their designs. That wasn't surprising, since every species had to follow the same rules of physics. Whether Dancers, enigmas, Kicks, humans, or Taon, their ships were roughly oval-shaped, with the main thrust at the rear to direct its power through the ship's center of mass. The rounded shapes were far stronger and more able to handle stress than other designs would be.

This new ship, though . . .

"That is not a ship," Desjani complained. "It looks like someone randomly stuck together a bunch of really big square blocks."

"It does," Geary said. "Can we identify their main propulsion?"

"Not in what we can see of that ship, Captain," Lieutenant Castries reported. "The cubes do have rounded edges and corners, but our sensors can't identify the function of the smaller cubes and the bumps on the outer surfaces of the, uh, primary cubes."

"Are those colored marks some kind of paint?" Geary asked. Unlike the uniform dark hulls of the Alliance warships, the new alien ship boasted bright, colorful symbols scattered over its cubes. Before anyone could answer, the reply came in the form of one of the shapes fading away. The bright orange symbol, resembling an underlined letter Y, had barely vanished when a blazing red sunburst silhouette grew in part of the space the giant Y had occupied.

"Whatever the coating on their outer surfaces is, it can be manipulated to show different things," Desjani observed. "Wait." A huge purple triangle bisected by a wavy green line had appeared on the side of one cube. "Are we seeing letters? Or symbols?"

"Or words," Geary said. "This could be one of those languages that uses logo- or pictographic forms instead of letters. Are the ones we're seeing random, or do those together form sentences or phrases of some kind?"

"If they're questions aimed at us, we're not going to be able to answer them," Desjani said.

"Captain?" Lieutenant Castries said. "Sensors are reporting some of the colors on the outer surfaces appear to show best in wavelengths longer than humans can see unaided."

"I wonder if they're going to talk to us," Desjani said. The first times they'd encountered Taon ships in Dancer star systems the Taon hadn't responded to messages.

As if triggered by her words, a comm alert sounded. "We have an incoming transmission from the new ship," the communications watch said. "It's not a broadcast. It's aimed directly at this ship."

"Does it look safe?" Desjani said.

"Yes, Captain. Our systems can't identify any malware or other dangers hidden in the message. It's . . ." The watch stander shook his head. "It exactly matches our message transmission standards and protocols. Technically, it should be a perfect match to our comm systems."

Geary exchanged a glance with Desjani, seeing she was also worried by the implications of this new ship being able to perfectly mimic human communications parameters. "Let's see what they have to say."

The image that appeared on the bridge displays caused everyone to fall silent for a moment.

"Octopuses?" Lieutenant Yuon gasped.

"Or squids," Captain Desjani said.

"They must have evolved from something like those," Geary said. He studied the creatures and their surroundings, a cubical compartment with what were probably control stations on the deck and walls. "Can we tell if they're surrounded by a gaseous atmosphere, or water?"

"No, Admiral. If it's water," Lieutenant Castries said, "it's very clear."

One of the individuals on the other ship began speaking, pastel patches of color blooming and fading across their skin in ways that called to mind the colors appearing on the outer hull. Geary heard what sounded like an electronic tone varying in frequency and intensity, ranging from eerie high-pitched squeals to very low-pitched moans. After a few moments the wavering sounds faded into the background as words the humans could understand began sounding.

"Hello, hello. The stars shine bright! Our greetings to humans, from Wave Breaks, representative of Wooareek people to human people."

"That is a frighteningly good translator," Desjani said.

"The Wooareek wish to greet and trade with humanity," Wave Breaks continued. "Before this, we must ask one of your ships to accompany us back to Uroolaaan. This is tradition/law/required."

"Just like with the Taon," Geary said, surprised. "Is that some sort of standard procedure for contacts with new species?"

"If so," Desjani said, "humanity didn't get the memo. Did the Dancers do things that way? The enigmas and the Kicks sure didn't. Maybe it's one of those standard-except-when-it-isn't procedures."

Wave Breaks continued speaking, the Wooareek's voice through the translator sounding breezily relaxed and confident. "There is no danger. Totally safe. Totally! Please tell us you are cool with this offer and will send your ship with us. Peace to all!"

The message ended, leaving Geary staring at the place where the Wooareek images had been. In their place, a depiction of the Alliance fleet had appeared, with one ship highlighted. "What ship is that?"

"Heavy cruiser *Sapphire*," Lieutenant Yuon announced.

"*Sapphire*," Geary repeated, calling up data on the ship. Commander Boudreaux was *Sapphire*'s captain. The cruiser had just restocked from the fast fleet auxiliary *Tanuki*, so all her food stores and fuel cell reserves were nearly at one hundred percent. There was nothing to indicate why the newly arrived aliens had picked out *Sapphire* from among the hundreds of ships in the Alliance fleet. "Why do they want *Sapphire* in particular to come with them?"

"Beats the hell out of me," Desjani said, frowning at her own display.

"Do you know Commander Boudreaux?"

"Not really," Desjani said, shaking her head. "I can't remember hearing anything negative about him."

"His record looks like that of a typically effective commanding officer," Geary said, sitting back in his seat with a scowl. "Nothing to indicate why they'd want him specifically, any more than why they'd want that specific ship."

"So," Desjani said, "are we cool with what the aliens want?" She shook her head in renewed disbelief. "That has to be the most laid-back translator we've encountered so far. Or the most laid-back aliens. Maybe it's both."

"And the best translator we've encountered so far. How did the, um, Wooareek know that this was the flagship?" Geary replied. "Were they able to analyze our fleet net and comm patterns that quickly?"

"Apparently. They also matched our technical comm specs perfectly."

He didn't want to think about what those things, as well as the design of their ship, implied regarding the technology level of the Wooareek. "Forward the message to Ambassador Rycerz," Geary said. "I'll go to my stateroom and call her so we can discuss what to do."

But as he left the bridge, Geary first headed toward the compartment where General Charban and his odd mix of assistants worked to communicate with and try to better understand the Dancers.

On the way he passed members of the crew of *Dauntless*, who gave him anxious looks. Only one called out a question, though.

"Are these new guys going to give us trouble, Admiral?"

The last thing he needed was for the fleet to get spooked by the Wooareek because the admiral acted like he was worried. Geary put on his best reassuring expression as he answered. "It doesn't look like it so far. We're talking to them."

Vague words, but honest ones. The sailors trusted him and relaxed at the news. "Are any of them good-looking this time?" one of the female sailors asked with a grin.

He couldn't help a short laugh. "No, I'm afraid not."

"Hell, Admiral, in the vids when humans meet aliens they're always really handsome," she mock-complained.

"Or beautiful," a man near her added.

"I know," Geary said. "Sorry, the real aliens are, well, alien. The Kicks are cute."

Those sailors within earshot laughed. "Cute and crazy dangerous!" one said. "I met a girl like that on Glenlyon."

"It's never a good idea to mess with women from Glenlyon," Geary said, walking onward as more laughter followed his comment. The fleet had been in this Dancer star system long enough for him to worry about morale as most days saw little but routine activity and no opportunity for shore leave on planets or orbiting facilities. Incidents of spying and a murder, followed by the failed attempt of the mutineers to trigger hostilities with the Dancers, had further rattled the fleet. But at the moment morale seemed to be doing fine. His ships' commanding officers had been reporting the same thing, but it never hurt to personally talk to the sailors to gauge their moods. And to engage in some conversation with them that implied the admiral wasn't worried in the slightest.

Maybe he was an awful liar, which Victoria Rione had accused him of, but sometimes good leadership required showing what needed to be shown regardless of whatever was beneath the surface.

General Charban and all his assistants except Lieutenant Iger were present in their working compartment. Iger was surely supervising his intelligence specialists as they sought to learn all they could from what could be detected of the newly arrived alien ship.

"Greetings, Admiral," Charban said. "We have new visitors?"

"We have," Geary said. He saw an image of the Wooareek ship floating in the center of the compartment, but Charban and his people wouldn't have seen the message yet. He called it up and waited while it played again.

"Well," Charban said when the message ended, "at least we won't have any translation challenges to deal with."

Lieutenant Jamenson bit her lip. "Understanding the words they're speaking isn't the same as understanding what they mean. We've learned that all too well from the Dancers."

"They sound . . . relaxed," John Senn said. "I mean, they're obviously not human, so they may not present emotional states in the same ways we do. But if they were human, I'd say they sound relaxed. Even though they're not human."

"Let's hope that emotion at least does convey accurately." Geary turned to Dr. Cresida, who after the message ended had returned her gaze to the image of the new ship. "Doctor, how does that ship design work with any physics we know?"

"It doesn't." Dr. Cresida looked at Geary as if he were a student slow to grasp the obvious. "They're clearly employing physics we don't know," she added, spacing out each word.

"Can you make any guesses as to what physics might be involved?" Charban asked.

"I don't like the word 'guess,'" Dr. Cresida said. "It implies a stab in the dark rather than carefully thought-out reasoning. But, in this case, anything I said would be nothing but a guess. There are several possible avenues that might lead to the physics those new aliens are making use of. I have no idea which might be involved, and it might in reality be something different from any of those. I need more data."

"We'll do our best to get that data," Geary told her. "We also need to know why the Wooareek want *Sapphire*, and *Sapphire* in particular, to return to their space with them."

"Maybe a randomly chosen ship representative of the species?" Lieutenant Jamenson suggested.

"That's plausible," General Charban said. "I assume if you send *Sapphire* that you'll also add some specialists to her crew?"

"Yes," Geary said. "Not too many. A heavy cruiser has a limited amount of space compared to a battle cruiser or battleship."

"May I assume," Dr. Cresida said, her earlier disdain replaced by interest, "that there will be room for me aboard *Sapphire*?"

"For you, we can make room," Geary said. "But I'll need the ambassador's approval for you to go."

"Why? This is an invaluable opportunity to learn more about the Wooareek science and technology," Cresida said.

"I agree. But this is a matter the ambassador has the final say on, and I'm afraid I know what the ambassador's answer will be."

"NO," Ambassador Rycerz said.

"Ambassador—" Geary began, using his most formal voice to avoid any emotion being apparent. He was in his stateroom, and Ambassador

Rycerz was in her office aboard *Boundless*, but they seemed to be sitting across from each other.

"No," Rycerz repeated. "I've already given Dr. Bron and Dr. Rajput the same answer. We cannot risk scientists who know our leading-edge theoretical work in a mission to space controlled by a newly contacted alien species whose motivations and intentions are unknown."

"Ambassador—"

"I have made my decision based upon my instructions from the Alliance government."

At the second interruption, Geary felt his expression hardening and let some of that feeling into his tone of voice. "I must insist on my right to express my professional opinion regarding this matter."

Rycerz sat back, rubbing her forehead, her eyes closed. "Certainly, Admiral. Express your opinion."

He tried to once more speak without apparent emotion. "All indications are that these Wooareek have technology, and therefore science, far superior to ours. It is extremely unlikely that they could learn anything from our most skilled scientists. But our most skilled scientists might be able to learn some very important things from them." He phrased his argument carefully, remembering the old adage to appeal not to someone's idealism but to their self-interest. "We could bring back invaluable information to the Alliance."

Her eyes opened and Ambassador Rycerz gave Geary a small smile devoid of humor. "You'll already be bringing back invaluable information. That star chart the Dancers gave us is priceless. Why risk our leading scientists on a single ship heading into the territory of a newly contacted alien species when the sensors on that ship can collect all of the information available and bring it back here where our scientists can analyze it all in safety?"

He wondered whether it would be worthwhile to point out that there had been resistance on Rycerz's staff to bringing the scientists here, inside Dancer territory, where they were now considered "safe." But he had a stronger argument to use. "One of the things that has been re-peatedly demonstrated to me in recent years is that our sensors can't spot everything. They can be fooled, and even if they are working per-fectly they can only see what we've designed them to see and pro-grammed them to see. Something outside those parameters is invisible to them, even though that thing might be extremely obvious to a hu-man looking at it with their own eyes. Our sensors can see a lot, but they cannot see something we don't expect them to see, and therefore didn't design them to see. That's why we need human observers."

Rycerz considered his words for a few seconds before shaking her head. "There will be plenty of human observers on that ship. They can bring their observations back here just as the sensors will."

"I disagree," Geary said. "Observers trained in different skills will see different things."

"You've made your disagreement obvious," Rycerz said. "Why haven't you proposed going along with *Sapphire* yourself? Surely you might see things others might miss."

The question took him aback for a moment. "I might see things others didn't," Geary finally said. "But my primary responsibility is here, with the fleet, and with *Boundless*. I can't go haring off with the Wooareek, no matter how much I might want to."

"You went with the group of ships to the Taon star system," Rycerz pointed out.

Was she trying to provoke him, or just pointing out the inconsisten-cies in his arguments? "That was a large group of ships," Geary said. "And it was the most effective means of dealing with other problems within the fleet. This . . . is not in any way the same. And we now know that other warships from other human governments may be showing up here, commanded by temporarily insane officers. I cannot depart on one ship for an extended period and leave those responsibilities to someone else."

Rycerz sighed and leaned forward. "Admiral, I understand your

arguments. But you understand that situations differ. I approved bringing Dr. Bron, Dr. Rajput, and Dr. Cresida into Dancer territory because
I knew they would be guarded by your entire fleet. I cannot do the
same with regard to one ship accompanying the Wooareek."

She looked down at her desk, then back at Geary. "I'll be completely
honest with you, Admiral. We knew the Dancers were more advanced
than us in technology. But their technology seems understandable to
us. Except for the translator and however their software works. These
Wooareek, though . . . Dr. Rajput said they could be a thousand years
ahead of us. That's the nightmare humanity has always feared, encountering an alien species so far advanced that they could do anything to
us they wanted to do. You know what human societies have done when
encountering other human societies much less technologically advanced."

"I'm worried about that, too," Geary said. "But the historian on my
ship pointed out something that gives me hope."

"What is that?"

"The Wooareek *aren't* human."

IN the end, after several more messages exchanged with the Wooareek,
there really hadn't been any choice. They couldn't risk not engaging
with these new aliens and learning as much about the Wooareek as
proved feasible. And, given the importance of the task, the cold, hard
fact was that a single heavy cruiser and the people aboard her were
possible sacrifices worth the risk that *Sapphire* would never return.

That didn't mean important questions went unasked. "Why did they
show up now?" Lieutenant Iger wondered.

It was a good question, so Geary presented it to the Wooareek.

"Why now?" Wave Breaks said. Wave Breaks seemed to be the primary Wooareek talking to the humans, though they had also been introduced to Cold Current and Whirlpool. "You humans got to know

the Taon, right? We've known the Taon like forever, so we swung by to visit. Their star group conductor Lokaa is totally cool with you. Lokaa told us all about you humans hanging out with the Tool People in the embrace of this star, and said we should look you up before you left. Lokaa didn't know how long you'd be here, so we decided to drop in right away and say hey."

"Tool People," General Charban commented. "An apt name for born engineers such as the Dancers. I wonder if that's what they call themselves."

"They talked to the Taon about us," Lieutenant Iger said, looking like someone who'd just fitted a difficult piece into a puzzle. "That's how they knew our message protocols and our flagship the moment they arrived in this star system. It wasn't some godlike technology that allowed them to instantly identify those things. They got that information from the Taon records of our visit there."

If the Wooareek were here at Lokaa's urging, that was reassuring on another count as well, Geary realized. When last seen, Lokaa had appeared to be well-disposed toward the Alliance. "Are the Taon telling other species about us being here?" Geary asked Wave Break. "Will others be coming here to meet us?"

Wave Break made a rippling motion of his many arms that probably corresponded to a human shrug. "Maybe. Maybe not. It's different, you know. Because different people are different, you know? The Tool People are a little standoffish, and the Not Seen don't want anybody coming around. I can't speak for others, but there's a good chance those others are going to wait to see how you do with the Tool People and us Wooareek."

"Are the, uh, Tool People those we call the Dancers?" Geary said. "Are they . . . well respected among other species?"

That question produced another multiarmed shrug. "Tool People are Tool People."

Geary exchanged surprised looks with Charban, Iger, Lieutenant Jamenson, and the others. The standard Dancer response to questions about other species, such as "Taon are Taon," had felt frustrating and meaningless. But hearing it from the Wooareek as well, it suddenly made sense.

"How would you explain what humans are like?" Lieutenant Jamenson said. "Humans are humans. It's that simple, and that complicated."

Charban nodded, looking rueful. "How do you sum up a species in a few words? You can't. Cats are cats. If you know cats, you understand, and if you don't know cats, how many books worth of explanations would you need to know what cats are like? And how do different persons' perceptions of cats alter what they think cats are? Why did we think another intelligent species could be summed up in a few sentences?"

"We've always done that," Jamenson said. "Humans, I mean. Cat aliens, or insect aliens, or dog aliens. Some simple shorthand to explain to us what they're like."

"Which means the Dancers haven't been blowing us off when they tell us 'Wooareek are Wooareek,' as they did about an hour ago. Why didn't we see that before this?" Charban wondered, scowling at himself.

Dr. Cresida answered in that teacher-to-a-dull-student tone she had mastered. "Because we only had one data set to work with, the Dancers. We couldn't generalize for all other species from that."

"It sounds like we can't generalize about other species at all," Jamenson said.

Cresida paused before answering, her expression thoughtful. "Not from our available data."

That obviously meant they should acquire more data, but the Wooareek proved to be just as vague in their answers as the Dancers could be. "It's, like, how we do things," Wave Breaks explained when asked about the need for a ship to visit Wooareek space. "Got to meet people. Reach out and touch. That tradition thing. Because it works, right? Sometimes you have to go with the flow, you know? No sense in fighting the current when you can let it take you where you need to go, am I right?"

"How does your translator do such an effective job of rendering your words into our language?" Geary asked, having decided to try another tack to get information. Given the distance to the Wooareek ship, it had taken nearly an hour for his question to reach them, and another hour for the reply to appear.

"You have to make the translator so it thinks about what you mean, you know?" Wave Breaks explained. "Not what you're saying. What you *mean*. That requires a thing that can xxrogzzzzzz. Did that come through? Sorry. Humans probably don't have a word for it yet. If you don't share the, you know, concept, the xxrogzzzzzz can't come across. Like, trying to explain eeddeetooppo. That's still just so out-there for you. Someday humans will get it and go, like, wow, and then when you get the concept you'll have a word for it like the Wooareek do. Cool, huh?"

"They cannot possibly be really talking like that," General Charban complained. "It must be some aspect of their translator that makes the Wooareek sound that way to humans."

Dr. Cresida gave him a flat look. "The xxrogzzzzzz. Which we don't get, yet."

"Totally," John Senn agreed.

Geary ran one hand through his hair, thinking. "Do you have any historical perspective on this? On why the Wooareek appear to be so . . . relaxed?"

Senn hesitated. "There's . . . well, everything I hear is that these Wooareek seem to be way ahead of our technology?"

"That's what it looks like."

"In human history," Senn explained, "when someone, I mean a group or an individual or a state, feels like they're superior, really superior, then they'd be confident. Overconfident, in many cases in human history. Which led to many disasters when the confidence was misplaced."

"You're saying the Wooareek are so relaxed because they're so superior to us in technology that they have nothing to fear from us?" Lieutenant Jamenson asked.

"Pretty much," John Senn agreed. "I mean, that's a possible interpretation from the perspective of human history. Though, as I said, in human history that confidence was very often mistaken."

Charban cast a speculative glance at Geary. "I'm thinking of the Kicks. So terrified of 'predators' and other challengers to the herd that they massacre them on sight, and commit suicide if captured. The opposite of the Wooareek, perhaps?"

"And maybe the enigmas," Lieutenant Jamenson said, her eyes hooded. "They're scared anyone else might learn anything about them, so everything they do reflects that. But the Wooareek aren't scared of us."

"They're not acting scared of us," Charban said. "That's either very mistaken, or the attitude of an adult human around a toddler that reflects the power difference between them."

"If the Wooareek are that far ahead of human technology," Geary said, "it keeps leading back to the same imperative. We have to send *Sapphire* to find out as much as they can."

"And I should be going," Dr. Cresida said, her angry gaze fixed on her personal pad.

"You know the admiral has attempted to arrange for that," General Charban said.

"And I'm still trying," Geary said. "You're free to try communicating with the Wooareek again."

Cresida's glower deepened.

Geary knew why. Cresida had already sent the Wooareek a carefully crafted message posing some questions about what were (for humans) the cutting edges of physics. The Wooareek reply had, literally, been:

Those are really cool questions. It's great humans are thinking about stuff like that. Good luck with your search for answers! As frustrated as Geary had grown with the evasive replies of the Dancers to questions, he had to admit that this time the Wooareek's direct and clear answer had, if anything, been worse. As Charban had just noted, it felt like the affectionate, indulgent reply of an adult to an inquisitive toddler wondering why the sky as seen from a habitable planet's surface was usually blue.

His sympathy for Dr. Cresida, though, was tempered by his experience with her. Cresida herself could also sound extremely patronizing at times. At least when she was talking to him.

He decided not to tell the others that Ambassador Rycerz had already requested room aboard *Sapphire* for two scientists from her staff, one a biologist and the other a sociologist. Dr. Cresida wouldn't mind hearing of the biologist but might explode when told a sociologist was being given preference over a physicist.

General Carabali also weighed in on the matter of who should go. "Some more Marines aboard *Sapphire* might prove very useful," she pointed out during a virtual meeting.

"They might," Geary said. "Though to be honest, if the Wooareek have even half the technological advantage over us they seem to have, no number of Marines would do any good. And since a heavy cruiser has much less space than a battle cruiser or battleship, I'd have to take someone else off the ship for every Marine I put aboard."

"And everyone else has important tasks," Carabali conceded. "I wanted to be sure the offer was on the table, Admiral."

"Understood." Geary waved about him, indicating the whole fleet. "How are the Marines doing? Morale is still all right?"

"Morale is fine," General Carabali said. She unexpectedly looked annoyed. "We are confronting one problem regarding the Wooareek and haven't figured out the answer to it yet."

"What problem is that? Do you need any special support?"

"No, Admiral, we need new terminology."

"Terminology?" Geary asked, thinking that his face must look as blank as he felt.

"Marines have always referred to fleet sailors as space squids," Carabali explained. "But now we've encountered real space squids. What do Marines call the Wooareek if we can't call them space squids? But what do we call sailors if we can't call *them* space squids?"

"That is a problem," Geary admitted, trying not to laugh. "But there are marines and Marines," he pointed out, emphasizing the capitalization the second time. "Why can't there be space squids and Space Squids?"

"That is . . . one solution," Carabali said after pondering the idea for a few seconds. "Of course, the rank-and-file Marines are going to come up with their own term no matter what is suggested to them, but I can feed that one down the line and see what happens."

"You can also feed down the line that if they come up with a term for the Wooareek that is obscene or wildly offensive, they won't want to see what happens," Geary said.

Carabali grinned. "I'll make sure they know that, Admiral."

DO you have any questions about your orders?" Geary asked. It was the next day, he was in his stateroom aboard *Dauntless*, and preparations were nearly complete for *Sapphire* to depart.

Aboard *Sapphire*, Commander Boudreaux shook his head. "No, sir. I understand that I might have to make some tough calls if the Wooareek change their attitude toward us. But I assure you that no actions by myself or anyone else aboard *Sapphire* will create any negative impressions among the Wooareek that might cause a harmful change in their approach to us."

"Kommodor Bradamont officially has no command authority over you," Geary emphasized. "She's going along with you to represent Midway Star System in accordance with agreements we've made with the leaders at Midway. But Kommodor Bradamont is also a qualified and extremely capable officer who served the Alliance well. If she offers advice, it's worth listening to."

"Understood, Admiral. I want to clarify that the kommodor is allowed to independently speak with the Wooareek using *Sapphire*'s comm systems."

"Yes. She knows such conversations will be monitored and recorded as usual." Ambassador Rycerz had not been happy about Bradamont accompanying *Sapphire* and being given the right to speak with them, but had finally agreed given the importance of Midway Star System to the Alliance, and Geary's assurance that everything Bradamont said would be overseen by *Sapphire*'s systems.

There wasn't much else meaningful to say, so Geary nodded to Boudreaux. "Good luck. I have every confidence in you and your crew. I look forward to the safe return of *Sapphire*. May the light of the living stars guide you, and our ancestors watch over you. To the honor of our ancestors, Geary, out."

He left his stateroom, heading for *Dauntless*'s shuttle dock, wanting to ensure he was there when Kommodor Bradamont and Lieutenant Iger departed for *Sapphire*. He found both already at the dock, along with Colonel Rogero and Lieutenant Jamenson. Geary stood back, waiting until Jamenson and Iger had said their goodbyes and exchanged a technically not-allowed-on-duty embrace that he intended taking no official notice of.

Iger came up to Geary, visibly a little nervous. "Are there any further instructions for me, Admiral?"

"Just do your best," he told Iger. "You know what we need. See what you can find out, and give Commander Boudreaux as much support as you can."

Iger nodded, his eyes intent. "If the Wooareek ask for information that the Alliance considers to be classified I'll have to deflect them."

"I agree that you shouldn't share military secrets, but rather than deflect I think you should be direct in saying you can't share that information," Geary said. "That's how the Wooareek have been with our questions. If that's how they think it's proper to handle things, we should do the same."

"Yes, Admiral. Dr. Cresida gave me some questions she wanted me to pose to the Wooareek. Am I authorized to do that?"

"Let me see the questions." Geary looked at Iger's pad, seeing words, letters, and numbers he could read arranged into sentences and equations he couldn't understand. It all looked like either high-end physics or some form of ceremonial magic, and not like anything that would create an incident. "Certainly. If the opportunity permits. Anything else?"

Iger hesitated. "Just, um, if we don't come back . . ." He glanced toward Lieutenant Jamenson.

"I'll look out for her," Geary said.

"Thank you, Admiral," Lieutenant Iger said. He saluted.

Geary returned the salute, watching Iger turn and walk onto the shuttle.

Bradamont finished exchanging parting words with Colonel Rogero. Looking his way, she paused, then saluted him, smiling. "See you when we get back, Admiral!"

"Have fun visiting the aliens," Geary called back to her, smiling as he returned the salute.

Once Bradamont had also boarded, Geary waited as the shuttle ramp closed and the shuttle rose before heading out into space. Colonel Rogero had come to stand on one side of him, watching the shuttle with a stoic expression, and to the other side of Geary stood Lieutenant Jamenson, her face impassive but her eyes filled with emotion.

"Odd how saying goodbyes never gets easier with repetition," Colonel Rogero remarked. "When Honore Bradamont and I first said farewells, neither of us expected to ever see the other again. I thought I was on my way to confinement at a Syndicate labor camp, and Honore thought she was being transferred to a different labor camp. We were on opposite sides in a war that had already lasted more than ninety years, and in which we'd already seen countless friends and loved ones die."

"I know that Bradamont was freed because Syndic Internal Security leaked information about the ship she and other prisoners were being transferred on," Geary said. "Part of that unsuccessful plot to force her to act as a mole within the Alliance fleet by playing on her feelings for you. Why didn't you end up in a labor camp?"

"General Drakon," Rogero said matter-of-factly, his eyes still following the shuttle. "CEO Artur Drakon had a reputation among other Syndicate CEOs for being soft. If no one else would accept a hard case, Drakon would, because he believed in second chances." Rogero canted a sardonic look at Geary. "That's also why he ended up with Roh Morgan on his staff. And why he's earned so much loyalty. He was never a good fit as a Syndicate CEO, but he got the job done better than most, so his eccentricity was tolerated. To a point. He did end up consigned to duty at Midway."

"That may have saved his life," Geary said.

Rogero shrugged. "We're all living on borrowed time. There are any number of battlefields where my time should have already ended." He smiled in a crooked way, tapping his head with one finger. "Instead, those battlefields live on up here. I'll never be free of them. That's the trade-off they demand for your living through them. It's like that for you, too, isn't it, Admiral? By all rights you should be dead a century ago by now."

Geary nodded, his eyes back on the shuttle as it swooped out of sight. "I suppose. Along with everyone else I once knew a century ago. Though that means everyone I knew is also still alive in my memory. I don't want to be free of them."

"No," Rogero said, his voice softening. "Does it really help? These beliefs in the Alliance about the living stars and your ancestors? I admit I don't entirely understand the Alliance and its worship of stars."

"It's not just the Alliance," Geary said. "Most of humanity aside from the Syndicate venerates the stars as the homes of our ancestors. It does help. The hope and the belief that we'll someday once again see those who we love, that the end of our physical lives isn't the end."

"But there's no proof."

"No," Geary said. "No proof it's true, no proof it isn't. That's why it's called faith."

"And that's why you send your dead into stars?"

"Whenever possible," Geary said. "How do Syndics mark or honor their dead?"

Rogero shrugged. "The Syndicate didn't want its people tallying up the cost of the war. There are mass columbaria where the ashes of the dead are mingled. Because we're all equals, you see. Except for CEOs, who get special monuments. The Syndicate has also built some large, heroic monuments to individual heroes of the Syndicate. All safely dead heroes, of course, who could not possibly challenge the Syndicate using their special status."

"I was supposedly safely dead, too," Geary remarked, thinking it was strange he could joke about that. "We have monuments to honor all the dead. Not necessarily heroic monuments." Geary almost flinched at the memory of the monument to him that he'd seen on Glenlyon. So heroic, and so ridiculous to his eyes. "The designs reflect the individual perspectives of whichever world they're built on, though all of them list the names of those who've been lost to the war. But those aren't seen as the true monuments to the dead."

He gestured toward the outside of the ship. "We see the true monuments every time we look at space, or look upward at night on a planet. Countless stars, shining to mark and commemorate those consigned to their fires."

"Eternal flames?" Rogero asked. "The Syndicate uses those."

"No," Geary said. "*Not* eternal. That's the point. Stars burn brightly, then die, casting their contents into the universe to form new stars, new worlds, new life. Just as humans die. But we do not end, any more than the stars end. We live on in our legacies, and someday we're reborn."

"The darkness is but an interval," Lieutenant Jamenson recited, nodding.

Colonel Rogero sighed. "It's a comforting belief, I guess. No farewell is final. I have trouble accepting it, though. Perhaps because it is comforting. I've seen too many die to find any consolation in the idea that their deaths are not the end."

"Not everybody in the Alliance believes, either," Lieutenant Jamenson said. "And there are countless variations in how the beliefs are interpreted. It's very personal, not one-size-fits-all."

"And what is your size, Lieutenant?" Rogero asked her.

"I know our ancestors watch over us," Jamenson said with calm confidence. "My mother has the sight. That's what we call the ability to see things science can't. She told us she could see our father after he died. She couldn't converse with him, but she'd see him come to watch over us as we grew up."

"Watch over you?" Rogero asked. "Could he do anything?"

"I think so," Jamenson said. She smiled. "Mum always claimed that if she had whiskey in the house the bottle would end up empty a lot faster than it should have, even if she locked it up. And one time . . . I was on my first ship. The *Amethyst*. We were getting shot up. I was on my way aft when I came to a cross passageway that would've led to a quicker route, so I started to go down it, but . . . found myself continuing on the one I was already in. I had meant to turn, told myself to turn, but I didn't. I told myself going back would waste time and went on and . . . I'd barely taken three steps when grapeshot hit the hull and vaporized the section I would've been in if I'd gone down that other passageway."

She looked at Rogero, still smiling. "I know it was my dad that stopped me from turning. No proof of it, like the admiral said, but I know."

Rogero gazed steadily back at her. "There are times I think such belief must be a burden, always being watched and judged by things we cannot see, but I admit it must also be a great comfort at other times." A slight smile formed on his lips. "How does *your* whiskey hold up?"

Jamenson grinned. "I've told Dad he'd best steer clear of my whiskey. He can have all he wants of Mum's. Since we kids left home, she keeps a full glass on the family altar for him. 'I don't want him wandering about bars trying to satisfy his thirst,' she says. 'I want him home drinking with me like an old love should.'"

As Geary and Rogero laughed, Jamenson's expression shifted, becoming pensive as she gazed toward where the shuttle had been. "She taught me not to live in fear, because if you worry too much, that's all your life is. Fear. 'Being smart is one thing, looking before you leap,' she says. 'Always being afraid is not the same thing.'" Jamenson let out a long breath. "By your leave, Admiral. I should get back to work."

"By all means," Geary said.

As Jamenson left, Rogero watched her and shook his head. "The Syndicate always claimed that the Alliance's weak culture produced weak individuals, no match for the strong workers created by the demands of the Syndicate. I wonder how Syndicate CEOs would explain someone like that lieutenant of yours?"

"In my experience," Geary said, "people like those Syndic CEOs simply refuse to believe things that contradict what they claim to be true. To be honest, there are people like that in the Alliance as well."

"There are probably people like that everywhere," Rogero said.

"I hope this mission is very successful," Geary said. "That it starts to help us get beneath the surface of aliens like the Wooareek and the Dancers. Get far enough down that we can really start to understand them. Maybe that'll help us better understand ourselves and other humans."

Rogero made a brief, sarcastic laugh. "That's where we differ, Admiral. I think we usually understand ourselves and other humans very well. Most of the time, though, we don't want to admit it."

◇

ALL new passengers loaded and supplies of food and fuel and spare parts topped off again, *Sapphire* accelerated away from the rest of the fleet. Despite Geary pressing the issue again with Ambassador Rycerz, none of the human physicists were on *Sapphire*. As a result, Dr. Cresida was simply ignoring Geary whenever he visited General Charban's work space. General Charban had confided in Geary that Cresida had nearly gone critical when she had learned that a *sociologist* had been given a space aboard *Sapphire*, and had refused to interact with anyone except John Senn for a day afterwards.

At which point Cresida had learned that Geary had tapped Lieutenant Iger to go, which had led to weaponized words from Cresida, which had led to Lieutenant Jamenson leaping to Iger's defense, and to General Charban having to separate the combatants into different compartments until they cooled down. "Sometimes," Charban told Geary, "running a small group can be more difficult than running a large division."

"Dr. Cresida does not have to stay aboard *Dauntless*," Geary said. "I can send her back to *Boundless*."

Charban shook his head, looking resigned to the situation. "She's simply too valuable to our work. And there is a good person inside her, even though Dr. Cresida sometimes seems to be bending every effort to avoid letting anyone else see that person."

"I knew someone else like that," Geary said.

"So you did. I got Dr. Cresida alone and explained why Lieutenant Iger was going, that his training and experience as an interrogator would allow him to ensure questions to the Wooareek were properly formulated to find out what we wanted, and allow him to better spot any evasiveness or misleading aspects in Wooareek replies. Once I identified Iger's practical skill sets, Cresida calmed down. She even apologized to Lieutenant Jamenson."

"Good," Geary said. "For the record, Ambassador Rycerz wasn't happy about Iger going along with *Sapphire*. She's worried about all of the Alliance secrets that Iger knows."

Charban laughed. "My impression of the Wooareek is that they haven't the slightest interest in human secrets. How were you able to convince the ambassador?"

"I didn't. But deciding what ship Lieutenant Iger is on falls under my command authority, so the ambassador had to accept my decision." Geary sighed, letting his uncertainty show. Usually he had to maintain a façade around others, always being the admiral, the hero Black Jack, they needed to see. Only with some, such as Tanya Desjani and General Charban, did he feel safe to let his inner doubts and worries appear. "Everyone has the impression the Wooareek are very eager for *Sapphire* to visit them. I hope *Sapphire* is able to learn just what it is the Wooareek want from humans."

"And we all hope whatever the Wooareek want is something humans will be happy to provide," Charban said. "Oh, you asked us to question the Dancers about the Wooareek, to see how much the Dancers might tell us about this new species."

"And?" Geary asked, suspecting that he already knew the answer.

"Wooareek are Wooareek." Charban shrugged. "Before the brief personnel conflict Dr. Cresida tried formulating some questions about Wooareek technology and science for the Dancers to see if they'd give us any useful information. They were formulated as really amazing arias, by the way. I personally would have told Dr. Cresida anything she wanted after hearing them. But the Dancer reply was to the effect that questions about Wooareek stuff had to be addressed to the Wooareek. There are no free lunches in alien space, and neither it seems are there any free data dumps."

AS usual in space, any action was followed by an extended period of waiting and watching. The odd-looking Wooareek ship had continued ambling around the Dancer star system at a sedate point zero five light speed, giving no clue that Alliance sensors could detect as to how it was maneuvering. It was forty-eight light minutes (roughly eight hundred sixty million kilometers) distant from the Alliance fleet when *Sapphire* intercepted it, taking up station as directed by the Wooareek about five kilometers from the alien ship.

Geary watched a message sent from the Wooareek ship forty-eight minutes ago when *Sapphire* had joined up. Wave Breaks seemed to be in a good mood, but then she always seemed to be in a good mood. "Everything is cool, humans! No problems. We're going to haul butt now. Catch you on the next phase shift! Peace to all!"

"They can't be real," Desjani grumbled.

"Sensors are picking up some odd readings around the Wooareek ship and *Sapphire*," Lieutenant Yuon said. "Whatever it is shows up as a slight space-time distortion."

Geary watched in disbelief as both ships disappeared from his display.

SIX

"WHERE—" Geary started to demand, before his display's image lurched and slightly distorted images of the alien ship and *Sapphire* appeared far from where they had been. The vector pointing along their path was impossibly long, indicating extreme velocity. "What just happened?"

"Captain?" Lieutenant Castries said, her voice filled with disbelief. "They went to point five light speed."

"They accelerated that fast?" Desjani asked. "Check your readings."

"I did, Captain. And, no, they didn't accelerate. Our sensors are reporting they went from their starting velocity of *point zero five* light speed to *point five* light speed instantaneously. And the Wooareek ship brought *Sapphire* along with them when they did that. That's why we lost them. Our sensors were focused on them and when they were suddenly a lot farther away the sensors took a moment to realize these were the ships they were supposed to be tracking."

"Ancestors save us," Desjani breathed, leaning to peer more closely at her own display. "If we'd tried to accelerate like that our ship would've disintegrated and we'd all be nothing but very thin layers of slime."

"But they didn't accelerate," Geary said. "Did our people aboard *Sapphire* survive that . . . whatever it was the Wooareek did?"

Nobody answered him. Nobody could. He stared at his display, furious with worry that he'd just watched the crew of *Sapphire* die, feeling a nearly overwhelming urge to lash out at someone for not knowing something they had no possible way of knowing.

The only thing holding him back was the memory of when he'd been the target of such an assault, screamed at by a superior officer for something that Geary himself could have had no way of preventing. He'd vowed back then never to do the same to anyone under his authority.

But, due to the shock of seeing *Sapphire* vanish until located again, it was still a near thing.

"Incoming message from *Sapphire*," the communications watch reported breathlessly.

Geary let out a gasped prayer of thanks, hearing similar sounds from the others on the bridge.

On the forty-eight-minute-old message the image of Commander Boudreaux shimmered as if being seen through water. Boudreaux's voice also sounded off, as if it were being filtered through layers of fabric. "We've successfully rendezvoused with the Wooareek ship, Admiral. I'm not sure what's happened. Our sensors show external views as if we were moving at a large fraction of the speed of light, but neither our bodies nor the ship's sensors detected any acceleration.

"As best as we can determine, *Sapphire* has been locked to the Wooareek ship. Not physically locked, but some sort of field that creates the same condition. Our sensors can't confirm it, but our bodies feel that *Sapphire* is now somehow linked to the alien ship, as if we were one ship. That's the best way I can explain how it feels.

"The Wooareek sent us a message just before things got weird. They said . . ." Boudreaux hesitated. "Admiral, Wave Breaks said, 'No worries. It's all good. Don't sweat it. Enjoy the ride.' That's what Wave Breaks told me."

"'Enjoy the ride'?" Desjani echoed in disbelief.

"Wave Breaks told us we're heading for the jump point," Commander Boudreaux added. "I just got confirmation from my people that our sensors detected some kind of minor energy surge just before things got weird. We'll send you a copy of our sensor readings. I . . . what? Admiral, our systems are estimating our velocity at point five light speed. We're not feeling anything, though. Um, no reports of any problems, any casualties aboard the ship. I'd think I was dreaming except as far as I know no one in a dream ever thinks they're in a dream. Boudreaux out."

The tension on the bridge of *Dauntless* had dropped almost as rapidly as it had shot up. "Why is the audio and video on this message so bad?" Geary asked, surprised to hear how calm his own voice sounded.

"Admiral," the comm watch said, "*Sapphire* is moving at point five light. At that velocity our systems can't compensate for the distortions caused by relativity. The quality problems in the message reflect the uncertainties that our systems can't precisely correct for. I can up the quality, get it looking and sounding good, but that would mean telling the systems to resolve uncertainties with guesses as to what the precise data should be. It'll *look* precise, but it won't really be precise."

"I understand," Geary said. "Don't set the systems to give us guesswork precision. I'd rather make any guesses about what we're seeing and hearing myself so I know I'm making them."

He forced himself to relax, trying not to focus too much on what the Wooareek had just done. But when he looked over at Captain Desjani he saw her watching him with a grim expression.

"That was . . . impressive," Geary said.

"That's one word for it." Desjani shook her head. "The Wooareek have got propulsion that makes ours look like oars and sails. I hope they really do want to be friends. Because if they want to fight, we're toast."

"We don't know anything about their weapons," Geary pointed out.

"It doesn't matter," she said, her voice flat. "They could only be armed with rocks. You know me. The Taon, the Dancers, they have systems better than ours. If we have to fight them, I will do my utmost to figure out a way to beat them despite their advantages. But these Wooareek? Our weapons couldn't even engage ships that can maneuver like that. We'd be helpless. You know I'm not exaggerating."

Geary nodded slowly, his stomach tightening at the thought of how badly outclassed humanity's latest warships would be in such a fight. "John Senn, the historian, guessed that the Wooareek were so relaxed because they had absolutely nothing to fear from us. It looks like he was right."

She narrowed her eyes as a thought hit her. "Why'd they show us? After arrival in this star system they just poked around. They didn't have to do that super jump start going back to the jump point. But they did. They wanted us to see what they can do."

"Or they simply didn't care whether we saw it," Geary said. "Maybe before they were concerned about scaring us."

"If that's so, it was a good concern. Because what that Wooareek ship did is scary as all hell."

THE amazing manner in which the Wooareek had departed hadn't done anything to reassure the diplomats aboard *Boundless*. "We're drafting possible responses to Wooareek demands," Ambassador Rycerz had grimly informed Geary. "I assume you agree with those aboard *Boundless* who say we would have no chance at all if we fought them."

"Yes," Geary said. "But nothing about the Wooareek to this point has indicated any interest in fighting us. What do we have that they could want?"

"We have something they want," Rycerz emphasized, rapping one finger on the desk before her. "The Wooareek were eager for that cruiser to accompany them back to their own star systems. We know it was important to them. We just don't know *why*."

He had no answer to that.

It didn't help that when Geary had General Charban ask the Dancers what they would do if the Wooareek were aggressive toward the human ships, the Dancer reply was once again all too familiar.

"Wooareek problem, Wooareek fix," Charban said, looking as if he'd developed another headache. "Have you noticed something, Admiral? Before Lieutenant Jamenson figured out that the Dancers expect rhythmic word combinations as signs of intelligence and understanding, they only used simple words and phrases in responding to our unartfully posed questions. Jamenson recently pointed out to me that when we ask about things such as what to do about the Syndics, or in this case what to do about the Wooareek if they attack, no matter how artfully our questions are framed the replies are as short and simple as when we were speaking the Dancer equivalent of baby talk."

"What does that remind me of?" Geary said, thinking. Once he considered the people assisting Charban, the answer came immediately. "Dr. Cresida, when she thinks I'm not grasping something simple."

"Yes," Charban said. "This feels very much as if the Dancers regard our questions about those particular things to be almost childish. As if we're expected to already know the answers."

"How are we supposed to know the answers when we've never before met species like the Taon and the Wooareek?" Geary demanded in frustration. "And why would the answers for those aliens be the same as the answer for the Syndics? Could this be a case where the Dancers expect some sort of trade or payment for information?"

"I asked them straight out," Charban admitted. "I asked the Dancers what they wanted in exchange for more information about the Wooareek. You may be hearing from the ambassador about that."

"She's already unhappy with me again," Geary said. "What did the Dancers reply?"

"'Wooareek are Wooareek,'" Charban said. "Sometimes I need to keep reminding myself that the Dancers are friendly aliens."

For at least the hundredth time since the Wooareek ship had first arrived, Geary called up the star chart the Dancers had provided. "This is Wooareek space," he said, indicating a substantial region of space containing hundreds of stars. "It's big, but it's not huge."

Charban nodded, moving his hand inside the projection floating above the table to outline the area controlled by the Wooareek. "They have fewer stars under their control than humanity does. If this chart indicates control and not just where a species has settled planets."

"That's the problem," Geary said. "Ambassador Rycerz is worried that nearby species might be under Wooareek control even though those other species occupy the stars in those regions."

"One of those other species on the Wooareek border are the Taon," General Charban pointed out. "Lokaa said nothing to us about the Wooareek and seemed to be making his decisions on his own."

Geary nodded, his eyes on the distant stars. "Those Taon xenophobes would also seem to be inconsistent with Wooareek control. They wouldn't settle for that."

"Maybe they're rebels against a Wooareek-controlled Taon government."

"Maybe," Geary said. "Just one more thing we know far too little about. All we can do is make guesses based on what little we do know."

Charban smiled. "In this case, what we know of the Wooareek implies they think of war as uncool. Peace to all, and all that."

"For the people," Geary muttered, the stock phrase of the Syndicate Worlds, which sounded humanitarian, but in reality didn't mean anything because the CEOs and executives and Internal Security agents saying it didn't believe a word of it.

"There is that possibility, too," Charban agreed.

AN impossibly short time later, the Wooareek ship, and *Sapphire* in company with it, abruptly and instantly shifted velocity down to point zero five light speed as it neared the same jump point it had arrived at. Moments later the Wooareek ship jumped, taking the Alliance heavy cruiser along with it.

Geary, in his command seat on the bridge of *Dauntless*, found himself gazing fixedly at the point in space where the ships had been before vanishing into jump space, wondering if he'd seen the first step in an interspecies contact with unlimited benefits, or if he'd just sacrificed a ship full of humans out of misplaced hope.

He couldn't do anything about that now. All he could do was try to gain some success here. "We need to figure out how to achieve another breakthrough with the Dancers," he told Captain Desjani.

"Agreed," she said. "I don't have any ideas, though. Do you?"

"Not a single one."

TO everyone's surprise, the next breakthrough came the very next day. Somehow, they'd done something right in their encounter with the Wooareek. No one had any idea exactly what they'd done right, but the Dancers seemed to be ready to finally take another step.

A step that involved Geary himself.

"The Dancers want *what*?"

General Charban had never before come to Geary's stateroom to personally deliver a message from the Dancers. But this time he had, and Geary was glad that he was already sitting down when Charban delivered it.

"The Dancers," Charban said, speaking slowly, "want you to visit the surface of the primary inhabited world in this star system."

"Me?"

"The invitation is specifically for you," Charban said. He took a deep breath. "And one other person. Captain Desjani."

"Captain—?" Geary rubbed his face with both hands. "Just the two of us? Visiting a Dancer planet?"

"That's correct, Admiral." Charban smiled encouragingly. "It will be the sort of opportunity to learn more about the Dancers that we've long sought. And you, of course, will go down in the history books."

"I'm already in history books," Geary said. "I'd be happy to let someone else get their name down there. Why do they want *me* to visit the planet?"

"They didn't say."

"Of course not." He glanced at his display, wondering why he hadn't already heard from Ambassador Rycerz about this. "I'll need to discuss it with the ambassador."

"I'm sure Ambassador Rycerz will be eager to discuss it," Charban said, unsuccessfully attempting to suppress a smile.

When Charban had left, Geary called Tanya. "Captain Desjani, I'd like to see you in my stateroom, please. It's urgent." This was the sort of news that would fly through the rumor mill faster than the speed of light. He didn't want her hearing it from someone else before he officially informed Tanya of the invitation from the Dancers.

A few minutes later she was standing in his stateroom, staring at him. "What did you say?"

"The Dancers want you and me to visit their planet in this star system," Geary repeated. "You and me. No one else."

"You and me," she repeated, then to Geary's surprise sat down. "Dancers. Why did they have to be spiders?"

"They also look like they're part wolf," Geary pointed out.

"That doesn't help." She gave him a resigned look. "I never mentioned this, but I have a thing about spiders."

"You—?" He gazed at her, bewildered and not bothering to try to hide it. "*You* have a thing about spiders? You're the most fearless warrior I've ever encountered."

"Thank you," Tanya said. "Syndics, hell lances, enigmas, exploding hypernet gates, Kicks, those I can handle without a problem. Bring 'em on. But spiders?"

"What would you do if . . ."

"If I saw a big spider on *Dauntless*?" Desjani asked. "I'd stomp on it. But it'd creep me out when I did it."

"Can you handle being down on that planet surrounded by Dancers?"

She looked and sounded insulted at the question. "Did you really ask me that? Of course I can handle it. There is *nothing* I can't handle. But I'm not going to be *happy* while I'm handling it."

"Understood," Geary said.

AMBASSADOR Rycerz was indeed eager to discuss the Dancer invitation. Desjani had no sooner left than Geary's display showed a call from the ambassador.

Seated in her office on *Boundless*, Rycerz fixed Geary with a demanding look. "How did you arrange this invitation?"

He didn't have to try to look both innocent and affronted. "I didn't. I have no idea why the Dancers extended the invitation at this time."

"We've been trying to get them to agree to a visit," Rycerz said. "A visit by me, and members of my staff who are trained in social protocols and can observe the details we need to know about the Dancers. And instead they invite you." She looked to one side, checking something in her office. "You and Desjani were closely involved in the Dancer visit to Old Earth." Rycerz squinted at whatever she was reading. "What is this Kansas mentioned in the report? Is that a star?"

"It's a place on Old Earth, where the Dancers returned the remains of the ancient human astronaut."

"Why Kansas?"

"It was his home."

"Oh." She read something else. "What about . . . Stone . . . hen . . . gee?"

"Stonehenge," Geary said. "Another place on Old Earth."

"What does Stonehenge have in common with Kansas?"

"We visited both places," Geary explained. "Tanya Desjani and I, and the Dancers who came to Old Earth to return the astronaut's remains. They wanted to go to Kansas, and were invited to Stonehenge among other places on Old Earth. Perhaps this invitation is seen by the Dancers as reciprocal. We were their hosts when they visited Old Earth, so they want to be hosts to Captain Desjani and me on a Dancer planet."

Rycerz made a face. "That's plausible."

"Captain Desjani and I," Geary added, "are the only humans in this fleet who were present at Kansas and Stonehenge."

"Hmm. That does fit." The ambassador sat back hard. "I'm proposing other people, from my staff, for the visit. We'll see how the Dancers respond to that."

"All right," Geary said.

"You're not objecting?"

"No," he said, shaking his head to emphasize the word. "I have no problem with someone else getting that opportunity. But I also don't have much confidence that the Dancers will change their invitation."

THEY didn't.

A few days later, Geary stood in the shuttle dock aboard *Dauntless*, waiting for Tanya and trying to convince himself to be grateful that the Dancer invitation had distracted him from worrying about *Sapphire* and those aboard her. Ambassador Rycerz had come to the battle cruiser in person for the historic mission, because this was the first time humans would be setting foot on a world occupied by the Dancers. "You'll be recording everything that happens on the surface?" she asked Geary anxiously, then flinched. "I'm sorry. I know your off-duty relationship with Captain Desjani. I don't expect you to record *everything*."

"That won't be an issue," Geary assured the ambassador. "This isn't a private getaway. We'll be on duty for this entire trip, so there won't be anything going on between Captain Desjani and me that wouldn't be suitable for recording."

Rycerz looked around to ensure no one else was close. "It's not very diplomatic of me to admit it, but I don't think being surrounded by Dancers would make anyone feel amorous." She shook her head. "Please remember your instructions. It is critically important that nothing is said or promised or implied that the Dancers would take as commitments on our part. We've given you some stock replies to use if any diplomatic issues come up."

"All of them referring the Dancers back to you and your staff for answers," Geary noted. "With so many limits on what I can say, I'm not sure I can even engage in small talk with the Dancers."

"The weather is usually a safe topic," Rycerz said, absolutely serious. "But don't criticize the weather. Not even 'it's a little chilly' or 'the sun is bright.' They might take that personally as criticism of the world they've occupied."

"I'll keep that in mind," Geary said, practicing trying not to sound sarcastic.

He must have been successful because Ambassador Rycerz nodded in approval. "If it gets too difficult to handle, we can cut this visit short. You have a stress word set up, right?"

"Yes," Geary said, knowing that Rycerz would love for the short visit to be cut even shorter so she wouldn't have to worry about him or Tanya creating a major diplomatic incident. But she also deserved to know he had taken reasonable precautions. "If I mention Major Gilbert Bougainvillea it will mean I'm worried but we don't need to be pulled out yet. If I ask them to pass a message to Captain Elizabeth Moon, it will mean we need to get lifted out of there as soon as possible. Only if I say the word 'Mameluke' will it mean the Dancers might oppose our extraction. I have no reason to expect to need that, but we still had to plan for the worst."

"We cannot afford any violence with the Dancers," Ambassador Rycerz said. "Especially not after what that Syndic flotilla did. And especially after seeing what the Wooareek can do. We need the Dancers as allies."

"We won't be responsible for any violence," Geary said. "Even if I activate Mameluke it will only mean they come in expecting the possibility of being shot at. It will not authorize returning fire. Captain Duellos, in charge of the fleet while I'm on the surface, has been clearly informed that he cannot order any firing on Dancer ships, facilities, or individuals without your express approval. Duellos can be counted on to follow those instructions."

"Good. It'll only be for two days and one night, but I doubt I'll sleep the entire time for worries about what might go wrong." Rycerz looked to one side, where a display showed the planet that Geary and Desjani would be heading for. "Why do you still do it, Admiral? A century in survival sleep. You lost everyone you'd ever known. You lost the universe you knew. I'm not sure I could've held myself together afterwards."

"I nearly didn't," Geary said. "But . . . I was needed. And even though my brother was gone . . . I still wanted him, and the rest of my ancestors, to be proud of me." He heard a sailor call out, "Captain's on deck!" and saw Tanya Desjani walking toward them. "And I found new people to not replace but carry on for those I'd lost."

"I see." Ambassador Rycerz nodded in greeting to Tanya, who like Geary was wearing a fleet service dress uniform. Also like him, she had a standard-issue bag slung over one shoulder holding essentials for their trip to the surface. "Good luck to both of you. There are a lot of people who wish they were in your shoes."

"There are also a lot who are glad they're not in our shoes," Geary remarked. He tapped his comm pad. "This is Admiral Geary. Captain Duellos is now in command of the fleet while I visit our Dancer friends. To the honor of our ancestors, Geary, out."

That essential task done, he walked onto the waiting shuttle along with Desjani, hearing the bongs of the ship's bell that heralded the ancient announcements identifying both him and Tanya by their professional roles. "Admiral, Alliance fleet, departing. *Dauntless*, departing."

They strapped into their seats as the shuttle ramp closed. "I'm glad that we're taking an Alliance shuttle down instead of a Dancer ship," Geary remarked.

"It might make the transition more abrupt when we step off and are surrounded by Dancers," Desjani replied.

"All of my uniform's weapons have been deactivated, right?"

"Removed," Desjani said. "There wasn't any sense in risking any incidents involving even deactivated weapons. We don't know how the Dancers would've reacted to your even having them. But the defenses are still active."

"Hopefully the Dancers won't take offense at that." Geary took a long, slow breath as the shuttle lifted and left the shuttle dock, twisting around before firing its main propulsion to put it on a vector toward the planet below. "Nervous?"

"Nah," Tanya said. "I'll try to act as if Black Jack himself is my commander," she added, citing one of the sayings the fleet had adopted during the century when Geary was assumed to be dead.

"Did you have to say that?" Geary asked.

"Yes. Yes, I did."

The compartment they were in was separated by a bulkhead from the flight deck where the pilots were, but displays before them showed a view from the front of the shuttle, as well as the situation in nearby space. Geary watched a half-dozen small Dancer ships swoop gracefully around the human shuttle, weaving back and forth in a display of agile movement that clearly showed why sailors in the fleet had named the species Dancers.

Escorted by the Dancer ships, the shuttle entered atmosphere, Geary abruptly feeling the sense of history fill him. Despite his earlier casual dismissal of the importance of this moment to the ambassador, he fully realized how significant it was. Humanity's encounters with the enigmas and then the Kicks had been marked by attacks and, so far, unrelenting hostility. Some of the fleet's Marines had been on the surface of a Taon-controlled world, but in an isolated location where they could learn little about the Taon. Victoria Rione had met a single Dancer in person during their first encounter with Dancer ships, but that had been a brief meeting in an air lock. This would be the first time any human had set foot on a world controlled by the Dancers. This would be the first time humans visited a city built and lived in by a different intelligent species.

As they neared touchdown, and the landing field came clearly into view, a different feeling filled him. There were perhaps a dozen Dancers lined up to one side of the field. Behind them was a large open structure of rods resembling a gigantic jungle gym, and filling the gym were a lot more Dancers. Hundreds of them, at least. It must be the Dancer equivalent of human grandstands.

"Ancestors," Tanya Desjani breathed as she took in the sight.

"They're not hundreds of giant hairy spiders with wolf heads," Geary said. "They're an intelligent, friendly species."

"I'll keep telling myself that." She glanced at him. "Have you ever wondered whether we're as hideous-looking to the Dancers as they are to us?"

"I don't think so. I guess I should have."

"I'm going to concentrate on thinking about those Dancers who went to Old Earth," Desjani continued. "Surrounded by millions of two-legged, bare-skinned, two-armed, worm-fingered monstrosities. And what do we smell like to them? If they could do it, so can I."

He didn't mention what she knew as well as he did, that the Dancers who came to Old Earth had never left the small craft they had used to come to the surface and move around on it. At the moment, looking at what seemed to be a massive pile of huge spiders awaiting them, he wished the two of them were going to do the same thing.

"Is that a Taon?" Desjani said, pointing.

As they drew closer, the single figure had grown more visible. Tall and wide in human terms, heavily built but basically human-shaped, the Taon was a welcome sight amid the Dancers.

"Do you think they're one of Lokaa's people?" Desjani asked.

"Most likely," Geary said. "We still don't know very much about the Taon, but Lokaa seems to be the Taon leader the Dancers prefer to work with. And since Lokaa has said they trust us, having one of their people here would be good for us."

"Maybe we can ask the Taon about the Wooareek."

"I'll be looking for a chance to do that," Geary said, trying to focus on the needs of the moment and not on the large number of Dancers awaiting their arrival. "Let's activate all of our personal sensors and recording devices. From this moment on, we're always going to be on-stage until we lift off the surface again."

"Got it," Desjani said, activating the sensors and recorders embedded in her own uniform. "Are you sure the Dancers agreed to us being loaded with surveillance devices?"

"General Charban swore the Dancers had given unequivocal approval for it."

The shuttle grounded with only the faintest jar, the human pilot doing her best to fly as gracefully as the Dancer ships did. "The air here is okay. Are you ready for me to drop the ramp, Admiral?" the pilot called to them, her voice sounding as if she expected Geary to say hell no and order her to take off again as fast as possible.

"Yes, drop the ramp," Geary said. "After we leave, seal it again. We'll see you tomorrow." The pilots wouldn't suffer even though they'd be confined to the shuttle for a couple of days. There was plenty of room inside for them to stretch out, a lot of onboard entertainment and reading options, and decent rations to heat up and enjoy. For them, this visit would be more like a two-day campout.

As the ramp fell, the air outside swept into the shuttle. Geary smelled the scent of vegetation, along with an aroma that reminded him of words Victoria Rione had spoken after breathing the air when she became the first human to physically encounter a Dancer. *Spicy*, she'd said. *Not too sharp or pungent. Almost pleasant.*

"Is that the Dancers?" Desjani said cautiously as she also breathed in the outside air.

"I think so. Not bad, is it?"

"Like some of those spice sticks they burn in Benten Star System," Desjani said.

"Ready?"

"Yes, Admiral. I'm telling myself it could be worse. There could be a whole bunch of lawyers waiting for us out there."

"That's the spirit." Geary, as required by his rank, led the way out of the shuttle, Desjani only one step behind.

SEVEN

THE sky outside was a pale blue, streamers of high clouds reflecting a sun that felt a little too dim by human standards but still left this part of the planet's surface comfortably warm enough at this time of day for a human in long sleeves or a coat. The vegetation seemed to be mostly dark green shading to almost black, what appeared to be large insects rather than birds flitting above treelike plants beyond the landing field.

But Geary had little time to take in his surroundings. The line of Dancers waited, facing him, each Dancer looking even bigger than he remembered. Though they stood on multiple legs with an abdomen almost parallel to the ground, the Dancers were still about a meter and a half tall and about two meters wide from leg tip to leg tip. Their fur, ranging in shade from dull gray to shiny black that had glints of blue in it, covered much of their bodies, including the heads, which were mostly wolflike except for the six eyes.

Like the first Dancer they'd encountered in a distant star system, these all wore brightly colored bands of what looked like silk cloth wrapped about them.

They looked terrifying. And beyond the line awaiting Geary and Desjani was that Dancer jungle gym / grandstand literally crawling with hundreds more Dancers.

Geary inhaled deeply and began walking toward the Dancers, Desjani coming up to walk beside him.

How close was he supposed to go to them?

Getting no signal from the Dancers, Geary stopped about two meters from them.

"Honored we both are,

"By your kind invitation,

"To visit your world," he said as clearly as he could, spacing out each set of words to make it clear he was using a haiku format. He had no idea how long he'd be able to keep speaking in any approximation of poetry or other rhyme, but at least he could greet the Dancers appropriately.

A rustling sound came as the Dancers facing them rubbed claws together.

"I hope that's applause," Desjani said with a bright, fixed smile.

One of the Dancers advanced.

Geary waited as the Dancer stopped directly in front of him. The foreclaws reached out, grasping Geary behind the shoulders, drawing him slightly closer as the Dancer raised up to touch their forehead against Geary's face. Geary held the contact, wondering if he should breathe, feeling stiff fur touching one side of his forehead and bare Dancer skin touching the other side, the small tentacles inside the Dancer's claws drumming lightly against the skin of his shoulders. The primeval monkey in the back of his mind screamed about spiders and snakes and monsters, but Geary tamped it down, trying to keep his heart from racing.

Releasing him, the Dancer stepped back slightly, then edged over to face Desjani.

"Hi," she said, the broad smile still fixed on her face. Geary noticed her eye nearest to him twitching slightly, but otherwise Desjani held herself rigid as the Dancer embraced her in the same way as they had Geary.

Then the other eleven Dancers did the same to both of them. Repetition didn't make the experience any easier.

The first Dancer finally spoke, words understandable to humans coming out of a device it wore.

"Welcome human friends,

"Our world greets you here this day,

"Happy all our hearts."

The Dancers didn't wait for any reply, returning to their line.

The Taon stepped forward, raising both open palms in greeting. "Darus," the Taon said, the words coming out of their own translation device worn on the chest, "surrogate to eight-legs. Hello, friend of Lokaa."

"Surrogate?" Geary said. "I guess he means ambassador or representative." Addressing the Taon, Geary held up one hand. "Hello, friend. We are happy to see you."

The Taon made the O-shape with their mouth, which seemed to be the Taon equivalent of a smile. "Eight-legs think you more happy/comfortable with Darus."

So the Dancers understood that humans might be discomforted at being surrounded only by Dancers. But Geary didn't want to openly admit that even if it was an unspoken truth. "We are happy with all here."

This close, in tandem with the Dancers, it was possible to see that the Taon translator was a bit larger than that of the Dancers, and to judge that the translations felt stiffer. Clearly, it wasn't a shared technology, but something each species had developed.

The twelve Dancers who had greeted them beckoned to Geary and Desjani before turning and walking toward a very wide low-slung vehicle with open sides.

Inside, the vehicle had a long, flat main body, the floor divided into what seemed more like nests than chairs arranged along the sides. But midway in the vehicle some of the nests had been replaced with seats that humans, and the Taon, could use.

The Dancer bus, or limousine, rolled into motion silently, no driver apparent up front. It moved smoothly off the landing field and down a wide street flanked on both sides by buildings interspersed with open areas holding local versions of trees, bushes, and grass as well as smaller forms of the jungle gym. There were a lot of Dancers on the sides of the street and in the open areas, all watching the humans pass by.

What Geary saw wasn't a surprise, but rather a confirmation of what the human ships had seen from far off in space. Observations of planetary surfaces were always hindered by atmosphere getting in the way, but many details could still be seen. In this case, that meant he knew the roads in this Dancer city had been laid out in a precise geometric grid, each running as straight as a laser guideline. Any underlying terrain had been meticulously flattened with slight gradients to encourage drainage. The buildings were all square on the bottom one or two stories, the most efficient design for use of materials and space, with top stories shaped into half-spherical domes, the most efficient design for energy use.

Every single building. Exactly the same on the outside, except for varying on having two or three stories.

"The planetary surveys were right. None of the buildings are more than three stories high," Desjani observed. "But there are a whole lot of Dancers lining the roads to watch us go by."

He nodded, knowing she was talking about speculation in the fleet that the relatively small buildings couldn't support a very large population of Dancers in this city. But the population looked plenty large from where they sat.

The answer came from an unexpected source. Darus had heard

Desjani's comment, and made an O with their mouth while pointing down. "Eight-leg buildings tall beneath ground."

It took Geary a moment to understand. "You mean there are many more levels of those buildings underground?"

"Yes. Not like human and Taon. Eight-legs go low to build high." The Taon mouth formed another O.

Desjani grinned. "Is that the first Taon joke we've heard?"

"Underground skyscrapers," Geary said. "This city is a lot bigger than it looks like on the surface."

Since the Taon seemed to be in a good mood, Geary decided to bring up another topic. "Do Taon know Wooareek?"

Darus took a moment before replying. "Taon know Wooareek."

"Are Taon and Wooareek friends?"

A longer pause followed before Darus finally answered. "Taon know Wooareek."

Geary pressed on further than he probably should, aggravated by another runaround. "Are Taon and Wooareek enemies?"

Darus's mouth formed into the O shape and a deep grunting sound emitted from deep inside them. Was it laughter? "Taon know Wooareek. Human will know Wooareek. Wooareek will decide."

Was that ominous, or reassuring? Darus clearly wasn't going to be any more specific than that. Geary looked at Desjani, who gave him a baffled expression in reply.

Though the crowds of Dancers on the edges of the streets didn't diminish, the wide streets themselves remained empty except for the bus carrying them. Geary kept waiting for the bus to accelerate, but it continued to move at an extremely sedate speed that felt not much faster than a walking pace.

Desjani must have felt the same way. "About ten kilometers per hour," she said. "If I guessed the distance we covered in the last minute right." She followed up by pointing to some nearby Dancers who were walking faster than the bus, passing it and pulling away, their multiple legs forming a strange-looking choreography. "A little better than a brisk walking speed for humans, but a little less than that for Dancers."

The slow speed did give plenty of time to study the passing buildings. Pulling out his personal pad, he typed a message for Desjani to see so that they wouldn't be saying anything the Dancers might find critical. The Dancers don't seem to like windows. On all the buildings, the ground-floor walls were unbroken except for solid doors, and strips of windows set high which were narrow in height and wide in width.

Desjani nodded, tapping on her own pad and then showing him the message. Closed-in buildings and open structures. Nothing in between. We humans like windows so we can see the outside and sort of feel outside even though we want to be inside. It's as if the Dancers want to feel inside when they're inside, and outside when they're outside.

The Dancer bus kept meandering through the city, the Dancers with Geary and Desjani staying quiet. Geary kept looking for distinctive features on the buildings. But the buildings were all surprisingly plain on the outside, with no ornamentation or special design features aside from bars of different colors forming flat rainbows near the doors.

He could hear the high-pitched buzz of Dancer talk, interspersed with claw clacks, from the crowds watching the bus pass. But the Dancers aboard the bus had remained silent. Were they waiting for him to say more?

Surely asking about the city constituted safe small talk.

Geary turned to the nearest Dancers on the bus, speaking slowly.

"Buildings have functions,

"Where are stores houses workplace,

"Manufacturing?"

One of the Dancers waved two claws toward the buildings they were passing.

"You see they are here,

"All of these places you ask,

"Are in these buildings."

Geary tried not to frown, looking from the Dancer to the outwardly identical buildings.

Darus the Taon pointed to those buildings as well. "All eight-leg houses same on outside, different inside."

"Oh." Geary unsuccessfully tried to spot any details through the small windows. "I guess the bars of colors indicate the function of each building."

"Sort of like human spaceships," Desjani said. "Basic hull shapes from the outside, but the interiors can vary a lot."

"It's very different than the human approach to buildings, though," Geary said. Which shouldn't be a surprise. The Dancers were aliens, after all. But he realized that humans had tended to assume that even aliens would do the same basic things the same ways that humans did.

Desjani was tapping out another message that she showed to Geary. Shouldn't we be talking more to the Dancers?

About all I can talk about is the weather, he typed in reply.

He could talk to the Taon, though. He nodded to Darus. "Are you the only Taon here?"

"Yes. Only Taon," Darus replied. But after a moment their expression shifted. The heavy Taon faces with their bony ridges made it hard for humans to figure out what an expression might mean, and this was no exception. "Human mean only Taon here," Darus said as they pointed to the floor of the bus, "or only Taon here?" They spread their arms wide to encompass the city and perhaps the planet.

Geary tried not to wince over how badly he'd framed that question. If Darus hadn't thought through what it might mean, the humans might have been left with a totally mistaken impression of how many Taon were on the planet. "Here," Geary said, spreading his arms wide as well.

"Thirty-two. Surrogate community," Darus said.

"A full embassy, then," Desjani remarked. "That's about thirty-two people, isn't it?"

"I don't know," Geary said. "I think it varies. Darus, are there other, um, surrogates on this planet? Representatives of other intelligent species?"

The Taon turned their head and gazed silently at the view outside the bus.

I guess that's a secret, Desjani typed. I've been looking closely at the Dancers. Those pale color changes on the places where they don't have fur. I think they're tattoos of some sort.

Color-changing tattoos? Geary typed in reply.

Why not? See how some Dancers have the exact same locations and shapes of colors? If those were natural wouldn't there be more variation? Maybe it's like the buildings, with the colors showing ID?

Maybe, Geary typed in reply. Rank or status or job.

They were passing a building with Dancers supervising robotic workers which seemed to be repairing part of the exterior. That reminded Geary of what should be a safe question. How long had the Dancers been on this planet?

Forming that question into a haiku proved particularly difficult, but he finally came up with something and spoke to the nearest Dancers.

"Cities have long lives,

"How many years since this place,

"First your people here?"

Desjani gave him a disbelieving look in silent comment on the quality of his latest haiku.

But if the Dancers were put off by the awkwardness of Geary's attempt, they gave no sign. After conferring among each other one began speaking through its translator.

"Humans measure time,

"In orbits of your home world,

"Nine hundred orbits."

Nine hundred standard years. This city had been founded before humans even left Old Earth for other stars. But it didn't look it.

Geary spoke again.

"Our cities show age,

"In different style buildings,

"Why here all the same?"

More discussion among the Dancers before one replied.

"Why different style,

"Best design does not alter,

"With time why change style?"

Again, a totally different perspective than the human way of doing things. The Dancers had settled on the most efficient shapes for building exteriors, and that was what they built. Why change? Looking about him, Geary guessed that the materials used had varied over time, but the basic exteriors hadn't. Humans made changes in exteriors based on changing aesthetics, different ways of doing the same things. Humans tore down old buildings, throwing away their materials, in order to build new ones of different design that might or might not be "improvements." That all must strike the Dancers as ridiculously wasteful and inefficient.

Desjani nudged Geary, pointing with her whole hand to mimic the Dancer claw-pointing gesture.

He looked, seeing a pillar rising from the center of an open area. Apparently perfectly round and with a multifaceted half sphere crowning it, the roughly ten-meter-tall pillar was about a meter across, and the first thing they'd seen that looked like public art.

Turning to ask the Dancers on the bus what the pillar represented, Geary was startled to see that all were gazing fixedly away from it. Looking back at the pillar, he noticed that every one of the dozens of Dancers near it was also avoiding looking at it in ways that were impossible to miss. Public art that no one is supposed to look at? he typed to Desjani.

Should you ask about it? Thinking not, she typed in reply.

It wasn't the weather, and anything that no Dancer looked at had to be a sensitive topic in some way. Not, Geary typed in agreement with her.

What did the pillar represent? Something the Dancers felt had to be commemorated, but something they didn't want to view. Did it mark some religious meaning, or was it a memorial to some past event? He burned to ask but knew that would violate his instructions from the ambassador. All he could do was watch until the pillar was lost to view, never seeing a Dancer look toward it.

Desjani tilted her pad so he could read it. Know what I'm not seeing? Kids. Where are Dancer kids? The Dancers we're seeing vary in size, but not as much as the difference between, say, a small human kid and an adult.

Geary frowned, searching his memory. Out of all the Dancers they'd seen so far, none had been significantly smaller in the way human children were compared to adults. Is that deliberate? he typed back. Or just result of the Dancer children being protected somehow?

Only way to find out is to ask, Desjani typed.

Was that too sensitive a topic? But they had no clue it might be. Desjani was right that the only way to learn if it was a sensitive topic was to ask. The answer might be purely innocuous, that Dancer children stayed inside during the day for education, for example.

Geary carefully composed his question before turning to face the nearest Dancer on the bus, who he thought was the same Dancer who'd first embraced him and Tanya.

"Children are special,

"The future of each species,

"Will we see any?"

The Dancer looked back at Geary without speaking, no expression a human could read apparent on the Dancer's face or in their eyes. Then the Dancer looked away without saying anything.

All the Dancers on the bus were looking away, not saying anything even among themselves.

Geary spread his hands toward Tanya.

I guess we don't talk about that, she typed.

Why would children be a sensitive topic? Geary wondered.

She paused before typing quickly. You've never had kids.

Eventually, after hours of slow progress down street after street, the bus entered a wide field and stopped next to a pavilion with open sides. Inside were rows of tables arranged in concentric hollow squares with nests/seats facing inward.

The exception was a slightly elevated platform in the middle, which boasted only one table with three chairs, one much wider and sturdier than the other two.

"I guess we know where our seats are," Desjani said. "But for what?"

Darus the Taon heard her question. Their mouth made the O shape as Darus gestured about at crowds of Dancers converging on the pavilion. "Feast."

"Feast," Geary repeated, looking at the rows of tables. "It looks like we're going to have a banquet."

Desjani bit her lip, typing quickly. Ancestors and the living stars save us.

There had been a lot of speculation among humans about what the Dancers ate, and how they ate it. Given the appearance of the Dancers, much of that speculation had been horrifying in one way or another, the most lurid guesses involving creatures still living who were paralyzed and helpless as the Dancers slowly ate them or sucked all their juices out. Geary had always downplayed such speculation, saying accurately that no human actually knew anything about what Dancers ate and how they did it.

But he was well aware that he had no more idea of the answer than anyone else. And the multi-jawed bear traps of the Dancer mouths seemed designed for serious chewing.

Darus the Taon led the way to the center table, waiting until Geary and Desjani had sat in the smaller chairs before settling into the heavy-duty chair designed to accommodate a Taon's mass and size. Dancers came in and took places at the tables, their foot claws making a sound like an endless series of tap dancers warming up, sitting to look at the humans and the Taon seated at the central table. It had gotten a little colder as the sun passed noon, enough so that Geary closed up his uniform jacket.

Several of the Dancers at the innermost tables closest to the humans stood up and began speaking in the high-pitched wavering tones of Dancer speech, interspersed with clacks as claws rapped together. Geary heard no human words from the Dancer translator, leaving him and Desjani to focus on the Dancer speech and movement.

"I wonder if they're giving speeches," Tanya said, watching the latest Dancer to speak declaiming in a way that felt oddly dramatic. "Or if they're singing or performing in some other way."

"Maybe both, if our guesses about how the Dancers communicate are right." The speechmaking/performances ended as other Dancers appeared, large trays balanced on their foremost arms.

"Here we go," Desjani muttered, her lips then continuing to move in silent prayer as the Dancers with the trays drew nearer.

Large, covered, shallow bowls were set before Geary, Desjani, and Darus the Taon. Also set before each of them were two utensils. "A fork and straw?" Geary said.

Desjani examined hers carefully. "That's a knork, not a fork. See the knife edges on both sides?"

"Yes." He'd been cautiously optimistic when the eating implements apparently didn't include a knife. "They're wood, I think, except for the cutting edges embedded in the knorks."

Desjani bent to look closely at the straw set before her, similar in diameter to those humans used for beverages with small "pearls" of treats in them. "Check out the designs carved into the straws." Both straws and knorks boasted intricate carving, geometric shapes that interwove and linked. "So, Admiral, how do we know what we're about to be served is safe for humans?"

"I talked to Dr. Nasr about that before we left the ship," Geary said. "We know the Dancers have been watching us for a long time. He's certain that they know a great deal about human biology. Given how careful they've been in everything else, it wouldn't be like the Dancers to serve us anything they didn't think was safe for us. But whatever it looks like, we'll still use our samplers to ensure it's safe."

Whether that something was food that humans would find attractive or tasty was another matter.

He realized that he'd been subconsciously listening, worried that he might hear something on the plate, under the lids, trying to escape.

Geary braced himself as the Dancers serving them reached to raise the lids on the bowls. *Don't react*, he told himself. *No matter how bad it is, don't react. Don't flinch or recoil or cry out.* Ambassador Rycerz had urged him to do his best to choke down at least a couple of bites of whatever it turned out to be, because every human culture set great importance in accepting food offered in hospitality. Aliens might be the same.

He hoped whatever it turned out to be wasn't still alive. He hoped he could manage a couple of bites of whatever it was without gagging.

The lid came up, vague shapes visible beneath it.

Geary nearly jerked with surprise at what he saw.

Neat, precisely cone-shaped mounds of food were arranged in a pattern of interlocking circles, each cone standing separate from the others. The largest cone seemed to be some kind of boiled grain. The other cones varied in size, showing a variety of what appeared to be natural colors that had been arranged to match a visible-light rainbow.

"Nothing looks like it's still alive," Desjani said after a moment. "Beans. Vegetables. Quite a variety. And fruit," she added, pointing to the brighter cones among the others. "I think."

Similar bowls were being placed before the Dancers now, similar arrangements of cones of food on them all.

Geary carefully brought out from his shoulder bag the food sampler he had been provided as Desjani did the same with hers. He pushed the filaments at the end of the sampler into different mounds of food, waiting as the mechanism analyzed and tested everything in the dish.

A green light came on. The food, whatever it was composed of, was safe for human consumption. Checking the readout on the sampler, Geary had to pause to read it again. "It's all plant origin. None of it contains any animal protein or insect protein, except the amounts that would be present if they were used as seasoning or oils."

"Plant origin." Desjani sounded as if she was strangling, before breaking into laughter. "Plant origin! They're vegetarians!"

Geary found himself laughing as well, both with relief and at the reality which was so ludicrously different from the horrible speculations humans had undertaken since first seeing the Dancers. "Vegetarians," he agreed, trying to stop his laughter.

The Dancers, who had been watching with what might have been suspense, appeared to relax at the humans' reaction. Did they recognize laughter? Did they realize it meant Geary and Desjani were happy?

He used the knork to try a cautious taste. The grains were slightly nutty, the various vegetables and fruits adding their own flavor tones. Geary worked his jaws as he realized the grains were chewy. Looking about, he saw Dancers eating with a daintiness that felt odd, and realized those bear-trap jaws were for thoroughly mashing undercooked grains.

"It's a bit bland for our tastes," Desjani observed. "Do you think the Dancers like food that way, or is their sense of taste more sensitive than ours?"

"Could be both," Geary said. "It's not bad, though."

"No, it's not. But my human taste buds still wish I had some salt, pepper, and hot sauce from Adowa." She cast a speculative glance at him. "Or they left out spices that are fine with them but might not play well with humans. Like if they use cyanide the way we use table salt."

"Also a possibility," Geary said.

The meal went on for a long time. Geary, his jaws tired, stopped eating after a while except to pick out pieces of vegetables and fruit from the diminished cones on his plate. The Dancers continued eating with meticulous care, the little tentacles inside their claws picking out small portions from their knorks, the mounds of food slowly being reduced. As the solid food diminished, some of the Dancers began using the elaborately carved straws to suck up the juices in the bottoms of the bowls.

Desjani laughed again for a moment after taking a drink of some of the juice. "This is really going to disappoint all of those people who wanted the Dancers to have, um, different food."

"At least we know for sure why none of our surveys from space spotted any ranches or other form of livestock facility," Geary said. "Just lots of farms."

Dancer waiters suddenly reappeared, depositing smaller trays in front of everyone.

The tray set in front of Geary had a lot of thin bread layers with something sticky spread between them, the whole thing then rolled. After the sampler gave it a thumbs up, he tried a taste. "That's pretty good. Is that honey spread between the layers?"

"Something like honey," Desjani said, smiling. She gave him a look. "Why don't we assume it's honey?"

"You know where honey comes from, right?" Geary said.

"Umm, yeah." She gasped another laugh, this one clearly aimed at herself. "But that's okay because we've always eaten it. Local customs, right?"

"Right."

The humans and Darus the Taon finished long before the Dancers, who continued eating with meticulous deliberation. "Is this a normal sort of meal for them?" Geary asked Darus.

Darus made an odd body motion that might have corresponded to a human shrug. "Fancy. Is right word? More fancy. Food always like this. Eight-legs make pictures with food."

"Food as art," Desjani commented. "That's something humans can identify with."

"Human also make fancy food?" Darus asked.

"Not every meal," Geary said. "Fancy food for . . . special meals."

The Taon made the odd body motion again. "To Taon, food is food. Why fancy? But human like eight-legs. Good to learn. I give you knowing in exchange. Taon eat simple. Food as it is. That is Taon."

"Thank you for the knowledge," Geary said. It sounded like the Taon ate their food raw. "Do you mean plants and vegetables like these?" Even though some Marines had spent a little time on a Taon planet, they'd been isolated and never seen Taon eat. Were the Taon also vegetarians?

"Food," Darus said, their manner that of someone unnecessarily repeating basic information. Or maybe that was the limit of what Darus was willing to give in exchange for what the humans had told them.

All told, by time as humans measured it, the meal took more than three hours, the local sun angling down toward the horizon. But when the meal ended, the Dancers began scurrying about quickly, clearing tables.

Let's hope they don't present us with a bill, Desjani typed.

That reminded him of something. Charban said there are no free lunches in alien space. Let's hope he was wrong about that, Geary typed in reply. Not that he expected what amounted to a diplomatic banquet to demand payment from the guests, but the truth was no one knew anything about how the Dancers did such things.

As it turned out, General Charban had been wrong. No sign was given that any payment for the meal was expected. Their escorts reappeared and led Geary and Desjani back to the bus. Somewhere in the hustle, Darus disappeared, presumably heading back to wherever the other Taon were staying.

Sunset was still a little ways off when the bus halted before a building that seemed like every other building. The exterior was as plain as that of other buildings, but once finally inside a Dancer structure Geary saw elaborate carvings and distinctive architectural features. The Dancers led Geary and Desjani inside, not letting them linger to examine the interior, before stopping at a very human-looking door leading farther into the building. One of the Dancers spoke, the translator quickly providing human words.

"This night stay safe here,

"Sleep and rest in happiness,

"Stay inside stay safe."

The Dancers moved back, plainly waiting.

Geary opened the inner door, stepped inside, and looked about, surprised. The room, and what he could see through openings into adjacent rooms, was filled with obviously human-designed furniture and other items.

The Dancers waited until Desjani had followed him into the room, then another spoke.

"This night stay safe here,

"Sleep and rest in happiness,

"Stay inside stay safe."

One of the Dancers closed the inner door, shutting off the view of the other Dancers quickly departing.

"What the hell?" Desjani said. She tried the door, pushing at it. "It opens easily, but after the first centimeter there's resistance to opening it more, resistance that grows the more it opens."

"Could you open it enough to get out?"

"I think so. But it'd take a big effort." She frowned slightly. "They're not locking us in. We're free to go. But it'd take a lot of work to get outside this door. What was that 'stay inside stay safe' stuff?"

"Repeated twice," Geary said. "I have no idea. But unless we have a good reason I suppose we should listen to that advice. How are you doing?"

For a moment, she let her expression clearly show her feelings. "I'm much better now. Because of that thing we discussed on the ship."

"The thing you have a thing about."

"That thing. But, now, we're in here. Just us. And that's . . . a relief."

"Because you're tired," Geary said, thinking that the Dancers might well be surveilling this entire set of rooms.

"Riiiight. Tired."

Geary looked about him, at the human furniture and human accessories and chairs and beds. "Some of this stuff looks familiar to me. The styles. Some of the design features." He touched the top of a chair. "Familiar to me from before."

"You mean more than a century old?" Desjani bent to study an end table. "I can believe that. My grandmother has something that looks like this. Um . . . sorry. Why does this place feel like it was designed at least a hundred years ago? We know the Dancers have a lot more recent records on us than that."

"I wonder," Geary said, walking slowly about the main room. "We were pushing toward the existing edges of human exploration a century ago. If the war with the Syndicate Worlds hadn't happened, we might've encountered the Dancers pretty soon back then."

Her laugh was low, soft, and bitter. "But the war started, and we spent a century fighting off the Syndics instead of exploring, and this set of rooms was left waiting for the humans who hadn't shown up when they were expected."

"That's probably what happened." There were two beds, each heaped with more pillows and blankets than they could possibly use. "We should be comfortable in here. Is that a kitchen?"

"Yeah. What's in here?" Desjani opened a cabinet and bent to look. "Oh, it's—" Her voice broke off.

"What's the matter?" Geary asked anxiously.

on a wistful tone. "Of course it was all junk. All fiction. But he couldn't get enough of things about aliens. It's too bad he never got a chance to meet a Dancer."

"I wish he had," Geary said.

She glanced at him for a moment. "It's too bad he never got a chance to meet you."

"If I'd been found sooner," Geary said. "If I'd been able to do something sooner—"

"You couldn't," Tanya said. "The living stars make their plans, and we have to live with them. They set when you'd be found, and that's all there is to it. You never had a chance to save my brother. You never could've had a chance. That's not anyone's fault."

She looked at him again, her eyes somber but a slight smile showing. "Someday we'll meet again, beyond the dark. And then I'll get to tell him about the aliens. And about you."

They spent a while more exploring the three rooms of their suite, testing the water in the faucets which proved to be safe, with a moderate mineral content, and then each taking a long shower. As Desjani was finishing up, Geary tried calling *Dauntless*.

The call was answered by Senior Chief Tarrani. "I've got the watch, Admiral. How's it going?"

"No problems so far," Geary said. "Is the data from the sensors in our uniforms reaching you okay?"

"Clear and strong, Admiral." Tarrani grinned. "It looks like you've had an interesting day."

"That's one way of putting it," Geary said. "Diplomacy is exhausting. Sitting on a bus going nowhere very slowly for a long time is exhausting, too." Should he have said that when the Dancers might be monitoring what was said in this room?

"About that, Admiral," Tarrani said. "Master Chief Gioninni and I were looking at some of the feed from your sensors earlier, and he said

"Have we been cursed by the living stars and abandoned by (ancestors?" Tanya said, her words freighted with horror.

"What is it?"

She held up a familiar-looking object. "Ration bars. Fleet rat bars. *All* of them are Danaka Yoruk ration bars."

"You're kidding."

"I wish I was." Desjani looked closer at the one she was holdi "Really stale Danaka Yoruk ration bars. In case you're wondering, taste doesn't get any better when they get stale. They're just harde choke down."

"I didn't know it could be any harder to get them down." He shrugg "At least if we were stuck in here we wouldn't starve."

"If I were given the choice of starving to death or surviving by (ing stale Danaka Yoruk ration bars I'd take the less painful opt of starvation," Desjani said. She checked other drawers and cabin "Dining utensils. Why have we got about a hundred spatulas? Wha the Dancers think humans do with spatulas? Glasses. These all l like they were made in human space." She paused, reaching into (cabinet and pulling out a plate. "Why does this look familiar?" Desj held up a plate with an elaborate multicolored pattern baked into i

He laughed briefly in mingled surprise and nostalgia. "Because th an antique design from the Old Colony Alfar. We have an heirlo bowl with that same pattern at home on Glenlyon. I think Rob Ge brought it with him from Alfar when he came with the first settlers Glenlyon."

She stood gazing at the plate. "My brother would've loved th Tanya said unexpectedly, startling him.

Geary stayed silent a moment, not sure how to react. Tanya ne talked about her little brother, who'd died in combat six years bef Geary himself had been found frozen in survival sleep. Before he co decide what to say, she spoke again.

"He was really into aliens when he was little." Her voice had tak to me, 'I betcha they're not showing the humans the city. What they're doing is showing the city the humans.'"

Geary paused to consider that, realizing that when he flipped his perspective on the day, Gioninni's suggestion made perfect sense. "It wasn't about us. It was about them. Thank the master chief for me."

"Will do, Admiral. Anything else? No worries?"

"No worries, yet, Senior Chief. We're going to turn in. Do not hesitate to notify us if needed."

"Understood, Admiral." Senior Chief Tarrani raised her hand in a salute before the call ended.

Desjani came in, yawning. "I might actually get a full night's sleep. That'd be amazing."

"Here's something else amazing." He told her Gioninni's idea.

"Oh, yeah," Desjani said. "That's exactly what they were doing. And during that feast, with us in the middle on a raised platform so every Dancer there could see us eat. But why? Every Dancer must have access to video recordings and pictures of humans."

"Videos and pictures can be manipulated," Geary said. "Faked."

"So we get paraded around to allow the average Dancer to see we're real?" Desjani shrugged. "That also makes some sense. Didn't the Wooa-reek say something about that when they were saying why *Sapphire* should come with them?"

"Yes," Geary said, remembering. "Wave Breaks said something about having to meet people. And Lokaa really wanted us to visit Taon space. Are we seeing a pattern?"

"Might be. I also wonder if they had Darus on the bus with us not just to keep us company but also to associate humans in the minds of the Dancers who saw us with the Taon, who are a known factor?"

"That's possible," Geary said. "We have to try to see things from the Dancer perspective, not just the human perspective."

She looked up toward one of the high, narrow windows. "Speaking of seeing things, the Dancer cities look dark at night from space. We didn't know if that was because they were dark, or if the Dancers directed light only where it was needed and avoided light scatter and pollution."

"Now's our chance to find out," Geary said. "From the look of the window, it's full dark out."

There wasn't any ladder in the room, but Tanya dragged a dresser to the wall under one of the windows, then carefully clambered on top and, standing, stretched to look out. "Yeah. Wicked dark. I can see a few more windows with light behind them, but it's not going very far. No streetlights or anything else. The only illumination is starlight, and from the looks of the clouds moving in before we came inside I'm guessing there's not much of that." She stretched up a little more, glancing about.

And froze, staring silently out and down.

"What is it?" Geary said.

"I don't know. Come up and take a look."

It took some effort to get up beside her without toppling the dresser, but Geary made it. Staring in the direction Desjani pointed, down toward the street muffled in darkness, Geary gradually made out movement. "What are we looking at?"

"I don't know. But there seem to be a lot of them."

As his eyes grew more accustomed to the darkness, Geary caught more and more suggestions of things moving below, in the street and next to the sides of the buildings. He couldn't make out any details, just a vague awareness of shapes moving in the dark.

EIGHT

"MAYBE this is why the Dancers don't have windows closer to ground level," Desjani said.

"But what are they? The Dancers should be able to cope with any wildlife that poses a danger to them."

"You'd think."

Geary frowned, chasing a memory. "There are places where certain animals are regarded as holy. No one is allowed to harm them."

"In human space?" Desjani asked. A child of constant war, she hadn't had the leisure to learn as much about different places outside the Alliance as Geary once had. "So these could be like that, or something like that pillar we saw that none of the Dancers would look at." She glanced toward the entry. "Even though the Dancers told us 'stay inside stay safe,' if we were Marines we'd probably go out that door and try to find out exactly what's out there."

"Probably," Geary agreed.

"Fortunately," Desjani continued, "we're sailors. So I suggest that we stay in here and let the sensors in our uniforms collect everything they can, so the specialists in the fleet can analyze it all later."

"I concur," Geary said.

They got carefully down off the dresser, Desjani sighing heavily. "Okay. There's something out there, probably the reason why the Dancers told us 'stay inside stay safe.' And whatever it is probably can't get through the walls. But it's still out there. So much for a full night's sleep. I'll take the first watch."

"Two hours," Geary said. "Wake me then." Was he hearing something scratching at the outside walls? That was probably just his imagination.

Stay inside stay safe. They were definitely going to do that. But it was still going to be a long night.

THE next morning the streets were empty of anything they hadn't seen in daylight the day before. There was no trace of whatever had been moving in the night.

"Breakfast," Desjani said as they pulled out ration bars (not stale and not Danaka Yoruk) from their bags. "There isn't any food in that kitchen area except those stale ration bars. Do you think maybe the Dancers only eat one meal a day? They took forever yesterday, eating so slowly."

"Could be," Geary said. He checked the label of his ration bar. Spicy Sweet Chicken. That explained why it tasted like pork. The only fleet ration bars with meat that didn't taste like chicken were the ones that supposedly contained chicken.

"Is there a diplomatic way to tell our hosts that Danaka Yoruk ration bars are not a good idea for snacks when humans are involved?" Desjani asked. "Especially not when they expired a decade ago?"

"I think we should leave that to Ambassador Rycerz and her people. She might think we shouldn't risk offending the Dancers over such an, um, minor issue."

Desjani snorted derisively. "Making people eat Danaka Yoruk bars is not a minor issue. Somebody's got to tell the Dancers."

Both he and Desjani were restless by the time the Dancer escorts showed up to collect them. They found themselves on the bus again, along with several Dancers, Geary wishing that Darus the Taon were along with them today as they had been yesterday.

He'd carefully worked out a question, not about the weather but about something he had to ask, and spoke to the Dancers just as the bus began moving.

"Something in the night,

"Not easy to see in dark,

"What was in the streets?"

No answer.

We don't talk about that, either, Desjani typed on her pad.

Geary dreaded another long, slow procession, but the ride this time lasted only about half an hour before the bus came to a halt before a structure that didn't appear to be any different from those around it. That made it all the more surprising when the humans got inside.

The building, designed to look unimposing from the outside, was huge inside, with wide ramps sweeping around the walls, vast open spaces, and floors set beneath ground level so that walls soared high around them.

And on the walls . . .

"Tapestries," Geary said. "Look at them."

"Awesome," Desjani agreed.

The tapestries ranged in size from some as small as the palm of a human hand, to vast sheets covering wide, tall walls from top to bottom. Some showed what were clearly nature scenes. Others were apparently abstract views of space. Several might depict scenes from Dancer history.

"Does that look like a stylized image of a major asteroid strike on a planet?" Geary said, pointing. Dominated by shades of red, orange, and black, the jagged lines of the images on the tapestry and silhouettes of what appeared to be various plants and creatures reinforced the sense of vast tragedy.

"I'd say so," Desjani said, studying the tapestry. "If the Dancers experienced, and survived, something like that on their home world during their recorded history, it would've had a huge influence on them."

"Like maybe building large structures mostly underground?" Geary said, looking about at the other tapestries. The largest were covered with intricate, interleaving patterns. When Geary tried to follow some of those patterns with his eyes he kept finding himself getting dizzy.

The tapestries were made of various threads, some extremely fine, some coarse and large, others a mix of various thicknesses that created a three-dimensional effect. Or perhaps more than three dimensions, Geary thought, thinking of how trying to follow some of the patterns made him light-headed.

"Huh," Desjani said. "That's odd. It's not finished." She pointed to one side of the nearest tapestry to them, where loose threads dangled in a waterfall of color. "None of them are finished," Desjani added, looking around.

Now that she'd pointed it out, Geary saw it, too. Every tapestry, large or small, hadn't been finished, every one instead ending in a tangle of unwoven thread. "That must have some significance."

Taking his eyes off the tapestries, he looked at the Dancers in the building. Aside from the escorts near him and Desjani, the other Dancers here were mostly gathered in front of various tapestries, their legs tucked under them, gazing silently at the tapestries before them.

"I was thinking this was an art museum," Desjani said, gazing about her. "Now I'm starting to wonder. Are those Dancers meditating or praying?"

"They might be," Geary said. "It feels like it, anyway. Maybe this is a religious building. But look at that tapestry over there. Isn't it displaying Newton's law of motion?"

She followed his gesture, studying the images woven into the tapestry. "Looks like it to me. Some of these tapestries might be showing scientific principles as the Dancers see them."

"I can't wait to hear what Dr. Cresida thinks when she sees them," Geary said.

"See, that's one way we're different," Desjani said. "Usually I'm happier not to hear what Dr. Cresida thinks. But I am curious as to what the Dancers are thinking. Why'd they bring us here? Why aren't our escorts explaining what we're seeing?"

Definitely not a weather question, but one Geary knew he had to ask.

"Beautiful in here,

"We see many fine works . . . art,

"What is the meaning?"

The Dancer escorts conferred among themselves briefly before one addressed Geary.

"What does human see?

"What meaning does human see?

"What does human hear?"

Geary looked at Desjani, who made a helpless gesture. "How do we answer that in three lines of five, seven, and five syllables?" she asked.

"How do we answer that when we're not certain what we're seeing?" Geary said, trying to sort out his thoughts in ways he could express to the Dancers. But his concentration was broken by Desjani, speaking in a low, urgent voice.

"What's up with this?"

Geary followed her gaze and saw what she meant. The other Dancers in the building, individually and in small groups, were coming closer to them. But, unlike the earlier encounters, something about them did not feel . . . comfortable. "Do they feel hostile to you?"

"Maybe just unwelcoming. They don't want us in here," Desjani said. "That's what I'm feeling."

They stood together, uncertain how to react, as the angry-seeming Dancers edged closer.

Geary was trying to decide whether a slow retreat would be wise when he realized that their escorts were moving to form a barrier between the humans and the unhappy Dancers, words being rapidly exchanged between both sides. Claws moved and clacked to emphasize the words in ways that made it clear this was a heated discussion.

It was odd to stand here, knowing he and Tanya were the objects of the argument, but also knowing he shouldn't do or say anything that might trigger more antagonism from the Dancers who clearly objected to humans being here. He could only guess why their presence was unwelcome, using his experience with humans, not Dancers, making it even harder to know what would make the situation better or worse.

Tanya stood next to him, outwardly relaxed, nothing about her revealing what she must be feeling inside as large, unfriendly spider-wolves pressed closer.

Not doing anything must have been the right thing in this case. The pace of the argument diminished, the unfriendly Dancers stopped advancing, and after a few more tense minutes the escorts ushered Geary and Desjani out of the building.

Once they were outside, the sense of growing tension fell away. "Not just an art museum," Desjani said firmly.

"Definitely not," Geary agreed. "I wonder how long it'll be before we learn exactly what it is. Any guesses why we were shown it? The Dancers didn't tell us."

"Maybe they did tell us," she said, pausing, her head slightly tilted as she looked back at the building. "When they answered you. They wanted to know what we thought of what we were seeing. What we 'heard' when we looked at those tapestries. Maybe what was important there wasn't for us to see the tapestries. Instead, it was for the Dancers to see how we responded to them."

He nodded, wondering why that hadn't occurred to him. "Was this whole visit a test? To see how humans responded to Dancers? Humans who the Dancers must know have conjured up all sorts of horrible alien threats out of our imaginations through all of our known history."

"If so, I think we did okay," Desjani said. "Those unfinished tapestries . . . have you ever heard that saying about how our stories are never finished? That every act leads to new things, every road to new roads? Do you think the unfinished tapestries might symbolize that sort of thing? We can't finish the picture because the picture is never finished."

"That might well be," Geary said. "What was in there certainly seems to confirm our earlier speculations about the Dancers seeing everything in terms of a tapestry, everything interwoven, and everything forming threads to make up the big picture of the universe."

After a moment, Desjani spoke again. "What did you think of those patterns?"

"The abstract ones?" Geary shook his head. "They made me dizzy."

"Yeah." She paused once more. "I felt my ancestors in one of them. As if they were speaking through it."

He started to reply to that, then himself paused to think, trying to sort out exactly how the patterns had affected him. "They made me dizzy," Geary repeated, speaking slowly, "as if the world was shifting about me, as if what I was seeing wasn't what was really there."

"Visual drugs?" Desjani asked.

"Is that possible?"

"Or aids to meditation, to seeing truth?" she continued. "How can something designed to mess with Dancer brains also mess with human brains?"

"Maybe there's something in common in those brains that no one has ever thought of," Geary said.

"It's not like we've been able to study any Dancer brains, yet," Desjani said. "What do you suppose our escorts are discussing?" They were on the bus once more, but it hadn't begun moving. The Dancers were clustered in the back speaking among themselves. She started typing. They're probably saying "Well, that didn't work." You'd think they'd have known what would happen when we went in there. We're not the first other species they've encountered.

Other species. He looked from the museum / cathedral / meditation center back to the Dancers talking together. Geary typed his reply slowly, his thoughts trying catch up with his words. Maybe they didn't know. So far we've encountered the enigmas, the Kicks, the Dancers, the Taon, and the Wooareek. What do they have in common?

She thought for a moment. Space travel. Sentience. That's about it. The Wooareek, the Dancers, and the Taon want personal meetings. Reasons unknown. The enigmas and the Kicks both want to kill us, but for different reasons.

And that's also true for how humans reacted to the aliens. It hasn't been the same in each case, Geary typed.

No. Desjani gave him a sidelong look. You're saying it's different every time. How they react, how your own species reacts. The Dancers didn't know what would happen when we went in there until we went in. How would we react to everything there, and how would their own people react to us.

"The ambassador's staff has been trying to develop a standard protocol for handling first contacts with alien species," Geary said, deliberately speaking out loud because he wanted the Dancers to overhear. "They haven't been able to because when they apply anything to one species we've met it doesn't work for others. Maybe a standard way of handling that is impossible, and even people like the Dancers with a lot of experience encountering new species have to wing it each time."

She eyed him, clearly trying to decide whether to also reply out loud. "How we react to them and their stuff, how they react to us and our stuff," Desjani finally said. "It'll always be a different mix for each species. That's going to be a hard sell, though. You know how bureaucracies work. No one back in Alliance space is going to want to hear that we can't make a one-size-fits-all approach to first contact. They want a checklist with some if-thens built into it, not a policy that treats each contact as unique."

"You're right," he said.

"I always am."

"But reality isn't going to adapt to bureaucratic imperatives," Geary continued. "We need arguments to convince them that flexibility is required. Maybe the Dancers can help us with that to ensure our contacts with them and others work out as well as possible." That was a major rewrite of one of the diplomatic talking points that Ambassador Rycerz had provided him, but one that he thought went to the heart of the matter. And it was something he'd wanted to flat out tell the Dancers for some time.

Desjani raised her eyebrows at him, smiling in a way that showed she knew he'd gone out on a limb with saying that last statement out loud. Shifting back to typing, she showed him her reply. Good luck with that, Admiral. Maybe it would help if we reproduce one of those Dancer tapestries that makes a human mind get wacked and make the human bureaucrats and the Dancer bureaucrats stare at it for a while.

He couldn't help smiling as well at the idea. I'm always open to new approaches, Captain.

But. She pointed upward. The Dancers, as General Charban keeps pointing out, insist they only want to talk to "one." One representative for all humanity. And when we had that fight with the Syndics in this star system, the Dancers told us it was a human problem for humans to fix. Those both sound like standard policies to me.

They do. He frowned up at the sky. So we have evidence to support unique approaches to each species, and evidence to support standard approaches to each species. Like Dr. Cresida says about relativity and quantum mechanics. Both are experimentally true, but they contradict each other.

Are you going to keep quoting her to me?

Only when necessary. Dr. Cresida had early on clearly communicated her opinion of the fleet her sister had served in and died in, and Tanya Desjani wasn't the sort to easily let go of something like that.

Having apparently made up their minds, and giving no sign they'd overheard anything Geary had said, the Dancer escorts returned to their nest seats as the bus surged into motion. Moving a bit faster than yesterday, but by no means fast, the bus turned and began heading for the edge of the city.

That edge was clean-cut. Unlike a typical human town or city that tapered off, going from dense development to less dense by stages, the Dancer city simply ended with city on one side of an imaginary line and countryside on the other. But the road kept straight on, and after a short time the bus turned off into a small area next to fields filled with vegetation that didn't look at all like the monoculture farms that Geary tended to think of.

The Dancers urged him and Desjani off the bus and toward the vegetation, where Geary saw many shapes of differing sizes moving amid the leaves and fronds and needles. Some were natural, the large insect-like creatures that here seemed to fill what were small mammal or bird ecological niches on many other habitable worlds. The others were bots, in what initial glances showed to be four standard models with different tool modifications for specific farming tasks. Geary wasn't surprised to see that just as human-made robots often mimicked human hands and bodies, the Dancer robots were built around copying the shapes of Dancers and their claw/tentacle hands.

One of the Dancers faced him, the translator instantly providing human words as the Dancer spoke.

"The world gives us life,

"We work with life to feed life,

"All is one design."

He didn't need further explanation. On one level, it was simple ecology. Everything was tied together. On another level, it described the

Dancer philosophy humans had already guessed at, that the Dancers saw everything in terms of its place in some grand pattern. In fact, Geary thought, looking at how the different kinds of plants were interspersed and arranged, they seemed to themselves make up a pattern or picture of some kind.

The farm didn't consist of rows or orchards of similar crops. Instead, clearly different types of "trees," "stalks," and lower-lying plants occupied the same area. The bot workers moved among the plants carrying out a variety of tasks, the smaller bots working around the roots, plucking up weeds and doing other tasks, while some large bots were picking higher-up fruit, their hands moving with impressive speed, precision, and delicacy.

"Mixed cropping," Desjani said. "Gunnery Sergeant Orvis made that guess from what we could observe from space. His family back home is involved in farming."

"Did Orvis say why he thought the Dancers would do this mixed cropping?" Geary asked.

"He said, when you factor in all the costs and all the requirements and all the benefits up and down the line, it's the most efficient way of growing crops. For a while it's also labor-intensive, but once robotics reaches a certain place there's no contest." She pointed around the area. "The crops support each other, some adding to the soil what others take, and protect each other from pests or too much sun or whatever."

"That sounds like a great way of doing things," Geary said. "It figures that the Dancers would employ the most efficient form of growing crops."

He watched as one of the big robots picking fruit paused in its work before turning and, its long legs stepping daintily as if it were a massive insect, approaching him and Desjani. None of the Dancers acted alarmed, so Geary waited until the robot stopped. Extending two arms, it offered him and Desjani each a fruit.

"Do you think it's ripe?" Geary asked, examining the gift.

"It's ripe," Desjani said, her voice so full of certainty that Geary looked at her in surprise.

She held up the fruit, giving Geary a flat look. "This is a paracot. Native to Kosatka, my home world. At least, we've always believed it was native to Kosatka."

"We're a long ways from Kosatka," Geary said. "Was any of this in what they served us yesterday?"

"Yes. I thought it tasted familiar, but also thought what are the odds? It turns out the odds were a lot better than I realized."

Geary looked to the nearest Dancer, trying to frame his question right.

"This . . . good fruit . . . grows here,

"Also very far from here,

"A . . . distant planet."

The Dancer made a sharp movement with one claw before they replied.

"Life knows no limit,

"All who travel carry life,

"And leave legacy."

"That sounds like an admission they've been dropping off seeds on worlds their ships visited," Desjani said.

"Or," Geary said, "an admission that any traveler carries contamination with them. Humanity long ago accepted that by traveling to other worlds we introduce new elements of life there. We can't prevent it."

"Same difference," Desjani said. She typed quickly. It means they were on Kosatka at some point. Long enough before humans got there for paracot trees to be well established in the wild. Why didn't the Dancers settle it themselves before humanity exploded into that sector of space?

That's a question we're probably not going to learn the answer to for some time, Geary typed in reply.

After a leisurely stroll through the plants of the mixed farm, the humans were urged back onto the bus.

Their destination this time only became clear when the bus rolled out onto the landing field where the Alliance shuttle was still grounded, awaiting Geary and Desjani's return. The day had gotten steadily more cloudy, with the feeling of rain threatening. With the sun obscured, the temperature had dropped to a level that was slightly cold even with Geary's jacket closed.

"I guess our tour is over," Desjani said. Do you get the feeling today's agenda was cut short after the incident at the museum/temple/whatever? she typed.

There's no way to tell since the Dancers never gave us an agenda for this visit. Geary looked about him, trying to judge the moods of the Dancers. They're not acting upset as far as I can tell. For what little that was worth. No human had yet developed much skill in sensing subtle emotions in the Dancers. Maybe they just want us to leave before it starts raining.

The bus stopped near the shuttle, the Dancers coming off to form the same line they'd been in when the humans arrived. Geary braced himself for another round of interspecies hugs, but to his relief the Dancers only waved the humans on, their claws rubbing together in "applause."

"Farewell human friends,

"Your time here very useful,

"Valuable as well."

That sounded good, though "useful" had a lot of possible connotations, not all of them good as far as humans were concerned. Geary had already memorized his own goodbye and tried to speak in a way that emphasized sincerity.

"We both are honored,

"By your hospitality,

"We sorrow to leave."

After waiting several awkward seconds to see if the Dancers would say or do anything else, Geary nodded to Desjani and they both walked to the shuttle. The ramp dropped as they approached. Geary paused at the foot of the ramp to render a salute toward the Dancers, wondering how they'd take that gesture.

Once he was inside, the ramp raised and the pilot called back. "Are we good to lift, Admiral?"

"I guess so," Geary said.

"There are six small Dancer ships hovering nearby. Probably our escort out. We'll lift as soon as you're strapped in, Admiral."

Shuttle pilots also had to practice forms of diplomacy, including how to tell admirals they needed to strap into their seats.

Geary, securely strapped in next to Desjani, felt the shuttle lift and watched on the displays as the planetary surface dropped away. He felt an odd melancholy, perhaps born of opportunities that hadn't appeared and answers that had often been ambiguous.

"At least we learned they were vegetarians," Desjani said. "And we learned they have mind-bending tapestries."

"And we learned they have a secret stockpile of stale Danaka Yoruk bars," Geary said.

"That's important, too."

What had they seen without realizing the importance of it? The sensor feeds back to the fleet should have recorded everything. Hopefully they had seen more than the unaided human eye could, and the experts among the fleet would be able to spot everything of significance.

Hopefully.

In the seat beside him, Desjani carefully deactivated the sensors and recording devices in her uniform, then shuddered. "Spiders," she muttered.

QUARANTINE after returning to *Dauntless* hadn't taken long, because the shuttle on the ground had been able to sample the outside for dangerous pathogens and had found none that humans weren't already protected against. After decontamination and a thorough screening from Dr. Nasr, Geary found himself in the familiar conference room aboard *Dauntless*, along with the real presences of General Charban and John Senn, the historian, as well as Senior Chief Tarrani. Ambassador Rycerz, back on *Boundless* once more, attended in virtual form from her office. So did Captain Smythe aboard *Tanuki*.

Captain Desjani was also present in person, but reluctantly, having concluded that *Dauntless*'s crew had gotten a bit loose during her brief absence and needed some tightening up.

"I assume you all saw and heard everything on the surface," Geary said.

"Everything you saw and heard," Rycerz said, resting her chin on one hand. "Sometimes nothing but what you could see. That unfortunately includes the things in the night."

"The sensors in our uniforms couldn't spot anything else?" Desjani asked, surprised.

"Whatever made up that window was transparent to some visible light and nothing else," Senior Chief Tarrani explained. "The wall wasn't transparent to *anything*. The best technicians in the fleet confirmed that, Admiral. Your sensors saw nothing more than what you could using the available light. Which is to say, pretty much nothing. Vague shapes that can't be exploited or fine-tuned or analyzed to come up with anything more precise or clearer."

"That's an interesting trick," Geary said. "Too bad we didn't get a sample of the window material. And the wall material."

Rycerz looked down, reading something on her desk. "Vegetarians. Vegetarians who arrange their food in artistic designs. That's going to shock a few people."

"That's going to shock a lot of people," Charban said.

"This thing about the fruit," Rycerz said, tapping her desk. "The . . . paracot. You brought back some of it? Did you have it tested?"

"Yes," Geary said. "It's genetically almost identical to a Kosatkan paracot. There are some minor differences that could be caused by genetic drift."

"Why would Kosatka be the only planet where we've seen this?"

"It's not," John Senn said, drawing startled looks. "There are a number of extremely similar plants that have been found on more than one planet we've explored. I mean genetically extremely similar. But those similarities have been attributed to coincidence. Chance." He smiled, his voice taking on a sarcastic tilt. "The official scientific term for the 'apparent' similarities is pseudosimilisorigo, false similar origin."

"Plants with that much similarity in their genetics were put down to coincidence?" Geary asked. It was exactly because of the fruit question that he'd asked that Senn be present for this meeting.

"Of course," John Senn replied. "Because it couldn't have been anyone nonhuman spreading those plants to other worlds before we reached them. Everyone *knew* that wasn't true. So it had to be something else. No matter how improbable that something else happened to be."

"Sometimes," Ambassador Rycerz said in a dry tone, "Occam's razor cuts the wrong way. These tapestries. You got some excellent scans of them."

"Dr. Cresida is examining them," Charban said. "She's already confirmed the speculation that some of the tapestries illustrate scientific principles. Others . . ."

"Fleet medical staff are trying to analyze the, um, hallucinogenic tapestries," Geary said. "They've confirmed the effects of looking at them, but have no idea how the tapestries are creating those effects."

Rycerz nodded slowly, her eyes lowered. "I'm wondering if the Dancers intended for you and Captain Desjani to gaze at those tapestries long enough to be strongly impacted by them. But I can't see why the Dancers would want that."

"I've been in the entry hall of the Alliance Senate on Unity," Geary said, "where exact reproductions of the greatest art in human history are on display. I felt there the same sort of awe that I felt in that Dancer building. If nothing else, it tells us that humans and Dancers share something in our ability to be moved by art."

"That is important," the ambassador agreed. "As is our apparent shared ability to have our minds bemused by some art. The fundamental question we're facing is why did the Dancers bother inviting you and Captain Desjani to the surface? I agree with you that this visit does not appear to have been intended to produce any breakthroughs or major developments. Some sort of incremental acceptance of humanity by the Dancers seems the most likely objective."

"Or another test of humanity," General Charban said. "The Dancers wanted to know what humans 'heard' when they saw those tapestries."

"If they really wanted to know that, why didn't they ask again afterwards?" Rycerz said, rapping one fist on her desk. "They could have put the question to Admiral Geary again once they were outside."

"Perhaps they thought we couldn't 'hear' the tapestries when we weren't viewing them," Geary suggested.

Ambassador Rycerz made a face but eventually added a reluctant nod. "That can't be ruled out. But why didn't the Dancers escorting you know that the Dancers visiting that tapestry place would object to your presence?" Ambassador Rycerz sounded as if she was asking the question of herself. "It seems a very amateurish mistake for the Dancers to make."

"Captain Desjani and I had some ideas about that," Geary said.

"Yes. I heard them." Rycerz sighed, sitting back in her chair. "Those ideas also can't be ruled out. But that doesn't mean your ideas are correct. We lack enough information to know. Why were there any hiccups at all? We were brought to this star system. The Dancers wanted us *here*, so they must have been prepared for our arrival. And the presence of the Taon on the surface means they are used to having other species around. The Dancers must have procedures for dealing with those other species. Why would they not have followed their own rules when humans were involved?"

"They have followed some rules," Geary said. "Only speak with one, and human problem, humans fix."

"How do we know that's not just a policy applied to humans in particular?"

"Governments and bureaucracies like to stick to fixed policies, if they have them," John Senn said, speaking carefully, as if uncertain he should be saying anything this time.

"Except when they have to do something different," Rycerz replied.

Senn made a gesture that was half shrug, half shaking of the head in disagreement. "When they have to do something different they may say they're following a different policy, but in fact they're usually following the same policy differently."

Rycerz gazed fixedly at Senn for a long moment. "I may have made a mistake letting you go to Admiral Geary's ship instead of keeping you with me," she finally said.

Senn stared at Rycerz as if trying to decide whether he'd been praised or threatened.

Charban, looking as if he was trying not to appear amused by Senn's words, gestured outward. "We need to keep in mind that while the Dancers brought us to this star system, the Dancers did not invite us to visit the regions of space they control. We showed up on their doorstep. They invited us in instead of sending us away, but we don't know why."

"We told them why we'd come," Rycerz said, her voice growing sharper. "To establish permanent diplomatic relations and closer ties."

"And they agreed to let us in," Charban repeated. "That doesn't mean the Dancers ever agreed to our agenda with them. The Dancers have never made clear their agenda with us. If we try to analyze Dancer actions in terms of how well they match the agenda *we* want to pursue, we may be barking up the wrong tree."

Rycerz sighed heavily this time, rubbing her eyes with one hand. "Let me say this plainly. I cannot accept that the Dancers have no interest in pursuing diplomatic relations, and perhaps only invited us here

to observe our reactions to events. Because if I accept that, it means my mission has failed, and all of your efforts to help it succeed were futile. I have to continue acting, and believing, that we can make this happen, even if that means convincing the Dancers to do something they didn't plan on agreeing to when they brought us here."

"You'll continue to have the fleet's full backing for that," Geary said, looking around to allow the others to nod in agreement when his eyes rested on them. "We all know how important this is for the Alliance and for humanity as a whole. I agree with General Charban that we can't assume the Dancers share our goals, but I also have to consider the possibility that the Dancers do want the same things we do and are sending us messages intended to convey that, messages which we are unable to understand properly."

"If I may," John Senn added, "I think we need to pay attention to that tapestry that seemed to depict a near-extinction-level event on a Dancer planet. If the Dancers experienced that within their historical memory, on their home world, it would have had a huge effect on how they view everything."

Desjani snorted. "I'm not disagreeing, I thought the same thing, but if the Dancers experienced that sort of random, horrible event, why would they have come up with this idea that the universe forms a meaningful pattern to which they contribute?"

"If the Dancers are anything like people," Senn said, "they have to try to make sense of something like that. Why did it happen? Why did our species survive something that could have wiped it out? Humans sometimes decide such things are random, and meaningless to the universe. But more often humans attempt to come up with reasons that make sense to them. Why did it happen? Saying it's part of some huge plan is comforting compared to it was just chance. Why did we survive as a species? Saying it's because we have some special role to play is more comforting than saying we were lucky."

Captain Smythe, silent up until now, finally spoke. "Speaking as an

engineer, and we still believe that the Dancers are born engineers, I always assume there's a reason when something happens. A reason I can analyze. If something goes wrong or doesn't work, I can take steps to fix it. It's not an engineer's approach to accept that something is random and unpredictable. We need to figure out the cause and what to do about it, and we always assume we can do that."

"Like what Dr. Cresida talked about," Geary said, surprised by how things were tying together. "With quantum mechanics. The Dancers don't accept unpredictable or uncertain elements. They view it all as certainties even though that seems totally wrong to us."

Ambassador Rycerz looked from Smythe to Geary. "If they assume they survived for a reason, they must assume every other space-faring species survived for a reason. And they think they know the reason."

"The tapestry of the universe," Charban said. "The unfinished picture they have to help finish."

"And we must be here to help that as well," Rycerz said. "Unless the Dancers have their own form of evil forces and assume some species, some actions in the universe, are driven by powers wanting to prevent the picture from being finished."

"That public art the Dancers wouldn't look at?" Desjani suggested.

Charban buried his face in his hands for a moment. "Everything we see and learn creates more questions and offers few certain answers. Are the tapestries ever supposed to be finished? That's a human conceit. Finish the project. Figure out how the universe will end. What if the Dancers believe the picture is an eternal work in progress, never to be completed?"

"That would really be a cool idea," John Senn remarked, his face lighting up with enthusiasm. "I need to mention that to Jazz."

"Jazz?" Geary asked, wondering who he meant.

"Dr. Cresida," Senn explained. "Her first name is Jasmine, and the way her mind works is like jazz, you know? Constant exploration and improvisation and testing boundaries and . . ." His expression shifted

to embarrassment as he realized that everyone else was staring at him. "You, uh, probably shouldn't call her that, though."

"Do you call her that?" Geary asked, amused.

"Umm . . . yes."

Ambassador Rycerz rapped her knuckles on her desk. "Getting back on topic. Admiral, I'm glad you asked the Taon representative about the Wooareek. The vague responses make it clear we're not just dealing with a Dancer attitude when it comes to other species. That and having the Taon there, but none of the other non-Dancer species that the Taon's presence implies might be in that city as ambassadors. There seems to be some protocol no one has told us about. If a new-to-us species chooses to make contact with us, the other species we know will acknowledge them to us, but they still won't share any information that new species hasn't chosen to tell us directly."

"It's an understandable policy," Charban pointed out. "Much like our own instructions regarding the Dancers. We're not supposed to give them data dumps about humans."

"That's correct," Rycerz conceded. "It would be immensely helpful, though, if the Dancers or anyone else explained that policy rather than leaving it to us to figure out. If we're even right about that. What's frustrating . . ." She paused, sighing. "*One* of the other things that are frustrating is the lack of any obvious diplomatic quarter in the city. The Taon are there, but where? And how many other species have ambassadors in that city, ambassadors we haven't seen any trace of?"

"Our historian," Charban said, nodding toward John Senn, "says there used to be parts of human cities where people of different cultures congregated, sometimes having different architecture."

"Shaniatowns," Senn said.

"Who was Shania?" Rycerz asked.

"No idea." Senn spread his hands. "It's one of those words that might have changed over time."

Captain Smythe was gazing at something in front of him. "Based on what the admiral saw, the inside of some of these buildings, behind the identical exteriors, might well be unique to different species."

"We might have rolled right past a dozen embassies like that," Captain Desjani said. "Since we couldn't see through the windows, and the signs were all those color bar codes and nothing else, there was no way to tell."

Rycerz nodded as if tired. "My staff will keep going over what you saw and heard, looking for insights. The Dancers considered your visit 'useful,' so maybe we'll see some more cracks in the dam after this. I . . . appreciate your continued support. All of you."

Desjani glanced down at her comm pad as it buzzed. "Another human ship has arrived at the hypernet gate, escorted by a Dancer ship. It's not a warship, though. It looks like a hybrid passenger and cargo ship manufactured in parts of the Alliance. That couldn't have made it through enigma space on its own."

"Meaning it used those long jumps," Geary said, his mind already generating many possible, ugly problems this ship's arrival might create. "If you'll excuse us, Ambassador, we need to find out what this ship is and how badly Severe Jump Space Syndrome might have impacted its crew."

NINE

AS Geary and Desjani walked quickly toward the bridge, she muttered something under her breath.

"What was that?" Geary asked.

"Jazz," Desjani said. "Ancestors help us. He *likes* her?"

"They're the only two civilians on the ship," Geary pointed out. "It was probably inevitable that they'd be drawn together."

"That sort of thing is never inevitable," Desjani said. "Remember when Lieutenant Castries and Lieutenant Yuon had to be confined together for decontamination? More than once Castries nearly murdered Yuon. The only way she was drawn to him was in imagining different ways to kill him."

Reaching the bridge, they both shifted fully into focusing on the new ship.

"We haven't received any message from the new ship yet?" Desjani asked.

"Nothing, Captain."

Geary tried not to frown as deeply as he wanted to. A message announcing your arrival, who you were, and why you were here was routine for ships reaching a new star system. Granted, the laws that required such a message didn't have standing in a Dancer-controlled star system, but it was still smart to follow them. Especially when the new ship must have seen how many Alliance warships were here the moment it arrived.

Unfortunately, there was a strong possible reason why the ship hadn't done the commonsense thing.

Desjani had reached the same conclusion. "Jump space syndrome."

"I think that's a certainty," Geary said. "What is that ship?"

"It's a *Volodymyr*-class mixed passenger and cargo vessel, Admiral," Lieutenant Castries reported. "A model six, constructed between twenty and thirty years ago. Our sensors have identified a symbol on the bow which corresponds to the logo of the Aurelius Corporation, a multi-star-system-spanning conglomerate inside the Alliance."

"Under normal circumstances," Geary said, "we wouldn't have to worry about them. But this isn't normal."

Desjani nodded, her mouth pursed. "Temporarily insane people controlling a large ship. And the engineering section of that large ship. They could override safeties and blow the power core. How do we make sure they don't kill each other, or someone else, or damage a Dancer orbital facility, without killing all of them?"

"Let's see if we can find out who we're dealing with." The Aurelius Corporation ship wasn't as slow as a typical freighter but was still moving at only point zero four light speed. At that velocity, it would take more than four and a half days for the ship to reach the vicinity of Geary's fleet. But that assumed he wouldn't have to try to intercept that ship as soon as possible to save the people aboard it from themselves. "Give me a tight transmission beam to intercept that ship."

"Ready, Admiral," the comms watch said. "Channel six."

Geary touched his comm controls. "Aurelius Corporation ship, this is Admiral Geary, senior Alliance military commander in this star system. In accordance with instructions from the Alliance Senate, I am directing you to identify yourself and to explain the purpose of your presence here. You are to maneuver onto a vector intercepting this fleet in orbit. I await your reply. To the honor of our ancestors, Geary, out."

There wasn't any sense in waiting for the reply, which would take at least nine hours, before planning for what was likely inevitable. Geary touched another comm control. "General Carabali, I want you to work up a plan for boarding that newly arrived ship. Control of the engineering section has to be achieved as quickly as possible to prevent any sabotage. Unless we learn otherwise, we need to plan for gaining control of the ship in a manner that minimizes any chance of injury to the people aboard it."

Carabali nodded, thoughts moving behind her eyes. "I assume this will be a noncooperative boarding operation?"

"Your planning has to assume that, yes," Geary said. "Everyone aboard that ship is probably temporarily insane."

"And all of them are probably Alliance civilians."

"All of them are probably Alliance civilians," Geary agreed.

"Admiral, I feel obligated to point out that this is the very definition of the sort of police action the Alliance military is supposed to avoid any involvement in," General Carabali said.

"I understand," Geary said. "But we don't have any police on hand, and the situation involves potentially life-threatening dangers to not only the humans on that ship but also Dancers in any of their ships or orbital facilities if the ship gets close to one of them and detonates its power core."

"Admiral, I still need a clear declaration from you that we are in a war zone. That's in order to protect my Marines from any legal fallout and to allow the use of a riot suppression agent against Alliance civilians. I wouldn't need such a declaration to use CRX gas against Syndic civilians. But I must have it to use CRX against Alliance civilians."

"We are in a war zone," Geary said. Saying that shouldn't have been necessary, not after the fight with the Syndics, but he knew legal requirements didn't always mesh well with common sense. "This action, if I order it, will be necessary to protect Alliance citizens."

"Thank you, Admiral. I will proceed with planning."

"Admiral," Captain Desjani said, "Ambassador Rycerz is trying to reach you."

"Of course she is." Geary accepted the link, seeing Rycerz's image appear before him. "We're still trying to identify the ship and who's on it."

"It looks like an Aurelius ship," Rycerz said.

"Are you familiar with that company?"

Rycerz made a face. "One of my co-workers had a run-in with them over some of the company's business practices. Our work also involves smoothing ruffled feathers among different star systems within the Alliance. Aurelius is . . . powerful."

"How powerful?" Geary asked.

"It wouldn't be diplomatic of me to say that Aurelius owns at least one Alliance senator, so I will not say that. But I'm not surprised it's one of their ships. If any Alliance conglomerate was going to try those long jumps to Dancer space, it would be Aurelius."

He tried to read between the lines of what she was saying. "Is that because the company is powerful or because it runs risks?"

"Both." Rycerz gestured outward. "If Aurelius sent a ship, there's a very good chance the senior person on that ship is their chief executive officer, Ronald Yangdi. He's that sort of showboater. I'm sure he intends trying to overawe me. How he plans to approach you, I don't know, but assume flattery."

"He's very likely temporarily insane," Geary said. "Do you know if he has armed bodyguards?"

"That's not a very common thing in the Alliance," Rycerz said with a frown. "It would look very bad for any corporate official to be parading around with armed bodyguards. Naturally, he does have bodyguards. He's extremely rich. Just not armed bodyguards."

"Got it. Do you think he came charging out here hoping to cut exclusive deals with the Dancers?"

"I'd guarantee it," Rycerz said.

"Unless Yangdi and the crew of that ship are somehow sane," Geary said, "I'm going to have to use Marines to board it and take control in order to protect everyone aboard and everyone else in this star system, Dancers included."

Rycerz froze for a long moment. "I hope that won't be necessary," she finally said.

"Me, too."

While waiting to hear from the new ship (if it replied at all), Geary went ahead with planning an operation that even Marines were reluctant to undertake. Fleet planning tools had suggested he use sailors instead because that would represent less force being used against civilians. But sailors lacked the training, the equipment, and the experience that Marines would bring to the job.

An assault transport would be needed to carry enough Marines for the (hopefully not required but unfortunately likely) boarding and takeover of the ship. General Carabali had already expressed a desire for *Tsunami* to take on that role, saying that Colonel Savchenko and her battalion aboard that ship had a lot of experience with boarding operations. But *Tsunami* would need an escort. Not too big an escort, but enough to handle the new ship if it did something dangerous.

That meant at least one heavy cruiser.

Or two?

Maybe a battle cruiser.

That might look like overkill.

Or like a sign of how concerned he was for the safety of the Alliance citizens aboard that ship.

No matter what happened, a battle cruiser could handle it.

Fine. Marines and a battle cruiser. He wasn't going to take any half measures for fear of being second-guessed far from here months from now.

Civilians were likely to get hurt.

But, then, given what had happened aboard the Syndic warships, civilians were probably already getting hurt on that ship.

It didn't seem like this could get any more complicated.

But then it did.

"WE finally got a response from the new ship," Captain Desjani told him.

Geary was already in a passageway, watching Ensign Duck parade by on the daily patrol, two Marines as watchful escorts, so he headed for the bridge to see the message.

Desjani was already there, of course. As soon as Geary sat down near her she called up the message.

The man whose image appeared before him was broadly built, his smile also broad. His eyes, though, squinted, as if he were facing a bright light. "Admiral! Black Jack! This is Ron! I am so excited to meet you at last! We've got so much to do!"

"We do?" Geary said, realizing that in his surprise at the statement he'd said that out loud.

"The deal," Ron said, almost as if answering Geary's question. "The deal! I'm glad you agreed to all my terms! It'll be epic! Nothing like it ever! But, listen, these, uh, aliens aren't talking! Gotta talk, right? I need you to hold up your end of things."

Geary stared at the man in bafflement, trying to figure out what he was talking about. Ron Yangdi wasn't on the bridge of the still-unidentified ship, but in some large room that, from what could be seen, was an elaborate office.

In the background, two people were struggling with a third.

A shape only partly visible on the floor behind some furniture might be a body.

Yangdi continued speaking as if nothing unusual was happening. "Get these aliens talking, Black Jack! They need to know who runs things around here, am I right? Of course I am! You're going to be rich! Waiting for your comeback!"

The message ended.

"Deal?" Geary said. "Terms? I've never spoken to him. Is he . . ."

"Crazy?" Desjani said. "We know he is. He broadcast that reply, by the way. It went to every ship in the fleet."

"He . . ." Geary struggled to control his temper. "He wants everyone in this fleet to think I negotiated some deal with him? When we've never exchanged any words before this?"

"It's just good business," someone said.

Geary looked to the back of the bridge, seeing that Colonel Rogero was there.

"Good business practices," Rogero continued. "At least as practiced in the Syndicate. Put your opponent off-balance, imply wrongdoing on their part, pretend to agreements that no one agreed to."

"This is an Alliance business," Captain Desjani said. "He's an Alliance business leader."

"A CEO is a CEO," Rogero stated flatly.

"CEOs in the Alliance aren't . . ." Desjani began. "I mean, not all CEOs in the Alliance are . . . Some CEOs . . . Admiral, he's right. We couldn't trust this guy even if he was sane."

"He's put you on the defensive," Colonel Rogero said. "Instead of simply refuting him, defending yourself, you need to make it clear why he cannot be trusted."

"I don't know anything about him as a person," Geary protested. "He might not be someone like a Syndic CEO."

"Even if he's a decent guy," Desjani said, "he's temporarily insane. He might honestly believe you and he talked and made some agreement even though it all happened inside his own head. You still have to make it clear it's all made-up."

"You'd think people would know that without my saying it," Geary said, hearing the resentment in his voice.

"Are you saying it's unfair?" Desjani asked in an innocent-sounding voice.

He gave her a lowered brow in response. "Yes. The universe is being unfair. Again. All right. You've made your point."

Yangdi's wild statements had forced his hand. He could no longer pass this off to any on-scene commander. And the more he thought about it, the less Geary liked having only a couple of ships far from the rest of the fleet.

Bringing too many resources against the problem was better than bringing too few.

Geary touched his fleet command controls. "All units in the Alliance fleet, this is Admiral Geary. We have finally received a communication from the newly arrived human ship and confirmed that it is a private vessel owned by the Aurelius Corporation. Unfortunately, the message also confirmed that the senior individual aboard, a Ronald Yangdi, is not rational. He spoke of some agreement with me that doesn't exist. We've never communicated prior to this. Background images in his message seem to show violence underway on the ship. We know from the Syndic prisoners what conditions were like aboard their ships when the crews were suffering from Severe Jump Space Syndrome. If anything like that is happening aboard this new ship, we have to take action to stop it and protect those aboard it.

"In light of this information, I am ordering an operation to board the civilian ship and ensure the safety of everyone on it. Given the uncertainties, even though the military threat appears minimal, the Second Battle Cruiser Division will escort *Tsunami* to intercept the new ship. Every possible precaution will be taken to minimize the danger to everyone involved. We have to save these people, and we will.

"To the honor of our ancestors, Geary, out."

"You're going to personally command this one?" Desjani asked.

"It looks like a unique opportunity to excel," Geary said, using fleet slang for a rough job no one wanted. "Given how worried everyone is about this op, I don't want anyone else to be stuck with any fallout from it. Speaking of things I don't want anyone else stuck with, I need to reply to 'Ron.' Do we still not have ID on that ship?"

"We don't have a solid ID, Admiral," Lieutenant Yuon said. "But based on details of the hull, fleet sensors are estimating with eighty-six percent confidence that the ship is the *Fortuna*, belonging to the Aurelius Corporation. He's still not broadcasting any standard identification, though."

"Those ID broadcasts are automatic," Desjani said. "Either someone shut it off deliberately, or it got disabled somehow and hasn't been fixed. Either way, that's not a good sign of what things are like on that ship."

Geary nodded, working to relax his grim expression so he appeared welcoming. "I want this message copied to Ambassador Rycerz." He waited a moment for that to be set up before touching the control to send another message to the new ship. "Citizen Yangdi aboard the Alliance commercial ship *Fortuna*, this is Admiral Geary. We are noticing indications that your ship is in distress, and will be sending ships to meet with you and escort you to meet up with the rest of the Alliance ships in this star system. Those ships will also carry personnel able to render assistance to you if needed. I want to clearly state that I have no knowledge of whatever deal you spoke of, nor did I ever agree to any terms. If you intend offering some . . . business opportunity, I have to remind you that as a fleet officer I am prohibited from engaging in such actions while on active duty. You are free to discuss your plans with Ambassador Rycerz, but since we are in a war zone outside of Alliance space your allowed actions will be limited by the security environment. Please have your ship's captain contact me as soon as possible to discuss the state of your ship, as we do have concerns."

He needed to say something calming, something to keep anyone aboard *Fortuna* from feeling threatened. "I promise you that any actions we take will be aimed at ensuring that everyone aboard the *Fortuna* is safe and remains safe. We will protect you, Citizen Yangdi, and your ship. To the honor of our ancestors, Geary, out."

That done, he sat back, waiting.

Desjani gave him an inquisitive look.

He pointed to his display as it alerted to an incoming call from Ambassador Rycerz.

Rycerz looked unhappy, but also wasn't directing that at Geary. "This is a very delicate situation, Admiral. I'm grateful that you are taking the responsibility for handling it on yourself."

"I don't think we have any alternative but to handle it this way," Geary said.

"There was something you told me about the Syndic ships," Rycerz said. "That when everyone was impacted by the Severe Jump Space Syndrome everything was 'more so.' It exaggerated problems that already existed. Looking at Ronald Yangdi's message, I'm seeing the same thing. He has a reputation as a glad-hander, being very enthusiastic and flattering. He's not a different person as a result of this syndrome. He's more Ronald Yangdi."

"How bad is that?" Geary asked.

Rycerz paused to think. "Yangdi is also a risk-taker, and by reputation will manipulate deals to his maximum benefit."

"'Just good business,'" Geary said. "I was already advised that we couldn't trust him. But it sounds like we need to worry about him deciding to undertake a risk that he would recognize as crazy under normal circumstances."

"Exactly," Rycerz said, nodding. "Because of the ugly legacy of the long war with the Syndics the average citizen of the Alliance isn't going to get worked up about some Syndic civilians dying as a byproduct of a necessary action. But Alliance citizens dying at the hands of Alliance forces is a whole different thing. If you haven't already learned about the Tiamat riots, you need to familiarize yourself with what happened then."

The call ended, Geary looked at Desjani. "Tiamat riots?"

Her face twisted in an expression of distaste. "Tiamat. Yes, you should read up on that."

WARNED by Desjani's reaction, Geary went to the privacy of his stateroom to look up the incident.

There were a lot of results to his search, including not only the official version that was marked as required reading for all new officers, but also many firsthand accounts and vids from the riots.

Eighty years ago, twenty years into the war with the Syndicate Worlds, twenty years after Geary's battle at Grendel and twenty years after he entered frozen survival sleep, frustration over the war and the losses the Alliance was already sustaining had led to mass demonstrations on the primary inhabited world of Tiamat Star System. The official summary of events was short and blunt, designed to hold the attention of senior officers, who often skimmed the first paragraph of a study before moving on to the next task.

> Faced with widespread protests by its citizens, Tiamat's government panicked, and demanded support from the Alliance military. Badly misinterpreting official policy regarding support to local governments, the commanding officer of a large recruit training facility at Tiamat armed the recruits and sent them to confront the protestors with orders to "shut down" the protests. Overreactions and confusing instructions to partially trained soldiers led to the deaths of over one thousand civilians as well as nearly fifty soldiers. This event nearly shattered the Alliance, dishonored the Alliance military, and is never to be repeated. All officers are reminded of their responsibilities under Article 16.

For good measure, the summary then cited Article 16 of the Alliance Military Code.

> Anytime an officer has reasonable grounds to believe an order
> is either issued in error, or improperly issued contrary to Alliance
> law or fleet regulations, that officer is obligated to confirm the
> accuracy of the order and its legitimacy before obeying it.

Article 16 dated to the formation of the Alliance and hadn't been changed in all the years since. Geary wondered if it was still called the Reasonable Article. And if officers were still told both of its importance and of the importance of never using it, because no commander wanted their orders to be questioned and anyone who did so would regret that for however much longer their career lasted. If anything, the consequences of invoking Article 16 had probably grown much more serious during the long war with the Syndics, opening up any officer who used it to potential charges of disobedience of orders in the face of the enemy, a field court-martial, and a quickly assembled firing squad.

But, clearly, what had happened on Tiamat eighty years ago still resonated within the Alliance military. Enough so that (like Article 16) it was something everyone knew about but no one talked about. Which was why he hadn't heard about Tiamat before this.

No wonder even the usually unflappable General Carabali was spooked at the idea of this boarding operation.

If anything, though, this was a reverse of the Tiamat situation, a case where not acting would result in more civilian deaths on top of however many had already died on the *Fortuna*.

TWO days later, having accelerated away from the rest of the fleet to intercept the *Fortuna* faster, the small task force began braking velocity to match the vector of the civilian ship. The battle cruisers *Dauntless*,

Daring, *Victorious*, and *Intemperate* were arranged around the assault transport *Tsunami*, protecting the less maneuverable, lightly armed transport and the Marines aboard her.

"Human problem, humans fix." General Charban had reported the Dancer response with weary resignation. "As directed, I asked them straight out why they kept bringing these human ships here instead of telling them to go home or just leaving them in the border star system until they left. The response to that was also 'human problem, humans fix.'"

Fortuna hadn't altered vector in any way since arriving in the star system, still heading inward at point zero four light speed, on a path that would bring the ship near the primary inhabited world as that planet orbited its star.

Ron Yangdi had exchanged a series of increasingly manic messages with Geary. "The entire galaxy, Black Jack. I've got the deal ready to go. And it's all leveraged! I'll get . . . I mean, *we'll* get the entire galaxy for the cost of a haircut! The keepers of the central stars are ready to sign."

"Keepers of the central stars?" Desjani asked.

"I guess you'd need them to sign on to a deal for the entire galaxy," Geary said. "Doctor?"

He was making sure Dr. Nasr viewed every message and offered suggestions on how to talk Yangdi down. "I would suggest not refusing the, um, deal," Nasr said. "Say you have to delay for some reason."

"Say you have to run it by legal," Colonel Rogero suggested. "Once you bring in lawyers you've got every excuse you need."

"Citizen Yangdi," Geary sent, "I am happy to hear of the proposed deal but we need to . . . run it by legal before I can give an answer. Is the captain of the *Fortuna* available to speak to me?"

They were close enough to *Fortuna* by now, only about eighteen million kilometers, that the delay for messages traveling at the speed of light to cover the distance was only about a minute long.

Ronald Yangdi's luxurious office could barely be seen in the latest reply. Yangdi had apparently shut off all the lights, himself only illuminated by reflected light from his display. "Legal? Legal? Do you want to kill this deal? Because you're going to kill this deal! And what's with all those warships? Don't play games with me!"

"We just want to be sure you and everyone on *Fortuna* is all right," Geary said. "We've got some medical personnel who can check on everyone's health, and some technicians who can take a look at some of the systems on your ship that don't seem to be working properly. Where is *Fortuna*'s captain?" The list of nonworking equipment had grown from the identification broadcast to include disturbing outputs from *Fortuna*'s power core as well as temperature readings that might mean life support wasn't working properly in some parts of the ship.

Even worse, every attempt to reach any other transmitter on *Fortuna* had failed. Aside from Yangdi's office and Yangdi himself, they hadn't seen any other part of the interior of the ship or anyone else except for occasional figures moving in the background.

Yangdi's next reply showed his office partially lit by portable lamps. "Don't try pressuring me! Do you know who I am? I can shut you down. Stop playing games. And, I'm going to be frank here, it's getting really annoying listening to you keep asking to talk to other people. You don't need to talk to anybody but me."

Dr. Nasr shook his head. "Admiral, the fact that he refuses to let the captain speak to you is not a good sign."

"I'm not aware of any sign that's been good," Geary said. "Captain, have we got any new readings on *Fortuna*'s point defense weapon?"

"Still inactive," Desjani replied. "We'll match vectors with *Fortuna* in twenty minutes."

Geary tabbed a comm channel. "Colonel Savchenko, prepare your boarding parties."

Savchenko replied, her hair knotted back in a tight braid, her attitude relaxed but her eyes intent. "We're ready to launch, Admiral. Confirm authorization to employ CRX gas against Alliance civilians."

"Confirmed," Geary said. "Knock out everyone you can and get them onto shuttles to *Tsunami* so they can be evaluated. We don't know how many were on board *Fortuna* or how many of them might have already died from various causes. If Yangdi brought along a large staff in addition to the crew, there might be as many as two hundred people on the ship."

"We'll access the ship's files as soon as we board," Savchenko said. "After securing the bridge and engineering, we'll fan out through the ship in fire teams to locate, sedate, and remove every civilian on the ship."

"Yangdi has made some statements implying he's well protected," Geary said. "That might just be Severe Jump Space Syndrome talking. His bodyguards are not legally allowed to be armed. But be aware that anyone trying to enter Yangdi's office might encounter defenses."

"Got it, Admiral."

"You have permission to launch shuttles as soon as *Tsunami* is in position," Geary said. "Commander Balboa," he added, tagging *Tsunami*'s commanding officer, "the Marines have permission to launch."

"I understand the Marines have permission to launch," Balboa repeated, his voice as calm as that of Colonel Savchenko. "Admiral, we will match *Fortuna*'s vector in five minutes, positioned five hundred meters from the main entry air locks. All medical personnel are standing by to receive evacuees from *Fortuna*."

"Excellent," Geary said. "The four battle cruisers will stand off two kilometers from *Fortuna*, ready to react if necessary."

Captain Desjani's hand was moving over her display. "All ships in the Second Battle Cruiser Division will be in position in three minutes, Admiral. Request confirm that all weapons should remain in standby."

"Yes," Geary said. "Keep all weapons in standby." This close to *Fortuna*, which was a large ship, but armed only with a single close-in defense pop gun, the presence of four battle cruisers felt a bit ridiculous. But given the uncertainties of the boarding operation, and what *Fortuna* might do, he didn't regret bringing them all along.

Ronald Yangdi chose that moment to send another message. "What's going on? What's with all of these warships? You're not trying to muscle me, are you, Black Jack?"

"They're escorts," Geary answered, which was true. The battle cruisers had other potential roles as well, but Yangdi didn't need to know about that. "Escorts suitable to . . . your status. And to ensure the safety of *Fortuna*."

"I don't need 'em here and I don't want 'em here," Yangdi declared. The lights in his office were on again, making it easy to spot the presence of a large individual in the background.

"That person in the back is former military," Colonel Rogero said. "Look how he's standing."

"One of Yangdi's bodyguards, then," Geary said before keying the circuit to call *Fortuna* again. "Citizen Yangdi—"

They were so close there was no delay in transmissions now, allowing Yangdi to interrupt Geary. "*Ron!* I told you to call me *Ron!*"

The friendly words combined with the threatening manner in which they were delivered felt so strange that Geary almost laughed despite the stress riding his nerves.

"Ron," Geary said. "It's a measure of your importance that I brought four battle cruisers as escorts."

"Then you should've brought eight!" Yangdi glared at something in his office. "What about the fifth one? Are they launching something?"

"Shuttles," Geary said. "We have to certify newly arrived ships as safe, so some people from that ship will come aboard *Fortuna* to—"

"No one comes aboard my ship unless I say so!"

"Ron, if you want any deals to proceed, you have to follow procedures." Would that get through to him?

"Procedures are for little people with little money," Yangdi said with a laugh. "You know who wants a deal with me? The Queen of the Dancers! She can't wait. I don't have time for you and your delays!"

Geary's last sight of Yangdi was him slamming down a hand to cut off the transmission. "The Queen of the Dancers?"

"Admiral," Colonel Rogero said, "you should take him out. For the safety of others."

"The CRX gas should do just that," Geary said.

"We're launching, Admiral," Colonel Savchenko reported.

Twenty shuttles shot out from *Tsunami*, heading for different locations on the nearby hull of *Fortuna*. Even though both ships were moving at well over five hundred thousand kilometers per minute, with their vectors exactly matched they appeared to be motionless compared to each other.

Geary quickly opened and rearranged virtual windows on his display, keeping the one that would show Yangdi centered in case he got through to "Ron" again. With no warship threat, he could focus his attention on the Marines boarding *Fortuna*.

One window offered a view from the battle armor of Captain Cayedito as his shuttle reached the ship. "Accesses are all locked," Cayedito reported.

"Crack them using nondestructive entry methods," Colonel Savchenko ordered. "Get inside without breaking anything."

Geary watched Marine hack-and-crack specialists position their equipment, analyzing locks, overriding control software, bypassing passwords and other security measures, in less time than it took the other Marines to position themselves for entry. The commercial lock software and hardware was a piece of cake for military specialists to break through after their experience dealing with Syndic physical security measures.

The same thing was happening elsewhere on *Fortuna*'s outer hull, access doors opening, Marines in battle armor crowding inside spacious entry air locks with luxurious fittings, scattered among the Marines fleet medical personnel and technicians in survival suits.

Ron Yangdi's image appeared again as he reconnected. "Black Jack! What the hell are you trying to do! This is my ship. Private property. Under Alliance law you need a warrant to enter my property. Back off or I'll call highly placed friends and your career will be *over.*"

"Do not directly refuse him," Dr. Nasr advised, who was monitoring the same circuit. "Try to stall."

"Gaslight him," Desjani suggested.

No one remembered where the ancient term had come from, but everyone knew what "gaslighting" meant. "I'm sorry," Geary said to Yangdi. "You already agreed to my people coming aboard for safety checks. Don't you remember?"

"Of course I remember! My memory is flawless!"

In another window, Captain Cayedito was reporting to Colonel Savchenko. The view from Cayedito's armor showed an eerily empty passageway inside *Fortuna.* The views from other Marines revealed the same strange vista of an apparently deserted ship. "The fleet techs with us have patched into the ship's control systems and carried out a remote shutdown of life support's air-filtering functions. We're starting to release the CRX into the closest air returns."

"What about control of the ship's power core?" Savchenko demanded.

"They say something is blocking them. Their best guess is a backup system independent of the rest of the ship's control systems."

Another group of Marines reported in. "We're at the bridge. Both doors are locked. Estimated time to entry less than a minute."

"Get them off my ship!" Yangdi shouted. "Get them off now! Do you know who I am?"

"How many people are aboard *Fortuna*?" Geary asked, hoping to distract Yangdi.

"Three hundred twelve!" Yangdi shouted in reply. "See? There's nothing wrong with me!"

"I didn't say there was anything wrong with you," Geary said. "Three hundred twelve? Why so many?"

Yangdi grinned, the exaggerated expression almost terrifying. "People paid to see the Dancers. See? See how smart I am? I sold tickets. Expensive tickets! Enough to cover the cost of this trip. See how smart I am?"

Geary muted the call with Yangdi. "Colonel Savchenko, I'm informed there are three hundred twelve people aboard *Fortuna*."

"I understand three hundred twelve," Savchenko replied. "I'll inform my teams on the ship. So far we haven't seen any of those three hundred twelve."

"We're going in!" the Marine leading the team at *Fortuna*'s bridge announced.

Geary ignored Yangdi's silent shouting for a moment to watch from the perspective of one of the Marines going onto the bridge.

"There's nobody . . . Hey, here's one. Doc, check this out."

A medical officer in a survival suit knelt by a woman lying on her back, her eyes closed. "She's unconscious due to the CRX," the officer said. "But she's also severely dehydrated."

"Here's another!"

A man had fallen from where he must have been seated on the deck in a corner of the bridge. "Dead," the medical officer announced. "Not from the CRX. Dehydration."

"Were they locked in here?" one of the Marines demanded, her voice carrying tones of disbelief.

"It looks like it," the doctor said, touching the hands of the man, which bore dried blood and extensive old bruises. "They couldn't get out."

"Every door and hatch we've encountered has locks engaged," Colonel Savchenko said. "I want all of those locks opened five minutes ago!"

Geary unmuted Yangdi just as the man paused to take a breath.

"Why are all of the doors locked, Citizen Yangdi? Why were the doors to the bridge locked?"

Yangdi paused, his face twisting as if he was having difficulty understanding the questions. "Rays," he finally said. "Cosmic rays, everywhere. I needed to protect everyone."

"Cosmic rays?" Geary asked, trying to keep his voice mild even though he had a growing fear of what things were like aboard *Fortuna*. "Are you saying your shields failed? There were people suffering radiation poisoning aboard your ship?"

"What, are you stupid? I said cosmic rays!" Yangdi waved an angry hand. "Making people act weird. One tried to attack me. Me! Others talking to nothing. One of my assistants killed themselves! Why would one of my assistants kill themselves? And my incompetent medical staff saying they can't find anything. Which had to be wrong, because people were acting wrong. Had to be cosmic rays. Had to lock everyone down."

"You can lock all of the locks on the ship from your office?" Geary said, sending the audio of the call to Colonel Savchenko. "What else can you do from your office?"

"My suite," Yangdi said. "I have a suite. A big suite. The best suite." He rapped the desk, smiling again. "I can control anything from here. Anything!"

"You mentioned medical staff," Geary said, doing his best to sound calm. "Where are they?"

"Locked up! They were part of the problem! Saying science this and tests that! Questioning my own judgment! I knew better." Yangdi's face contorted with rage. "Get those people off my ship!"

Geary looked at the other windows open on his display. Every Marine team was now opening every door they encountered, finding some living persons, badly physically stressed in most cases from lack of food or water or both but knocked out by the CRX, and too many dead ones, either from deprivation or from violent acts committed while confined behind locked doors.

CRX. Why wasn't Yangdi out?

"Colonel," Geary called after muting his end of the conversation with Yangdi. "Citizen Yangdi must have an independent filtration system for his suite. He's still aware, awake, and paranoid. He claims he can control anything on the ship from there."

"We've got a team near the engineering spaces," Savchenko began. "Once we control that, we can—"

"You think I won't do it?" Yangdi shouted. "I'll do it!" His hands moved. "See? Nobody ignores me! Nobody!"

"We're getting emergency readings from the power core aboard *Fortuna*," Lieutenant Castries announced as alerts pulsed on displays.

"Citizen Yangdi—" Geary started.

"RON!"

"Back it off, Ron. You could kill yourself and everybody else aboard *Fortuna*."

"Get them off my ship!"

"Engineering assesses that safeties on *Fortuna*'s power core are being bypassed," Lieutenant Castries said.

"Colonel," Geary said, "get your people off that ship!"

"Admiral, my people say they can breach engineering in ten more minutes—"

"A power core could become unstable and blow apart at any moment when the safeties are bypassed," Captain Desjani said, her eyes haunted by memories.

Geary called Colonel Savchenko again. "Get your people off now!"

TEN

"EMERGENCY evacuation!" Colonel Savchenko sent to all of her Marines. "Everyone off the ship, on the double."

"Colonel," Captain Cayedito protested, "we're—"

"The ship's power core is about to blow. Get to the shuttles. Bring all the civilians you can carry with you, but get to the shuttles!"

On the virtual windows before Geary, the views from Marine armor began jerking quickly as the Marines scooped up any living but unconscious civilians within reach and dashed back for the air lock accesses.

Geary gestured to Desjani. "Move the battle cruisers to a safe distance from *Fortuna*." If the civilian ship's power core blew up it might seriously damage other ships if they were too close.

"Moving them now," Desjani said, passing orders to the rest of the battle cruisers.

"I'm going to do it!" Yangdi was screaming. "I'm going to do it better than anyone else ever did it!"

"Ron," Geary said, "everybody is leaving the ship. You don't have to do it. Please don't do it."

"You don't think I can do it!"

He didn't have to lie this time. "I think you can. I very much think you can. You don't need to prove it." Yangdi paused, breathing heavily, eyeing Geary. "Ron, please. Reactivate the safeties on the power core." What argument would convince him?

Colonel Rogero spoke in a low voice. "Point out how much his ship is worth."

"You've got a very expensive ship here," Geary said. "A . . . magnificent ship. It'd be a shame to . . . lose that ship. Lose that investment."

Yangdi's eyes widened, then narrowed. "I spent a lot of money on it," he bragged. "Highest-quality fittings everywhere on it." His hands moved on the desk, but paused. "Those people are still on the ship."

Geary checked the armor views, seeing the Marines had crowded into the big air locks. While they were inside, other Marines had rigged tubes from the air locks into the shuttles so everyone, including the unconscious civilians, could go straight from air lock to shuttle without being exposed to space and without the need to wait for the air locks to depressurize. "They're leaving as fast as they can," Geary said.

"Power core readings from *Fortuna* are fluctuating," Lieutenant Castries said.

"Abandon the access tubes," Geary told Colonel Savchenko. "Don't waste time recovering them. Commander Balboa, the moment you get the last shuttle aboard, get *Tsunami* away from that ship."

"The shuttles are overloaded," Balboa pointed out. "Some of those aboard them might get beat up."

"Better beat up than dead."

"I agree, Admiral."

Geary had heard that assault transport captains and crews tended to be cool in even the hottest situations, and took pride in never failing to drop their Marines where intended, or recover them regardless of risk. Watching Commander Balboa handle this evacuation so calmly, Geary wondered again why those traits hadn't earned the assault transports higher status in the fleet.

"Our chief engineer says *Fortuna*'s power core is wobbly," Lieutenant Castries reported. "It could blow any second. She recommends all units clear the danger region as quickly as possible."

Geary tried not to despair as he saw how close the shuttles and *Tsunami* still were to *Fortuna*. "Ron, your power core is going unstable. If you don't back it off now you might not be able to do it at all."

Yangdi laughed. "You think I can't do it? You think it's too late?"

"It might be," Geary said. "For the love of our ancestors, Ron, please reactivate the power core safeties. Why waste such a beautiful, expensive ship?"

"Half a minute until the last shuttle docks on *Tsunami*," Commander Balboa reported. "Colonel, tell your people to brace themselves as best they can. I'm going to kick in full acceleration."

"Marines," Colonel Savchenko ordered, "the space squids are going to blast out of here. Grab on and hold on."

"I could do it," Yangdi insisted. "I could do it right now."

Which "it" was he referring to? Geary wondered. "Can you reengage the power core safeties?"

"I . . . I . . ." Yangdi's expression and voice wavered. Geary heard alarms sounding aboard *Fortuna*, a recorded voice warning of extreme danger. Someone else in Yangdi's office called out, the words garbled by the privacy software so Geary couldn't grasp anything except urgent tones.

"Shut up!" Yangdi roared.

Tsunami's main propulsion lit off on full, the assault transport accelerating rapidly away from *Fortuna*.

Geary saw someone struggling with Yangdi.

"Systems estimate *Fortuna*'s power core is certain to overload within forty-five seconds," Lieutenant Castries reported, her voice tightly controlled. "Highest probability of overload is estimated at fifteen seconds from now."

Desjani had already moved the four battle cruisers out more than a hundred kilometers from *Fortuna*, and turned them so the four warships were bow on toward the civilian ship, presenting their heaviest shields to the danger.

On Geary's display, a red bubble appeared around *Fortuna* as *Dauntless*'s system automatically portrayed the danger radius from a power core explosion. *Tsunami* was still inside it, but moving away with increasing speed. "This is going to be way too close."

Yangdi was no longer visible. At his desk, a man was frantically moving his hands over controls. "How do I do this?" he pleaded with Geary.

Feeling sick inside, knowing it was too late for anything to help, Geary opened his mouth to reply.

The link disappeared, the virtual window blanking.

"Power core overload on *Fortuna*," Lieutenant Castries said, her voice still unemotional except for a slight tremor.

Tsunami was near the edge of the danger radius, still accelerating for all she was worth.

The shock wave of the power core overload reached *Dauntless*, the high-velocity dust that had once been a ship and the people aboard it impacting the bow shields and causing the battle cruiser to shudder.

An alert pulsed near *Tsunami* on Geary's display.

"She got hit," Desjani observed.

How badly? Geary waited, nerves taut, for an update to show how serious the damage to *Tsunami* had been.

"The hit was on the stern," Colonel Rogero said. "Your assault transports are well protected from that angle so they can survive emergency evacuations under fire."

That was strange, learning something about his own ships from someone who'd once fought against forces using those ships.

Geary's display updated. He let out a slow breath. "It's not too bad."

Commander Balboa's image appeared on Geary's display. "We got shook up, Admiral. One of my main propulsion units is offline. Initial assessments are that we may require support from one of the auxiliaries to get it working again. I'll get you status reports from the shuttles as soon as possible."

Status reports from the shuttles. Finding out how many civilians aboard *Fortuna* the Marines had been able to save in the too-brief time they'd had. "Thank you, Commander," Geary said, hearing the flatness of his own voice. "Well done, to you and your crew. Colonel Savchenko, well done to your Marines. You did all that could possibly be done."

Savchenko shook her head, her mouth tight. "There were still people aboard that ship, Admiral. We couldn't get everywhere. There were still people aboard."

"You did all that could possibly be done," Geary repeated. He knew what small comfort that was, because he'd also done all he possibly could, and knowing that was no comfort at all.

"ONE hundred and five," Ambassador Rycerz said, her voice heavy. "Out of three hundred twelve. I wish the information your Marines copied from the files aboard *Fortuna* hadn't confirmed Yangdi's number. At least those files gave us the names of everyone you weren't able to rescue. I'm glad to hear the people you could save from *Fortuna* are all out of physical danger, though it's distressing to hear how many are suffering symptoms of Severe Jump Space Syndrome.

"There'll be a lot of questions raised about this back in Alliance space. Yangdi was not the only Big Name on that ship. His boast of having sold a lot of very expensive tickets on the trip appears to have been true."

Rycerz sighed, rubbing her face with one hand before continuing. "I wish I could tell you the focus back home will be on the efforts that managed to save more than a hundred Alliance citizens. I am extending official thanks for that on behalf of the Alliance government. But I won't sugarcoat things. There's a good chance the attention will instead be turned to the two hundred you couldn't save. The conspiracy-minded will accuse the military of having killed those two hundred and then blown up the ship to cover up the act, despite having no evidence for such charges, and despite all of the evidence you've provided to the necessity of your actions. It's likely the only reward to you and your Marines will be suspicion and investigations, especially since most of those you saved were crew members of the ship living in the lower decks since you didn't have time to get to the luxury suites occupied by the Very Important People.

"For now, all we can do is hope your expedition back to Midway delivers their warning before any more ships leave Alliance space to try those long jumps."

Ambassador Rycerz's message over, Geary leaned back in his chair in his stateroom aboard *Dauntless*, closing his eyes. That only served to bring to his mind's eye images of Yangdi's last moments and of *Fortuna* exploding, though.

With *Tsunami*'s ability to maneuver limited by her damaged main propulsion, the trip back had taken longer than the trip out to meet *Fortuna*. They were still a day out from rejoining the rest of the Alliance fleet.

He called up the latest status report from *Tsunami*. Numerous minor injuries had been suffered among Marines and sailors packed into shuttles and unable to properly brace themselves when the ship had bolted away from *Fortuna*. The majority of the rescued civilians were doing well physically with carefully monitored food and liquids intake, though all of them were suffering various degrees of Severe Jump Space Syndrome. Fortunately, in most cases the temporary insanity wasn't hazardous to themselves or others so meds could keep them under control. Unfortunately, the combination of the syndrome with Yangdi's confinement of everyone had traumatized every survivor.

The senior doctor aboard *Tsunami* had confided to Geary that he suspected those suffering the worst from the syndrome had not survived the enforced isolation and being deprived of food and water for days. He had strongly advised everyone aboard *Tsunami* not to dwell on what had happened aboard *Fortuna* before the Marines arrived.

Geary had sent a copy of information downloaded from *Fortuna*'s internal files to Captain Smythe for an engineering analysis. Smythe's report had been scathing. "He broke dozens of rules and regulations when that ship was overhauled to his specifications. Duplicate controls in his office that could override every control elsewhere in the ship! I'd like to know how many bribes he paid to have that overlooked. All of those locks! And the secondary life-support system for his suite was worthy of a Class Alpha quarantine facility. You said he ranted about cosmic rays at one point? Citizen Yangdi, for all of his bravado and for all of his wealth and power, must have been a very frightened man."

There was considerable irony in that, Geary thought. Someone without all that money probably would have had his fear issues identified and treated somehow. But Yangdi had instead been able to indulge his internal terrors in ways that ultimately proved fatal to him.

A knock on his stateroom door brought him out of his dark reverie.

"I'm just making my rounds of the ship," Tanya Desjani said. "I thought I'd check on you as well as my crew."

"I'm doing all right," Geary said. "Just thinking about what a waste it all was."

"I have considerable sympathy for the crew of that ship," Desjani said. "For Yangdi and his friends, not so much. Do you know what *Fortuna* means, by the way? *Good luck.* That had to be one of the most badly named ships in human history."

"You can say that again. I was thinking of the Marines, being so careful to enter and move about that ship, making sure they didn't break or damage anything."

"And then Yangdi blew it all to hell."

"And then Yangdi blew it all to hell." He shifted his gaze to the starscape on one bulkhead. "I hope *Sapphire* gets back safe and sound soon. I could use the lift. Hoping no more uninvited human ships show up here, that'll leave one loose end for me, the ships we sent back to Midway. Once Jane Geary returns with the warships we sent to warn everyone about the long jumps, I'll be able to stop worrying about them. Things should feel a lot more secure here then," Geary said.

Later on, he would look back on those words as bitter irony.

"SAPPHIRE is back."

It had been over a week since the rescue mission had joined up with the rest of the fleet again. Geary hit his comm panel to thank Desjani for the alert, blinked away the last vestiges of sleep, and quickly checked his stateroom display.

The heavy cruiser had indeed returned, along with a Wooareek ship. He couldn't tell if it was the same one. But the Wooareek ship was hauling *Sapphire* along with it at point five light speed, on an intercept with the Alliance formation. They were three light hours distant, but at their current velocity they'd cover that immense distance in six hours.

His mind had trouble with that timeline. Accustomed to the capabilities of human propulsion technology, he kept thinking that a distance of three light hours would take at least fifteen hours to cover even at point two light speed.

Was point five light speed the limit of what the Wooareek could do, or were they just doing their equivalent of lazing along?

"We have a message from *Sapphire*, Admiral."

"Link it to my stateroom," Geary ordered.

The image of Commander Boudreaux appeared, once again looking swathed in layers of gauze, but this time also oddly thinned. Boudreaux's voice sounded not only muted but also pitched slightly too high. "This is Commander Boudreaux for Admiral Geary. I wish to

report *Sapphire*'s safe return. Our mission was, I think, successful. I will provide a full report when we reach the fleet. I believe trying to transmit it while at this velocity will introduce too many errors into the message. Our navigation system keeps trying to reset because this velocity throws off its error parameters, but between resets projects our arrival at the fleet in five hours forty-eight minutes. To the honor of our ancestors, Boudreaux, out."

Successful. That could mean any number of things, but none of them were bad.

Geary pulled on his uniform and headed for the worship spaces. This was definitely the right time to burn a candle of thanks.

FIVE and a half hours later, he was on the bridge of *Dauntless*, watching the alien ship approach.

"They're still moving at point five light speed," Lieutenant Yuon said, his voice not quite steady.

Even Tanya Desjani was having trouble hiding her concern as the Wooareek ship with *Sapphire* in tow continued charging for an intercept with the Alliance fleet. There was something terrifying about seeing something heading for you moving that swiftly, knowing that light itself was only moving twice as fast as that ship. Knowing that ship was covering about one hundred fifty thousand kilometers every time you blinked.

"They're twenty million kilometers out," Lieutenant Yuon added. "Estimated time of intercept is . . ."

Geary looked at his display, which kept updating, the human systems estimating the Wooareek ship had to start braking right then and then immediately having to redo the calculations when it didn't. The normally slowly changing numbers for estimated times were jumping around.

"Two and half minutes, maybe," Desjani said. "Do the math in your head, Lieutenant Yuon."

"But, Captain, if he has to brake velocity—"

"He doesn't," Desjani said. "We've seen this."

"I want every sensor in the fleet trying to track that ship when it slows," Geary said.

"Yes, Admiral," Lieutenant Castries said. "The Wooareek ship has been given maximum priority on all sensors."

"Do you think we'll detect anything useful this time?" Desjani asked Geary.

"Probably not," Geary said. The minor energy and distortion readings they'd picked up last time hadn't provided any clues to the propulsion method being used by the Wooareek. Even Dr. Cresida hadn't been able to derive anything meaningful from them. "But we have to try our best."

"Admiral, some of the fleet's ships are asking whether we should go to combat standby status."

Geary weighed that question for about half a second before realizing such a move would be meaningless given the technological advantages of the aliens, but might still rub the Wooareek the wrong way. "All units in the Alliance fleet, this is Admiral Geary. Remain in current alert status. The Wooareek ship is not a threat."

"Wooareek ship is seven million kilometers out," Lieutenant Yuon said. "Still at point five light speed."

"Less than a minute to go," Desjani said. "How much margin of error would it take at that velocity to end up impacting one of our ships instead of stopping in open space?"

"I don't want to think about it," Geary said. "I do know our maneuvering systems couldn't handle that problem."

"I don't like how this makes me feel," Desjani said, rubbing her chin, her eyes on her display. "Like the adults have finally shown up, and the children are watching them wondering how they do what they're doing."

"It's definitely an ego check," Geary said.

An instant later alerts sounded as the Wooareek ship and heavy cruiser *Sapphire* suddenly appeared in the midst of the Alliance formation, their motion exactly matched to the vectors of the other ships, both of them only eight hundred meters from *Dauntless*. Spitting distance, in space terms. They hadn't actually teleported into position, but the speed with which they'd arrived had been so fast it felt just as if that had happened.

Geary jerked in involuntary reaction when the ships were suddenly there, and so close. He thought everyone else on the bridge had done the same.

"Damn," Lieutenant Castries breathed.

Geary touched his comm controls. "Commander Boudreaux, are you with us?"

Boudreaux responded immediately. "Yes, Admiral. *Sapphire* is perfectly all right. Everyone aboard her is perfectly all right."

"What did that feel like?"

"Uh, Admiral, it didn't feel like anything. Like watching a program. No sense of movement or stopping. Just one moment moving like a bat out of hell and the next . . . not."

"Sensors have picked up minor energy readings that appear to exactly match those seen last time," Lieutenant Castries said.

Meaning those readings would be just as unrevealing as the earlier ones.

A call from the Wooareek appeared. Geary accepted it, seeing one of the aliens waving two tentacles as if in greeting.

"Hey, humans! Miss us? This is your old pal Wave Breaks. Here's your ship back, good as new. Had a wild time, lots of good talk, made friends. Your guy Farmer has all the news. We have to fade now, got other chores, you know? We'll be back. Talk things over. Looking forward to dealing with you guys! Cool? Cool. Peace to all!"

Geary didn't have any time to decide whether to reply.

Dauntless's alarms wailed in puzzlement as the Wooareek ship seemed to vanish.

"They're already a million kilometers away from us," Lieutenant Yuon said. "Velocity point five light speed. Their estimated vector is back to the jump point."

"Who the hell is Farmer?" Geary asked.

It wasn't until Commander Boudreaux answered that Geary realized the call was still active. "Admiral, I've been told that my last name meant 'farmer' in an Old Earth language. The Wooareek kept calling me that."

"That's one good translator," Desjani said. "What kind of deals do you think the Wooareek are talking about? Because we may not have many options in terms of agreeing."

"Peace to all," Geary said, his voice grim. Whether deliberately or not, the Wooareek had just put on a breathtaking demonstration of how one-sided any competition between them and humans would be. "Let's hope they mean that."

RUMORS were running wild through the fleet. When *Sapphire* had left, the events had been far-off, glimpsed well after they occurred, easy to put aside. But this time, the dramatic and casual display put on by the Wooareek had taken place right in the middle of the fleet. Every sailor and Marine could easily reach the same conclusion as Captain Desjani, that these Wooareek were awesomely powerful, with tools compared to which humanity's greatest technology seemed like toys. To call such a revelation unsettling was putting it mildly.

Geary had decided he couldn't sit on what Boudreaux and the rest of *Sapphire*'s complement had learned. As much as possible had to be shared as quickly as possible in order to keep a handle on things.

To that end, and to allow as many different perspectives as could reasonably be accommodated, Geary had made use of *Dauntless*'s fleet conference room, which could be virtually expanded to allow as many guests as wanted. He invited not only his senior captains to attend Boudreaux's report, but also General Charban's entire group, Dr. Nasr, the three leading-edge human physicists, and Colonel Rogero, as well as Kommodor Bradamont and Lieutenant Iger. Ambassador Rycerz and a few senior members of her staff were also present in virtual form, as was Colonel Webb. Also virtually sitting at the table were the biologist and the sociologist sent along on *Sapphire* by the ambassador.

Sapphire and all aboard her were still in total quarantine, so Commander Boudreaux, Bradamont, and Iger attended virtually as well. The only things currently being allowed off *Sapphire* were the electrons transmitting messages, and even those were being scanned carefully.

"I want to begin with a summary of quarantine activity," Geary said. "Dr. Nasr?"

Nasr gestured toward Commander Boudreaux's virtual presence. "We have thus far detected no organisms or other contamination that might have been introduced while the ship was in Wooareek space."

Captain Smythe, head of the fleet's engineers, nodded in agreement. "Physically, we haven't found anything, either. We've scanned at a molecular level but found no bugs or any other sort of equipment that wasn't already on *Sapphire* when she left. If the Wooareek planted anything on her, it's something beyond our ability to detect."

"The enigmas did just that with our software," Captain Armus noted with a glum expression. "Has Dr. Cresida been given an opportunity to examine *Sapphire*?"

Cresida, for the first time in Geary's experience, seemed bewildered as everyone turned eyes on her. "Why would you ask that of me?"

"Your sister," Armus said, "may her memory always be honored, found something in our software that no one else had even thought of looking for. I understand that you're her equal."

"I'm . . ." Dr. Cresida breathed in and out slowly. "I'm more theoretical than my sister, who . . . was more involved with practical applications. I doubt that I could help in this matter."

"If I may second that," Dr. Bron added, "Dr. Cresida and the rest of us are theoreticians primarily. We've studied practical applications as they apply to the hypernet and have some expertise with software, but otherwise you're far better off consulting someone like, um, Captain Smythe there."

"Dr. Nasr, Captain Smythe, is there any reason we should maintain the quarantine of *Sapphire*?" Geary asked.

"I would like to continue the quarantine for another forty-eight hours," Dr. Nasr said. "After that, I would have no objections to lifting it. As Captain Smythe said, if we have not found anything by then, it will have been something we could never detect."

"I agree with the doctor," Smythe said.

"Dr. Yarovets?" Ambassador Rycerz asked the biologist.

"I have nothing to add," Yarovets said, sounding annoyed. "How could I when I had no opportunity to examine any organisms or environments except from distances of billions of kilometers?"

Geary gave Ambassador Rycerz a glance, but she said nothing else, so he addressed the whole group. "*Sapphire*'s quarantine will last another forty-eight hours, then be lifted unless any contrary information surfaces before then. Now, we've received detailed reports from those aboard *Sapphire*. I'd like those present to summarize what they consider the most important aspects of their reports and answer questions from the rest of us. Dr. Nkosi?"

The sociologist shook her head. "I have little to say. The Wooareek didn't respond to any of my questions in any meaningful way, and I can't even judge whether that was due to privacy taboos or an unwillingness to share information with us."

"What did they say?" Rycerz asked.

Nkosi looked pained. "A typical reply was when I asked about their social hierarchies. Their reply"—she looked down at her notes—"was 'We don't really do that kind of stuff, you know? We just get it done, and whoever can do it, does it.'"

"That answer does tell you something," Rycerz said.

"It rules out rigid hierarchies," Dr. Nkosi said. "But what does it mean in practice? I could never observe them. We only saw a few individuals, who appear to have passed on questions from others observing remotely. Yes, their social hierarchy appears to be very loose based on what few interactions I saw, but that's as far as it goes. And that's about as much information as I got about anything."

"Did they seem aggressive at any point?" Ambassador Rycerz asked. "Domineering?"

"No. Quite the opposite."

"Lieutenant Iger?" Geary asked, knowing that both his officers and the ambassador wanted to know anything learned about the Wooareek from a military perspective, as well as whatever Iger might have learned using his interrogation experience.

Iger also shook his head, looking unhappy. "If the models we use to judge human responses apply to the Wooareek and their translator, then I could not spot evasions or lies in their replies. If they didn't want to answer something, they said so. Most of their answers were vague and all of them were informal, but that felt natural, not evasive. I did ask the Wooareek directly about their defenses, asking if a species such as the Kicks worried them."

"What did the Wooareek say?" Rycerz pressed.

"They said . . ." Iger sighed. "The one I was speaking to, Warm Clear Waters, answered me by saying 'No problem.' When I asked for a clarification, Waters replied, 'We don't waste time worrying about those guys.'"

"They knew who the Kicks were?" Captain Armus pressed Iger. "And they didn't worry about them at all?"

"They knew the species," Iger said. "And they claimed not to worry about them at all." Another pause. "And that is essentially all I was able to learn. Whatever the Wooareek military capabilities are, we couldn't spot any through our sensors, and couldn't get the Wooareek to talk about them."

"You could detect no defenses?" Geary asked.

"Nothing, Admiral," Lieutenant Iger said. "Either they are hidden in ways we can't spot, or they take forms we couldn't identify, or they don't exist. I personally believe it's a combination of the first and the second. The Wooareek are so confident, so relaxed. They'd either have to be hopelessly naïve, or so powerful they don't have to worry about what others might do."

General Charban spoke up. "That's what our historian here speculated much earlier, that the Wooareek are so relaxed they're either badly mistaken or greatly superior to us."

"I agree with Lieutenant Iger," Kommodor Bradamont said. "And I guess the historian. I've gained some extra experience with double-talking and false fronts from my time interacting with the Syndicate and some of those on Midway, and I couldn't spot any defensiveness or concern or deceit. They simply didn't tell us things they didn't want to talk about, and apparently told us the truth when they did answer. They never got upset; they never seemed worried. There was nothing that could be interpreted as a threat or a demand."

"Commander Boudreaux?" Geary asked.

"I agree as well," Boudreaux said. "Even when it was time to return here, the Wooareek asked us if it was okay to leave now, if we were 'cool' with going back to the fleet. He didn't tell us it was time to go."

Ambassador Rycerz sat back and slapped one hand against the table. Even though the table she sat at was on *Boundless* and the conference taking place aboard *Dauntless*, the conferencing software provided not only the sound but the vibration of the blow to those seated at the table. "Did we learn anything useful?"

"Their jump drives are different than ours," Boudreaux said. "Much better, somehow. We made three jumps to reach Wooareek space. Each time we came out of jump our navigation systems figured out where we were. Based on the distances covered, the Wooareek jump drives somehow moved us about twice as fast as our own jump drives do."

"Twice as fast?" Captain Smythe demanded.

"Yes, Captain. We couldn't measure velocity in jump space, but we knew about how long a journey across a certain number of light years should take. We got there twice as fast as we would've using our own jump drives."

Smythe shook his head. "I have no idea how you'd even go about doing that."

"We don't, either," Dr. Bron said. "Our theories of how jump space works don't allow for such different travel times."

"But then," Dr. Cresida added dryly, "most of our theories about jump space remain pure speculation."

Ambassador Rycerz turned back to Boudreaux. "Commander, what about the questions the Wooareek asked of you? Didn't those tell us anything about them?"

"The Wooareek asked us many questions about human history," Commander Boudreaux said. "They knew a lot of events and personalities. However they've been watching us, it's been thorough and exhaustive, though the Wooareek didn't give us any details beyond saying they respected the privacy of persons."

"Whatever that means to them," Dr. Nkosi the sociologist muttered.

"I asked them why they cared so much about our history," Boudreaux continued, "and why they cared about what we thought about our history. And they said, 'You can't know where you are unless you know where you came from.'"

John Senn sat up straight and grinned. "I wholeheartedly endorse that sentiment!"

"Did they mean that?" Ambassador Rycerz asked, looking skeptical.

"Yes," Kommodor Bradamont replied. "At one point they asked me why the Alliance had stopped bombarding enemy cities from space. The Wooareek didn't ask why we'd *started* doing that in the later decades of the war with the Syndics. They wanted to know why we'd stopped. I used their earlier answer to frame my reply, saying that Admiral Geary had reminded us of where we'd been, and that caused us to realize where we were, and once we did that we knew we didn't want to be there."

"The Wooareek liked that answer," Commander Boudreaux said. "It's in my report. When they were happy, we'd see dark patches on their skin. This really bright purple seemed to be when they were most happy. If the colors got pale, it meant they weren't so happy."

"I have an extensive analysis of that in my report," Dr. Yarovets grumbled.

"Do you agree with what Commander Boudreaux said about the coloration?" Rycerz asked.

"It's overly simplified, but . . . not *wholly* inaccurate."

"At one point," Bradamont said, "we felt they were really unhappy, even though they didn't say so, and it was almost as if they faded into the background."

Dr. Nasr made an intrigued sound. "On Old Earth, species such as the octopus could change the color of their skin to blend in to their environment. I read up on them after we saw the Wooareek. Perhaps the Wooareek are the same, and when feeling worried or unhappy hide themselves."

"I have a detailed analysis of that as well," Dr. Yarovets hastily interjected. "An informed analysis."

"So they wanted to know why we'd done things in our history," Ambassador Rycerz said. "What else did they want? Why did they even want *Sapphire* there instead of asking us those questions here?"

"I have a guess on that," Dr. Nkosi said, speaking cautiously. "I don't have anything like sufficient grounds to speak definitively. But I believe it may have been a type of interview. The Wooareek, including members who may not have wanted to or couldn't leave their own star systems, wanted to see firsthand what humans were like."

"The Wooareek kept telling us they wanted *Sapphire* there so they could talk to us," Bradamont said. "So they could see us. I gained the impression that also meant judging us based on how we answered and what we asked them."

"There's insufficient data to support that conclusion," Dr. Nkosi said.

Rycerz shook her head, looking thoughtful. "While you were gone, the Dancers invited Admiral Geary and Captain Desjani to visit the primary inhabited world here. Our impression of that short visit was about the same, that it was aimed at allowing many Dancers to see humans for themselves."

"What about these deals the Wooareek mentioned?" Geary said. "Did they make it clear what they wanted from humanity?"

It was the question no one had wanted to ask because everyone was afraid to hear the answer. He felt the way tension rose as his question went home, the way the climate-controlled compartment seemed to chill.

Kommodor Bradamont laughed softly, startling everyone. "Yes. Yes, they told us what they wanted."

ELEVEN

"WHAT is it, then?" Ambassador Rycerz demanded, clearly puzzled by Bradamont's attitude. "What do they want from us?"

"The Wooareek want our stories," Bradamont said. "Our books, our music, our videos, our art. The products of human imagination and creativity."

Several seconds of stunned silence were finally broken by Geary. "Our books?"

Commander Boudreaux nodded. "Yes, Admiral. The Wooareek desire agreements for the sharing of what they called 'creations.' That's what the Wooareek call things like music, movies, books, art, anything like that."

"Why?" Captain Badaya spread his hands in bafflement. "Why would someone like the Wooareek care about human books and movies and pictures?"

Bradamont smiled. "The Wooareek told us, 'Your stories are windows into how you think, your art shows how you see, your music shows how you feel.' Apparently, they're fascinated by the different perspectives different species bring to such things. How they view the universe and each other."

"Sort of like how humans enjoy experiencing other human cultures?" Captain Duellos said.

"That's a rough comparison," Dr. Nkosi said. "But roughly accurate, as far as we can tell."

Captain Armus leaned forward, plainly skeptical. "The Wooareek made it clear to you that they had closely surveilled us for who knows how long. That means they must already have had plenty of access to our music and movies and such."

"Yes, sir," Commander Boudreaux said. "We brought that up. The Wooareek said they'd used those things for scientific purposes. But the Wooareek claimed they haven't sold or exchanged or distributed any of that music or other things within their society. Because, they said, they haven't paid for it."

"They haven't *paid* for it?" Rycerz stared at Boudreaux. "They want to *pay* for it?"

"Yes, Ambassador," Kommodor Bradamont said. "The Wooareek told us they need to have agreements with the creators of the 'creations' that allow them to distribute those things. And they said they'd pay for those agreements."

"They already have them," Captain Badaya said, openly skeptical, "but they think they still have to pay for them?"

"Yes," Commander Boudreaux said. "They insisted on it."

"Ethical aliens," Captain Duellos said, looking torn between amusement and disbelief.

"If their technology is that advanced, and we can trade them popular songs for it, why wouldn't we do that?" Captain Smythe said, smiling.

Everyone turned eager looks on Commander Boudreaux, who shook his head, looking unhappy. "We asked the Wooareek about technology. They said . . ." He grimaced. "The words were polite enough, but they amounted to *absolutely not*."

"'No way,'" Bradamont quoted. "Maybe it was just how their translator worked, but listening to their reply, I and the others had the distinct impression of adults telling an eager child, 'Maybe we'll talk about that when you're older.' They're not going to transfer technology."

The silence following Boudreaux's and Bradamont's statements was broken by Captain Smythe, speaking in a plaintive voice. "But I want it *now!*"

Once the laughter had died down, Geary looked at Ambassador Rycerz. "I guess getting access to any of the Wooareek technology will be a long-term diplomatic issue."

"And a business issue," Rycerz said. "If the Wooareek want deals for creative products such as songs and books, that would mean negotiations with those holding the rights to those things. All the Alliance government could legally do is exert oversight of such business negotiations."

"What were they talking about paying, if not knowledge or tech?" Captain Duellos asked.

Kommodor Bradamont smiled slightly. "Precious metals. Jewels. Other precious natural items. Their own art. They showed us some amazing carvings of what seemed like corals. And, of course, the deals would create sales access for the human creators to all of the Wooareek-occupied star systems."

Tanya Desjani spoke up. "I don't get it. These Wooareek appear to be incredibly powerful. They control awesome technology. Why are they asking us about making deals? Why aren't they telling us what deals we're going to get?"

"That's what humans would do," Captain Badaya agreed matter-of-factly.

"But instead they want peace and mutual agreements?" Desjani asked. "They want to pay us for what they already have? What is up with that?"

"They're ethical," Captain Duellos repeated.

"So? I'm pretty ethical, too. I think most if not all of us here are ethical. Or mostly ethical, anyway. But the Wooareek seem way too good to be true."

"You're sure they have weapons?" Geary asked Bradamont, Boudreaux, and Iger. "Did you say they confirmed they have weapons?"

Boudreaux grimaced. "They admitted they'd developed weapons to defend themselves against dangerous creatures in their home world, and dangers they've encountered in space. That was as specific as they got."

"The Wooareek didn't act ashamed of having weapons," Bradamont added. "It was just, 'Yeah, we've got that sort of thing. No, we're not worried about anyone else attacking us.' It wasn't bravado. No waving around of weapons or boasting of what they could do. We've all seen that sort of posturing. It was . . . confidence. The sort of deep-rooted confidence that comes from being the best at something."

"That same impression was shared by nearly everyone aboard *Sapphire*," Commander Boudreaux said.

Lieutenant Iger nodded. "My assessment is that the Wooareek are at peace because no one dares pick a fight with them. And if anyone does attack, as the Kicks or the enigmas might, the Wooareek could easily make short work of them. More likely, the Wooareek simply avoid them so they don't have to deal with species like the Kicks."

"So," Captain Badaya said in arch tones, "these Wooareek are armed to the teeth but also ethical? Why?"

"I also don't understand the connection between ethics and peace," Captain Armus said, frowning. "It seems to me the ethical always get stomped on by the unethical. If these Wooareek are so powerful, they can do whatever they want. The fact that they seek agreements with us for things they can take seems an admission of weakness." There were murmurs of agreement following his words.

Dr. Cresida, frowning, looked about her. "Ethics is often mistaken for weakness."

John Senn nodded quickly. "That's been a frequent error through-out human history."

"Then explain the Wooareek behavior," Captain Armus said.

Kommodor Bradamont shook her head. "What is there to explain? Why are you all questioning this? Of course an ethical species would be a peaceful species! None of them would ever decide to take some-thing belonging to someone else just because they wanted it. None of them would go to war to take things by force instead of negotiating a mutual agreement. None of them would let others suffer by withhold-ing things they have which they could easily part with to help another!"

"You mean like the Syndics would," Captain Badaya said pointedly.

"Yes, like the Syndicate Worlds," Bradamont agreed.

"No one would describe the Syndicate as ethical," Colonel Rogero said. "I had to look up the word just now to understand what you were talking about."

"If the Wooareek are that ethical," Duellos said, "why do they even want to do business with humanity?"

"I asked them why they'd make agreements with us," Bradamont said. "Because I wondered the same thing. And they said 'You're not always Melos.' None of us have been able to figure out what that meant. It doesn't seem to match any person or world in our databases. There's just some ancient historical reference to an island on Old Earth."

"Melos?!" John Senn said in surprise before looking abashed as every-one switched their attention to him. "The Melian Dialogue. That must be what the Wooareek meant. Yes, it's ancient history on Old Earth. Thucydides wrote about it. There was a city called Melos that remained neutral in a war between . . . Athens and Sparta. Athens sent a strong force to attack Melos anyway, and in their demand that Melos surren-der didn't pretend to make any ethical arguments. They just said, 'The strong do what they want, and the weak endure what they must.'"

"Power politics at its most basic and most brutal," Ambassador Ry-cerz observed.

"And an awful lot of human history reflects that attitude," Senn said. "Not all of it, though. If the Wooareek said we're not always Melos, then they must mean humans aren't always . . . unethical. So they're willing to at least give us a chance." He looked even more surprised. "The Wooareek know Thucydides? They must have already acquired a *lot* of knowledge about us."

"The enigmas proved how easy that was," Captain Duellos said. "How long ago was this Melos thing?"

"Thousands of years old before humans even left Old Earth."

"I wonder how long they've been watching us. Did the Wooareek give any indication of how long they've had interstellar space travel?"

"They wouldn't say," Lieutenant Iger replied.

Duellos made a face. "But we do know they know a great deal about us. They must have been collecting that information for a long time. Why wait until now to contact us?"

"That's the same question we've asked the Dancers," General Charban said. "The answer is always something along the lines of 'the time was right.'"

"We contacted the Dancers," Desjani pointed out. "They didn't reveal themselves to us. We came knocking on their door. Maybe we need to knock on doors before any of these species will deal with us."

"The enigmas and the Kicks have responded to knocks on their doors by trying to kill us," Badaya said.

Lieutenant Jamenson pointed to the star chart floating above the conference table. "We've never seen enigmas or Kicks in Dancer space, except when the Kicks followed us and the Dancers helped us fight them off. But the Taon and the Wooareek both seem to have free passage through Dancer-controlled space. Maybe they're all part of some association, and knocking on one of their doors is the same as knocking on all of them?"

"That is entirely plausible," Ambassador Rycerz said. "Not necessarily something as closely bound as star systems belonging to the Alliance, but some association allowing contact and trade. If so, when we entered Dancer space we may have knocked on the doors of every species belonging to such an association."

"But they're all judging us independently," Geary said. "The Taon certainly did, and it seems the Wooareek are doing so as well."

Rycerz nodded. "An association in which each member species retains considerable autonomy. Did the Wooareek say how they intended to get our response to their requests?"

"They said they'd be back here," Commander Boudreaux replied. "They said they realized it might not be feasible for now, but ultimately they wanted to be able to visit human space to negotiate directly with creators."

"That'd go over great," Captain Badaya said, his voice heavy with sarcasm. "Can you imagine the reactions in human star systems to the sort of show that the Wooareek put on when they brought *Sapphire* back?"

Captain Smythe snorted. "That kind of display of superiority wouldn't play well."

"I don't believe a display of superiority was what the Wooareek intended," Bradamont said, gesturing to emphasize her words. "I think they did it because they could and because it was fun. Just like humans having fun maneuvering battle cruisers all out or those warbird aerospace pilots doing stunts."

"What they intend matters less than what humans would think," Ambassador Rycerz pointed out. "There's going to have to be a lot of groundwork laid to make that happen. Does anyone disagree with the need to reach these deals with the Wooareek?"

"I think," General Charban said, "we need to consider how the Wooareek would react to dealing with the likes of Ronald Yangdi."

"There comes a point where we cannot control that," Rycerz said. "Not under the laws of the Alliance."

"Realistically," Captain Smythe said, "we can't keep the Wooareek out of human space except by negotiations and reaching agreements. As it stands, if the Wooareek wanted to visit Unity, we couldn't stop them."

"We'd fight to the last if it came to that," Captain Armus said. "Even it was hopeless, we would not submit without fighting as long as we could."

"Even if it was hopeless," Captain Desjani agreed.

"But surely it would be better not to fight," Ambassador Rycerz said. "Not if we can reach agreements that, as far as I can see, would not harm humanity."

Geary looked around, wondering if anyone would openly disagree.

No one did. Not even Colonel Webb, who, given his past distrust of aliens, Geary had thought would be leery of dealing with the Wooareek.

But Webb sat, silent, his eyes hooded. Something about his demeanor didn't feel right to Geary, who made a mental note to check up on Webb after this.

Captain Armus nodded toward the ambassador. "I wouldn't object. There have been too many deaths already."

"Midway will need to have a place at the table when these agreements are made," Colonel Rogero said. "Did the Wooareek indicate a willingness to deal with us?" he asked Bradamont.

"They did," Bradamont said. "Though they kept making a reference to an umbrella. That's how their translator rendered their word. Umbrella."

"Specifically in reference to an agreement?" Rycerz asked. "I see. An umbrella agreement is basically something written broadly enough to cover both current issues and any future issues that might arise. It could also refer to an agreement that covers all Wooareek and human interactions."

"But is that what the Wooareek meant?" General Charban wondered.

Bradamont shrugged. "Their translator seemed to be remarkably accurate when it used other words. Those words matched what humans would use."

"I see," Rycerz repeated. She paused. "My staff and I have been speaking with the Dancers about an agreement governing contact and travel through each other's territory and trade. The Dancers approached us with their own proposals, which seemed to be very broad. They could be characterized as an umbrella agreement. Perhaps those proposals are the same which govern the Dancers' association with other species, and how other species interact with each other. But there seems to be some other meaning to the term as they're using it that we're not getting."

"Why not just tell us, then?" Captain Badaya said, exasperated. "Why can't the Dancers simply tell you that? And what about other humans? The Dancers know the Alliance doesn't represent all of humanity. No one does! What happens when other humans don't abide by the 'umbrella' agreement between the Alliance and the Dancers? Do we get accused of violating the agreement?"

General Charban answered, his expression unhappy. "'Human problem, humans fix.' That's what the Dancers told us about the Syndic flotilla we dealt with. That's what they told us about *Fortuna*. Maybe the Dancers expect us to enforce whatever deal we make. Enforce it against any other humans," he added with heavy emphasis.

"Lokaa," Geary said, as Charban's words reminded him of earlier thoughts along those lines. "The Taon led by Lokaa were welcome in Dancer space. But there were other Taon who attacked Lokaa's force. Lokaa said those other Taon were xenophobes. Is Lokaa's fleet in that star system to enforce an agreement with the Dancers about contacts between their species?"

Ambassador Rycerz gave Geary a worried look. "Which might indeed mean the Dancers expect us to do the same with regard to any human actors not part of the Alliance."

"Have the Dancers flat out told you that?"

Rycerz's reply came out reluctantly, as if she regretted the need to share the information. "There are parts of the Dancer proposals whose meaning is . . . unclear to us. We've been trying to get their meaning, as understood by the Dancers, nailed down. But it is a reasonable interpretation of them that the Dancers do expect *us* to enforce the agreement."

"You realize," Colonel Rogero said, "that Midway could not accept such an agreement."

"Even parts of the Alliance, such as the Callas Republic, might not," Captain Hiyen said, speaking up for the first time.

"Old Earth wouldn't," Captain Duellos said. "Nor the Old Colonies. The smaller associations of stars between the Alliance and the Old Colonies wouldn't accept it. And, of course, the Syndics would never buy into such an agreement."

"Not to mention Mr. Medals and his fellow nutcases on the other side of the galactic arm from Old Earth," Desjani said. "We haven't heard from any of them since *Dauntless* visited Old Earth, but news like this will spread through every place humans have reached."

"Amid all the uncertainties," Captain Smythe said, "we do have one certainty. Some humans will try to do unethical things to the Wooareek, as well as to the Dancers, and to the Taon. Try to cheat them on a deal, try to steal technology, try to break any rules the Wooareek or the Taon or the Dancers have established."

"The Syndicate will do all of those things," Bradamont agreed.

"As I reminded the admiral regarding the *Fortuna*," Colonel Rogero said, "what you just described are considered nothing but good business practices in the Syndicate."

"Right there!" Smythe said, pointing to Rogero. "So, we make these deals, sign these agreements, and then what happens when other humans break them? Are we, the Alliance, willing to go to war with the rest of humanity in order to keep the peace?"

"That," said Ambassador Rycerz, "is one of the most bizarre statements I've ever heard. And I've heard many in my diplomatic career.

But it also may sum up our choices. I hope we're not interpreting them correctly."

"The Wooareek didn't seem worried about anything like that," Lieutenant Iger said. "They may have special means of keeping out unwanted visitors."

"That still leaves us with the Dancers and the Taon," Smythe commented.

"There are grounds for hope," Geary said, drawing surprised looks from everyone but Tanya Desjani. "The Dancers, the Taon, and the Wooareek have found ways to make this sort of thing work. If they can do it, humanity should be able to figure out an answer."

Captain Duellos arched his eyebrows at Geary. "Admiral, if former senator Victoria Rione were here I think I can easily imagine what her response to those optimistic words would be."

Geary smiled in reply, again startling the others. "Rione was as cynical and manipulative as they come. But she always believed there was an angle, a way to handle any situation that came up. You just had to be, uh, creative in looking at the problem and thinking of solutions."

"I feel obligated to remind you, Admiral," Captain Armus said, his voice heavy, "that her last solution, may her memory be honored, required her to sacrifice herself."

"We're not at that point yet," Geary said. "Think, people. For all of our flaws, humans find solutions. We want to find a good one."

"How long do we have?" Captain Smythe asked. "The fleet can't stay here indefinitely."

"I will emphasize that to the Dancers," Rycerz said. "That's all I can promise."

COLONEL Webb answered Geary's call quickly, displaying his usual élan rather than any appearance of misgivings as during the meeting on the Wooareek. "To what do I owe the pleasure, Admiral?"

"I'm just checking in with you," Geary said. He'd made this call from the now otherwise empty conference room, wanting to have more security than even his stateroom offered. "I know you're not under my command, but I still feel obligated to keep an eye on any military here. How are things going?"

Webb paused, not answering for several seconds. "Admiral," he finally said, "I'm waiting for the other shoe to drop."

"Which shoe would that be?"

"The one wielded by the people who have made your life, and my life, far too interesting on this op," Webb said. "That attempt a while back by a few of your ship captains to start a war with the Dancers while you were off with part of the fleet visiting the Taon seemed way too amateurish, if you'll forgive my saying so."

"It could've done damage," Geary said.

"It still felt sloppy to me," Webb said. "And under-resourced. We've got a lot of enemies trying to undermine what we're doing." Webb shook his head, looking unhappy. "I'm still waiting. I can feel it. Like a thunderstorm coming. Maybe I've been doing this too long and I'm getting jumpy. We'll see. How did you manage it down on that planet?"

"With the Dancers, you mean?" Geary smiled slightly. "It was interesting."

"I bet. Ambassador Rycerz has told me that if the Dancers want our embassy to be on the planet's surface, she'll want me and my soldiers to stay aboard *Boundless*. Between you and me, I'm okay with that."

After a couple more exchanges of vague pleasantries, Geary ended the call. Webb had been unusually open about his worries, but that might be attributed to those worries. At least he seemed to be sure he and Geary were on the same side again.

A few days later the shoe dropped, though it would be a while before Geary realized it had happened.

"The task force is back from Midway," Captain Desjani told him from where she was on the bridge. "It's bigger than when it left. You've a message from Captain Jane Geary that was sent on their arrival."

Geary got out of his bunk quickly, wondering what Desjani could mean. His stateroom display quickly supplied an answer.

The task force contained four more battleships, four more battle cruisers, seven more heavy cruisers, and twenty more destroyers than it had set out with. The new ships, rather than being mixed in with the older ships, were in a separate formation.

He didn't want to analyze all of this alone. Settling his uniform, Geary headed for the bridge.

"Jane has gained a lot of new ships," Desjani noted as she gazed at her display.

"I noticed. Why are they in a separate formation?" Jane Geary's ships were arrayed in a wide box. But the new ships formed a spherical formation far enough from the others to make it clear that they were not part of the other force. "Who are they?"

"Ship identification broadcasts show them as Improved *Audacious*-class battleships," Lieutenant Castries called out. "*Audacious, Implacable, Defiant*, and *Paladin*. The battle cruisers are Improved *Renown*-class. *Renown, Intrepid, Invincible*, and *Fearless*."

"Improved," Geary muttered, wondering why hearing that bothered him. It was natural for ship designs to be modified, incorporating lessons from earlier designs and experience in battle. But while he had managed to get his ships overhauled, very little in the way of modifications had come their way even though they had been bearing so much of the burden of carrying out fleet missions. "Do we know exactly what 'improved' means?"

Desjani glanced at him. "From what we're getting on them it looks like mostly marginal improvements to shield strength and weapons."

"Fine. Why did they have to name them after ships we've lost in battle?"

Desjani had looked away, but now focused on him again, surprised. "We're used to that. It became common during the war, because so many ships were being destroyed."

"All right." He'd been told that plenty of times before, but didn't want to discuss how seeing those names evoked for him those who had died aboard them, unwelcome reminders of how many casualties this fleet had suffered since he'd assumed command. "I didn't realize we were still building at this rate."

"Roberto Duellos was saying some of the planned cutbacks were reversed because star systems didn't want to lose all of the space-dock jobs depending on new warship construction. But I don't think even he realized this much was still being built." She sighed. "They built another *Invincible*. Of course they did."

Geary confined his response to a nod. During the war, a superstition had developed in the fleet that ships named *Invincible* were bad luck because the living stars didn't like that humans were claiming something they built couldn't be destroyed. And *Invincible*s really had been hard-luck ships, with average service lives before being lost in battle that were shorter than those of other battle cruisers. But, as Desjani had noted, the fleet brass refused to give in to the superstition and instead kept naming new ships *Invincible* as fast as the old ones were destroyed. It made the fleet leadership happy, even if it made everyone assigned to an *Invincible* feel like their lives were even more imperiled than those on other warships.

But he realized he should be focusing on the question of why the new ships were in a separate, different formation. That was odd. "You said we've already received a message from Jane?"

Desjani gestured. "It's ready for you."

He accepted the message, seeing the image of his grandniece seated in her stateroom aboard the battleship *Dreadnaught*. "I'm happy to report the mission to Midway was carried out without any losses," Jane Geary reported. "The enigmas had minimal forces in Lalotai when we passed through en route Midway. We encountered no enigma presence at Pele except a single picket ship that remained near the jump point to Hina. On our return trip there were substantial enigma forces in Lalotai but they did not attempt to close on us, standing off at a distance of one light hour until we jumped out of the system.

"After we delivered Kommodor Bradamont's report to President Iceni, she approved using Midway's hypernet gate to send *Mistral* with the warning to Alliance space. President Iceni sends her thanks for alerting Midway and their, um, associated star systems of the dangers posed by the jump drive modifications. It seems that same technology had mysteriously been 'discovered' in a nearby star system and there was debate going on as to whether to attempt the jumps."

Captain Jane Geary paused. "Just before *Mistral* entered the hypernet gate, a large formation of Alliance warships arrived through it. Captain Constantine Rogov on *Implacable* informed me that the ships were under his command. Captain Rogov, who is junior to me, refused to place his ships under my command, saying he was acting under orders of General Arnold Julian, who is aboard *Implacable*. I was told General Julian is bringing additional orders for you.

"Unless instructed otherwise my force will proceed to a rendezvous with the rest of the fleet. I do not have control of the new ships commanded by Captain Rogov and am unsure as to their intentions. To the honor of our ancestors, Geary, out."

Desjani raised her eyebrows as the message ended. "'I am unsure as to their intentions'? That's a pretty blatant red flag."

Before he could comment in turn, another message arrived, this one from *Implacable*. Captain Constantine Rogov was not a large man, but he carried himself as if he were three meters tall. Geary, trying to decide whether that reflected laudable confidence or dangerous self-assurance, studied Rogov intently as he spoke.

"This is Captain Rogov, notifying Admiral Geary of my forces' arrival in this star system. We are conveying General Julian to you in order to deliver critical new orders, and will proceed to orbit near *Boundless*. To the honor of our ancestors! Rogov, out."

Desjani sat back, raising her eyebrows once more. "He's notifying you of his arrival, not reporting to you? And telling us what he'll do instead of outlining his initial actions and requesting further instructions?"

"Do you know anything about him? Rogov?" Geary said, trying to decide on the right response.

"Rogov? No, not really. I barely know the name."

"What about this General Julian?" Geary called up data on the name. "Malphas Star System. He was in command there not long before I was found in survival sleep."

"Malphas?" Desjani shook her head, looking unhappy.

"Should I read the details?"

"Only if you want to. Officially, Malphas was an Alliance victory."

"And unofficially?" Geary asked, afraid that he already knew the answer.

"Unofficially it's called Bloody Malphas." She gave him a sidelong look. "The word going around before you were found was that our losses at Malphas were so bad they helped motivate the Senate to approve Admiral Bloch's desperation plan to strike the Syndic capital star system. We know how that turned out."

Geary squinted at the data. "If Julian was in command of that big of a disaster, why is he here doing something important?"

"Probably because Malphas was officially a victory."

"He got a medal?" Geary said in astonishment as he read. "Why would the Senate have chosen Julian to bring me new orders?"

"Don't ask me," Desjani said. "I don't pal around with senators like you do."

He couldn't do anything about General Julian, but he could about Captain Rogov. "Where's a good place to park Rogov and his ships?"

"How about here?" Desjani suggested, highlighting an area beneath the main formation. "That's a good spot while you wait to decide whether to distribute them throughout the formation."

"Yes. I like that." Tapping the reply command, Geary spoke like someone who knew his orders would be followed. "Captain Rogov, this is Admiral Geary. *Boundless* is not the guide ship for this formation. You and the ships under your command are to proceed to intercept the main formation, taking position as indicated relative to *Dauntless*. If you are carrying orders for me, that will place you in a better location to deliver them. I expect a full, standard arrival status report from you covering all of your ships. Geary, out."

"Rogov ought to feel that burn," Desjani murmured.

"Did you say something, Captain?"

"No, Admiral. Not a thing." She gave him a sidelong look. "If I may, it might be a good idea to send a personal message to Captain Geary on *Dreadnaught* asking her why she included that 'unsure of their intentions' thing in her arrival report to you."

"Another good idea," Geary said. He stood up. It would be several hours before he could receive any reply from Captain Rogov. "I'm going back to my stateroom to send a personal message."

JANE Geary's reply came before Captain Rogov's, which didn't do anything to further endear Geary to Rogov.

"Admiral," Jane said, remaining formal since this was an official, even though personal, communication, "I can't offer any specific concerns regarding Captain Rogov and his ships. More than anything else, it's been his attitude, which from the beginning with me was borderline insubordinate, as if he didn't need to worry about obeying orders from me. His communications have also implied some sort of special secrets to which he is privy. It's probably related to the presence of General

Julian on his ship. I never received any communications directly from the general, which is a bit odd as well, and haven't received any clues as to what his orders for you might be."

Jane took a moment to order her thoughts. "I used a back channel to speak with an officer I know aboard the new *Intrepid*. We'd served together a couple of years ago. He definitely had an attitude of anticipation and told me something big was coming before asking me not to mention that to anyone else.

"Oh, one other thing. I was giving Captain Rogov a rundown on how the Dancers did things with us, and Rogov gave me a brush-off. He didn't outright say he didn't care how the Dancers operated, but that was the impression he gave. This again struck me as odd for someone given command of a substantial force being sent into Dancer territory. If my task force hadn't happened to meet up with them at Midway, they would've encountered the Dancers on their own. Again, not a smoking gun. For all they knew, the fleet was still in that Dancer border star system we first jumped into. It still struck me as just . . . odd. You asked me for my impressions, and that's what they are. I hope I'm just being overly cautious. Geary, out."

He sat looking at his display for a long time, trying to think things through. But he didn't know enough to come up with any conclusions.

While he was there, Captain Rogov's reply finally arrived.

"This is Captain Constantine Rogov for Admiral Geary. I regret that I was unclear in my earlier transmission and apologize for the misunderstanding. The orders I was given to deliver require me to rendezvous with *Boundless*. Once that is done, and after General Julian provides you with your new orders, I will of course be under your command. Rogov, out."

There wasn't anything he could object to in that. But it still bothered Geary. Now that he'd been sensitized to it by Jane's message, Geary thought he felt in Rogov the same anticipation, the same sense of eagerness, that she had mentioned. Was that just his imagination?

In any case, it wasn't grounds for fighting the issue or attacking Rogov. He would have to wait to see what Rogov was like once he joined with the rest of the fleet.

"Admiral?"

"General Charban," Geary said, looking at where Charban stood in the stateroom door. "What brings you here? Not another invitation for me from the Dancers, I hope."

"It's the Dancers," Charban said, coming inside. "But not an invitation." He grimaced. "They've sent us a message which, boiled down to basics, expresses unhappiness with these reinforcements to your fleet. The Dancers want to know why we've brought more warships here. Lieutenant Jamenson thinks they are also hinting we should send some away. They're not happy."

"I'm not exactly thrilled myself," Geary said. "I can't tell the Dancers why those new ships are here because I don't know myself. They're supposedly bringing me new orders."

Charban looked like a man trying not to frown and not quite succeeding. "Orders carried by General Arnold Julian? Is that right?"

"Yes." Geary examined Charban. "Do you know Julian?"

"I've never been closely acquainted with him," Charban said. "Our paths did cross a few times."

"Then please tell me what you're trying to avoid saying."

Charban smiled slightly. "Julian struck me as the sort of person who never doubts their own special destiny or their own decisions. Other officers joked he suffered from G—" Charban choked off the word he'd been about to say, looking uncomfortable again.

"Were you going to say 'Geary Syndrome'?" Geary asked.

"I was."

He'd never expected to have a syndrome named after him, but then it hadn't really been named after *him*. It had been named after the Black Jack Geary the government had created, the perfect hero, the perfect officer, the one who legend said would someday return from the dead to save the Alliance. As the war with the Syndicate Worlds had dragged on for decade after decade, Geary had been told that more than one senior officer had decided they were that person, that perfect officer, the one fated to save the Alliance. Enough senior officers that it had become an official medical disorder.

One of the odder things he'd experienced since waking from nearly a century of survival sleep had been having a fleet doctor wonder if he himself was suffering from the malady named after himself.

And, in truth, there were still some who believed the imaginary Geary who'd inspired Geary Syndrome was the real one.

Geary smiled crookedly at Charban to show he wasn't offended and could see the perverse humor in the situation. "Do you have any idea why they'd have sent Julian to deliver orders to me?"

Charban shrugged. "Perhaps just to get him out of their hair for a while?"

"I hope you're right." Geary rested his head in his hands, thinking. "I'm going to talk to Ambassador Rycerz about the Dancers' concerns. Do you have any idea what we should tell them?"

"Vague reassurances?" Charban suggested.

"I'll see what Rycerz wants to say."

AS it turned out, Ambassador Rycerz shared the Dancers' unhappiness. "Why did they send you all of these new warships? It looks bad, like we're planning something aggressive."

"I don't know why they were sent," Geary said for the third time. "I have not asked for reinforcements since we left Alliance space. I don't even know if they're going to be added to the force I have, or go home once these orders are delivered."

Rycerz eventually promised to try to reassure the Dancers. They had to leave it at that until Rogov's task force reached the fleet.

Which would be quicker than expected, since the new task force had made a show of ramping up velocity quickly past point two light speed. It made for a flashy approach, but one that unnecessarily wasted fuel cells, and one that further lowered his opinion of Captain Rogov before he'd even met the officer face-to-face.

Unless Rogov had a good reason for wanting to get those orders to Geary as quickly as possible. That possibility only increased the feeling of vague unease Geary felt whenever he checked on the progress of the new ships.

Tomorrow Rogov's ships would join up, and he'd learn what was in those orders.

TWELVE

CAPTAIN Rogov's formation matched orbital vectors with the rest of the fleet, positioned behind the formation, lined up on *Boundless*.

Naturally, and annoyingly, the new orders had to be delivered in person.

Geary, despite an urge to let General Julian be greeted by Captain Desjani, which would've been seen as a bit of a slight but also saddled Tanya with delivering it, instead waited in *Dauntless*'s shuttle dock. He had nixed the idea of an honor guard, though, telling Desjani this was a routine official trip by Julian, not a special visit.

He'd reckoned without the general, however. As soon as the shuttle grounded and its ramp dropped, a dozen soldiers in dress uniforms marched down the ramp and took up position, six to a side, standing rigidly at attention. Geary noticed, off to the side, the two Marines providing routine security and the sailors in the dock crew exchanging comments accompanied by smiles, doubtless mocking the ground forces' display.

General Julian came down the ramp in full dress uniform, his medals sparkling in the light of the shuttle dock. Taking no apparent notice of the honor guard, he strode up to Geary.

The general smiled as he extended his hand in greeting. "Arnold Julian, Admiral. It's a great pleasure to meet you."

"Thank you, General," Geary said, shaking the offered hand, and noting that General Julian's grip was much tighter than necessary, as if the general were trying to impress Geary with his strength. If Julian had hoped for a squeeze-off to see who could exert the most hand pressure, he was disappointed, though. Geary simply maintained his usual grip until Julian dropped the handshake. "I understand you have something for me." The sooner he got the orders, the sooner Julian could leave.

But the general shook his head. "These orders have to be delivered in a secure compartment." He looked about at the sailors and Marines, shaking his head. "No unauthorized personnel should be present. You understand, I'm sure."

"Of course," Geary said. Deciding to use the secure conference room, Geary led the way.

Feeling the silence awkward as they walked, Geary tried some conversation. "That's a nice collection of new warships that came with you."

"New and better," General Julian said, sounding as if they were his ships to be proud of. "Better all around. Weapons, armor, maneuverability. And the officers and crews have been handpicked."

Geary managed to keep his face from showing his reaction to that boast. Because if the crews of these new ships had been "handpicked," that meant the replacements he'd received for his ships had been those who hadn't measured up to whatever requirements had been used.

Reaching the secure conference room, Geary led the way inside.

General Julian, though, paused outside it, looking around. "I could use some coffee."

"There's a break room right down the passageway," Geary said. "I'll show you the way."

"Umm . . ." The general looked at Geary as if trying to determine whether or not he was serious. "Never mind." Julian came into the compartment. Rather than sit down, he walked about, appearing to examine the walls, as the door sealed and the security measures activated. "I'm bringing important orders."

"So I understand," Geary said.

"There are some major policy changes being implemented." He had been carrying a data pad and now offered it to Geary.

He looked it over, seeing the High Security Restricted Access Eyes Only labels on the cover.

"Major changes?" Geary asked as he opened the cover and waited for the data pad to confirm his biometrics.

"This mission is being militarized," the general said, smiling. "You no longer have to pay any attention to that ambassador."

"Militarized?" Geary demanded, staring at Julian.

"That's right. I'm in overall charge of the region."

"What region?"

Julian made an expansive gesture. "Everything from Midway out to here, and extending into the various alien-controlled star systems."

"That . . . is a very large region of space," Geary said, trying to grasp what he'd just been told.

"Don't worry," General Julian said, smiling reassuringly. "You're still in charge of all the fleet assets. Your expertise will be needed in carrying out our missions."

"Missions." Geary began reading the orders, thinking that Julian must be overstating things, but almost immediately stopped in disbelief. "An ultimatum? To the Dancers?"

"Yes. The, uh, spider-wolves," General Julian said. "The Alliance is done messing around with them."

"You do realize that the Dancers have aided us in the past? And that they are technologically superior to us?"

"They haven't demonstrated any major military advantage over us," the general said, waving away the objection. "If they make the mistake of resisting our demands, human courage, human genius, will more than compensate for any minor capability shortfall."

"How can you—?" Geary forced himself to stop speaking and start again. "Who are these orders from?"

"The Senate, of course."

The orders looked like they had come from the Senate. But it made no sense. Why would the Senate, war-weary for the most part, and argumentative as they debated the Unity Alternate and Defender Fleet scandals, have agreed to deliver an ultimatum to the Dancers?

And what about what the Senate didn't know, couldn't have known, when Julian left Alliance space? "What about the Taon?"

"The what?" General Julian appeared annoyed at the question.

"Another alien species we've made contact with, one which we know has significant military advantages over us. Ship for ship, their weapons are more powerful, their shields stronger, and their ability to maneuver is superior to ours."

"Oh." Julian waved off Geary's statement. It appeared to be a favorite gesture for handling unwelcome information. "They can't fight better than us. That's what matters."

It was as if he was back talking to Captain Falco, years ago, listening to the guiding military philosophy that had developed from despair rather than lessons learned, and had led to repeated bloodbaths as the war with the Syndicate Worlds ground on without end. The fact that military way of thinking had been justified as "what Black Jack would do" only made it more insane to him. He'd shown everyone the importance of fighting smarter, not harder, that every life had to count instead of being just a name on an endless list of casualties.

And yet, only a short time later, he was being confronted with that same thinking again, from a highly ranked officer selected for a major command.

He'd been warned of this, long ago, by an instructor at Fleet Officers

School, a warrant officer who didn't care whether his lessons met with official approval. *Militaries are conservative when it comes to traditions, and when it comes to lessons learned in blood that they'll toss out in a heartbeat so they can go back to doing what they used to do even if it was stupid.* Young, idealistic John Geary had scoffed at the words, certain that common sense would rule out something like that. Because young, idealistic John Geary hadn't yet learned how often common sense seemed to have nothing to do with military decisions.

But he still couldn't believe this, and still protested. "And the Wooareek?"

"Wooareek?" General Julian's annoyance increased. "What are Wooareek?"

"Another alien species. So far ahead of us technologically our best physicists can't even conceive of how they are doing things we've watched them do."

"Such as?" Julian asked skeptically.

"Instantly go from orbital velocity to point five light speed. No acceleration. Just an instant change in velocity."

Julian twitched his lips in a very brief smile. "They can't outrun a hell lance, can they?"

"We can't target them at that velocity, General. Our systems aren't capable of it."

"You're not afraid of these nonhuman species, are you?" General Julian asked, his voicing mixing apparent disbelief with a clear taunt.

"I don't pick fights with people stronger than me unless I have to," Geary said, refusing to respond to the mockery.

Julian grinned, showing his canines. "Then I assume you won't pick a fight with me, Admiral. We have a lot to do, together, after we've dealt with these spider-wolves."

A lot to do *after* provoking war with the Dancers? Ignoring the general's claim that he had superior strength, Geary looked down, reading more. "Midway Star System is included in this militarized region? Midway is not part of the Alliance. We can't simply assert control over their star system."

"That says we can," General Julian said, reaching out to tap the data pad that Geary was holding. "There are no neutrals when the survival of the human race, and the Alliance, is on the line. Midway will either join the Alliance, under terms we dictate, or be treated as an enemy star system. We don't anticipate any problems. Midway's leaders are Syndic CEOs. They can always be bought. And if the price is too high they can be replaced by leaders who'll follow orders."

Geary took a long moment to calm himself before speaking again. "General Drakon and President Iceni are not typical Syndic CEOs. They will fight rather than submit to these demands."

"Then they'll be crushed," General Julian said. "Their forces are no match for our fleet. They must have known this would happen when we linked their hypernet gate to the Alliance. Now they either accept it, or we get rid of them and impose direct rule."

He had thought nothing else in these orders would surprise him, but still gazed in disbelief at the next section. "We're to carry out a campaign to weaponize enigma hypernet gates and destroy enigma-controlled star systems?"

"That's right. No more games. They've attacked humanity." Julian smiled again, showing a lot of teeth. "I have some experts with me who think they have worked out how to take control of the alien hypernet gates, disable any safeguards, and ensure the gates' collapses wipe out any and all enigmas in each star system." He paused, tapping the data pad again. "You might not have noticed this yet, but this also calls for the immediate arrest of Captain Honore Bradamont on charges of treason and espionage. You'll want to get that done as soon as possible."

Geary breathed in slowly, skipping to the end of the orders. "Issued by authority granted under the Alliance Wartime Emergency Act. Who issued these orders? Do they really come from the Senate?"

"Of course they do," General Julian said. "I understand these policy shifts are a little hard to grasp after the weak-kneed actions the Alliance government has followed since we defeated the Syndics. But now we're going to act from strength. Humanity can no longer afford half measures and blind hope when faced with real aliens and the dangers they represent."

Geary stared at Julian, then heard himself saying something he'd never expected to say, claiming credit for the end of the war. "*We* didn't defeat the Syndics, General. I did. With the critical support of the personnel in this fleet."

Julian seemed taken aback for a moment, then grinned again. "Which means you understand the need for us to act now. I'm looking forward to having you under my command. Now, I need to get back to *Implacable*. There are some things that need to be done regarding *Boundless*. Let me know when you want to discuss our plans for dealing with Midway and the enigma campaign. I won't need your input when issuing the ultimatum to the spider-wolves." His smile grew. "Great times, eh? Humanity is going to make sure other species respect it, and we're going to make sure any species that doesn't respect us is going to regret it."

It took every bit of Geary's control to remain outwardly calm while he saw General Julian back to his shuttle.

Captain Desjani was waiting at the shuttle dock, and instantly sensed his mood. "What's going on?" Desjani asked him in a low voice the moment the ramp sealed on Julian's shuttle.

"I need a status report on *Boundless*. Talk to someone on the ship and find out if anything is going on."

"Yes, Admiral. You're about to explode inside. I can tell. What's going on?"

"I'll let you know in a little while." He already knew what he had to do. The one thing he'd always sworn not to do. But he was finally being forced into it. "Talk to *Boundless*, and then please ask Kommodor Bradamont and Colonel Rogero to come to my stateroom as quickly as possible."

Desjani saluted. "Yes, Admiral."

Less than five minutes later, Desjani knocked on the door to Geary's stateroom. "Something's not right on *Boundless*," she said. "I asked to talk to Captain Matson and one of Colonel Webb's people told me Matson wasn't available."

"I just tried to speak with Ambassador Rycerz," Geary said. "A sergeant informed me that the ambassador was not available."

"What's going on?"

Geary sat down, rubbing his forehead. "Article 16 of fleet regulations hasn't changed since I was first commissioned over a century ago, and Alliance law still provides backup to that article."

"Article 16?" Desjani asked. "The Reasonable Article?"

"Yes," Geary said. So it was still called that. "Anytime an officer has reasonable grounds to believe an order is either issued in error, or improperly issued contrary to Alliance law or fleet regulations, that officer is obligated to confirm the accuracy of the order and its legitimacy before obeying it."

"Why would you be talking about Article 16?" Desjani asked, her eyes wary.

"Because of this," Geary said, gesturing to the high-security data pad holding the new orders.

"I don't know how it was a century ago, Admiral," Desjani said, spacing her words carefully, "but in recent decades at least we've been warned that anyone invoking Article 16 had better have very, very good grounds for it. And even if they do they're probably going to get kicked out of the fleet afterwards."

"That's the way it was a century ago," Geary said. "But Article 16 is in there for a reason. Its use wasn't exactly encouraged a century ago, either, but we were taught that the founding members of the Alliance insisted on it being part of military regulations for any Alliance forces. They didn't want any officer being able to claim they had no alternative but to obey orders. Maybe that's another thing that was forgotten in a hundred years of war. But if I have to choose a hill to die on, I will not hesitate if that hill is Article 16."

Desjani stared at him. "Just how bad are these orders that you're talking about Article 16?"

"Extremely bad. Contrary to reason and contrary to the principles of the Alliance." He paused as Bradamont and Rogero arrived. "I'm going to call a meeting of all the fleet's commanding officers, but before I do that there's something I have to let you know."

"Does this pertain to Midway?" Bradamont asked.

"Yes. And to you, personally. Kommodor, I was brought new orders by General Julian. Orders purportedly approved by the Alliance Senate. I have asked you here to inform you that one of those orders requires me to have you immediately arrested and returned to the Alliance for trial."

Bradamont and Rogero both stared at him in shock. Rogero recovered quickly, though, his face tightening with anger. He opened his mouth, but Bradamont held out a restraining hand. "Let the admiral speak. He asked us here for a reason."

"I have no intention of carrying out that order," Geary continued. "It would be a betrayal of our agreement with Midway, and a violation of my own personal word of honor. You have done nothing to negate our deal and *will* be returned safely to Midway, Kommodor. As I promised."

Colonel Rogero relaxed. "General Drakon judged you right, Admiral. You keep the deals you make."

"I'm glad someone will be happy about what I'm doing," Geary said.

"That's only one of the orders you've received?" Desjani said, not bothering to hide her disbelief.

"And not the worst," Geary said. "General Charban," he added as Charban also arrived. "Please inform the Dancers as quickly as possible to disregard any transmissions from *Boundless*. They should only pay attention to anything sent from *Dauntless*."

Charban jerked with surprise. "You're going to freeze out Ambassador Rycerz?"

"No, General, I'm going to try to rescue the ambassador and salvage a mission that others are about to sabotage. Get that message out."

"On my way," Charban said, walking quickly out of the stateroom.

"Captain Desjani, please arrange a fleet conference as soon as possible. I do not want General Julian there, but General Carabali should attend. Besides Carabali, every commanding officer of every ship. I want to tell them what's happening, and what I will do. But given the . . . nature of the betrayal of trust in my orders regarding you, Kommodor, I wanted you to know going in what was going to be said, and what I was going to do."

"What is happening, Admiral?" Bradamont asked, her eyes worried.

"I don't know for certain. The most likely possibilities are either someone is trying to stage a coup and trick me into playing along, or the Alliance government has forfeited its right to govern," Geary said, knowing full well the weight of his words.

"I hope it's the first thing," Desjani said, her expression hardening. "That's something we can fight."

"Yes," Geary said. "It is."

"What if it's the second thing, Admiral?" Bradamont asked.

"Then I will honor my ancestors by my actions," Geary said.

TWENTY minutes later, Geary stood at the head of the table in the conference room. Just as when he'd first assumed command of the fleet years ago when it teetered on the edge of disaster at the Syndicate Worlds home star system, every commanding officer in the fleet was virtually "seated" at the table, the more senior closest to Geary, the most junior down at the other "end." But if he looked at any one officer, their virtual self would be brought close, and anything anyone said would be heard as clearly as if they were seated next to every other person.

Back then, the fleet whose command he'd inherited had teetered on the edge of mutiny, battered and bled by a century of war, the officers increasingly convinced that their failure to win must be laid at the feet of the Alliance government. Geary had bent every effort to convince them otherwise, to remind them what the Alliance was supposed to be, to show them that taking over the government to save the Alliance would just be another way of destroying the Alliance. And he'd succeeded in that.

But now . . .

He hadn't called such meetings of the fleet's commanding officers very often, and rarely on such short notice. Geary could feel the tension coming off even the virtual presences as they waited for him to speak.

Aside from Geary, those physically attending the meeting were Captain Desjani, General Charban, and (to her bafflement at having her presence requested) Dr. Jasmine Cresida. Besides the fleet's commanding officers, General Carabali was also present in virtual form.

There were thirty-five new faces, the officers commanding the ships which had brought General Julian. Of them, Captain Constantine Rogov was closest, eyeing Admiral Geary with a slight smile, as if happily anticipating what he would say.

"I have called this meeting," Geary said, speaking calmly and firmly, "because I am in receipt of new orders. As nearly as I can determine, those orders are authentic. However, in my judgment these orders were either issued in error, or improperly issued contrary to Alliance law or fleet regulations," he said, deliberately quoting the words. "Therefore, in accordance with my responsibility as an officer of the Alliance, I am invoking Article 16 of the Alliance Military Code."

He paused to let a shocked ripple of reaction run through those listening. If he'd pulled out a sidearm and shot Dr. Cresida it might have generated the same reaction.

Captain Rogov's smile had disappeared.

"I am well aware that Article 16 is not to be lightly invoked," Geary continued. "I am well aware of the potential personal consequences to me for taking such action. But I do not feel I have any alternative in light of the orders brought to me by General Julian."

He noticed people quickly looking around, trying to see if Julian was present at the meeting, and just as quickly realizing that he was not.

"The responsibility for this decision is mine alone," Geary said. "The consequences should fall nowhere but on me. I am aware that you all must decide whether to continue following my orders. I hope that you will do so, for the good of the Alliance. But rather than demanding your continued loyalty I will explain the reasons for my decision.

"These orders," Geary said, holding up the high-security data pad, "contradict the orders I personally received from the Senate at Unity Star System. While apparently valid, with all proper verification, and declaring they are issued in accordance with the Alliance Wartime Emergency Act, they do *not* explicitly state that these orders supersede or replace my earlier orders. Given how extreme the difference between the orders I personally received and these orders, I have serious doubts as to their validity. For those reasons alone, I would hesitate to accept that these orders are both correct and legitimate."

He paused once more, feeling how everyone was hanging on his words. "But you deserve to know the content of the orders themselves. They claim the entire region of space beyond current Alliance territory has been placed under exclusive military control." Geary heard surprised gasps as he continued. "Including this star system. Including all star systems controlled by all alien species, even though when these orders must have been written no one in the Alliance knew we had made contact with either the Taon or the Wooareek."

He paused again for just a moment. "The orders remove Ambassador Rycerz from any position of authority and place all such authority in the hands of General Julian. I am supposed to remain in command of all fleet assets, but under General Julian's control. Again, this contradicts orders I received directly from the Alliance Senate."

Captain Duellos was shocked into speaking out of turn. "Why would they militarize this star system?"

"Because," Geary said, "as part of these orders, General Julian intends giving an ultimatum to the Dancers, demanding they submit to certain agreements with the Alliance government, including technology transfer."

"An ultimatum?" Duellos said, looking stunned. "And what are we supposed to do when the Dancers refuse?"

"According to these orders," Geary said, "if the Dancers refuse the ultimatum, they are to be regarded as hostile and treated as an enemy to humanity."

He wasn't sure a fleet meeting had ever gotten this quiet. Utter silence reigned as officers stared at him and at each other.

"If I may," General Charban said, "I was not surprised by the admiral's news because that ultimatum has already been issued from the transmitter aboard *Boundless*. *Boundless* itself appears to have been taken over by Colonel Webb's soldiers under orders from General Julian and is totally under their control."

"We sent the Dancers an ultimatum?" Captain Parr of the *Incredible* demanded. "Did you actually say that?"

"I did," Charban said. "The ultimatum wasn't formatted properly, so the Dancers would have probably ignored it anyway. But, on orders from Admiral Geary, I had already told the Dancers to disregard any transmissions from *Boundless*."

"We're going to declare war on the Dancers?" Captain Armus asked, speaking even more slowly and deliberately than usual. "Why?"

"To try to force them to share their technology with us," General Charban said. "That's the gist of the ultimatum."

"The Dancers fought alongside us at Unity Alternate," Armus said. "That is not how battle comrades are treated."

"I agree," Geary said. "I also see no possibility that the Dancers will submit, which would mean war with the Dancers, starting in this star system."

"Nonetheless, Admiral," Armus continued, frowning mightily. "To invoke Article 16 is an extreme measure. As you have reminded us, just because we don't like an order, or think it unwise, is not grounds for refusing to obey it."

Captain Plant nodded. "Captain Armus is right. I don't see the wisdom in your orders, Admiral, but to refuse to carry out orders from the Alliance government would be even more unwise."

"Exactly! That is not our decision to make!" Captain Rogov had recovered from his surprise enough to finally join the debate. "We have orders to carry out."

Geary waited to see if anyone else would reply.

Armus did, speaking with the firmness of the rock he had sometimes been compared to. "What do the Marines say?"

Every eye turned toward General Carabali. She looked back at them, her expression unrevealing. "The Marines are awaiting the outcome of this discussion to decide the appropriate action."

Desjani leaned close to Geary to whisper. "You've got about half of them. The other half are scared of using Article 16. The junior ship commanders are waiting to see how the senior captains go. This could tip either way."

He thought her estimate was right, but he had a powerful tool yet to employ. "I should provide you with the other measures called for by these orders," Geary said, using the meeting software to mute the other voices trying to chime in. "These orders also call for us to return to Midway Star System with sufficient force to deliver a different ultimatum there, demanding that Midway join the Alliance or else submit to occupation by Alliance forces."

"What?" Captain Parr cried out, no longer just baffled, but outraged. He'd been one of those who seemed on the fence, not happy with the orders about the Dancers but also distressed by the idea of using Article 16. "We can't force someone to join the Alliance. That's a violation of the founding principles. Star system membership in the Alliance is and remains voluntary."

"I am aware of that," Geary said. "That is another reason for me to distrust these orders. Why would the Senate demand such an action? You all know how many of the star systems in the Alliance would react to the use of the fleet to coerce a star system into joining."

General Carabali gestured slightly. "Occupation? You're talking about landing and seizing control of the primary planet and all orbital facilities?"

"That's correct," Geary said.

"We do not have sufficient Marines to carry out that operation," Carabali said. "Not against General Drakon's ground forces."

Armus frowned again. "You would have full fleet support backed by control of all space within the star system."

"If you want to bombard the planet to dust, fine," Carabali said. "If you want to take possession of a habitable planet and usable facilities, no."

"Syndics—" someone started to say.

"They aren't Syndics. Not anymore. My Marines have gotten to know the quality of Drakon's soldiers. They're good."

"Why do we need Midway so badly?" General Charban asked.

"It's to serve as a forward base for operations," Geary said.

"Operations?" Duellos asked. "For war against the Dancers?"

"Not only that," Geary said. "Following the . . . forced occupation of Midway, we are supposed to use that star system as a forward base for . . ." He had to take a moment before saying the next words. "For exterminating the enigma presence at every star system we can reach."

"Exterminate?" Captain Badaya said. "How? Bombardment from space?"

"By taking control of enigma hypernet gates, weaponizing them, and causing them to collapse at full nova-scale strength."

Once again, the conference room had become silent.

"Admiral," Captain Vitali of the battle cruiser *Daring* said, "those instructions are clearly spelled out in these new orders? They're not an interpretation?"

"They are clearly spelled out," Geary said.

"Admiral, I was not prepared to support your arguments, but . . . haven't they seen what Kalixa is like? They want to do that again and again?"

"Extermination?" General Charban said. "Are we Syndics?"

Captain Rogov spoke up again. "I realize these orders are surprising, but, Admiral, if it is the decision of the Alliance to carry out such actions, we have no grounds for failing to obey orders."

"Orders to commit genocide?" Captain Parr demanded of Rogov. "Orders to force a neutral star system to join the Alliance or become occupied territory?"

"It is not our place to argue the wisdom of orders from higher authority," Rogov replied. "We are not aware of their reasons. But we all know what a danger the enigmas pose. Midway knows as well. They will surely agree to join the Alliance, not have to be forced, when told that doing so will result in the elimination of the enigma threat."

"Will they?" Parr asked, skeptical. "Has this idea been presented to Honore Bradamont? She could tell us how Midway's leaders will react."

"Bradamont should already be under arrest for treason," Rogov said, looking to Geary for confirmation.

"That action is also contained in these orders," Geary said.

"Captain Bradamont has done nothing against the Alliance," Duellos argued.

"Then she has nothing to fear from a court-martial," Captain Rogov said.

"I am uncomfortable with this," Captain Vitali said. "My father told me about the spy hunts in the fleet thirty years ago. How much damage they did and how many officers were dishonored without cause."

Geary muted everyone else again as arguments erupted. Bradamont had served in this fleet, and been well respected. She still had a lot of friends. "I should clarify that Honore Bradamont has not been arrested. She is with this fleet as part of a diplomatic agreement with Midway. Arresting her would violate that agreement, which I also promised to honor. It is required of us by Article 16 to question orders that give every appearance of error or being improperly issued. I am doing so. I will not carry out orders that do not appear to be legitimate, not until I can personally confirm that they were issued appropriately by authorities authorized to issue such orders."

"Admiral," General Carabali said, "what will you do if those orders are eventually confirmed by Fleet Headquarters and the Alliance Senate?"

Geary inhaled deeply before replying. "If that happens, I will resign rather than carry out actions contrary to the laws and principles of the Alliance, and I will urge every other officer in the fleet to do the same, and I will issue public statements that the government of the Alliance no longer has my support." He waited a few seconds, seeing all of the eyes riveted on him. "I must add that I consider it highly unlikely that the Alliance Senate has approved these orders."

"Who sent them, then?" Captain Rogov protested. "The orders are in proper format and came to you through proper channels."

"I intend finding out exactly who sent them," Geary said.

Rogov shook his head vigorously, looking about the conference table. "This is about Desjani's orders, isn't it, Admiral? Isn't that what this is about?"

Desjani gave Geary a curious look.

He nodded to her. "The orders do also relieve Captain Desjani of command of *Dauntless*, replacing her with an officer currently serving with General Julian," Geary said. "That, too, conflicts with my orders directly from the Senate that I have full authority over every person under my command. I am curious, Captain Rogov. General Julian assured me that only he knew the contents of those orders. How is it that you are aware of so many of the actions contained in them?"

Rogov looked at Geary, his mouth opening, then closing, with no words coming out.

Captain Armus spoke up, his voice rougher than usual. "With all due respect to *Dauntless*'s commanding officer, Captain Desjani's fate is a very minor issue here. The rest of the orders sent to the admiral are what matters."

"That is not our call to make," another officer spoke up.

Geary focused on her, the software obligingly popping up a box with identifying data. Captain Petra Bai, commanding officer of the newly arrived battle cruiser *Invincible*.

"Article 16 says it is our call to make," Captain Duellos said, his voice cool.

Captain Rogov shook his head. "You heard the admiral. General Julian has been appointed overall commander of this region of space. It is his right, and only his, to make such a determination."

"Until these orders are confirmed," Geary said, "I consider myself to remain in command of every fleet asset in this star system, in accordance with my orders from the Alliance Senate."

Rogov turned toward General Carabali, gesturing about him. "Surely the Marines will not sit still for this refusal to accept the legitimacy of orders from higher authority!"

Carabali turned an icy look on Rogov. "Do not presume to lecture Marines on loyalty to the Alliance."

"This man," Rogov insisted, pointing at Geary, "is refusing orders. He is betraying the Alliance!"

Captain Badaya, uncharacteristically almost silent until now, burst out into laughter. "Really! You're accusing Black Jack Geary, greatest hero of the Alliance, of betraying it? We were taught he was the perfect officer!"

"There's no humor in this," Captain Bai shot back at Badaya. "And you of all people should know it. I am aware of conversations you have had in the past, Captain, conversations regarding overthrowing legitimate authority. You should walk carefully here. If such things were to become public knowledge, it would create major problems for you."

Silence again, until Badaya laughed once more. "You're aware of such things, are you? Then be aware of this. Publish it and be damned! I've *done* nothing, undertaken no action, not consistent with my oath to the Alliance." He pointed at Geary. "The admiral, Black Jack—if you'll forgive me for once more bringing up that nickname, Admiral— has not proposed taking any action against the Alliance. He has invoked Article 16, which is his right and responsibility under Alliance law, and is refusing to carry out orders he has not confirmed are proper. I'll go one step beyond the admiral, though, and say what I know a lot of those here are thinking. These orders don't just appear suspicious; they also seem to be the work of total idiots. That might be regarded by some as proof they did come from Fleet Headquarters. But that is not sufficient proof for me!"

Captain Jane Geary had been quiet until now, knowing that her loyalty to the admiral would be assumed. "The Gearys stand together. For the Alliance."

"For the Alliance?" Captain Plant asked. "We have our orders. Our default is that orders must be obeyed."

Geary shook his head. "The Alliance was not founded on blind obedience to orders. Especially when those orders would violate the laws of the Alliance."

"You cannot know—" Rogov began.

"He's Black Jack, you idiot!" Captain Badaya yelled. "My apologies, Admiral, for my unprofessional behavior just now," he added in a normal voice.

Geary had rushed the meeting with his fleet commanding officers to get it going while General Julian was still aboard *Boundless* sending his ultimatum. It had been easy to block anyone on *Boundless* from joining the meeting. But he knew Julian would rush back to *Implacable* when informed of it.

So it was at that moment that General Julian's virtual presence appeared in the meeting. "What is going on here?" he demanded in loud tones that had probably sent shivers down the backs of countless subordinates. "I should have been informed of this meeting." He looked around, narrow eyed, as if memorizing faces.

"I called this meeting," Geary said. "To inform my officers that I am invoking Article 16 in regard to those orders you delivered."

Julian turned a bristling glare on Geary. "The contents of those orders are for your eyes only. If you have shared any information from them . . ." He let the words trail off in a vaguely menacing way.

Geary smiled in a way that didn't touch his eyes. "How strange that Captain Rogov seems to know a great deal of the information from those orders. How is that, General?"

"I order you—"

"You do not have authority over me. My orders come directly from the Senate." Geary touched the data pad. "I have no idea where these orders came from." He looked from General Julian over at Rogov and Bai. "And, pursuant to my orders from the Senate, I am directing all ships in this star system to report only to me and accept orders only from me. I am also directing you, General, to release *Boundless* and all aboard her from your control."

"You're either crazy or a fool," General Julian said. He turned to look down the conference table. Geary could have silenced him, but decided to let Julian talk. "You all learned the same lesson that I did from our long war with the Syndics. Any sign of weakness provokes danger. Only strength can create the kind of respect that will protect the Alliance from its enemies." He turned a hard gaze on Geary. "Enemies both human and alien, and those humans who place their love for aliens above their loyalty to humanity."

Captain Duellos spoke in almost a drawl. "You mean the sort of strength that would force a star system to either join the Alliance or be conquered?"

"It's for their own good, and the good of humanity," Julian said.

Captain Hiyen stood up, his voice heavy. "If the Callas Republic hears of such orders, of intent to force any star system into membership in the Alliance, I am certain it will sever all remaining ties with the Alliance."

"That would be a serious mistake," General Julian said.

"Is that a threat?" Hiyen asked as if unable to believe his ears. "Did you just threaten the Callas Republic?"

"It wasn't a threat," Julian said, looking as if he wanted to backpedal but wouldn't. "I'm simply reminding you, and everyone here, that all of humanity, every star system, has to stand united against the alien threat."

"Stand united whether they like it or not?" Captain Badaya said. Always a verbal bomb thrower by nature, Badaya seemed to be enjoying this meeting a great deal.

Hiyen had the appearance of someone trying to control growing anger. "What you describe is not an Alliance, General. It is an empire. As the senior representative of the Callas Republic in this fleet I tell you that we will have no part in it."

"You are relieved of command," General Julian said. "I'll send another officer to take command of . . . *Reprisal.*"

"Are you insane?" Hiyen asked. "No one can relieve me of command except the Callas Republic. That is clearly spelled out in the terms under which the republic joined the war against the Syndicate Worlds."

Julian looked around again, focusing on General Carabali. "Send Marines to that ship and arrest that officer," he said, pointing at Hiyen.

Carabali gave Julian a bland look, shaking her head. "I do not have authority to carry out such an arrest of an officer of an allied government."

"General," Captain Armus said, his frown deeper than ever, "has an ultimatum indeed been sent to the Dancers?"

"That's correct. We're letting them know who's boss."

"And if the Dancers do not comply with this ultimatum, we will attack them?"

"If necessary," General Julian said. "Any minor Dancer advantages in terms of technology will be easily overcome by human fighting spirit and our numerical advantages in this star system. We will prevail."

"What if the Dancers have a mutual defense agreement with the Taon?" Commander Boudreaux called out. "Or with the Wooareek?"

"Are you scared of these aliens?" Julian scoffed.

"Yes, General, I am," Boudreaux said. "If I want to commit suicide, I'll do it on my own rather than take my entire crew with me by trying to attack the Wooareek."

Captain Smythe, who had been sitting on the sidelines, watching and waiting, finally erupted. "You want to start a war with the Dancers here? We're isolated deep inside Dancer-controlled space! What happens after we 'prevail' in this star system?"

"We have the auxiliaries," Captain Bai said. "We can fight our way through as many spider-wolf star systems as needed."

"The Dancer ships are faster than ours," Duellos said, "and their weapons more accurate. And, as engineers, they know those auxiliaries are our weak point. The Dancers will destroy the auxiliaries first."

"That's not a problem," General Julian said, his voice dripping with scorn. "Why would we have to use jump drives? Think about it! There's a hypernet gate here. We linked the hypernet gate at Midway to the Alliance hypernet. We have the same expertise here. We can do the same thing in this star system with the alien hypernet gate."

"Are you a complete idiot?"

Geary had asked Dr. Cresida to be at this meeting because he thought that issue might come up. And, as he had hoped, when it did she didn't hold back.

"Who the hell are you?" Julian demanded.

"Dr. Jasmine Cresida! The person who developed the theoretical basis for linking Midway's gate to the Alliance hypernet, and the person who led the team that carried out that linkage!"

General Charban, used to dealing with Cresida, spoke up while General Julian fumbled for a reply. "Doctor, are you saying that any plan to make use of the Dancer hypernet by taking control of it is unrealistic?"

"I am saying it is total fantasy! The Dancer hypernet employs the same theoretical basis as ours, but it implements that using a different technological approach. An approach of which we know effectively nothing except that remote analysis of the Dancer gates confirmed they are not constructed along the same lines as ours."

Julian had finally found his voice. "Just because you can't—"

"No one can! Were those words small enough for you to understand?"

The general's glare looked as if it could have melted its way through a meter of armor. "My experts say otherwise. They say we can do it."

"Experts? What experts?" Cresida demanded.

"Dr. Frederick Lobachevski and Dr. Deena Resandia!" Julian announced triumphantly.

Cresida actually managed to look more angry. "Lobachevski is a moron who thinks if he makes up things to balance an equation it proves he's right! And Resandia nearly bankrupted an entire star system by promising to deliver a next-generation hypernet that never worked! Your experts are scientific snake-oil peddlers."

Geary, despite enjoying seeing Julian's smugness dressed down, didn't want Cresida to generate any reflexive support for a military officer being chewed out by a civilian. Especially a civilian with the chewing-out gifts of Dr. Cresida. "Thank you, Doctor. I think you've made your point very clear. We cannot use the Dancer gates without their full cooperation."

General Julian shook his head, pointing at Cresida. "Why would we credit the words of this civilian? Someone with no connection to the military? Someone who does not understand our ability to get things done? Someone who never sacrificed as we have?"

"Excuse me." Captain Armus rarely looked angry. He did now. "General, you should be aware that Dr. Cresida's sister died as part of this fleet. Her sister, may her memory always be honored, was a fine battle cruiser commander who served with distinction and died valiantly fighting the Syndics. It is unbecoming of a senior officer to defame her family."

Watching Julian, Geary saw the knowledge that he'd made a big mistake flash across his face. An attack on Dr. Cresida was viewed by the fleet as an attack on her sister, Jaylen Cresida, whose memory was indeed honored. Did Julian also realize that Geary had laid that trap for him, hoping he'd step into it?

Armus, at first not at all supportive of Geary invoking Article 16, was clearly wavering. But he had yet to express support for Geary's position, or a willingness to follow Geary's orders after this. And a rough estimate of attitudes among the other commanding officers was that perhaps a third were still in the same boat with Armus, not happy at all with the new orders, but unwilling to commit to not following those orders.

He needed another lever. But what?

THIRTEEN

"HOLD on," an officer said.

Geary focused on her. Commander Thalente Hasan of the new heavy cruiser *Gusoku*, the same name as a ship that had been destroyed at Cavalos Star System fighting the Syndics.

"This is not adding up," Commander Hasan continued. "We were told that this mission had the strong backing of Admiral Geary, and that the orders had been issued at the urging of Admiral Geary. Yet he is telling us he had no knowledge of these orders before this, and does not seem at all pleased with them."

"Do *you* have a problem with your orders?" General Julian demanded.

"No, sir. Yes, sir," Hasan said. "I agree with what needs to be done. But there is something wrong here. I think it should be clarified."

"It should be clarified," another new voice said. Lieutenant Commander Banoy Genji from the heavy cruiser *Citadel*, replacing a namesake lost in battle at Vidha Star System. "Admiral Geary's example, and support, are critical to this mission, aren't they? I don't understand why he is objecting so strongly to this if the whole thing is his idea."

Captain Rogov turned a glare on Lieutenant Commander Genji. "Do you understand *your* orders?"

"Yes, sir."

"Then why are you questioning them?"

Genji's face tightened with anger at the rebuke delivered in front of so many others. "Admiral Geary—"

"Is not in command here!"

"The orders say he's supposed to be!" Commander Hasan protested. "Don't they? All *Citadel*'s commanding officer and I are trying to—" She stopped speaking as Lieutenant Commander Genji's virtual presence vanished from the meeting.

General Julian spoke in the surprised quiet that followed Genji's disappearance. "Lieutenant Commander Genji has been relieved of command."

Geary moved to silence the babble of voices that arose but paused as Commander Hasan shouted. "The ground forces detachment aboard my ship is trying to break into my stateroom! My crew is resisting but unable to stop them."

"Ground forces?" General Carabali's parade-ground voice easily rode over all others. "Not Marines?"

"We don't have Marine detachments on our ships!" Hasan said, speaking quickly. "They're some sort of special forces without unit identification or patches. Wait, what—"

Commander Hasan's virtual presence vanished.

"Special forces without unit identification or patches?" Captain Parr said. "Arresting commanding officers in the middle of a fleet conference? What the hell is going on?"

"This is what happens on Syndic ships, I've been told," Captain Armus said, his voice a low, low rumble. "With special security forces aboard to ensure loyalty."

"Why aren't there Marines on those ships?" General Carabali demanded. "Fleet regulations call for Marines, not ground forces without unit identification."

"This," Captain Rogov announced, "is what happens when a senior officer starts questioning orders. Soon everyone is doing it. Even simple personnel decisions are questioned! Don't you see where this kind of anarchy will leave us?"

"I wish to speak with Commander Hasan," Captain Armus said. "Now."

"You will follow orders," General Julian said.

"I will follow orders," Captain Plant said. Heads turned to look at her, while Geary tried not to show his disappointment.

"I am an officer of the Alliance," Plant continued. "Sworn to uphold the laws and principles of the Alliance."

"But—" Captain Badaya began.

Captain Plant silenced Badaya with a gesture and a stern look. "I've made my decision. Which, as has been pointed out, is my responsibility under Article 16." She looked at Geary. "I will follow *your* orders, Admiral."

Badaya barked a relieved laugh. "You did that on purpose, Nanami."

"I do everything on purpose," Captain Plant replied.

"And you are now also relieved of command," General Julian said.

Captain Armus exhaled like a bull seeing a red flag. "That is enough. Despite my respect for Admiral Geary, I was not prepared to endorse his decision. Even though these orders seem designed to cause new wars and to force the Alliance into a different entity than it has always been. But Admiral Geary reminded us of something soon after he assumed command. He reminded us that we cannot become like our enemies. We cannot justify our actions by necessity. We must look to what the living stars demand of us, to what our ancestors would view with pride, to what our honor requires. And we must look to what the founders of the Alliance believed, and how they incorporated those beliefs into our laws and regulations. Including Article 16."

Armus fixed Julian with a hard look. "I will not be party to turning the Alliance fleet into something indistinguishable from a Syndic flotilla. Run by those who demand obedience to every order without question. I also now question the legitimacy of these orders. Either they are divorced from any consideration of their terrible consequences, or else they are designed to produce exactly those consequences. Admiral Geary is right to refuse to follow them without confirmation of their accuracy and confirmation of whether they were genuinely issued by the government as claimed."

Captain Armus came to his feet, slowly and steadily, turning to face Geary. "I await your orders, Admiral."

Duellos and Badaya stood up quickly, Desjani joining them, along with Parr, Smythe, Jane Geary, Vitali, and the other senior fleet captains. Geary saw ripples of movement down the table. Whether from peer pressure or genuine commitment, the other commanding officers of the fleet stood up en masse, looking to Geary. "That decides me as well," one announced. "I'm taking orders from the admiral."

But, aside from the now-gone commanding officers of *Gusoku* and *Citadel*, the other captains who had come with General Julian remained seated.

General Julian glared down the table. "So, you've made your decisions, have you? You're going to surrender the Alliance, surrender all humanity, to these ugly aliens? To these monsters? You're willing to have your families, your children, turned into meals for their ravenous appetites?"

"The Dancers are vegetarians," General Charban said.

"They— That's irrelevant!"

Geary shook his head, letting his feelings about Julian show. "You don't know even basic facts about the aliens, yet you feel confident you know exactly how to handle them, exactly what we should do. That is lousy tactics and horrible strategy. I saved this fleet once when reckless thinking trapped it deep inside enemy space. I won't see this fleet destroyed because you want to repeat that mistake with a species that isn't even our enemy. If you want to fight some aliens that badly, go visit a

Kick star system. They'll be happy to accommodate you with a battle to the death."

He gazed at the still-seated officers. "If you change your minds, you will be welcomed by your fellow officers. If you are afraid to change your minds, you might ask yourselves why you would follow the orders of someone who threatens you for standing up for the Alliance."

"This meeting is over," General Julian announced. He sent a demanding look along the row of seated officers, waiting as their virtual presences rapidly disappeared. When Captain Rogov, the last, had gone, Julian pointed at Geary. "I trust that you know the fate of traitors."

"I trust that you know that fate as well," Geary said. "To the honor of our ancestors."

The other remaining officers chorused the phrase en masse. The last reverberations of "ancestors" were still ringing through the compartment when General Julian's presence vanished.

It was a great moment.

It was a great moment that might mark the beginning of a civil war within the Alliance, unless he managed to defang Julian and deal with the substantial number of warships following his commands.

ENDING the meeting (which would all too likely also go down in the history books, though hopefully as a good thing) took a while. "Let your crews know what has happened, what my decision was, and why I made that decision. If you think I should speak to your crew, let me know." When it was done, Geary still had with him General Charban, Captain Desjani, and Dr. Cresida in person, and the virtual presences of the rest of the fleet's senior captains.

"What's the plan, Admiral?" Captain Badaya asked.

"The plan," Geary admitted, "had to wait on the outcome of the meeting. I didn't know what situation I'd face when it was over."

"Your opponents made the case for you," Captain Jane Geary said.

He knew why she hadn't jumped in more forcefully during the debate. Her support for him would be assumed, but too much vocal support from her could well have been seen as the Gearys trying to muscle the others present.

"Do you believe General Julian will order an attack on us?" Captain Armus said, still looking unhappy.

"No," Geary said. "I think he's capable of such an act, but even someone like Captain Rogov would push back against an order like that. Given the odds against the forces answering to Julian's orders, an attack on the rest of the fleet could have only one end."

"Shouldn't we go to alert status, anyway?" Captain Duellos asked. "So we won't be caught flat-footed if it comes?"

"No," Geary said again. "That might be read by Julian's ships as preparations by us to attack. I don't want to do anything to provoke combat between us and Julian's ships."

"Good," Armus said.

"It might still come to that," Captain Plant cautioned.

"Two of Julian's loyalists were coming around before they were relieved," General Charban said. "We should try to convince the others to listen to the admiral."

"Those others seemed pretty hard-core in support of General Julian," Captain Smythe observed.

"General Julian boasted to me that the officers and crews of those ships had been handpicked," Geary said.

"Is that so?" Captain Duellos said. "It's not very hard to guess what qualities they were handpicked for, is it?"

"No wonder we saw so few new replacements who were rabidly anti-alien," Desjani said. "As many as possible were being identified and sent to those new-construction warships."

"They're still vulnerable to argument," Charban said. "Those two ship commanders were surprised by the admiral's objections and wanted to find out more."

"How do we get through to them?"

"There are always channels," Geary said. "We need to get the senior enlisted talking to their counterparts on those ships."

"Are we certain the senior enlisted on our ships will follow our lead?" Armus asked.

"That's highly likely when it comes to the admiral leading this," Captain Duellos said. "But we should still be alert for, um, internal problems."

"The last thing anyone wanted was for it ever to come to this," Captain Plant said. She glanced at Badaya. "Most of us, anyway."

Badaya grinned in reply. "I am a loyal supporter of the admiral and of the government."

"*Boundless* is a problem," Captain Jane Geary said. "She's in Julian's hands now?"

Geary nodded. "Apparently. We need to find out if it's just Colonel Webb's soldiers enforcing martial law on *Boundless*, or if other ground forces troops have been sent to reinforce them."

General Carabali spread her open hands, palms down, in a warning gesture. "I see the need to retake *Boundless*, but doing that without creating combat between Webb's soldiers and my Marines might be impossible. And if fighting starts on *Boundless*, it could easily spread. General Julian would try to reinforce Webb and move warships to interdict any movement by us toward *Boundless*. That's not even bringing in the fact that *Boundless* is a very large hostage situation, with a lot of civilians we have to worry about."

"Any losses of civilians on *Boundless* would look particularly bad after *Fortuna*," Captain Plant added.

"Agreed. We need to avoid that," Geary said. "See what options you can come up with that might allow us to regain control of *Boundless* and free the ambassador. Without triggering a big fight with Colonel Webb's soldiers or creating conditions where the civilians aboard will be further endangered. I know how difficult this will be to carry off, if we can do it. I know it'll take a miracle. But see what you can give me."

"Certainly, Admiral. I'll see what can be done." General Carabali stood up, preparing to leave the meeting. "The Marines are used to being called on when someone needs a miracle."

After Carabali's virtual image vanished, Captain Duellos shook his head. "Do you suppose Marines ever have existential crises where they wonder if they're good enough for the job?"

"You're kidding, right?" Captain Desjani said.

Geary looked over at Dr. Cresida. "Doctor?"

She'd been listening silently since lambasting General Julian, but now turned a sharp gaze on him. "Admiral?"

"Thank you for making clear how unrealistic parts of General Julian's plans are."

"It was a pleasure," Cresida said. "Really. It was."

"Is what those orders called for possible, taking over the enigma hypernet gates and causing them to destructively collapse?"

Cresida hesitated for a long moment as if deciding what to reply. "I don't know. Probably not. Surely you don't expect me to assist in such an atrocity?"

"I am certain that you wouldn't," Geary said. "Others might. If those actions are possible, I want to know how they can be prevented. Your sister created the means to prevent using hypernet gates as weapons in human-occupied star systems. I want you, if possible, to help me ensure those gates can't be used as weapons anywhere no matter who built them."

"That's probably impossible," Dr. Cresida said.

"Then you're probably the best person to see if it can be done," Geary said. "Will you?"

Cresida eyed him for a long moment. "Since you're asking, I'll take a look at it. Am I right that all of you here have put your lives on the line by not following those apparently real orders?"

"I don't think they are real," Geary said. "But, yes."

"You have my thanks. I'm sure my sister would be pleased."

"Your sister would've been the first to stand by the admiral," Captain Armus said.

Dr. Cresida stared at Armus for a moment before finally nodding once. Rising, she left the compartment.

"What do you need from me?" Charban asked.

"General," Geary said, "I need you to get across to the Dancers that anything done by the ships responding to General Julian's orders are not signs that any of my ships are a threat. Let them know we're going to do everything we can to defuse this situation without any violence."

Charban nodded. "The Dancers will just tell us 'human problem, humans fix,' but it won't hurt to inform them of our current situation."

"I'd also like you and your unique set of co-workers," Geary added, "to put your minds to ways we can resolve this."

"We will do so." Charban saluted and left.

Geary looked at those remaining. "Thank you all. I know this wasn't an easy decision."

Armus made a face. "As Captain Geary said, General Julian himself was your greatest ally in convincing us to accept your arguments. Admiral, if we end up shooting at other Alliance warships, it will open rifts that may never heal."

"I know," Geary said. "I'm going to do my best to avoid that happening." He didn't say, because they all knew, that awful outcome might happen anyway, because avoiding it might be beyond anyone's power.

"CAPTAIN Rogov's ships are increasing their shield strength."

Geary had gone to *Dauntless*'s bridge to look at his display, viewing the formation that now consisted of the Alliance ships answering to his orders, and the bulge near the back of the formation that was made up of the ships answering to General Julian's orders. The opposed sides were close enough to each other to make anyone nervous. And nervous people and weapons were usually a bad mix.

Either Julian or Rogov or both might feel the same. Their ships had braked a little, just enough so that those ships were drifting farther behind the main Alliance formation with every minute.

Every ship they controlled except *Boundless*, that is. *Boundless* remained in the back center of Geary's formation, slightly cut off from Rogov's ships, but close enough for them easily to react if they saw any attack developing against *Boundless*.

Captain Desjani, in her command seat next to his, looked over at him. "Should we raise shields to match?"

"No," Geary said. "Rogov, and Julian, want to provoke something. If we match their moves we'll be doing what they want. I bet once enough time goes by without us matching their increase in shield strength they'll try powering up their hell lances."

"That would certainly concern me," Desjani said.

"If it comes to shooting," Geary said, "there has to be absolutely no question that it was initiated without cause by Rogov and Julian."

"Admiral?" Lieutenant Castries asked. "What are they going to do?"

He knew that question was also about *What are we going to do?* Which was more than fair, given that these officers had entrusted their fates to him in a situation that no one should have had to face.

"I think," Geary said, "that they don't know what they're going to do. Their plan was to have me buy into those false orders." He had decided from now on to simply call the orders false, because that was how they felt to him, and the Senate he had last met could not possibly have approved them. Which didn't mean there wasn't a chance some arms had been twisted and opponents sidelined to produce those orders. But if that was the case he would deal with it when the time came.

"Now they're stuck," Geary said. "They don't have sufficient numbers to attack those ships loyal to the Alliance." He had also decided to describe his ships in those terms from now on. "Their commanding officers may well be uncertain as to whether their crews would go along with orders to attack other Alliance ships. Without my backing, the

Dancers are ignoring the ultimatum that General Julian sent. So the general is doubtless trying to come up with another set of ideas to advance their plan to start a war with the Dancers."

"But why start a war with the Dancers?" Lieutenant Castries asked. "What would that gain us?"

"They're ugly aliens," Captain Desjani said. "And they have things we want. Their technology. What would a war accomplish? Maybe get us access to that technology. But it would also serve as justification for other actions."

"Such as forcing Midway Star System to join the Alliance," Geary said. "And, back in the Alliance, once the war begins it would considerably strengthen the hands of people who would use the war and the fear of aliens as reasons for gaining more power."

"Admiral, they wouldn't . . ." Castries paused. "The word going around is that General Julian threatened to take over the Callas Republic if they objected to any of this."

"That word is accurate," Geary said. "That's what whoever issued those orders wants. To have the excuse and the power to remake the Alliance."

"They won't get what they want," Lieutenant Castries said.

Desjani glanced at Geary and smiled: "My crew."

"Any readouts so far about the reactions among other crews?" Geary said.

"Everything I'm hearing is they're worried, but they're putting their trust in you. They know Admiral Geary cares about them, and their lives. Having the alternative be the lead butcher at Bloody Malphas made that decision easier." Desjani let her own concern show for a moment. "But I don't know how far you can push that."

"I understand. That's why I want to avoid ordering any offensive action."

"Then how do we get *Boundless* back?"

"Let's hope General Carabali comes up with a brilliant idea." Geary studied the image of *Boundless*, knowing his expression was as bleak as his thoughts. But something was teasing at his memory. Something . . . "Sergeant Tyminska."

"Admiral?"

"I need to talk to Gunnery Sergeant Orvis. And Master Chief Gioninni."

Ten minutes later, in Geary's stateroom, Orvis listened intently, his brow furrowed. "Yes, Admiral. Sergeant Tyminska and I talked a bit when she was aboard to check on that prisoner."

"What was your impression of her?" Geary asked.

"I thought she came across as a good, competent sergeant."

"Is there any way you know of to get in contact with her?" Geary nodded toward Gioninni, who had been listening with a calculating expression. "Any back-channel, unauthorized means to allow you to talk to Sergeant Tyminska?"

Orvis glanced at Gioninni. "There might be such a means, Admiral. Why?"

"I need to have someone Tyminska knows talk to her." Geary pointed at Orvis, then toward the image of *Boundless* on the display over his desk. "Someone she might listen to, who can find out how much Tyminska and the rest of Webb's people know about what's really going on."

"You think she might agree to help us?" Sergeant Orvis frowned heavily, taking on the aspect of someone about to say something difficult. "Admiral, I wouldn't count on it. There's a lot of unit loyalty involved in something like that."

Master Chief Gioninni nodded. "Special forces units tend to be really tight."

"Normally," Geary said. "But you both know what's gone on aboard *Boundless*. Colonel Webb's witch hunts. He did a lot of damage to the cohesion of his own unit. Maybe enough damage. If his own people's trust in Webb has been battered badly enough, maybe Tyminska will listen to you. I'm going to be trying to get through to Webb. Based on his actions when dealing with problems within the fleet, I don't think he was in on whatever General Julian is doing.

"Even if all you can do is confirm that it's only Webb's people controlling *Boundless*, that they haven't been reinforced by any soldiers Julian brought, that will be extremely valuable."

"Got it, Admiral."

"Is there any room for deals?" Gioninni asked hopefully.

Geary sat back, resting his chin on one fist as he regarded the master chief. "Yes. Our goal is to resolve everything without any combat, without anyone getting hurt. If someone is willing to cut a deal, I want to know about it."

"I got you, Admiral," Gioninni said. "And I won't need any piece of any deal. Just knowing you're grateful for my assistance in difficult circumstances, and might help me out if I ever got brought up on charges for something I'd never do."

"Let's see what you can swing, Master Chief," Geary said.

HE couldn't take anything for granted.

When General Julian's ships were five light seconds behind Geary's main fleet in their orbit about the star, they accelerated just enough to once again match velocity to the fleet and remain at that distance.

Geary roamed the passageways of *Dauntless*, trying his best to get a personal feel for how the sailors were reacting to the crisis.

They were understandably worried. But they also seemed ready and willing to continue following the orders of the officers who were following orders from Geary.

As Desjani said, they trusted him. They believed in him.

It should have been a nice thing to know, but instead it reinforced something he'd tried to deny ever since he'd assumed command of the fleet. Because, as far as he could tell, these sailors would've followed his orders even under much different circumstances.

What he was doing now was something many had feared he would do after being found and awakened, something that many others had hoped he would do. Black Jack, they thought, would use his enormous popularity and heroic reputation, ironically created by the government itself, to overthrow that government. "Fixing" the Alliance by shredding its founding principles. "Saving" the Alliance by destroying it.

Had this been inevitable ever since that day he found himself aboard *Dauntless*, being told that he'd been frozen in survival sleep for nearly a century in a damaged escape pod? Still reeling from the destruction of his heavy cruiser *Merlon* and the deaths of many of her crew in a legendary battle which to him had happened only the day before. Trying to grasp that everyone he'd once known was long dead in subsequent battles or just from old age. Trying to understand the awe and admiration and hope with which these people born long after his supposed death looked at him.

Being told by Victoria Rione exactly what those people expected of him.

What he was doing now was what Rione had been afraid Black Jack would do. Would she approve of this, though? Because if his suspicions were right and those orders were false, he wasn't acting against the government.

On the other hand, if those orders were authentic, if the Senate really had approved such actions, then Rione would agree that Black Jack had no Alliance left to save. It was already dead. And he would not serve the corpse of those dead dreams as it flailed about, killing those it had once served.

Not entirely by chance, he found himself near the worship spaces. He got in line to wait for one to be free, listening to the talk among the others waiting their turn. These sailors were more anxious, wanting to consult with their ancestors or beg them for guidance or help.

If he ordered them to attack Rogov's ships, Geary thought most would obey. Maybe. Maybe not. He couldn't let it come to that.

His turn finally came, Geary entering one of the small rooms and taking a seat on the plain wooden bench along one side. Before him a candle sat, ready to be lit with one of the matches. Setting the candle alight, he sat looking at the flame, letting his thoughts drift, finding them repeatedly veering back to his ancestor Rob Geary, the first Geary to come to Glenlyon.

In the past, he'd never thought that much about Rob Geary. Family lore limited his role on early Glenlyon to some time spent protecting the planet as part of an improvised space defense force. In fact, Geary had not long ago learned that his ancestor had played a critical role in defending Glenlyon and Kosatka, Tanya Desjani's home star system. But his reputation had been badly damaged during the last attack on Glenlyon, when Rob Geary had refused to sacrifice his ship and crew in a hopeless attack, knowing that he would be blamed for "doing nothing" even though his ship had been the only thing limiting the invaders' ability to act.

He could have been a gloriously dead hero of early Glenlyon. Instead, he chose to do the right thing, and paid the price for that. *I guess we Gearys tend to be stubborn that way*, Geary thought.

Almost exiled, Rob Geary had helped stand up the beginnings of the Alliance fleet, pulling together warships hastily acquired from places like Old Earth, which had been disbanding the fabled Earth Fleet. Star systems which had jealously guarded their independence had been willing to cooperate in providing forces for the Alliance, knowing that would protect them all.

Something about that thought teased at Geary, as if it mattered more than as a piece of old history. But whatever it was didn't come forward, leaving his thoughts free to drift again.

Rob Geary must have also played a role in drafting the regulations guiding the new Alliance fleet. Had he helped write Article 16? Were his own actions today bringing his ancestor's work full circle, employing the rule which his ancestor might have helped create?

If that was what was happening, did his ancestors approve? Would Rob Geary tell him he was doing the right thing?

Was the candle flame before him much brighter now, growing larger? Or was that just his imagination seeking validation?

It didn't seem right to ask for miracles.

Help me make the right decisions.

THE next day, Captain Rogov's ships started powering up their hell lances. Those ships had already strengthened their shields to near maximum.

"It sure looks like they're preparing to attack," Captain Desjani observed.

Geary was once again on the bridge of *Dauntless*, not because he needed to be there but because he needed to be seen there, handling the crisis where everyone could see. "They won't."

Captain Badaya called in. "This is another bluff, Admiral. I can feel it."

"I agree with you. We won't respond."

Desjani shook her head as she leaned back in her captain's seat. "When did Badaya start thinking about things before charging in all out?"

"He's probably been watching you and learning," Geary said.

"Oh, yeah, that's it." She gave him an inquiring look. "Are we going to do anything? I'm thinking it might not hurt to broadcast to Rogov's ships that we're not matching their moves."

"I have something I recorded to broadcast to them," Geary said. "No time like the present."

He'd given a lot of thought to it, wanting to avoid threats. "This is Admiral Geary. This message is addressed to the officers and crews of the Alliance warships currently responding to orders from General Julian. You were told that the orders General Julian brought were written at my urging. That I approved of those courses of action. That's not true. I have never proposed or supported any of the actions contained in those orders. I did not ask for those orders to be written. In fact, it is my firm belief that they are false, created to fool loyal personnel into believing the Alliance expects its people to carry out actions that are contrary to the Alliance's oldest beliefs."

He went on, telling everyone on those ships that he had invoked Article 16, explaining his reasoning, urging them to not act against their fellow Alliance sailors on other ships, telling them that they also had the same responsibilities under Article 16 that he did.

The broadcast was surely jammed as soon as Rogov and Julian saw it, but there were ways for junior officers and the enlisted sailors to get access to content that was supposedly banned. Geary hoped they'd use those methods.

What else could he do?

Geary called his ships. "If anyone knows anybody on those new ships, someone from home, someone you trained with, someone you served with on another ship, try to get through to them using any means available. Talk to them. Let them know they have an option. Let them know nothing will happen to anyone who in good faith followed orders they thought were legitimate."

The only problem with such tactics was that they might take a very long time to bear fruit. Did he have that time?

STALEMATE. He couldn't make any new moves. Neither could Julian or Rogov. How long would it be before someone made a mistake, did something that was misinterpreted and resulted in ships firing on each other? How long would the Dancers wait before they did something that might trigger conflict between the Alliance ships? Even a Dancer ship coming too close to the Alliance formation might set off a nasty fight.

The two sides had been facing off for four days now. Aside from broadcasting messages at each other's ships, they had remained passive.

Even General Julian, it seemed, didn't want to trigger a war between Alliance ships. Not when he had no hope of winning it, anyway.

"Admiral?"

Geary tried not to get his hopes up when Gunnery Sergeant Orvis and Master Chief Gioninni showed up at his stateroom. "Any luck?"

Gunny Orvis twisted his face up a bit. "Not exactly, Admiral. We did learn a few things. We finally got through to Sergeant Tyminska, Admiral. She was willing to talk. Things are pretty bad over there."

Master Chief Gioninni nodded. "Twenty-one soldiers trying to keep a lid on everybody aboard a ship the size of *Boundless*. They're being run ragged."

"Standing duty four hours on, two off," Orvis said. "Ever since Webb took over the ship per orders from General Julian. The only way they've kept going is through plenty of Up meds."

"According to Tyminska," Gioninni added, "morale has disappeared beneath an event horizon. But they're still following orders."

"Webb's people are being run that hard?" Geary asked. "They're still the only soldiers aboard *Boundless*?"

"That's right, Admiral," Orvis said.

"Were you able to find out why Webb hasn't requested reinforcements from General Julian? Or has Webb requested them and been turned down?" If that had happened, it would mean Julian's resources were already stretched as far as they could go maintaining control of the warships under Captain Rogov's command.

"Sergeant Tyminska wasn't sure whether or not her colonel had requested reinforcements," Gunny Orvis said. "She thinks Colonel Webb isn't too happy about this whole thing, and doesn't want to surrender control to Julian, which is what'll happen if a bunch more troops come aboard *Boundless*. But that's just Tyminska's impression of things."

"Did you ask her what would happen if we came aboard *Boundless* to regain control?" Geary asked.

"Yes, Admiral, I did." Orvis shook his head slowly. "Tyminska said they'd fight. She wouldn't even consider helping us get Marines aboard, or helping stir up trouble for Colonel Webb. As far as her unit is concerned, they're family. And she's positive all the rest of her unit feels the same way. That's what she said. None of them are happy with what's going on. But they'll all fight if they're pushed."

"She wouldn't talk deals," Master Chief Gioninni said, appearing mildly scandalized that someone would refuse to bargain over anything. "One other piece of bad news, though. Tyminska also said the civilians on *Boundless* are not happy, and they're starting to push back against the soldiers. Little stuff, mostly, so far. But it's escalating. She's worried about that, because the longer those ground pounders are on Up meds the more wired they'll get."

Orvis nodded grimly. "Restive civilians and armed soldiers is trouble anywhere and anywhen. When the soldiers are nervous wrecks, it's just a matter of time before people get shot up."

And, Geary thought, if any of Webb's soldiers shot civilians, there wouldn't be any way they could be pardoned if they surrendered, which would make them that much less likely to be talked into surrendering. It added another layer of urgency to the situation, one more thing that couldn't be allowed to fester much longer.

So far all the solutions he'd been offered would just make the problem worse. But now he knew continuing to do nothing was also making the problem worse. He had to do something. But what?

"Pass your information on to General Carabali," Geary told Orvis and Gioninni. "Make sure she knows everything you told me, and if she asks for you to try to find out more, do what you can."

THREE hours later, General Carabali asked to speak with Geary.

She took a shuttle to *Dauntless*. Routine shuttle flights between ships had continued throughout the standoff, even though those shuttle paths coming within weapons range of the other side were nerve-racking. By unspoken mutual consent, neither side had fired on the other's shuttles. But that was one more thing that might fall apart at any time.

Geary welcomed Carabali to his stateroom, gesturing to a seat. "Have you got anything for me? I'd be happy to hear even bad options at this point."

General Carabali sat carefully. She clenched one hand into a fist, raising it to her mouth, before lowering it again and meeting Geary's gaze. "Admiral, you asked me how we can resolve the situation on *Boundless* without causing a violent reaction aboard that ship and elsewhere among Alliance forces in this star system. The information Gunnery Sergeant Orvis provided confirmed what other sources have told me. Any attempt to regain control of *Boundless* by my Marines will result in Webb's soldiers violently resisting. Webb's soldiers have the means to spot my scouts in stealth suits, which would otherwise be our best hope to overwhelm them by surprise. There is only one course of action I can propose which offers the best chance of minimizing the possibility of Webb's soldiers fighting. Not a certainty by any means. But the best chance."

A way Carabali was clearly reluctant to state. "Something not involving your Marines? Go on," Geary said.

"You, sir." She turned her fist into two fingers pointed at him. "If you openly approach and board *Boundless*. Unarmed. And personally tell Webb and his soldiers to stand down. No one but Black Jack could do that and have a chance of success. And you, sir, are Black Jack."

Geary tried not to let show his initial negative reaction to the suggestion. Was Carabali right? He realized that her advice sounded uncomfortably similar to what Victoria Rione might be telling him if she were still alive.

But it would mean exposing himself to capture, or assassination, by Webb's soldiers. And Colonel Webb himself had been erratic at times. How would he react to such a situation?

If it was anyone else, even Carabali, Webb probably would just place them under arrest. But Black Jack was different. Rione had always insisted on reminding him that Black Jack was different. Even Tanya Desjani had told him more than once that Black Jack in many ways had become the Alliance, a symbol of what was supposed to be right about it. That was what had allowed him to convince so many warships to follow his lead in rejecting the orders General Julian had brought.

Now that might also mean walking off a shuttle unarmed and unprotected to face a group of strung-out, trigger-happy soldiers commanded by a colonel suspicious of everyone.

General Carabali was waiting, not saying anything.

He'd always insisted that his life wasn't more important than anyone else's.

Had he meant that? Or had it been a way for a senior officer to deal with the guilt of how many had died following his orders?

There were other reasons to be worried about the suggestion, though. "If something happened to me, what would happen to resistance against General Julian?"

Carabali frowned. "I can't predict that with absolute certainty, Admiral. I do know if soldiers responding to General Julian's orders are responsible for attacking you, it would guarantee that no one in the forces currently commanded by you would follow any direction from Julian." She shrugged uncomfortably. "It might generate immediate demands for revenge. An all-out assault on the forces loyal to Julian that would have only one outcome, Admiral. They'd be annihilated."

"Alliance forces wiping out other Alliance forces," Geary said.

"Yes, Admiral. It would bring all of that to a head." Carabali spread her hands. "You asked me for any possible course of action that might prevent fighting. That is the only one I can think of. It comes with substantial risk, not only to you personally, but to the entire situation. It could trigger what we've been trying to avoid. But I do not think any better options exist. Even a forceful occupation of *Boundless* that miraculously didn't result in casualties on either side would still likely trigger more fighting, which would very likely quickly escalate."

Geary nodded slowly. "Thank you for your candor and your estimate, General. Given the risks, I need to consider whether to try the option you've proposed. Stalemate might well be preferable, but I have a feeling that stalemate is growing increasingly unstable. If it breaks down, we'll probably face that worst case."

"I agree, Admiral."

"I'll let you know my decision, General."

FOURTEEN

CARABALI had left. Geary sat in his stateroom, alone, realizing he didn't really have a choice, but still very reluctant to take such a risk.

A knock on his door caused him to scowl and look up.

Dr. Jasmine Cresida stood there, appearing unhappy to have had to make this visit, her attitude that of someone doing an unwelcome but necessary task.

"Come in," Geary said, trying to smooth out his expression into something approaching welcoming. "What brings you here, Doctor?"

"You asked me to look into whether alien hypernet gates might be taken over and destructively collapsed," Cresida said in a flat voice, having come only a couple of steps inside.

"Oh, yes." Geary nodded apologetically to her. "I'm sorry. What did you find out?"

"Nothing definitive," Cresida said. "There are two possible approaches that I thought of which, in theory, might allow it."

"Can those approaches be blocked?"

"I don't even know if they exist," Cresida said, her voice growing sharper. "I can't speculate on details when I don't know if the general concepts are even valid."

"Of course."

"But," Cresida added, "if species such as the Dancers and the enigmas have viewed hypernet gate technology as a means for nova-scale bombs for much longer than humanity has, they should have already identified and protected against any ways in which an enemy can use their weapons against them. The only way to confirm that is to discuss the matter with the Dancers. Charban thought I should clear that with you before we ask."

Geary nodded again. "He's right. As of now, General Julian can find out anything we talk to the Dancers about because of the duplicate transmitter/translator aboard *Boundless*. We need to regain control of *Boundless* before we ask those questions."

"Regain control?" Dr. Cresida said, her voice suddenly gone extremely cold.

"Yes," Geary said, meeting her gaze, which had turned hostile. "Without triggering fighting among the Alliance forces here. There may be a way to do that, but it will involve a lot of risk."

"Are you worried some of your minions may die?"

He almost snapped back at her over that, but instead shook his head. "I always worry about whether people might die. My worry here is about what happens if the worst possibilities play out. About how many may die if I'm wrong, or if someone makes a mistake that can't be taken back. I know you don't like me and never will. That's fine, because what you're doing is so valuable not just to the Alliance but to humanity. I hope you will continue those efforts."

"As long as you ask nicely. So, you have to make a decision, and if you're wrong everything goes pear-shaped?"

"Pretty much."

"Why do you think you wouldn't be able to find a solution to that?"

He looked at her, judging what he should say, what he could say. He didn't know what decided him, but it was probably her resemblance to her sister Jaylen. "Because if it goes that badly, I won't be around to find a solution. Others will have to try to fix the mess I'm leaving for them."

"I see. Why are you still considering it, then?"

"Because," Geary said, "as risky as it is, it may be the only chance to start resolving this situation, to free Ambassador Rycerz and everyone else on *Boundless*, without triggering all-out violence. We can't keep waiting indefinitely, because conditions aboard *Boundless* appear to be deteriorating. To prevent anyone dying on that ship, I may have to risk triggering the conflict I'm doing my best to avoid."

Dr. Cresida gave Geary a speculative look, remaining silent for a moment before speaking in a different tone of voice. "You have always been candid with me. I will return the favor by being honest with you. Admiral, if I may paraphrase one of the greatest detectives in literary history, once you have eliminated all other options as worse, whatever option remains, no matter how unpleasant, must be the right one."

He thought about that for a few seconds. "That's true. That does sum up the scope of my choices, doesn't it? Who was that detective?"

"Sherlock Holmes."

"Holmes?" Geary surprised himself by smiling more. "That's right. I remember now. *The Hound*. I love that story."

"You've read *The Hound of the Baskervilles*?" Cresida said, staring at Geary as if he had suddenly grown a second head.

"Well, it was more than a century ago."

"That still counts." Dr. Cresida shook her head at him. "You're very confusing, Admiral. Good luck."

"Thank you." He looked at the door to his stateroom after she had left. *Whatever option remains, no matter how unpleasant . . .* That really did say it all.

Geary touched his comm pad. "Captain Desjani, I need to see you in my stateroom."

◊

"YOU'RE..." Desjani struggled for control. "That is . . . With all due respect . . . *Are you out of your mind?*"

"There's only one way to resolve the situation on *Boundless* without potentially triggering civil war between the Alliance forces in this star system," Geary said. "Only Black Jack can do this, so I have to take that chance."

"If you're murdered by Webb's fanatics it'll all fall apart anyway!"

"No. It won't." Geary kept his voice calm. "I am leaving orders that if anything happens to me Captain Jane Geary is to assume command of all Alliance forces in this star system. With backing from you and Captain Duellos and the other senior officers in this fleet, Jane will be able to hold it all together and take any necessary actions to deal with General Julian and his followers."

"Who suggested this?" Desjani demanded.

"General Carabali."

"But—" Desjani covered her face with one hand, breathing in and out slowly. "Please forgive me for my unprofessional outburst, Admiral."

"Of course."

"But I still strongly advise against this course of action."

"Your objection is noted for the record." Geary had felt his own resolve wavering a bit, so he pushed on. "I'll need a shuttle. Not one of *Dauntless*'s. I want to be able to approach *Boundless* without them guessing I'm aboard until it's too late to block me. And an honor guard. Gunny Orvis, and seven more Marines as an honor guard. Dress uniforms. No weapons."

"Understood, Admiral." Desjani lowered her hand but avoided looking at him. "I'll get it set up and notify you when the shuttle is ready to depart."

"Thank you, Captain."

She turned to go, but paused partway through the door. "Try not to die."

"I'll do my best."

OVER a century ago, as a young lieutenant, Geary had ridden with a half-dozen Marines in a shuttle heading to intercept a merchant ship suspected of smuggling contraband. In an Alliance that hadn't fought a significant war in decades, those Marines had carried only sidearms as weapons and had only been exposed to a handful of potentially dangerous situations in their careers. They had joked on the approach to the merchant ship, relaxed in the certainty that this was just one more routine search and they'd be back aboard their own ship in a few hours, eating dinner and looking forward to a decent night's sleep.

It was funny, in a way that wasn't really funny, to recall how nervous he'd been back then.

This time, Geary was accompanied by eight Marines from the detachment aboard *Dauntless*. All had seen, and survived, brutal combat situations. All but one of them had been wounded at least once. They'd worn battle armor in earnest too many times to count. They knew they were headed to confront heavily armed soldiers, but they themselves carried no weapons. Instead of battle armor, they wore dress uniforms. And instead of joking, they sat mostly silent, keeping their thoughts to themselves as the shuttle swooped upward toward *Boundless*.

The quiet in the main compartment of the shuttle was broken by a call from the pilots up front. "Admiral, *Boundless* is warning us off. Their shuttle dock isn't opening."

"Give me a few seconds," Geary said, leaning toward the nearest comm pad. Blasting their way inside *Boundless*, or even breaking in as Marines might do in a typical boarding operation like that on the *Fortuna*, would be a very bad idea this time.

Seeing Gunnery Sergeant Orvis and the other Marines watching him intently, Geary gave them a tight-lipped smile. "Being fleet commander comes with certain perks," he explained. "Including special override codes." He was tapping the comm screen as he spoke. Finishing, he checked over the code before hitting the transmit command.

A moment later, the pilot called back again. "The shuttle dock is opening, Admiral. We still don't have approach clearance, though."

"Go ahead and enter the dock," Geary ordered. "Notify *Boundless* that this shuttle is carrying me." He tried to sound as if he wasn't worried. *Boundless* did have point defense weapons installed, though. Would Colonel Webb think of those? Would he employ them against a shuttle he'd been told carried Admiral Geary? It seemed unlikely Webb would take that step, but it wasn't impossible. So Geary sat with a calm expression and a crawling sensation inside as he wondered if the shuttle would be ripped apart as it made its final approach to *Boundless*'s dock.

"We've got a reception committee waiting," the pilot warned.

"We see them," Geary said. One of the displays was showing the view inside the dock, revealing six soldiers in battle armor, their weapons at the ready. One of the soldiers was unsuccessfully trying to wave off the shuttle.

The pilot brought the shuttle in to land, using a routine approach as Geary had ordered rather than a combat landing coming in fast and braking hard. "Should we drop the ramp, Admiral?"

No one had opened fire yet. Geary stood up slowly, feeling the tension around him climb. "Yes. Drop the ramp. Normal loading speed."

In combat operations the ramp would slam down quickly to allow Marines to exit in a rush. But a fast-dropping ramp would look like an increased threat to the waiting soldiers. Instead, the ramp began lowering at the pace used in non-threat situations, slowly offering a direct view of the shuttle dock outside.

The six soldiers in full battle armor had taken up position to fire on anyone leaving the shuttle, and so were easily visible in what could be seen of *Boundless*'s shuttle dock beyond the shuttle ramp. All the soldiers' weapons were leveled, aimed toward the shuttle.

The Marines with Geary had all stood up as well, automatically straightening their dress uniforms as they waited for orders, their eyes on Geary and the gunnery sergeant.

Geary had been able to choose to do this. All the Marines were supposedly volunteers, but he knew that meant they'd been told they were volunteering. They were here, unarmed, facing armed soldiers, knowing just how perilous this was. But they waited for orders, steady, the only outward signs of tension their quickened breathing and eyes both alert and worried. "There's no one else I'd rather have with me right now," Geary told them, meaning every word of it. Knowing they were watching him gave him the resolve to keep on with this even though his common sense was screaming at him to raise that ramp and run away. "Follow me."

Gunnery Sergeant Orvis nodded to Geary. "We'll be right behind you, sir. Admiral, I've always maintained that no sailor could ever be the equal of a Marine, let alone better than one. I guess after this I'll have to make one exception to that rule, and buy you a beer next time we have liberty."

"I'll look forward to that," Geary said, trying not to let the quivering in his guts sound in his voice.

Taking a deep breath and squaring his shoulders, Geary walked slowly down the ramp, timing each step to ensure he didn't rush, seeing the soldiers' weapons shift slightly to aim directly at him. He heard the Marines lining up behind him in two rows, shoulder to shoulder, as an honor guard should, following him, trusting him.

He'd never realized just how long a shuttle ramp was.

Geary stepped off the bottom of the shuttle ramp, his feet touching the deck of *Boundless*'s shuttle dock.

The soldiers were about four meters away, faceless in their battle armor, their weapons pointed straight at him.

It took every bit of Geary's courage and will to speak in the calm tones of someone who simply expected to be obeyed. "I'm Admiral Geary. Lower your weapons, soldiers. There are no enemies here."

He heard the Marine honor guard behind him come to a halt, Gunny Orvis and the other seven Marines standing at attention on the ramp, the only variation from routine the way the Marines had their open hands turned toward the front so that it was clear they held no weapons.

Geary saw each of the soldiers' weapons twitching nervously from one target to another, restlessly lining up on him, then one of the Marines, back to him, another Marine . . .

He deepened his voice a little, also raising its volume slightly. "Is there a problem? Who's in charge here?"

After a very long moment, with the weapons of the soldiers still agitatedly shifting rapidly from one target to the next, the voice of one came out through the speaker on his armor. "Drop your . . ." The voice trailed off as the soldier realized the rote command to drop their weapons made no sense when Geary and the Marines had none.

It still heartened Geary, who was trying to maintain his calm, authoritative appearance despite the growing tension inside him. One wrong step and this could go badly wrong very quickly. But the leader of these soldiers had fallen back on routine, on the standard procedures in such a situation, and right now Geary believed that routine was his friend. Because routine meant responding to the orders of an admiral, and not firing on friendly forces.

He looked directly at the soldier who'd spoken. "Sergeant . . . ?"

The soldier's weapon wavered a bit as he automatically straightened to attention. "Sergeant Hayden Quinn, sir."

"Sergeant Quinn," Geary repeated, smiling slightly. "Good. You can lower your weapons."

"Um . . . Admiral . . . our orders . . ."

"Do you see any hostile forces before you, Sergeant?"

A long pause. "No, Admiral."

"There's been some miscommunication," Geary said. "Confusion. None of that is your fault. I'm here to clear it up, and I give my word that no one who in good faith obeyed apparently legitimate orders has anything to fear." He noticed the aim of another of the soldiers drifting away from the shuttle. "Who are you, soldier?"

"Corporal Riley Quinn, sir." The voice sounded exactly like that of Sergeant Quinn.

The strangeness of it, his relief at not getting shot yet, prompted Geary to smile a bit more. "Are you and the sergeant related?"

"Yes, Admiral. We're brothers."

"Twins," Sergeant Quinn said. "I'm two minutes older," he added, as if feeling the need to explain.

"That explains why you're the sergeant," Geary said. One of the things he'd learned from Tanya Desjani was how jokes in the middle of tense situations would calm everyone down, get them thinking instead of reacting.

The soldiers all abruptly stiffened, their aim steadying again. Geary guessed that orders had come to them through their armor's comm systems, most likely something along the lines of *What are you idiots doing?*

"Admiral," Sergeant Quinn began, his voice strained, "we have orders to place you under arrest."

"On what grounds?" Geary said, keeping his voice relaxed.

"I . . . I don't know, Admiral."

What was Colonel Webb doing? Probably on his way down here. Would it be wiser to wait, or try to force the issue before Webb arrived?

The need for that decision was preempted as Webb and five more soldiers, neither Webb nor the others in battle armor but all carrying weapons, burst onto the shuttle dock.

Geary heard some shuffling from the Marines behind him. "Steady, Marines," he said in a low voice.

Webb came closer to Geary, staying out of the line of fire from the armored soldiers who'd greeted the shuttle. "What are you doing here?" Webb looked like hell, his face drawn with tension, blinking as if his eyes hurt.

"Excuse me, Colonel?" Geary said. The tension in the shuttle dock had rocketed upward once again. He could see the soldiers with Webb, see how strung out they looked, confirmation that what Sergeant Tyminska had told Gunny Orvis about them being on Up meds too long was true. Twitchy, their nerves on edge, their minds hyped beyond safe levels, those soldiers too were aiming their weapons toward Geary and his Marines.

One nervous finger tightening on one trigger, and he'd probably be dead before he knew what had happened. And this fleet would probably end up in exactly the brother-against-sister war that he'd most feared.

Routine was his friend. Habit was his friend. These soldiers were disciplined and skilled. They'd spent years following orders, doing their duty. He needed to have them focusing on those things.

Geary looked around, his expression growing disapproving. "Colonel Webb, this isn't the reception I expect when visiting an Alliance ship. I expect better of Alliance soldiers, especially soldiers with the reputations and experience that yours have. You're the best the Alliance has, aren't you?" Geary demanded, letting his gaze rest on each soldier in turn. "Act like it. Lower your weapons, get into formation, and prepare for inspection."

The command was so unexpected that every soldier simply gaped at Geary, even Webb too stunned to reply at first.

"Did I not speak clearly?" Geary said. "Move it, soldiers!"

The soldiers who'd arrived with Webb, probably having been awakened from their too-brief rest periods and probably even more mentally off-balance because of that, moved first, lining up shoulder to shoulder, the butts of their weapons on the deck.

Those in battle armor hesitated, then, at an order from Sergeant Quinn, also clomped into line, their weapons lowering.

Colonel Webb shook his head as if trying to settle into order thoughts that refused to unscramble. "Admiral, you don't . . . you can't . . ."

"Colonel," Geary said, gesturing slightly toward the line of soldiers. "I'm waiting."

"Yes, sir." Webb straightened to attention, saluted, and turned to lead Geary toward the soldiers.

"Wait here," Geary told Orvis, catching a glimpse of wide-eyed Marines watching him.

He followed Webb. Standing in front of the first soldier, Geary gave her a narrow-eyed look-over. "When was the last time this uniform was cleaned?"

"Five days ago, Admiral!" she responded, her eyes properly fixed straight ahead, but one of them twitching uncontrollably, showing a side effect of too many Up meds.

"That's not acceptable," Geary said. "Is there a problem with the ship's laundry?"

"No, Admiral! Operational tempo did not permit time for laundry."

Geary shook his head. "Colonel Webb, if you needed some extra forces on hand you should have let me know. Your people are the best, and I expect them to look it."

"Yes . . . Admiral," Colonel Webb said, looking as if were still trying to figure out what was happening.

Geary paused in front of the next soldier, recognizing a specialty badge. "You're a hack and crack?" he asked, using the popular nickname for those trained to break into anything that could be broken into either electronically or physically.

"Yes, Admiral!" she replied.

"You should talk to General Carabali's hack-and-crack teams," Geary said. "You could probably give each other a lot of pointers from your experiences. We should set that up," Geary told Webb. "Let me know if there are any problems getting that done."

"Yes . . . Admiral."

He noted a few uniform discrepancies on her, then moved to the third soldier, who clearly hadn't shaved. "Came down here in a hurry, did you?" Geary asked.

"Yes, Admiral!" the soldier replied, his eyes worried but his face properly expressionless.

"Don't let it happen again," Geary said. "When was your weapon last maintenance checked?"

"Zero six hundred this morning, Admiral!"

"Good." Geary commented on a couple more items on the soldier's uniform before moving on.

He couldn't do much in the way of inspecting those in battle armor, but he went through the motions, finally finishing the last. Counting Colonel Webb, there were twelve soldiers down here. That meant nine were elsewhere on *Boundless*, probably standing guard in places like the bridge and engineering control to ensure the ship's crew didn't try anything. "We need to talk, Colonel," Geary said.

Webb, still trying to figure out what had happened, licked his lips. "Admiral, I have orders."

"Who gives the orders in this fleet, Colonel? What do your orders assigning you to Ambassador Rycerz for her protection say about that?"

Webb hesitated. "We are assigned to the ambassador," he finally said. "But those orders have been changed."

"Have they? Who has authority to do that, Colonel? My orders came directly from the Senate. I have every reason to believe the new orders brought here did not come from the Senate."

Webb's face shifted as he struggled to reply. "The . . . the aliens . . ."

"Colonel, I've fought the enigmas and the Kicks, and Taon who attacked us, and I'll fight any other alien species that poses a threat to the Alliance. Do you doubt my record? Do you doubt *me*?"

A long silence followed until a very low voice spoke. "He's *Black Jack*."

Geary looked that way, seeing Corporal Riley Quinn. "Yes, I am.

And I *will* save the Alliance." He looked down the line of soldiers. "But I can't do it alone. Are you with me?" he said to the group, before looking directly at Colonel Webb again.

Webb stared at Geary. His hand came up in a rigidly correct salute. "Hell, yes, Admiral. If you'll have me."

"Hell, yes," Geary said, deliberately echoing Webb. He slowly reached up to lay a comradely grip on Webb's shoulder. "Your whole unit. Let's go see the ambassador and get this straightened out. Your soldiers can stand down and return control of *Boundless* to her crew."

Webb nodded, pointing to Sergeant Quinn. "Pass the word, Sergeant. Everyone stand down." He paused, his face sagging with weariness. "Everyone get some rest." Looking back at the shuttle, he bared his teeth in a tight grin. "The Marines are here, so we can all relax now, right?"

Webb's soldiers laughed, relief flowing off them in a wave so strong even the waiting Marines smiled in response. "Stand easy, Gunny," Geary called to the Marines. "I'll be back after I talk to the ambassador and Captain Matson."

As Webb led Geary out of the shuttle dock, he shook his head. "Admiral, you're either the craziest man I've ever met, or you really are blessed by the living stars. Either way, I guess I should be on your good side."

"You need some rest, too, Colonel," Geary said. "What I told Sergeant Quinn is true of you as well. Anyone following in good faith orders they believed to be legitimate will not face punishment."

"It's my job to know what to do," Webb said, looking unhappy. "What's the right thing to do."

"That's not ever an easy thing," Geary said.

"Tell me something, Admiral. Were you scared in there?"

Sometimes lies were necessary for even the most honorable. "Why should I have been scared around Alliance soldiers, Colonel? I knew I had nothing to fear from those who believed in the Alliance as much as I do."

Maybe Webb believed him. Maybe not. But Webb nodded and smiled tightly and led the way to where Ambassador Rycerz had been under confinement in her stateroom.

AMBASSADOR Rycerz proved more difficult to pacify than Colonel Webb and his soldiers. "How can I possibly trust them again?" she demanded. "They should all be disarmed and under arrest! I want Marines guarding me!"

The fact that she had every right to feel that way didn't make it easier for Geary to convince her otherwise. "The example we set here is critical to resolving this situation."

"What kind of example is it to preemptively pardon soldiers who held me at gunpoint?" Rycerz said, glowering at him. She'd left her stateroom, where she'd been confined for days, as soon as the guard departed. In her office, she sat at her desk, constantly looking about and checking things to see what might have been messed with while she and her staff were unable to come here.

Geary pointed outward. "We've got a bunch of warships out there, crewed by people who thought they had to follow General Julian's orders. Any of them who want to shift allegiance now are afraid to surrender to my authority because they think if they do, they'll be charged with all sorts of crimes, including treason on the battlefield. We have to demonstrate to them that it is a safe option to come over to me, that they can abandon Julian without earning themselves certain imprisonment, dishonor, and likely death sentences. Colonel Webb's soldiers are the example everyone will be looking to. How do we handle them? That's why I risked my life coming to this ship unarmed, because any armed subjugation of Webb's soldiers would've confirmed the fears of everyone else who's listened to Julian."

Rycerz flexed her hand as if wanting to hit someone or something. "So we just let them get away with kidnapping me and my staff, and pirating control of this ship from its lawful captain and crew? That's what you're saying?"

"Yes," Geary said, not trying to sugarcoat the deal. "If we punish them, imprison them, there's no telling how many others will die. Because our only chance to convince the crews of those warships to end this peacefully is if they feel safe to do so. Otherwise, they will fight out of despair and a certainty they have no other option. And we'll probably have thousands of dead as a result, plus setting the awful example of Alliance military forces firing on each other for the first time in the history of the Alliance. That's not a price I want to pay for the satisfaction of revenge on Colonel Webb and his soldiers."

"Don't put it in terms of personal satisfaction!" Ambassador Rycerz snapped angrily. "You know that's not what's involved. This is about respecting the rule of law, of following the regulations your fleet holds so dear."

Geary made a deliberately vague gesture. "That is exactly the argument used by those who claimed that we had no choice but to obey the orders General Julian brought with him. This is a situation that requires us to use our personal judgment."

"By forgiving soldiers who turned their weapons on civilian authority?"

"Yes," Geary said. "I'll remind you that there are those who claim I am defying civilian authority. Of course, I'm an admiral. Even if I wasn't Black Jack I'd probably get off for that with a slap on the wrist and at worst have to retire. But Webb's soldiers, lower-ranked enlisted, are expected to obey orders without question, and expect to be severely punished if they make a mistake when doing so. Put yourself in their place, Ambassador. What would you have done? I've already confirmed with Captain Matson that none of the soldiers inflicted injuries on any of the crew."

"No physical injuries," Rycerz pointed out. "Being menaced with weapons inflicts other kinds of injuries. Admiral, the crew of this ship is not going to forgive and forget. One way or another we need to get Colonel Webb and his soldiers off this ship, and replace them with a security force that can be trusted."

He didn't have a simple, quick answer to that, because he knew it was true. "It can't be done immediately. That would be widely perceived as punishment and lack of trust. Yes, I know it would be perceived that way because that's what it would be. I will work to identify some role, some assignment, I can transfer Webb and his people to that will be of sufficient importance that it won't be perceived as exile. That will take time."

"And in the meanwhile we're just supposed to trust them?"

"Ambassador, this is about symbolism, about the perceptions our actions will create," Geary said. "You of all people should understand the importance of that."

She snorted out an angry breath. "Using the arts of diplomacy against me? That's a low blow, Admiral. Tell me this. Why are you working to convince me? This is a security matter. You could be simply telling me what you were going to do and informing me that I had no choice but to go along. And you would be legally within your command authority to do so. Why aren't you doing that?"

He took a moment to think through his reply. "Because when it comes to symbolism, I think it is critically important that we be seen as working together. That I be seen as consulting with you, and us making decisions jointly. If I were to be seen as ordering you around, it would reinforce the sort of actions that General Julian claims are required by the orders he brought. It would make it seem that I was overriding Alliance civil authorities."

Ambassador Rycerz looked away from him, drumming her fingers on her desk. After several seconds, she turned her head to look at him again. "Clarify one thing for me. You want these soldiers forgiven for following orders, and you say they are afraid of being prosecuted for following orders. I thought the military expected its people to always follow orders."

"It does," Geary said. "The military demands that its members follow orders. Except when they shouldn't. It all sounds simple. But it's not."

"As with you refusing General Julian's orders."

"Partly," Geary said, leaning back with a sigh. "Article 16 exists even though I've never met an officer who liked it. And no one is ever supposed to use it. But the founders of the Alliance put it in there for a reason. I believe a situation like this is such a reason."

Rycerz's sigh was much louder than Geary's. "Are you guaranteeing that this example, the way we treat Webb and his soldiers, will succeed in ending this confrontation peacefully?"

"You know I can't do that."

"Yes." She actually smiled, though in a bitter way. "I wanted to see if you'd be honest about that. As soon as possible, Admiral. Are we clear on that? Get Webb and his soldiers off this ship as soon as you can make it happen without making it obvious no one aboard this ship trusts them anymore."

"You have my word," Geary said, feeling himself relax again. He had wondered if Rycerz would agree, and what sort of stalling he might have to do if she'd insisted on Webb being shipped off immediately.

"Now." Rycerz leaned forward, resting her elbows on her desk, her eyes fixed on Geary. "Can you do the same thing on each of Julian's ships that you did here?"

His stomach felt hollow at the thought. "No," Geary said quickly. "Perhaps if I could get aboard them, I could talk enough of the officers and crews around, but I'd never make it. It would only take one officer, such as Captain Rogov, using automated fire control and weapons to destroy my shuttle before it reached any of those ships. The most important thing now is to slowly move *Boundless* deeper within the formation, out of easy range of Captain Rogov's ships. I'm going to have Captain Matson coordinate that movement with Captain Armus, whose battleships are the closest to *Boundless* in the formation. Ambassador, this situation remains balanced on a knife-edge. Please do not take any action, make any statements, without discussing them with me first. The wrong thing could be the match that sets off the explosion we need to avoid if at all possible."

TAKING over *Boundless* might prove to have been the easiest part, Geary thought. Moving the ship far enough from Rogov's ships to take it out of immediate danger without triggering impulsive action by Rogov was going to be a delicate operation.

Especially when Captain Matson was among those trying to throw a lit match into the combustible situation.

"Not on my bridge," Matson growled at Geary. "I won't have him up here."

Geary matched Matson glare for glare. "It is vital that Colonel Webb be shown up here, free and armed with his weapons, telling all of Rogov's ships that this ship was not retaken by force, and that none of Webb's soldiers have been harmed or confined."

"I don't care what you consider vital!"

When he wanted to, Geary could look every inch an admiral. "You'd better care," he said, his voice a low growl. "What's more important to you, Captain? That wave of outrage you're surfing, or the safety of this ship and everyone aboard her?"

Matson held Geary's gaze for a moment before dropping his eyes. "I don't like it."

"You don't have to like it. You can hate every minute of it, and tell anyone you want. After this is over. Right now, we have to save this ship."

"All right. Under protest," Captain Matson added.

"I need a comm relay through *Dauntless*, making it appear I'm transmitting from that ship," Geary said. "And a broadcast transmission set up for Colonel Webb. I want you in the picture with Webb. You don't have to smile. You do have to look like you are in command and working with Webb."

"I can do that. Why don't you want them to know you're on *Boundless*?"

"It might make this ship look like entirely too attractive a target," Geary said.

"Captain?" One of the watch standers on the bridge of *Boundless* was looking at Matson. "We're getting another message from that battleship demanding to know who was aboard that shuttle."

"Tell them it was delivering some necessary parts," Matson said.

A few moments later, the watch stander called out again. "They want Colonel Webb to confirm that in person."

Matson made a face. "It seems you were right, Admiral."

Webb, already summoned by Geary, came onto the bridge, looking about warily. "What do you need, Admiral?"

Geary gestured toward the communications controls. "First off, you need to tell them you're okay and that the shuttle that landed didn't contain any dangerous material."

"That's technically true," Webb mumbled. Walking to the controls, appearing to be unaware of the gazes of the civilian crew, he keyed the transmitter. "*Implacable*, this is Colonel Webb. We're all right."

"What was on that shuttle? Why did you let it land?"

"Parts," Captain Matson said.

"The shuttle carried some things we needed," Webb told *Implacable*. "Everything aboard is fine now."

"From now on coordinate things like that with us beforehand! Do you understand?"

Webb smiled humorlessly. "I understand. Webb, out."

"Your relay is ready, Admiral," Matson said.

"Thank you," Geary said. "Captain Desjani?"

Her image gazed at him. "Admiral Geary. I see you're not dead."

"Not yet. Patch me through to Armus."

"Done."

Captain Armus's image smiled at Geary. "My ships are ready, Admiral. Once *Boundless* begins moving we will slowly converge toward blocking positions between her and Rogov's ships. It will not look like a chase or an attempted intercept."

"Thank you, Captain. The moment *Boundless* starts maneuvering you are free to maneuver as well. Geary, out."

Captain Matson shook his head. "Why would they attack us? So what if *Boundless* is no longer under their control? We're not a warship."

"It's the symbolism, Captain," Geary said. "They'll have lost control of the only ship they managed to take over. We'll have regained control. That's a loss for General Julian no matter how it's viewed, and Julian isn't the sort to easily accept even a minor loss. Taking *Boundless* and silencing the ambassador was also the only one of their objectives that they'd succeeded in carrying out. That success is now going to be reversed. Win-win for us, lose-lose for Julian and Rogov. Attacking us as a result would be a dangerous overreaction, but from Julian's record we have to assume he might try it to salve his pride."

"You're moving four battleships into position to block an attack?" Matson said. "That should deter any attack."

"It should," Geary said. He turned back to the comm controls. "*Dauntless*, give me a secure transmission to the fleet. All units, this is Admiral Geary. *Boundless* is once again under our control, without any boarding operation or casualties. We are going to maneuver *Boundless* deeper into our formation, an action which could trigger an impulsive attack by some of General Julian's ships. Do not strengthen your own shields, do not power up weapons. We will not take the first aggressive steps. But be prepared to rapidly reach maximum defensive readiness on very short notice if General Julian decides to attack ships loyal to the Alliance. Geary, out."

Webb gave Geary a raised eyebrow. "Wasn't what you did technically a boarding action, Admiral?"

"I came aboard for a surprise personnel inspection," Geary said.

"My mistake," Webb said, his grin exposing his canines.

"Captain Matson, are you ready?"

Matson nodded, looking extremely unhappy. But he smoothed out his expression, changing it to a blandly calm, nothing-out-of-the-ordinary look, before walking to stand next to Colonel Webb.

Webb nodded to Matson, his own discomfort clear, but then also changed his look to that of someone confident and in control. "All Alliance forces, this is Colonel Webb aboard the *Boundless*. I am notifying everyone that myself and my unit are responding to the orders of Admiral Geary. *Boundless* is once again under the control of Captain Matson and the civilian crew. There has not been any action. No one has been harmed. As you can see I remain armed and free, as do my soldiers. Admiral Geary has expressed his confidence in us. We will protect this ship, and all of the Alliance citizens aboard it, in accordance with orders issued by Admiral Geary. I freely urge all of my fellow officers on other ships, and all of the enlisted with them, to do the same. To the honor of our ancestors. Webb, out."

Geary gestured to Matson. "Let's get moving."

Matson nodded. "Lauren," he called to one of the crew. "Get us going. Make it as gentle as if there was a diplomatic banquet underway and we didn't want any wine to spill."

"Yes, Captain."

Thrusters fired to shift *Boundless* onto a slightly different heading, then the main propulsion lit off at so low a setting that Geary had to check nearby displays to confirm that the ship was very slowly being nudged onto a new vector, moving away from the ships controlled by Captain Rogov, and deeper in among Geary's fleet.

Alerts flashed on the same displays, showing that the battleships *Colossus, Encroach, Redoubtable*, and *Spartan* had also begun maneuvering. Spread out behind and to all sides of *Boundless*'s original position, the four battleships were converging, easing into new positions that would form a diamond between *Boundless* and Rogov's ships.

"When will we know if we're safe?" Matson asked Geary, his eyes on the displays as he tracked the relative movements of all the nearby ships.

"If nothing happens within the next few minutes—" Geary began.

More alerts flashed.

Thrusters were firing on *Renown, Intrepid, Invincible*, and *Fearless*. Rogov's battle cruisers were about to move.

FIFTEEN

HIS link to *Dauntless* was still open. "Admiral, their shields are at maximum and they're charging up their hell lances," Desjani said. "If they accelerate you're only going to have a few minutes before intercept."

She didn't say the obvious, that he was not aboard a battle cruiser, or any other warship. The famous Black Jack was facing a potential intercept by four battle cruisers aboard a converted passenger ship with minimal shields, no armor, and only a few close-in defense weapons that wouldn't stress the shields on any warship.

"They want us to shoot first," Geary said.

"If we don't," Desjani warned, "their first shots might rip apart *Boundless*. Admiral, we're between a black hole and a supernova here."

"I've noticed that." He gazed at the displays on *Boundless*, trying to think through options. How desperate would General Julian be to avoid the symbolic loss of *Boundless*? How much influence would Rogov have to caution Julian against taking that last critical step that would result in open warfare? How willing would the officers and crews on those battle cruisers be to open fire on other Alliance ships?

Unknown after unknown. What could he do that might deter attack and not provoke it?

Battleships were cumbersome as warships went. They weren't used in swift attacks. In the Alliance fleet, battleships were widely viewed as defensive, mobile fortresses in a way, whereas battle cruisers were seen as swift offensive weapons.

"Captain Armus," Geary transmitted, "I want you to power up the shields on your ships and turn them to face the vector Captain Rogov's battle cruisers would have to come down to reach *Boundless*. Continue to move into blocking positions."

"Understood, Admiral," Armus said, looking and sounding grimmer than usual. "Powering up the shields on the ships of the Fourth Battleship Division."

"What about the rest of the fleet, Admiral?" Captain Desjani asked.

"The rest of the fleet will remain at their current readiness status," Geary said.

Colonel Webb had come to stand closer to Geary, aware of how the civilians on the bridge of *Boundless* felt about Webb now and probably seeing Geary as a refuge of sorts. "Will you open fire, Admiral?"

"Only if I have to."

Captain Matson turned a worried gaze on Geary. "Should we increase velocity?"

"No," Geary said. "You can't outrun them, but if it looks like you're trying it might encourage an attack."

"Admiral," Captain Desjani called in, "Rogov's battle cruisers have finished powering up weapons. All four are lined up on the right vector, but none have lit off main propulsion yet. Captain Armus's battleships are at seventy-five percent shield strength and building. His hell lances are not powered up."

"Incoming call from General Julian," one of *Boundless*'s crew called out.

Geary nodded to Matson to tell him he should accept the call, then stepped out to the side so he wouldn't be visible to Julian.

"This is Captain Matson."

General Julian didn't waste time on pleasantries. "Where is Colonel Webb?"

"Here." Webb stepped into Julian's view.

"Get that ship back where it belongs! In fact, bring it in among my ships!"

Webb inhaled slowly. "General, with all due respect, I regret to inform you that my orders come from Admiral Geary."

"What did he promise you, Webb?" General Julian demanded. "What did Geary offer you to make you turn traitor and dishonor your family?"

Geary could have told Julian that sort of frontal attack was a bad idea against Webb. Colonel Webb straightened, his eyes fixed on Julian. "The only thing the admiral offered me was respect, General. Respect, and the opportunity to ensure my honor was not tarnished."

"You're a coward, Webb! Weak!"

"Anytime you wish to measure my courage against yours on a field of honor, I will be happy to accommodate you," Colonel Webb shot back, his jaw tight.

Challenges to duels of honor between officers had been outlawed. But, Geary realized, Webb hadn't challenged Julian. He'd stated his willingness to accept such a challenge.

Julian turned his head to speak to someone else. "Get them moving!"

A pause while someone replied.

"I told you to get them moving!"

Geary made a call of his own. "Captain Armus, power up the hell lances on your battleships."

"Understood, Admiral. My ships are going to full combat readiness."

Alerts appeared on the displays as the main propulsion units on Julian's battle cruisers lit off.

"Are we authorized to engage any attacking ships, Admiral?" Captain Armus added.

"No," Geary said, his eyes fixed on the displays. "Not yet."

The four "enemy" battle cruisers were accelerating, but not all out. They were charging ahead at roughly three-quarters full propulsion. But they were coming right along the vector that would lead *Renown*, *Intrepid*, *Invincible*, and *Fearless* between the battleships *Colossus*, *Encroach*, *Redoubtable*, and *Spartan* in order to reach *Boundless*.

Tactically, it was a stupid move. One on one, battleship versus battle cruiser, sacrificing the battle cruisers' advantages in maneuverability and maximizing the battleships' advantages in shield strength, armor, and weapons. The battleships probably wouldn't stop any of the battle cruisers, but they'd do a lot of damage.

Physical damage, that is. The other damage that would do, Alliance warships firing on Alliance warships, Alliance sailors killing other Alliance sailors, was impossible to calculate.

"The battle cruisers will be within firing range of the battleships in eight minutes, Admiral," Captain Desjani told him.

Was that outcome now inevitable, impossible to stop?

He heard Victoria Rione's voice in his memory. From their first meeting, long ago. *I've heard all about you. You're a Hero. I don't like Heroes, Captain. Heroes lead armies and fleets to their deaths.*

He should have died a century ago. Maybe that long-ago debt had still to be paid. Geary looked at the displays, knowing only one thing might be able to stop what was about to happen.

"Give me a broadcast to every ship out there," Geary told Matson. "From this ship."

"Very well," Matson said. "You're on."

Geary looked steadily ahead, speaking as calmly as he could. "This is Admiral Geary. As you can see, I am aboard the *Boundless*. Any attack on the *Boundless* will be an attack not only directly on me, but on the Alliance. Not just the physical Alliance, but the ideals, the honor, of the Alliance. If four battle cruisers strike *Boundless*, they will probably destroy the ship in a single pass. They will also certainly destroy the Alliance."

He took a deep breath. "I am standing on the bridge of *Boundless*. I will not leave it. I will not depart this ship and allow the Alliance citizens on board it, and the soldiers commanded by Colonel Webb, to die while I seek safety. They are my responsibility. Every Alliance citizen, every Alliance sailor, Marine, soldier, aerospace member, is my responsibility. I will stand with them. I will stand with the Alliance. I will not order my ships to fire. Because the crews of those battle cruisers are also my responsibility.

"The eyes of our ancestors are upon us all. Do what is right, to honor them, and to honor our actions this day. To the honor of our ancestors, Geary, out."

A moment of silence followed.

"Four minutes until the battle cruisers are within weapons range," Captain Armus sent. "Request instructions."

"Hold fire," Geary said. "Do not engage."

"I understand do *not* engage," Armus said. "May the living stars stand with you, Admiral."

The four battle cruisers were coming on, still accelerating, swooping along the vector aimed at an intercept with *Boundless*.

Ambassador Rycerz called up to the bridge. "Admiral? What is going on?"

"You saw my message?" Geary asked. "That's what is going on. I'm sorry we didn't have time to get you to safety."

Rycerz took a moment to reply. "I guess I should close out my files. Do you think there's a chance it will work?"

"There's a chance," Geary said.

A chance that seemed to recede in the next instant. "*Renown, Intrepid, Invincible,* and *Fearless* have locked their fire control systems on *Boundless*," Captain Desjani reported.

He had trouble looking her in the eyes, knowing it might well be the last time. "Thank you, Captain." He paused. "Thank you for everything."

She met his gaze steadily. "It was an honor, Admiral."

Damn. I didn't deserve her, Geary thought, looking back at the displays.

"Is this accurate?" Captain Matson asked, his voice rough. "We'll be within range of those battle cruisers thirty seconds after they pass the battleships?"

"That's correct," Geary said.

"Isn't there anything you can do?"

"I'm doing it."

Colonel Webb took another step closer. "Thank you for the honor of dying in such good company, Admiral."

"You're welcome," Geary said. "But there's still a chance you may be denied that honor this day."

"Sure." Webb didn't sound like he believed that.

The bridge of *Boundless* was silent, the crew members staring at the displays, their horrified feelings plain to see. Webb said nothing more, standing by Geary's side as if prepared to escort him into the dark.

And Geary himself waited, not even praying because it was too late for that. *These are Alliance. All of them. They can still do the right thing.*

And, if not, his example would hopefully ensure that any civil war would be extinguished in a heartbeat.

It was really the last thing he could do, the last thing he could hope for.

He saw the four battle cruisers tear past Armus's four battleships. As ordered, Armus held fire.

Less than thirty seconds.

Geary breathed in slowly, nerving himself to stand still, to not flinch.

Ten seconds.

He kept his eyes open despite an instinctive urge to shut them as the battle cruisers roared within range.

And flashed by on all sides.

For perhaps several seconds after the battle cruisers tore past *Boundless*, not releasing a single shot, everyone stood silently, as if all were unable to believe they were still alive.

"The four battle cruisers are altering vectors," Captain Desjani called, her voice sounding just a little rushed. "It looks like they're going to climb out of the top of our formation. We're detecting a lot of messages being exchanged between the battle cruisers and their main body, but can't break the encryption yet."

Geary finally let out his breath, feeling dazed.

Others on the bridge of *Boundless* were laughing, crying, and shouting at each other.

Colonel Webb spread his hands. "You were right, Admiral. It'll have to wait for another day. By your leave, I'm going to check on my people."

"Do so, Colonel," Geary said. "Well done."

Webb grinned, saluted, and hastened off.

"Something's going on in Rogov's formation," Desjani reported. "Some ships are powering up hell lances. Others aren't. There doesn't appear to be any pattern."

"Incoming message from, um, Commander Hasan on the *Gusoku*," one of *Boundless*'s crew announced.

Geary saw the image of the woman he'd only seen once before, during the meeting where he'd invoked Article 16 and she'd been relieved of command and arrested by special forces on her ship at General Julian's orders.

"Admiral Geary," Hasan said. "This is once again the commanding officer of the heavy cruiser *Gusoku*. My crew released me from confinement. The special forces did not resist. Our war is not with others loyal to the Alliance. *Gusoku* is at your command, Admiral."

Other ships were broadcasting, the messages showing up at different times depending on how far off the ships were and when they transmitted.

"This is *Renown*! We do not fire on other Alliance ships! Article 16!"

"This is *Topaz*. We are not blindly obedient robots. Awaiting orders from Admiral Geary."

"Julian is losing them," Desjani said. "He pushed them too far, and you didn't take the bait."

"It was a brilliant and courageous plan, Admiral!" Captain Armus sent.

He didn't feel particularly brilliant or courageous. "I guess I should take the shuttle back to *Dauntless* now," Geary said.

AS soon as the shuttle docked on *Dauntless*, Geary raced up to the bridge, still escorted by Gunnery Sergeant Orvis and the other Marines clearing a path for him, hearing cheers following him down the passageways. "It's a bit premature to celebrate victory," Geary grumbled.

"Admiral," Gunny Orvis said, "they're not cheering victory."

He reached the bridge, pausing only to dismiss the Marines and thank them, then hastening to his fleet command seat. "How does it look?"

Desjani gave him a calm glance, as if he'd just come from his stateroom. "Three of the battle cruisers, two of the battleships, six of the heavy cruisers, and all of the destroyers have asked for your orders. Rogov and Julian still, technically, command two battleships, a battle cruiser, and a heavy cruiser."

"No one has fired at anyone yet?"

"Nope. My guess is the two battleships went over to you when they were told to fire on the heavy cruisers that had already shifted allegiance."

It wasn't over. Not even close. Anyone controlling even one battleship had an immense amount of firepower at their command.

He took a moment to reorient himself, checking where everyone was relative to everyone else.

Thankfully, during this entire crisis the Dancers had for once responded clearly to General Charban's requests, and had kept all of the ships in orbits or transiting along vectors between planets or facilities from coming anywhere near any of the human ships. The closest approach to the humans by a Dancer ship had been more than five light minutes, which must have made for a lot of work by the Dancers to avoid crossing into a sphere with a radius of roughly ninety million kilometers that was centered on the human ships and was moving around their star as the human ships orbited. That was an engineering problem of sorts, though, and the Dancers were brilliant engineers.

His fleet was still in an immense rectangular box formation, the long side facing "ahead" along their orbit about the star, the battle cruisers and battleships forming strong points within the lattice of overlapping fire, the vulnerable auxiliaries and assault transports, as well as *Boundless* now, occupying a much smaller box along the center of the big formation, protected from attackers coming in at any angle.

The four battle cruisers that had made a run on *Boundless* had altered their vectors after passing *Boundless*, climbing up through the top of the formation and curving over in what would be an immense loop. So far, all four of them had remained together even though *Renown*, *Intrepid*, and *Fearless* had announced they would take orders from Geary, while *Invincible* apparently still remained loyal to General Julian.

The rest of the warships in General Julian's formation were still five light seconds "behind" Geary's, following Geary's ships in orbit. So far, none of them had altered vectors to break from the formation even though many had declared they would no longer respond to Julian's orders. He tried to imagine the level of tension on those ships, and the potential for someone making a decision that could still blow up everything. "Should I try to disentangle the ships now answering to me from the ones still listening to Julian and Rogov?"

"Oh, are you asking for advice this time, Admiral?" Desjani shook her head. "It's still playing out. The battle cruisers are staying clear of the other ships, so you can probably direct them safely. The others are still close in to Rogov's ship *Implacable*, so any movement by them could trigger someone opening fire. They haven't actually broken with General Julian yet in terms of openly leaving his formation."

She paused as alerts sounded. "Never mind. Here comes *Topaz*." The heavy cruiser was accelerating away from its station not far from *Implacable*. Moments later both *Gusoku* and *Presidio* started accelerating to follow *Topaz*. Behind them in a ragged series of main propulsions lighting off on low came *Macuahuital, Falcata, Serpentine*, and the other seventeen destroyers like ducklings coming after their parents. "Where are they going? Looks like they're accelerating just enough onto vectors to slowly catch up with us and eventually merge with our formation. That means they're only slowly opening the distance between them and General Julian's ships. We're too far off to help if *Implacable* or *Audacious* fires on them."

"Do you think Rogov would risk giving those orders after what's already happened?" Geary wondered. "No. It'd be General Julian giving that order, like he did to the battle cruisers. Right now is he more angry at losing control of more ships, or more afraid of losing even more?"

"He hasn't got any reinforcements to call on," Desjani said. "Julian kept feeding soldiers into the fight at Malphas because he had a bunch in reserve. This time he's down to his last available assets."

"*Invincible* is altering vector," Lieutenant Yuon warned.

Invincible. Whose commanding officer was Captain Petra Bai, along with Captain Rogov the most insistent supporter of the need to obey the almost certainly fake orders. Small wonder that *Invincible* was the only battle cruiser still responding to Rogov's and Julian's orders.

"*Invincible* is estimated to be maneuvering for an intercept of *Topaz*," Yuon added.

Desjani was running possible maneuvers through her display. "Even our battle cruisers couldn't get there in time to intercept *Invincible* before it reaches *Topaz*. But we could prevent *Invincible* from making a second attack. To do that we'd have to start moving within the next two minutes."

It was odd how making a decision about the fates of others was in some ways harder than making a decision that directly affected his own fate. "*Invincible* won't shoot," Geary said. "It didn't shoot at *Boundless*, and this time they're intercepting one of the ships they considered their own. This is another attempt to get us to react and justify their own actions afterwards."

"Julian might be getting desperate," Desjani reminded him. "Or angry enough to be really, really, stupid."

"Then why didn't *Implacable* and *Audacious* fire on those ships while they were within range?" Geary said. "Why aren't they maneuvering now to engage those heavy cruisers and destroyers?"

"Good point," Desjani admitted. More alerts appeared on their displays. "And here come *Defiant* and *Paladin*. It looks like those battleships are moving to block any intercept attempt by *Implacable* and *Audacious*."

Civil war between Alliance ships once answering to General Julian and those still loyal to Julian would still be civil war.

"We're going to get our answer here," Geary said. "I think you're right that Julian is probably losing it from anger right now, and ordering his ships to fire on each other. Whatever happens is going to happen before I can intervene."

"You already have intervened," Desjani said. "With that bit while you were on *Boundless*. This is just the end stages of what that caused playing out."

"*Audacious* is maneuvering," Lieutenant Yuon reported. "She's either trying to intercept *Defiant* and *Paladin*, or trying to join up with them. Heavy cruiser *Oppida* is matching the movement of *Audacious*."

Aside from *Implacable*, which had yet to alter vector, all the ships formerly or currently under General Julian's command were converging toward the same region of space. All except the three battle cruisers.

"*Renown*, *Intrepid*, and *Fearless* are requesting orders," Lieutenant Castries said.

Geary took another couple of seconds to look at his display, trying to decide. "I should handle this like the inspection," he finally said.

"What?" Desjani gave him a confused look.

"On *Boundless*," Geary said. "Treat this as if some newly arrived ships are making routine requests to know where they should take up station in our formation."

"Okay, Admiral." Desjani gestured to her display. "I already made up some options for you."

"Of course you have."

"Do you want them isolated from the other ships, which will make them feel like pariahs, or buried in the formation surrounded by the rest of our ships, which will make them feel threatened, or added on along the top of the formation in a natural extension of the formation?"

"It sounds like you're making a recommendation," Geary said. "I agree with it. Let me see that third option." It immediately popped up on his display. "Great work, Captain."

She shrugged. "I had to do something that might be useful to occupy my time while waiting to see if you were going to die, Admiral."

Geary keyed his command circuit. "This is Admiral Geary calling all newly arrived units." He phrased it as if the other ships had just gotten here and the last several days hadn't happened. "I'm assigning you stations together along the top of the current formation where you will reinforce combat capabilities. Take up stations as indicated. Welcome to my command. I am very happy to have you. Geary, out."

Desjani smiled wickedly. "You included *Invincible* and *Implacable* in that order."

"I'm still extending an open hand to every Alliance ship," Geary said.

"I hope it works. *Invincible* is still on intercept with *Topaz*."

"Six minutes until *Invincible* reaches firing range for *Topaz*," Lieutenant Yuon reported.

Over the next few minutes, while Geary tried not to look nervous, one after another of the new ships acknowledged his command, shifting vectors, in some cases accelerating more to proceed to their newly assigned stations quicker.

Among those accelerating was *Topaz*, altering her vector.

"*Invincible* has adjusted vector to maintain intercept course on *Topaz*," Lieutenant Yuon said. "Two minutes to intercept."

Geary checked the data on his display. *Topaz* and the ships with her had their shields at maximum, but all of them had powered down their hell lances.

"*Topaz* is broadcasting," Lieutenant Castries said. "They're repeating the message . . . um . . ."

"Lieutenant?" Desjani asked sharply.

"'Like Black Jack, we will not fire on Alliance ships. Black Jack is our commander,'" Castries finished, avoiding looking at Geary.

Desjani gave Geary an innocent look and spread her hands. "*Topaz* is saying it, not me."

"I'm never going to get away from that, am I?" Geary muttered.

"No, not when you just did on *Boundless* the most Black Jack thing that anyone could possibly do."

Invincible was still coming down on a clean intercept aimed at *Topaz*, all weapons active, hell lances powered at full.

And *Topaz* was determined to do a Black Jack, waiting for the blow, refusing to fire on another Alliance ship.

How strange it was to feel both guilty and proud at the same time. Guilty because of the sailors who might die aboard *Topaz* because of his example, and proud of those sailors for facing possible death without sacrificing their ideals or raising a hand against their brothers and sisters.

"*Invincible* is entering firing range of *Topaz*," Lieutenant Yuon said.

Geary waited, watching, his stomach tight.

The battle cruiser tore past the heavy cruiser without firing.

Everyone on the bridge of *Dauntless* seemed to exhale at once.

"We have an incoming message from *Invincible*," Lieutenant Castries said.

The image that appeared in Geary's display was not Commander Petra Bai. It was another woman, looking nervous and agitated. But she spoke clearly and calmly. "This is Lieutenant Commander Grace Lopez, acting commanding officer of *Invincible*, reporting to Admiral Geary. *Invincible* will proceed to the main formation, joining up as ordered with our fellow Alliance warships. Our former commander, Captain Bai, is . . . indisposed. We await instructions for dealing with her." Lopez raised her voice, speaking defiantly. "To the honor of our ancestors! Lopez, out."

"Bai must have intended firing on *Topaz*," Desjani observed. "Her officers and crew felt otherwise. That means they effectively mutinied against their commanding officer." She gave Geary a meaningful look.

"There are provisions for commanding officers to be relieved if they lose the confidence of their crews," Geary said.

"Which are applied about as often as Article 16."

"I know." He gave her a level gaze back. "Are you saying you don't think *Invincible*'s crew had grounds for removing Captain Bai?"

"No, I'm not saying that." Desjani laughed. "This is going to be another one of those cases where the fleet tells Lopez she did the right thing, and then tells her and everybody else they'd better never do it again. So, General Julian's mighty task force has shrunk to one battleship."

"One battleship is nothing to scoff at," Geary said. "Maybe Captain Rogov will abandon a losing cause if given time."

"Let's hope so. Otherwise we'll be back at stalemate again."

"Let's see if Rogov will talk to me," Geary said, touching his comm controls.

He was a bit surprised when Captain Rogov accepted the call. With *Implacable* still five light seconds from *Dauntless*, there was a noticeable delay in each side of the conversation. While it was very annoying to wait at least ten seconds for your message to reach the other person and their reply to come back, it was possible to talk that way.

"This is Captain Rogov of the *Implacable*. What do you want to say? Rogov, over."

It wasn't exactly a respectful response, but Geary saw no reason to call Rogov on it. "Captain, you can see how the situation has developed. The other ships once with you have come to agree with me that the orders brought by General Julian are suspect and must be questioned. You're at a dead end. There is no possible victorious outcome for you if you follow your original plan. As with the other ships and their commanders, I am guaranteeing that no officer will face punishment or reprimand for following orders they thought appropriate, or for refusing to follow orders they knew were not appropriate, such as firing on other Alliance ships. Let's bring this dangerous situation to an end without any further risks of loss of Alliance life. Geary, over."

A long minute crawled by, then thirty more seconds. Rogov's reply finally came back. "A man of honor does not yield his principles because of the odds. If you think *Implacable* will so easily yield, you are sadly mistaken. It is not too late for you to reevaluate your own course of action, your defiance of lawful orders by Alliance authorities, and submit to the overall command of General Julian. *Implacable* will not—"

Shouting sounded in the background, causing Captain Rogov to glance behind him with a scowl.

A man and a woman wearing special forces working uniforms without any identifying markers, both carrying rifles, came onto the bridge, visible behind Rogov.

"What the hell—" Rogov began.

More shouts. The sound of rifle or pistol shots. Screams.

"Who is firing!? Who is firing!?" Rogov shouted. "Stop! Immediately! Who gave orders to fire?"

One of the newly arrived guards called out a reply, only partially audible to Geary. ". . . members of crew . . . to bridge . . . refused to disperse . . . General Julian . . ."

"Julian?" Rogov shouted. "He gave orders to fire on my crew?"

One of the bridge watch standers on *Implacable* called out loudly. "I just got a report of at least seven dead! Maybe more!"

"The penalty for mutiny is death." General Julian came striding onto the bridge, pointing toward Captain Rogov's display, looking as if he were pointing straight at Geary. "Shut that off!"

The window blanked.

Geary sat, his eyes fixed on the spot where the image of Captain Rogov and *Implacable*'s bridge had been, unable to believe what he'd just heard and seen.

"Ancestors save us," Captain Desjani breathed, looking as shocked as Geary had ever seen her. "Those special security types shot some of *Implacable*'s crew. How can that happen on an Alliance ship?"

She locked her gaze on Geary. "We can't just sit and wait now. We have to do something."

He nodded, feeling the weight of at least seven lives lost at the hands of fellow Alliance personnel. "We will."

SIXTEEN

EVERYONE viewing the recording of Rogov's last call agreed that it could only mean a number of *Implacable*'s crew had been marching to the bridge to insist that the ship defer to Admiral Geary. And that General Julian had reacted by using the special security forces to "restore order" by firing on the crew and effectively take control of the ship.

Geary knew he had two basic options. One was to demand *Implacable*'s surrender, and if that didn't happen, attack. That option couldn't be considered for even a moment, both because of the loss of life it would surely cause and because Geary himself had just gone to the mat for the principle that Alliance warships did not fire on each other.

That left a boarding action. With all the potential for more members of the crew dying in the crossfire, and the problem of trying to get shuttles close enough to board the battleship without them being blown to pieces by the immense armament of the warship.

Knowing he needed more information on the "special security forces" aboard *Implacable*, Geary asked the ships that had come over to him, and who carried similar contingents, to provide him with all the information they could.

Since they were supposedly special forces from the ground forces, Geary then tasked Colonel Webb with analyzing the information, telling Geary exactly what they faced, and offering suggestions.

It had taken only a couple of hours for all that, with the crews of the new ships as appalled by what had happened aboard *Implacable* as everyone else. If Geary had been in the mood to consider silver linings he might have been grateful for an event that had solidified his control over the other ships that had come with Julian.

But not at that cost.

Geary was brooding in his stateroom when Colonel Webb called.

He accepted the call immediately, the image of Colonel Webb appearing to stand in his stateroom. "I have the report you needed, Admiral."

"Good," Geary said. "Let's have it."

"The special security forces aboard *Implacable* are stronger than those on the other new ships because they were also tasked with guarding General Julian, who apparently thought he needed special guards even on an Alliance battleship. There's a total of fifty officers and enlisted in the special security force." Webb displayed a pad in his hand. "We don't just have raw numbers. The ships that came over to us had classified personnel files on them that allowed us to identify every one of the so-called special forces people aboard *Implacable*."

"So-called?" Geary asked.

Webb tapped the pad. "Like on the other ships that came with General Julian. Most of them are either regular ground forces who volunteered, washouts from special training, or wannabes who never served in special ops. Julian must have had a lot of good veterans to draw on, people let go after the war ended, but from what I've learned the general apparently didn't think they were reliable enough. Among the fifty on *Implacable* there's a half dozen who are an exception to the washouts and wannabes, a hard core of dirtballs who were kicked out of special forces for various reasons."

He pointed to one particular name. "This one. Strasser. He was court-martialed for killing people who weren't targets, just because he liked it. He should've faced a firing squad, but I guess someone pardoned him. And this one. Wanasinghe. Shot her sergeant because he'd written her up for drug use. And Gerasimov. Rape and attempted murder. None of them should've been allowed to wear a uniform again."

"How did people like that even get in special forces?" Geary wondered.

Webb grimaced. "The Alliance needed a lot of people in the special forces during the war with the Syndics. Standards slipped. They took people they shouldn't have."

"I can understand that," Geary said.

"Based on where the special security forces are bedded down on the other three battleships, we've got a picture of exactly where their counterparts on *Implacable* will be sleeping," Webb added.

Geary nodded, glad that he had people like Webb and Carabali to handle this kind of operation. It wasn't his skill set. "Thank you, Colonel. This information will be very valuable to the Marines."

"About that, Admiral," Webb said, looking uncomfortable. "I want to ask a big favor."

Would Webb actually request mercy for the people he'd just described as dirtballs? "Go on," Geary said.

"I request that I and my unit be the ones who go aboard *Implacable* and take down these guys," Colonel Webb said. "We can take out discreet targets so quietly it won't raise alarms. Then we can bag General Julian. He's a criminal now, right? Ordering that Alliance personnel be shot?"

"Yes," Geary said. "If we can get our hands on him, he'll be under arrest."

"Do you want to take control of the ship, Admiral?"

He'd been trying to sort that out. "I'd much rather the officers and crew made that choice. After what happened I'm sure they'd refuse to obey General Julian if he wasn't holding them at gunpoint."

"Fine," Webb said. "If my unit goes in, the dirtballs would be dead before they knew it, the wannabes will be sleeping off tranquilizer rounds, we'll take all their weapons with us, and with the fake special operators disarmed and out of the picture, and Julian in our hands, the crew of the ship can regain control."

Not a request for mercy, after all. Geary stopped an initial reflexive denial of Webb's request, thinking about it. "Why, Colonel? Why do you want this mission?"

"We screwed up bad, Admiral," Webb said. "Me and my unit. We let down you, we let down the ambassador, we let down the other civilians counting on us to protect them. We want to make it right."

"Your unit agrees with you on that?"

"They do, Admiral. All of them."

Geary leaned back, considering the offer. "Why shouldn't I use Marines?"

Webb gusted a short laugh. "Admiral, Marines can kick butt. But that's not what you need here. They go on a ship to capture that ship. That's what they do. And that means lots more potential for casualties among the crew of *Implacable*. My guys take out pinpoint targets."

"Assassinations," Geary said.

"When so ordered," Webb admitted without trying to deny it. "That's what you need here. These guys, like Strasser, have already bought themselves firing squads by killing some of the sailors on that ship. You can bet he's one of those who pulled the trigger. We'll just be getting the firing squads' jobs done quicker. Take out the hard core, and the wannabes will be a piece of cake. Then we bag Julian, egress, and the crew of that ship is free."

He hated ordering the deaths of specific people, but what Webb was saying was all true. Anyone involved in the "executions" aboard *Implacable* already had a death sentence hanging over them. Trying to spare them while increasing the danger to members of *Implacable*'s crew made no moral sense at all.

"I need to talk to General Carabali," Geary said. "I'll get back to you, Colonel."

"Thank you, Admiral. We want to do this." Webb saluted before his image vanished.

TO Geary's surprise, General Carabali had no objections to Colonel Webb's proposal. "We're trained to capture enemy ships," Carabali said. "We can also handle hostage situations. But a hostage situation the size of a battleship is pretty tough. Webb is right. His soldiers have a better chance than my Marines do of taking out a few important targets without raising a fuss. And his small force has a better chance of getting aboard that ship without being spotted."

"They'll need one of your stealth shuttles to approach *Implacable*," Geary said.

"That's not a problem," Carabali said. "What is a problem is that an Alliance ship's sensors will be keyed to spot subtle but critical signs of the stealth shuttle's presence. If we can't do something to disable or at least degrade the sensors on *Implacable*, it's going to be really risky getting anyone onto that ship."

"They didn't fully link in with our command network," Geary said. "I can't use my fleet override codes for anything aboard *Implacable*."

"Maybe we can get a single saboteur aboard? That'll also be a very risky deal, of course."

Geary rubbed his forehead, thinking. A deal. Maybe that was the answer. "There's someone I need to talk to, General. I'll get back with you."

Five minutes later he was looking at Master Chief Gioninni. "Master Chief, I need you to find someone aboard *Implacable* who wants to make a deal."

"There are a lot of unhappy people aboard *Implacable*, Admiral," Gioninni said. "We're talking to them on all kinds of unofficial channels. But they're scared. What kind of deal are we talking about?"

"Someone who can make sure *Implacable*'s sensors aren't working quite right, or if the sensors do work, making sure no one notices something coming their way."

"And what can I offer? I start low, but some of them aboard that ship might be asking for major deals."

That was a harder one to answer. "I don't want to promise a free ride to anyone guilty of involvement with the killing of those sailors. That's out of the question. See what you can wrangle with anyone else. If you think they want more than I'd be willing to give, let me hear about it and decide."

"You can count on me, Admiral."

Geary waited until Gioninni had left, then called Webb. "Colonel, you've got your wish. Start planning. Your unit will be going in."

BUT then he had to wait. Webb was planning, Gioninni was cutting deals, a stealth shuttle had to be transferred to *Boundless* as part of apparently routine shuttle flights around the fleet, and it was necessary to plan the operation to coincide with "night" aboard *Implacable* so as few people as possible would be awake and moving around. Even when standing watches around the clock, humans needed the regularity of a day/night cycle. During the period when most of the crew should be asleep, most of the "special security force" should also be, and anyone awake should be at their watch stations rather than roaming the passageways.

A visit to his stateroom by Kommodor Bradamont was a welcome distraction from waiting while others did the tasks assigned to them. "Do you have time to talk, Admiral?"

"Right now it would beat worrying over things I have to let other people get done," Geary said. "Have a seat. What's bothering you?"

Bradamont sat with a sigh. "Colonel Rogero and I have been keeping a low profile while this mess with General Julian plays out. Anything we did or said might be construed as shoving an oar into Alliance matters. But the Alliance still holds a place in my heart, and it was very painful to see what happened aboard *Implacable*."

"I think it shocked everyone," Geary said.

"But I've seen that kind of thing," Bradamont said. "Midway has been trying to change their system, but I've seen what happens when Syndicate 'workers' riot, and the officers wade in firing live ammunition to force them into compliance. What happens when Syndicate snakes battle crews who've had enough. And here was a version of all that aboard an Alliance ship."

She shook her head, sadness apparent. "We think of the Alliance as a forever thing. We know it isn't. Like a parent, who also seems to always be there, but one day won't be. Hopefully replaced by something with the same aspirations, but maybe not. We don't want to think about that. We want to think what we have is strong enough to stand against any challenges."

Bradamont looked at him. "But then this happens, and very suddenly it becomes obvious just how fragile the whole thing is. How in the blink of an eye the wall separating us from the Syndicate vanishes and our own security agents are shooting our own sailors. And we see how a single person can break what we thought was unbreakable."

"It's not a single person," Geary said. "That person always needs helpers. People willing to break important things. But they can be stopped, by people who see the value in those things, by people willing to listen to others and learn that maybe they don't know everything they think they do. We're going to stop General Julian. Not me. We. I could not possibly have done it alone."

"Without you it might not have happened," Bradamont said. "We might not have gotten this far. Julian might be commanding the entire fleet, starting a senseless war with the Dancers, using that as a springboard for more 'emergency' measures to curtail rights within the Alliance. Admiral, you may have needed the help of a lot of people, but without you those people might have lacked the leader they needed. What if you hadn't been found when you were? What would have become of the Alliance?"

Geary tried to deflect the idea. "Tanya would say I was meant to be found when I was."

"Maybe you were."

"I can't say." Geary leaned back, trying to order his thoughts. "It bothers me for something of the same reason you spoke of earlier. The idea that the Alliance is so fragile that one person made the difference in whether it continued or ended makes me unhappy. It should be stronger than that."

"People matter," Bradamont said. "Individuals matter. That's something the Syndicate never understood, still doesn't understand. It sees people as tools. Interchangeable. Unless they're a CEO, and then they're unique and special and deserve all of the benefits denied everyone else. But it's incredibly scary to know how much one individual can matter."

"If I hadn't been there," Geary said, "maybe another individual would have stepped up. Or maybe enough other individuals. I guess what bothers me is the idea that only one person can save the day."

Bradamont shook her head. "The idea that only one person can save the day is embraced by a lot of people, including people like General Julian."

"Anyone who really thinks they're that one person should be disqualified from being that person," Geary replied with a wry smile. "I wish we'd been able to find out more about how the Dancers, and the Taon, and even the Wooareek handle such things. Maybe we'd have seen things that helped us figure out better ways to handle it."

"Maybe," Bradamont said, frowning a bit.

He thought he knew why. "How are negotiations going with the Dancers from your perspective?"

"Badly. We still get the 'only talk to one' response from the Dancers when we try to talk about Midway as separate from Alliance negotiations." She gusted an ironic laugh. "That at least has had the benefit of convincing Donal Rogero that it really is the Dancers' position and not something the Alliance set up. But it's a nonstarter. Not just for Midway. Every non-Alliance human entity is going to want the right to talk to the Dancers."

"I know." He grimaced, remembering the *Fortuna*. "There has to be an answer. The Taon found it."

"It feels like one of those special clubs kids make up, where you can only get in if you know the password, and no one wants to tell us the password."

After Bradamont left, Geary fended off another call from Ambassador Rycerz wanting to know why Colonel Webb and his unit weren't already gone from *Boundless*. At least that reminded him that he needed to send some Marines to *Boundless* to provide security while Webb's unit was gone on their mission to *Implacable*. As simple as that sounded, it needed to be done in such a way that it didn't look like Webb and his unit were being placed under Marine supervision. The crews of the new ships were still nervously watching everything that happened, wondering if they'd be punished despite assurances otherwise.

Webb himself provided the answer, at Geary's prompting making an open request for some Marines to be placed on *Boundless* to take some of the strain off his soldiers. "We're too small a unit for our responsibilities," Webb had sent, knowing how many people would be listening in throughout the fleet. "Having some Marines around to assist would be a big help. Not too many. Say a platoon?"

"I'm sure we can free up a platoon," Geary said. "They'll be under your command."

"Good. Send them over as soon as you can, Admiral. My guys need a break."

The platoon of Marines selected by Carabali grumbled and complained right up until they reached *Boundless*, where they learned they'd be bunked in staterooms like those used by officers aboard the assault transports and eat the food prepared by the diplomatic-dinner-quality cook staff on the ship. In exchange for that, they were willing to accept working with ground forces for a while.

"Admiral, I got some good news," Master Chief Gioninni said with a grin as he knocked on Geary's door.

Geary checked how long it was before Webb's soldiers were supposed to launch from *Boundless*. "Very good timing, Master Chief. What've you got for me?"

GIONINNI had made a lot of deals. "There are a lot of unhappy people after those killings. Most of them didn't want much of anything. They just wanted to get back at those special security guys."

One of those deals had involved minor adjustments to the sensor settings aboard *Implacable* during "routine maintenance." On Geary's display on the bridge of *Dauntless*, the stealth shuttle with all its protective measures activated was marked by a blob indicating its probable position based on tiny detections that hinted to its presence. On *Implacable*, nothing should show at all.

It was deep into ship's night on board *Implacable*. Even keyed up by recent events, everyone should be tired. And everyone should be depending on their sensors to issue automated alerts if any danger threatened.

Veterans knew not to trust in automated alerts. They kept their eyes out for trouble. But a lot of *Implacable*'s crew were new.

Unfortunately, the only way to confirm that *Implacable*'s sensors had been "adjusted" as arranged was to send the shuttle in and hope it didn't get shot at. Even a stealth shuttle would have a great deal of trouble surviving near a hostile battleship that could fill space with grapeshot.

"That shuttle is well within range of *Implacable*," Desjani commented from her ship captain's seat.

"How close would you let them get before opening fire?" Geary asked.

She considered the question. "I wouldn't want them too close. People have been known to use automated stealth shuttles as bombs. I'd definitely open fire about now."

Geary watched, tense, as the shuttle drew nearer to *Implacable*.

"We can see an access hatch opening on *Implacable*," General Carabali called. She was monitoring the operation, linked in with Geary, visible in one of the windows on his display. "Right where it's supposed to be."

Another deal that, so far, seemed to be working.

"The shuttle should be reaching *Implacable*'s hull and docking right about now," Desjani said.

A highly directional feed that should be invisible to anyone aboard *Implacable* sprung to life. That feed might have been spotted by sensors on another ship, but with *Implacable* isolated and alone, there was nobody else to link with her sensors.

Geary saw a view from inside the shuttle as Webb and his soldiers tumbled off and into the air lock beyond. Instead of battle armor, they were all wearing standard Alliance crew working uniforms that had badges identifying them as crew members of *Implacable*, and carrying bags that appeared to be normal carryalls.

A single sailor awaited them. "I disabled the hatch notification," she told Webb, who wasn't wearing a special rank insignia. "They shouldn't have any idea this is open."

"I need a system access panel," Webb said.

"Right there."

Geary watched Sergeant Hayden Quinn open the panel and plug in, working quickly. "I'm inside the ship's internal surveillance system.

Linked. Taking over. All it will show to those aboard is a repeat of the last two hours of saved data."

"Link the real internal picture to the off-ship feed," Webb ordered.

"Got it. Done."

Geary saw a nest of new data appear in one corner of his display. Internal views from all over *Implacable*.

"I need confirmation of where the goons are," Webb said.

"Hold on, Colonel," Carabali announced. "I've got someone analyzing the feed you're sending us." A brief pause. "Confirmed. The data we got from the other ships is accurate. You'll have to pull up the names of those in each compartment."

"Getting it," Sergeant Tyminska said. "Here we go."

"Everybody get your targets confirmed," Webb ordered. "Names and compartments." He then looked to the sailor again. "We good on this hatch, too?" Webb asked, pointing to the one leading farther inside *Implacable*.

"You're good," the sailor said.

"Thanks."

"Don't thank me. One of my friends was killed by those scum. Make them pay. That's all the thanks I want."

"You're on," Webb said. "Don't go wandering around before we get back."

"I'm staying right here."

Webb made a sweeping gesture encompassing all twenty of his waiting soldiers. "Everybody got their targets?" All nodded in reply. "Any questions? Let's get this done."

Webb cracked the hatch, and moments later the disguised soldiers went through in a rush.

"Is everything okay around us?" Geary asked Desjani.

"Still quiet," she said. "You can dive into those feeds."

Geary searched through the real-time surveillance feeds from

Implacable, finding one group of three soldiers in crew uniforms moving along a passageway at a steady pace that wasn't fast enough to arouse suspicion. There wasn't anyone to see them, though. The passageway held the hushed solitude of most parts of the ship at this time of *Implacable*'s night. He followed the group around a corner, down another passageway . . .

Two men in special forces uniforms without patches or unit markers came around the corner up ahead, their weapons held at the ready. Both of the men looked worried and tired. "Hey!" one of them shouted. "What are you doing out during curfew?"

"Curfew," Desjani muttered in disgust. "On an Alliance ship."

"Maintenance," Sergeant Tyminska said, sounding tired and put out. "If something breaks we can't wait to fix it."

"What broke?"

"The high-pressure flux capacitor," Tyminska said.

"The what? Show me your work order!"

"Sure." Tyminska strolled closer to the two men, the soldiers with her following casually to either side of her. Stopping, Tyminska reached into her carryall, the eyes of the men watching her movements nervously and intently.

Their concentration on Tyminska meant they didn't notice the hands of the other two moving until shots were fired silently from two pistols. Jerking from several hits, both men fell, Tyminska lunging forward to catch their weapons before they noisily hit the deck.

"What did they hit them with?" Desjani asked.

"They're supposed to use tranquilizer rounds on most of the security force," Geary said.

"Two down," Tyminska said. "We need a place."

Carabali spoke again. "That door to your left has the ship code for a storage space. No. Your other left."

"Got it. You guys get it open," Sergeant Tyminska told her companions.

Less than a minute later both unconscious bodies had been hidden in the storeroom, their conspicuous weapons concealed in a larger bag carried by one of Tyminska's soldiers, and the team was on their way again.

Geary shifted his windows, finding another group of Webb's soldiers poised outside a sleeping compartment.

"Alarm is disabled," one murmured, sounding like one of the Quinn twins.

Another soldier made a gesture, noiselessly yanked open the door of the darkened compartment, and the whole group entered in a silent rush. Geary couldn't figure out how to follow the surveillance feed inside because of the privacy settings. But he heard low thuds and a single, strangled gasp.

"That's all four," someone said.

"Is Strasser dead?"

"Mostly."

Another low thud. "This time he won't get pardoned before the firing squad can do its work."

Geary switched back to looking at Sergeant Tyminska's group just as they entered another berthing compartment. He heard only small rustling noises before the soldiers emerged again with more large bags carrying more weapons, followed by a ragged snore from inside before Tyminska closed the door. "Next," she said, pointing onward.

While some teams of Webb's soldiers were killing or tranquilizing the off-duty special security guards, one of the teams taking out a second roving patrol before those two guards even knew there was anyone else nearby, three other teams had headed for the most critical compartments on the ship. Timing their entries, all three walked into engineering control, the bridge, and weapons control at the same moment.

Geary had windows open for all those spaces, switching his attention rapidly among them.

"What the hell are you doing here?" one of the security guards in engineering yelled at the three soldiers who'd just walked in, looking like typical sailors carrying typical bags.

"We got a repair call," the corporal in charge replied.

"A repair call?" Both guards had their weapons leveled at the corporal. "From who?"

"That guy." The corporal pointed to a startled ensign at the other end of the compartment.

Both guards spun to look. One had time to realize what they'd done before both jerked from multiple impacts by trank rounds fired by the soldiers.

The corporal looked at the stunned sailors watching his soldiers disarm the comatose bodies of the guards. "Relax. We're good guys. And we're leaving now."

In the weapons system control compartment, the two soldiers who entered encountered a single guard, having already tranked a second sentry who'd made an ill-advised and unauthorized dash to a washroom. "We got a repair call."

"Why? What's broken?"

"That thing. It's going to explode."

The guard stared at the indicated piece of equipment before collapsing as trank rounds lodged in her.

"Another one went to the head," a chief petty officer standing watch told the soldiers.

"Yeah, we already got him. He's asleep out there."

"You guys Marines?"

"Excuse me?" Webb's corporal said. "Marines? We nail these guys for you and you insult us?"

"Oh. You're ground forces." The chief grinned. "Thanks, anyway. What about the rest of these dirtbags?"

"Getting the same treatment. We gotta go."

On the bridge, the three soldiers who entered were led by Sergeant Hayden Quinn. As they stepped onto the bridge the two special security sentries were engaged in a vehement argument with a lieutenant, and barely spared a glance at the three new "sailors."

Moments later both sentries dropped senseless as the lieutenant stopped yelling in mid-sentence, watching them fall in disbelief.

A commander who'd been in the captain's seat jumped to her feet, staring at the fallen security sentries and at the three sailors who'd dropped them. "Who are you?"

Sergeant Quinn saluted as his two companions swiftly stripped every weapon from the tranquilized security personnel. "Ground forces, here by order of the admiral."

The lieutenant who'd been arguing knelt to check the incapacitated special security man and woman. "They're still alive."

"Tranked," Quinn explained. "They'll be out for several hours, and they'll have nasty hangovers after that."

"What are you going to do with them?"

"Take all of their weapons, and leave those two. What happens after that is your call."

"Where is Captain Rogov?" the commander demanded.

"Probably in his bunk. I don't know. Our orders are to take out these guys"—Quinn indicated the passed-out soldiers on the deck—"and not harm any of the crew."

The commander studied Quinn and his companions. "What are we supposed to do now?"

"My understanding," Sergeant Quinn said, "is that is entirely up to you. We're leaving."

"Wait! Who is your commanding officer and where are they?"

"Colonel Webb," Quinn said. "And he should be getting his own errand done right now. We'll be pulling out. Admiral Geary sends his respects."

Two more sentries outside the stateroom suite occupied by General Julian had been more suspicious and more alert. Webb himself acted harmless and confused until close enough to inflict a fatal stab on one of them. "Wanasinghe," he told the soldiers with him who had dropped the second sentry an instant later. "What about Gerasimov?"

"Heart failure," one of the other soldiers said.

"Too bad." Webb checked the door for alarms, disabled them, and led the way inside.

General Julian was awake, with the look of someone who had been having trouble sleeping for a while, glaring at a display showing the local stars. He shifted his glower to the soldiers. "What are you doing here?"

Webb raised a pistol. "Asserting legal authority under Alliance regulations, General. You are under arrest." He fired, knocking out the shocked Julian before the general could finish rising.

In what seemed an amazingly short time, Webb's soldiers had finished their work and were falling back toward the air lock they'd arrived at, where the shuttle still awaited them. Even given the quick work, though, sailors were starting to rouse as word of something unusual happening spread rapidly through the battleship. The soldiers encountered more and more sailors spilling into the passageways, sometimes giving puzzled looks to the unfamiliar sailors moving purposefully and each now hefting a number of large bags.

Three teams had converged on the route where Colonel Webb was transporting the unconscious General Julian toward the waiting shuttle, reinforcing his group to make sure they got through. Webb's soldiers had requisitioned a nearby emergency stretcher on which Julian was firmly strapped, snoring loudly, his face covered. As they walked quickly through the passageways they got a lot of attention, finally having their way blocked by a lieutenant. "Who is that? Where are you going?"

"Medical," Webb said.

"Sick bay is that way!"

"It's a medical evacuation," Webb said. "Unknown disease, unknown how contagious it is."

The lieutenant had been reaching for the cover over Julian's face but now yanked that hand back as Colonel Webb shouldered past the lieutenant, who continued to hesitate long enough for all the disguised soldiers to get by.

The air lock was crowded when Webb and his group reached it, closing and locking the hatch in the face of a chief petty officer demanding to know what they thought they were doing. "Give me a count," Webb ordered.

Sergeant Tyminska waved around her. "Everyone's here. You're the last."

"Let's go." Webb waited as the other soldiers scrambled into the shuttle, hauling General Julian with them. "Thanks again," he told the sailor who was still waiting.

"Did you get them?" the sailor asked.

"Yeah."

"Thank *you*. I'll seal the outer hatch after you go."

Seconds later, the stealth shuttle broke away from *Implacable*, accelerating toward safety.

Geary still had access to the internal surveillance feed from *Implacable*, which hadn't been cut off yet. His attention was yanked back to the view of the bridge as a watch stander called out.

"Commander, there's something out there. Our sensors just did a scheduled reset and this thing popped up."

Damn. Of all times. "How's the shuttle doing?" Geary asked.

"Still too close," Desjani said.

The female commander studied her display. "That's a stealth craft."

"Should we engage? It's within grapeshot range."

SEVENTEEN

A long, tense moment passed.

"It's moving away," the commander said. "Captain—" she began as Rogov stormed onto the bridge.

Another voice interrupted her. "Somebody's tapped into our internal systems! We're—"

The windows from *Implacable* on Geary's display went blank.

Why had everything gone to hell at this particular moment?

Think, Geary told himself.

Give several seconds for Captain Rogov to be told what had happened to the special security guards lying unconscious on the bridge. Give a few more seconds for him to be told about the stealth craft detection. Give at least a few more seconds for Rogov to try to decide what to do. "He's going to call General Julian," Geary said.

"Excuse me?" Desjani said.

"Captain Rogov. Instead of himself ordering *Implacable* to fire on that stealth shuttle moving away from his ship, he's going to call Julian and ask for orders, placing responsibility for the decision on General

Julian's head. Julian won't answer. Rogov will send someone to find out why not."

"And by the time he finds out, the shuttle will be clear of *Implacable*'s hell lances and grapeshot," Desjani said. "Not missiles, but Rogov will know if he orders a missile fired it might miss anyway, and the decision will be laid at his feet and no one else's."

"That's what I'm thinking," Geary said.

General Carabali was still linked in. "They're also going to be worried about whether all of Colonel Webb's soldiers left. All they know is that they were disguised as crew members of the ship. There's going to be a big scramble to muster all personnel and see if there are any extras aboard."

It all made sense. But it was also all a guess.

Geary could only watch, still worried, until the shuttle had passed beyond the range of any missile that *Implacable* might fire.

CAPTAIN Rogov seemed deflated. That was the best word Geary could think of, deflated like a balloon that had lost a good part of its air and was now sagging. "What are your terms, Admiral? Rogov, over."

Hoping for just this, and having given Rogov hours to decide what to do, Geary already had the terms ready. "Acknowledge my authority, Captain. Obey my orders. I will need a thorough investigation into the deaths aboard *Implacable*, exactly who gave the order to fire on your crew, and whether any of the special security force members still alive were among those who fired and killed your sailors. Geary, over."

A long, long ten seconds later, after light had crawled both ways along the distance between the ships, Geary saw Rogov's response. "I would not be comfortable serving under you, Admiral. I still believe you are wrong, and your use of Article 16 was especially wrong. Nor can I believe that you would be comfortable with me remaining in command. I am notifying you that as soon as this message is complete I will relinquish command of *Implacable* to my executive officer, Commander Hana Sasorith, and await reassignment. I am still confident that what needs to be done will eventually be done, or the Alliance will be swept away. Unfortunately, my crew overwhelmingly disagrees."

Rogov paused, his face twisting. "Despite all of that, I never would have ordered anyone to fire on my crew. I deeply regret that, and will do all I can to help bring those responsible to justice. Rogov, out."

"He did you a big favor," Desjani said. "Having Rogov still in command of *Implacable* would have made a lot of people uncomfortable."

"Don't tell Rogov that, okay?" Geary said before keying his communications again. "Commander Sasorith, this is Admiral Geary. I am sending you the position for *Implacable* to assume in the formation. Advise me as soon as possible whether you need any special assistance in light of the unlawful killings aboard your ship. Geary, out."

Desjani was listening to another report. "Admiral, Chief Master-at-Arms Slonaker informs me that General Julian has finally awakened in the brig. General Julian is most unhappy and is expressing that loudly and continuously. Chief Slonaker wants to know if you want to see the general."

"Oh, hell, no," Geary said. "Not until he's worn out his voice, anyway."

"We're going to need a statement from Julian as part of the investigation into the deaths aboard *Implacable*," she reminded him. "Who gets handed that hot impact crater?"

Who, indeed? "We need someone impartial."

"Yeah, there are a lot of people like that in this star system," Desjani commented sarcastically. "Maybe you can get a Dancer to do the investigation."

Geary looked over at an alert. Ambassador Rycerz wanted to talk to him.

Ambassador Rycerz.

"*Boundless*," he said. "There a lot of people aboard *Boundless*."

"People who could be tapped to do the investigation?" Desjani asked, obviously skeptical.

"Rycerz has lawyers on her staff."

"Lawyers? Do we have to go there?"

AFTER the events of the last few weeks it felt surreal to walk about *Dauntless* without worrying about what might happen at any moment.

Geary stopped by General Charban's workplace to talk to everyone. "Thank you for the support you gave. Keeping the Dancers out of this may have been the critical factor in getting it resolved with . . . minimal loss of life."

Lieutenant Iger, still sleep deprived after devoting every possible moment to trying to learn about General Julian's ships and plans, didn't look happy. "We didn't do nearly enough, Admiral."

"You did what was needed," Geary said.

"But did we do what was right, Admiral?" Iger asked. "I'm still wrestling with that."

"Do you think war with the Dancers would have benefitted us?"

Iger didn't hesitate. "No. That would have been a disaster."

"Do you think we should have tried to force Midway to join the Alliance?"

"No."

"We did the right thing," Geary said. "Have you seen any feedback from the Dancers about all this? About what they're thinking?"

Charban almost rolled his eyes. "Human problem, humans fix."

"I think there's something else in there, though," Lieutenant Jamenson said. "It's subtle. A shift in the way they're addressing things. Like they're analyzing what we did and are starting to add that into their intentions. That's my impression."

Geary nodded, studying Jamenson. "If you see that, it might well be there. See how it develops."

"I wish I could have contributed more," John Senn said. "But the stakes seemed a bit high for me to stick my nose into it."

"Did you understand what the dispute was about?" Geary asked.

"Oh, sure. That was easy. Kadavergehorsam. That's what it was about."

Everyone else stared at him in various stages of perplexity. Everyone else except Dr. Cresida, who nodded toward Senn. "Corpse-like obedience. Blindly following orders to the letter. The dream of authoritarians for thousands of years summed up in a single word."

"I've never heard it," Geary said. "Corpse-like obedience. I've met people who expected it, though."

"Article 16," General Charban said, "was written to avoid anyone being able to claim that as an excuse for their actions."

"But the military still loves the idea," Dr. Cresida said.

"Of course it does," Charban said with a wry smile. "The military wants smart, capable, versatile individuals who can think for themselves and will only do precisely what they're told to do. Militaries are like that. So are some forms of government, and any number of businesses."

"Perhaps militaries present it in its clearest form," John Senn remarked. "And, yet . . . I saw our fleet, our people, think for themselves. Those other ships were told to attack us, right?"

Geary nodded. "The four battle cruisers were supposed to destroy *Boundless* to keep it from our hands. Even on *Invincible* they wouldn't do that, though Captain Bai tried again when she charged *Topaz*."

"Bai did try to fire on *Boundless*?" Charban asked.

"Yes. Members of her crew took it upon themselves to abort the firing commands."

Dr. Cresida gave Geary an arch look. "But you still expect obedience to *your* orders."

"Yes, I do. It's important." Geary scratched his head, thinking. "It's critical, really, that I know people will do what I tell them to do under normal circumstances. But, at the same time, there has to be a mental and moral kill switch in there. Something that can say no when an order crosses a line."

"Such as being ordered to fire on other Alliance ships," Lieutenant Jamenson said.

"Like that," Geary agreed. "Like Article 16. Without that, we'd just be robots, like one of the new ships said when shifting command authority to me. I understand the contradiction, Doctor. Yes, you're expected to obey, but you're also expected to think. All I can say is it seems to be the best system humans have been able to develop. Oh, speaking of systems, you're free to ask the Dancers about those possible gate modifications."

Charban gave an exasperated groan. "Anything for a straight answer, even if it's an answer only Dr. Cresida might be able to understand. What is it that all of us are missing when dealing with the Dancers?"

"They are aliens," Lieutenant Iger said.

"Yes. But I can't help thinking our problem is less one of alien thought patterns than it is of something we ought to be able to grasp as easily as Dr. Cresida does all those equations. Pragmatism. There are certain requirements to get things done. Regardless of how you view the universe. There's what we want to do, what we can do, and what we must do. Those often conflict, but there's always a way to reconcile them."

He paused, his brow creased in thought. "Admiral, the two lieutenants and I joined the military because we thought we had to, because the Syndics attacked and kept attacking and it felt like we had to help stop them. But, Admiral Geary, a century ago before the war, you could make a choice to serve in the fleet based on your personal desires. Dr. Cresida is here, on a warship. So is our resident historian. In an ideal universe, they would be working on other things, I would never have worn battle armor into combat, and Tanya Desjani never would have commanded a battle cruiser in action."

"I think your vision of an ideal universe differs from Tanya Desjani's," Geary said. "What's the point?"

"We all ended up here, in the same place, dealing with the same problems. And, so far, we've been in agreement about what to do. Even though we came from very different places and experienced different things. Why doesn't that work with the Dancers?"

"Because we haven't figured out the pragmatic solution," Jamenson said. "The Dancers are waiting for us to do that."

"Why not just tell us?" Geary said wearily.

"Maybe that's the test," Jamenson said. "The big test. Can they figure out something that ought to be obvious? If not, how can they be trusted?"

"Trust does seem to play a big role," Lieutenant Iger said. "Lokaa of the Taon made a huge deal of it. And the Wooareek wanted to see a bunch of humans in person in one of their star systems to see what they thought of us. At least, we think that's what they wanted."

"And the Dancers," Geary said. "That visit Captain Desjani and I had on the surface. How would we react to them? How would a lot of Dancers react to us? In person, not in virtual form. Maybe that's a prerequisite for a deal. As close to personal contact as possible. The Kicks and enigmas couldn't do it, and they also couldn't make any live-and-let-live arrangement with another species. But how does that lead us to the deal?"

"Whatever it is has to be something that includes room for Midway," Charban said. "Bradamont and Rogero have been very patient, but they're also frustrated. That 'only speak to one' thing. What solution meets the needs of the Dancers and of different parts of humanity?"

"A pragmatic one," Geary said. "As you said, General, you all have different backgrounds. Maybe the answer we're seeking will come from one of those."

THE lawyer sent from *Boundless* to lead the investigation into the deaths aboard *Implacable* didn't look dangerous. That is, her appearance was pleasant enough, nothing about her indicating any kinship with sharks or other merciless predators. Eyeing her, Geary wondered if she was like that writer he'd met a long time ago, a kind-looking woman who wrote blood-soaked stories about vampires and zombies. Perhaps this woman, despite her outwardly open appearance, also secretly wrote stories of death and despair and entire worlds dying. Because she was definitely a lawyer. "Citizen Thompson?"

She nodded, all business. "Mary Thompson. I'm only here to interview General Julian. No one else aboard this ship has firsthand knowledge about the shootings beyond what you viewed in the message from *Implacable*, correct?"

"That is correct," Geary said. "If you've viewed the record of that message, you know as much as I do. Do you think General Julian will actually cooperate in the investigation?"

Thompson shrugged. "People like him tend to fall into two categories. Either they refuse to say a thing, or else they insist on telling you at great length exactly what they did and why they did it and why this whole thing is unfair because it's obvious they did nothing wrong."

"General Julian strikes me as the sort who'll do the second thing," Geary said, escorting the lawyer to the vicinity of the brig. "This is Chief Master-at-Arms Slonaker. He'll provide anything you need. If there is anything else I can do, please let me know." He paused, fighting down a wave of anger. "If General Julian did give the orders, I want him to pay for every life taken."

Mary Thompson nodded. "I'll do my best to ascertain the facts. Is it correct that every living member of the special security force from *Implacable* is currently imprisoned on . . . *Typhoon*?"

"They are all there," Geary said. "Along with the remains of the special security force members who died during the disarming of their force."

"Deaths during a military operation are a different issue," Thompson said. "It's not part of the investigation I'm doing. I'd appreciate

Typhoon being notified that I'll be going there next. Have you talked to any of those people?"

"No," Geary said. "I've made visits to a number of the new ships to meet their crews, but not *Implacable* given the need for the investigation, and I haven't been to *Typhoon* since the prisoners from *Implacable* were brought there."

"Good." The lawyer looked about her. "You should feel free to visit *Implacable* now. The people on that ship were walking around like those expecting a hammer to fall at any minute. Frankly, I don't expect to learn much from those being held on *Typhoon*. Most likely they'll all try to throw their dead comrades under the bugs by blaming all of the killings on them."

"Under the bugs?" Geary asked. "I thought the expression was 'under the bunk.' That's what they say in Glenlyon, as in 'hiding the evidence.'"

"No, no," Thompson said, "it's 'under the bugs.' Not just hidden but hurting them, too. That's what we say on Wotan."

Geary watched the lawyer and Chief Slonaker walking toward the brig cell holding General Julian. He thought about whether he should go with them, exchange some words with Julian, but decided against it. He'd either gloat, or try to punch Julian. Either action might hinder the investigation.

He turned back toward his stateroom, hoping that he'd never have to speak to General Julian again.

The next day he made sure to visit *Implacable*. The battleship wasn't that far off now, part of the Alliance formation. The crew was indeed nervous and unhappy. Geary did his best to reassure them, to express shared sorrow for the loss of their shipmates, and to let them feel like they were fully part of the fleet from which they'd been temporarily separated. He also told Commander Sasorith that she'd remain in command and made sure Captain Rogov wasn't being a problem.

"No problem," Sasorith told him. "He barely speaks to anyone. He blames himself for the sailors who died."

"Should I speak to him?" Geary asked.

"I don't think that would be a good idea. Captain Rogov still feels you created the conditions that led to the shootings."

There wasn't much he could say to that, because in a way it was true. It was also false in very important ways, because Geary didn't think he'd had any choice, and Rogov himself had been willing to order other ships to fire on their Alliance comrades when told to do so by General Julian. Maybe it was Rogov's knowledge of his own guilt that contributed to his depression. "Have medical personnel seen Captain Rogov to assess his mental and emotional state?"

"Yes, Admiral," Commander Sasorith said.

There wasn't anything else he could do.

The next day, Commander Sasorith called to inform him that Captain Rogov had killed himself.

"It's not your fault," Desjani said.

"Yes, it is. He was one of my officers. I was responsible for him."

"He made his own choices. Sasorith said they discovered he wasn't taking the meds he'd been prescribed."

"I'm still responsible," Geary said, his voice low, his eyes focused on nothing.

She sighed heavily. "Yes, as fleet commanding officer the welfare and health of everyone in the fleet is part of your duties. But you're not one of the living stars. You can only do so much. Don't beat yourself up because you couldn't do more."

He gave her a glance. "You know exactly how I feel because you feel it, too."

Desjani didn't reply for a moment. "Of course I do. I've never stopped wishing I could've saved more from the *Fleche*. Everybody told me how great I was for saving so few. And I never believed that. Any more than you can believe what I'm telling you about Rogov. But you have to accept it. It's the only way to keep going. You know that as well as I do. We do our best. And when that's not enough . . . we suck it up and try harder. No one tries harder than you. It's not your fault."

She was right, he knew. But, as with her, that knowledge was a cold comfort. Like her, he'd never stop wishing he could've done something more, even if that something was not humanly possible.

And so he made a call he didn't want to have to make but felt he had to. "Dr. Nasr, I wanted to ensure that General Julian is being medically evaluated on a regular basis."

Dr. Nasr nodded, his expression somber. "This is about Captain Rogov? I have heard. You need not fear that General Julian will attempt the same act. There are people who keenly feel their responsibility for the impact their words and actions have on others and on events. Such was Captain Rogov. And there are those who never spare a thought for such things, whose only concerns are for themselves. Such is General Julian. He continues to express the firm belief that his actions were perfect, and once back in the Alliance he will be freed, celebrated, and his opponents will be punished in the most severe manner. He is looking forward to that, and will do nothing that might prevent him from witnessing the triumph he is certain will come."

It wasn't exactly welcome news to hear, but it was one less thing to worry about.

THERE were ways to distract himself from dark thoughts. Paperwork was one of those ways, and there was always paperwork to do for someone commanding a fleet.

At the end of a long day, having finally caught up on the latest paperwork, Geary was looking forward to hopefully getting a decent night's sleep. But the moment he prepared to crawl into bed a call came from General Charban.

"I'm sorry to bother you, Admiral, but this is urgent," Charban said. "John Senn was watching the transmitter when something unusual came in. The Dancers sent the same message to us and to *Boundless*. Specifically addressed to both ships. They've never done that before."

"What's the message?" Geary asked.

"I asked Lieutenant Jamenson if she agreed with me on my interpretation, and she did."

"What is the message?" Geary repeated, growing more concerned.

"I'd have to call it an ultimatum. Yes, the Dancers sent us an ultimatum. As Lieutenant Jamenson summarized it, they're tired of messing around, they want us to present a proposal for long-term relationships they can deal with, and if we can't come up with that within six more days they'd like us to leave. Of course, the Dancers said it much more poetically than that. But it doesn't require a degree in literature to get the meaning."

"Oh, hell." Geary's comm panel buzzed. "Hold on, General. Yes?"

"Ambassador Rycerz wants to speak with you, Admiral. She says it's urgent."

It had been a long day, and it was also going to be a long night.

THE next couple of days were filled with a different kind of stress. It was one thing to have a goal in sight and try to find a way to reach it. It was much different when the goal itself was uncertain beyond the vague need to meet whatever requirements the Dancers had.

Every discussion seemed to go in circles, bouncing variations on the same ideas off the same problems and getting nowhere.

Not wanting to pressure Charban and his people, Geary nonetheless dragged himself down to their work area to see if he could contribute anything useful. He hadn't gotten enough sleep since the Dancers issued their ultimatum, but neither had a lot of other people.

The compartment had a full complement inside. In addition to

General Charban's usual group, Kommodor Bradamont and Colonel Rogero were present. Everyone was sprawled in their seats in the postures of mentally and physically weary individuals who had been running steadily for too long and still couldn't see a finish line anywhere.

Everyone except Dr. Cresida, who still sat as if unaffected by the crisis. But Charban had told Geary that she was working at least as hard as anyone else, trying to come up with proposals from a different perspective.

"Relax," Geary said as he joined them. "Go ahead and keep working."

"I feel like we're trying to stack marbles," Charban said. "Lots of effort, but the same result every time."

"I wish the pressure was generating new ideas," Geary said. "But I understand why it's not. I certainly haven't thought of anything new. If my ancestors plan on dropping any hints, I hope they do it soon."

Lieutenant Jamenson, her eyes bleary, looked at him. "One of your ancestors helped form the Alliance fleet. Didn't you tell us that, Admiral? That must have been hard, too."

"It was. They did find a way to work together."

John Senn gazed from Jamenson to Geary, his brow lowered in thought. "Admiral, you did mention that before. It's been stuck in the back of my brain for some reason."

"How can that example help?" Charban asked. "We don't want to talk the Dancers into joining the Alliance, and if we did there's no reason to think they'd agree."

"But . . ." Senn made a vague gesture. "That cooperation back then . . .

"When did it start? Didn't some of it happen before the Alliance was actually formed?"

"It depends how you look at it," Geary said. "I've discovered some histories claim the first allied defensive action was when my ancestor prevented an attack on Kosatka by an unidentified warship. Others say it was later when Glenlyon helped defend Kosatka against a worse attack, and some say it wasn't until a force made up of ships from three different star systems combined to defeat an attack on Glenlyon."

"That was all before the Alliance formed?"

"Yes," Geary said.

"How did they do that?" John Senn asked, looking perplexed. "Everything I've seen of this fleet is one person in command and we're all part of the Alliance and basically we're this one thing. But back then they weren't?"

"Not yet," Geary said. "The 'one thing' came later. There must have been some kinds of agreements that let them work together, but I don't know the details."

"It's history," Senn stated. "I'll find the details." Looking down, he started entering some searches into his pad.

Watching someone else enter search terms was guaranteed to produce a weird combination of boredom and frustration. Geary nodded to Cresida. "Have we received any replies from the Dancers about the ways they protect their hypernet gates?"

"Yes," Dr. Cresida said, stifling a yawn. "The gist of it was that they had protected against the theoretical dangers I'd suggested. I asked if they could share their methods of protection with us to ensure our gates were as safe as possible, but they haven't answered yet."

"Thank you, Doctor," Geary said. He tried to think of something else appropriate to say but his weary brain couldn't come up with anything.

"I think . . . I think I've got an idea. A new idea. Well, it's an old idea. The same idea they used to work together before the Alliance." John Senn, blinking away fatigue, was gazing at his pad where some text was displayed.

Charban roused himself with a groan. "Please tell us."

"This is from history, from Old Earth," Senn continued. "What the admiral said, and what Shamrock said," he added, using Lieutenant Jamenson's nickname, "made me sort of remember something, and I looked to find it and I think I might have. Maybe it can't help us now, but—"

"Please tell us," Charban repeated, an edge in his voice.

"Back then, on Old Earth, they'd have things called multinational forces, usually with ships."

"Multi-*national*?" Geary said.

"Like different countries. Like Old Earth still is, divided into lots of different governments," Senn explained. "And those governments didn't want to give up being independent of each other. But sometimes there'd be something they wanted to do without, um, surrendering any of their autonomy. And then they'd put together a multinational force, where anyone who wanted to be part of it provided a ship or money or whatever to support the effort and give them a voice in what was done. That's what Earth Fleet was. Old Earth wasn't united at all, but everybody saw the need for Earth Fleet so they all kicked in for it."

"Who was in charge if it was all these otherwise nonaffiliated governments working together?" Charban asked, sitting up straighter.

"Sometimes whoever contributed the most. Sometimes they'd, uh, rotate the command among those who contributed." Senn pointed to his pad. "The thing is, these weren't always part of some, um, alliance. The force would be one thing, but the different powers contributing to the multi-force wouldn't be bound by any other treaties or whatever unless they wanted to be."

General Charban sat up completely, his eyes fully awake. "One. They'd be one. Even though they were many."

"I'm not following this," Geary said. "How does this solve the problem with the Dancers?"

Lieutenant Jamenson gasped. "I get it. The Dancers want humans to deal with other humans wanting to enter Dancer space. Maybe a multi-something force like that could be the answer."

Charban nodded slowly. "The Dancers keep saying they'll only speak with one, and we've been thinking that *one* has to mean one government like the Alliance. But the one could be something like a multi-force where anyone who contributes is a member and can speak as part of it."

Colonel Rogero, still leaning back far in his seat, frowned. "If you're talking about having to join some organization controlled by the Alliance in order to talk to the Dancers, Midway's leaders would never agree to that."

"Wait," Kommodor Bradamont said, also sitting up. "I think I understand. Midway might contribute, say, a single light cruiser. Or even a single Hunter-Killer. And that ship would be part of a single force. But that would be as far as any association between Midway and any other part of the force, any other star system or association of star systems, would have to go."

"And," Jamenson added, "when Midway wanted to talk to the Dancers about Midway issues, it would approach them as a member of the *one* multi-force, yet still be able to speak fully for Midway."

Dr. Cresida cleared her throat. "One of the ancient forms of theater involves the use of masks for the characters. Sometimes, there'd be a large mask, and multiple characters would take turns speaking from behind it. It sounds as if this multi-creation would be such a mask." She smiled at John Senn, startling Geary, who couldn't recall if he'd ever seen Cresida smile before.

Jamenson nodded quickly. "And it's something everyone, all human governments, should agree on the need for. All of us want to interact with the Dancers, but to do that we need to have a sort of border guard, a border guard that anyone can participate in so that anyone can speak through that mask to the Dancers about their own issues."

Geary eyed the others in the room, trying to find flaws in the proposal. "But that issue of command, of who's in charge . . ."

"That's a matter for diplomats to work out, isn't it?" Charban said.

Colonel Rogero was finally sitting straight as well. "That sounds like something Midway could accept. Participation when it comes to dealing with the Dancers, but not in a way that binds us from talking about whatever we want. The big problem is the Syndicate. They'll never agree to something like that."

"Even if they did," Bradamont said, looking a bit dejected, "no one else would want the Syndicate Worlds to participate."

"The Syndicate Worlds will quickly learn that the Dancers won't even talk to them if they don't," Charban said. "There'd be no upside to them refusing to participate. And, maybe, if the Syndics have to work with others, they'll learn how to do that without being bullies."

"The Syndicate could attack that . . . multi-force," Bradamont said. "Just to break things for everyone else."

"Everyone else," Geary repeated. "That's what it would be, wouldn't it? Attacking that force would mean attacking every human entity that had contributed ships or funding to it. Would even the Syndicate Worlds want to declare war on nearly the entirety of humanity?"

Rogero rubbed his chin, glancing at Bradamont. "Possibly not," he finally said.

Lieutenant Iger had been listening, and now spoke up. "The Dancers brought the Syndic flotilla to this star system, and *Fortuna*, because our fleet was here. They'd want this human multi-force to be in one of their border star systems or one of our border systems. Like Lokaa's force with the Taon. If someone just showed up and wouldn't be part of the human multi-force, why would the Dancers escort them through the Dancer hypernet? Or speak to them, or interact at all, or let them transit through Dancer-controlled space?"

"This would be the next step," Charban said. "The aliens get a personal feel for what we're like. The Dancers. The Taon. The Wooareek. Then they're willing to set up mutual security arrangements, but not with every little fragment of the other species. They want us to handle that part of the deal. And this is a way to do that which could work even with humans."

"This is . . . pragmatic," Geary said, feeling hope stir inside him. "Exactly like General Charban spoke of earlier. A way to get something done. There are a lot of specific questions I can think of that will need to be tackled, but it feels like a usable framework. Humanity doesn't get along with each other much of the time, and we all cherish our own freedom. But we can cooperate when the need exists. That's how the Alliance fleet started, as something like this multi-force, different planets kicking in ships to defend against aggression, even though those planets didn't have any other agreements between them. And that first group of ships . . ." He dug at the memory, trying to find what he needed. "I think Benten was in command. Even though Benten only contributed one ship."

"That's right," John Senn added. "That's one of the examples I just looked up."

"So this has worked before?" General Charban said. "We have a working example of how this can happen?"

"Yes," Geary said. "Not just in the far past on Old Earth. And not to say it's going to be easy to make it happen now. But we've done it before."

"That's where we were," Bradamont said, smiling, "and that tells us where we can be now. As the Wooareek might say."

"It's so simple," Jamenson said. "No wonder the Dancers have gotten frustrated with us for not figuring it out."

"Or," Charban said, "maybe the Dancers think we have figured it out and are trying to avoid doing it for . . . human reasons. Which would explain the ultimatum. 'Stop wasting our time. You know what we want. If you won't do it, just go.'"

"I need to speak with Ambassador Rycerz," Geary said, getting up. "I don't know what the history books will say about this agreement, who will get the credit for it, but all of you in this room figured it out, and that's what I'll tell everyone. Damn good job, people."

◇

GEARY called *Boundless* from his stateroom. He wasn't surprised to find that Ambassador Rycerz was in a meeting, sitting at the head of a table lined with various people from her staff, looking as worn-out as Geary was. Rycerz also appeared to be trying to hide the same despair that Geary had felt a half hour before.

"We have an idea," Geary told her. "I think it's promising."

He'd been worried she'd just blow off him and his nonexperts, as she had in the past when they presumed to tread on diplomatic ground, but Rycerz seemed beyond such games. "Anything, Admiral. We can use some new ideas. Please tell us."

He tried to summarize what John Senn had come up with, and the discussion that had filled in the gaps of the general idea. Finishing, he waited.

Ambassador Rycerz stayed silent for a long time after Geary finished explaining the idea. No one else around the table with her spoke.

Finally, she buried her face in both hands.

"So simple," Rycerz said. "That's what the Dancers have been trying to say. But myself and my entire negotiating team knew humanity would never agree to form itself into a single entity, no matter what the reward, so we kept trying to find alternate explanations for what the Dancers were suggesting, alternate proposals that might feel the same to the Dancers.

"And the answer is something that doesn't involve any commitments beyond what's needed to create a single umbrella for humans to use when approaching the Dancers." Rycerz laughed. "Umbrella. The exact term the Wooareek used. It's been right in front of our faces and we couldn't see it."

"So you think it might be the answer we need?" Geary asked, surprised that Rycerz had accepted the idea without argument.

"It'll take a lot of work to make it work, but, yes, that idea could get us where we need to be. I think it will." She looked around her. "Does anyone think it's not worth trying?"

One of her staff spoke carefully. "There are a lot of details that will need to be worked out, especially back home."

"As the admiral noted," Ambassador Rycerz said, "working out details is what we diplomats are supposed to be good at. And he says this idea has been implemented before. If our ancestors did it, we can do it."

"But will other governments buy into a plan that the Alliance insists on?"

"The Alliance isn't demanding that only 'one' speak for humanity. That's the Dancers. What the Alliance will be doing is telling other governments that the aliens only wanted to deal with one, but look at this way we came up with to let everyone else play in the sandbox. We could've tried to monopolize this, but we *won't*. We will share with every portion of humanity that wants to contribute to the effort."

"In practical terms we couldn't monopolize it," another staffer said.

"So what?" Rycerz said. "We could've tried. It's still a generous offer to anyone who wants a piece of it. Admiral, you did say that Midway's representatives have already bought into the idea?"

"The general idea, yes," Geary said, "pending working out the details."

"If we agree on the big things, details can be worked out. The fact that one very much not an Alliance player likes this is a very good sign." She rapped the table. "I need these ideas distilled into a clean proposal, then rendered into the proper format for transmission to the Dancers. We're well into the third twenty-four-hour period since the Dancer ultimatum. I want to try to get this to them before that ends so we have three days left to negotiate any items the Dancers want done differently."

Another of Rycerz's staff spoke up cautiously. "We don't know the Dancers will accept this idea. I agree it seems very promising, but I'm not a Dancer. We do have to come up with an acceptable term for the multi-whatever."

"A tapestry," Geary said. "We'll form human ships from many star systems into a single picture, and that's the picture that the Dancers will see and address."

Rycerz grinned, spreading her arms triumphantly. "The visit to the surface of the planet finally produces a definite result! Humans might want another term, but 'tapestry force' should sell the Dancers."

"'Mosaic force,'" another staffer suggested. "For human consumption. One picture, discreet elements."

"Excellent! Run with this, people! We're short on time." As her staffers scrambled to leave the room, Rycerz smiled at Geary. "You said this idea came from General Charban's people? Please give them my thanks."

"The historian provided the core idea," Geary said.

"The historian." Rycerz laughed. "I really need an historian on my staff. Would you be willing to part with yours?"

"That would be up to him, but I have a feeling Citizen Senn wants to be on whichever ship Dr. Cresida is on," Geary said.

"Really? How does Dr. Cresida feel about that?"

"She seems to like him."

"Amazing," Ambassador Rycerz said. "The living stars lay out our paths in mysterious ways, don't they? The people who didn't want this mission to succeed paired you and me along with instructions designed to get us so busy fighting each other we'd never cooperate to get the job done. But instead they may have created the conditions that will allow it to succeed. I'll let you know what the Dancers say, Admiral."

"Thank you. I'm going to go light a candle."

"Good idea. We still need all the help we can get."

EIGHTEEN

GEARY spent the next twelve hours trying not to think about what the Dancers would do with the new offer from the ambassador.

It reminded him of the old joke that the way to turn rocks into gold required boiling them for half a day while watching the rocks and never once thinking of cows, because knowing you shouldn't think of cows made it impossible not to.

Oddly enough, the call from Charban still startled him.

"They like it," Charban said.

"The Dancers?"

"Yes. The Dancers like the proposal. They want to discuss a few items in it, the six-day deadline is gone, and they have accepted *Boundless* as an embassy for the Alliance which can remain orbiting in this star system indefinitely."

Geary ticked off each item in his head. "That's everything we were going for, isn't it?"

"That is everything," Charban said. "All else, technology transfer, trade agreements, what have you, is supposed to come later, flowing from the permanent diplomatic presence."

Ambassador Rycerz's call came moments later. Rycerz was beaming as she spoke to Geary. "Success!"

"So I understand," Geary said.

"When will your ships depart?" Rycerz said. "I understand you're eager to get home, but I would like Captain Matson to be able to put in a request for any resupply he needs before you go."

"It'll take a few days," Geary said. "But we need to clarify one issue. Colonel Webb. I can probably get enough Marines to volunteer to stay on *Boundless*. Real volunteers, that is, not Marine 'volunteers.' If you still want Colonel Webb and his unit off your ship."

"Colonel Webb." Rycerz sighed. "Admiral, there's something of which I believe you remain unaware. Something that happened during that time when it seemed *Boundless* would be attacked and possibly destroyed by General Julian's battle cruisers. I called you where you were on *Boundless*'s bridge."

"Yes," Geary said, remembering. "You called from your office."

"I wasn't in my office." Rycerz spread her hands. "I'd been waylaid by four of Colonel Webb's soldiers and was being rapidly escorted to the shuttle you'd arrived on. The soldiers told me they'd been ordered to get me off *Boundless* safely if possible. Colonel Webb himself was going to stay on the bridge with you to make it appear I was definitely still aboard the ship, and the rest of his soldiers were either guarding my office to make it seem I was still there or running interference for me and my escort. None of them, except the four with me, expected to live."

"I had no idea that had happened," Geary said.

"I'm not surprised Colonel Webb didn't inform you. He's not the sort to brag." Rycerz gazed steadily at Geary. "So, here were the officer and soldiers who had imprisoned me, now prepared to sacrifice themselves to try to get me to safety. It created a bit of emotional whiplash.

But, in the aftermath, it also allowed me to understand that devotion to duty can lead otherwise good people astray sometimes.

"There has been a lot to repair in terms of working and professional relationships. But the colonel has done everything he can. And he and his soldiers demonstrated in the clearest possible way they were willing to die to protect me. It has also occurred to me that the same people who wanted us to fail also wanted the colonel to fail. Knowing he instead succeeded would twist the knife of our success in our opponents' bellies, don't you think?"

"That's an interesting metaphor," Geary said. "For my part, I do trust the colonel. Having erred, he's going to work extra hard to avoid failing again. And his people did amazing work on *Implacable*, preventing further loss of life. Innocent life, that is."

Rycerz pondered for a few seconds. "We'll keep him and his unit, Admiral. I'll let him know, and tell him that you recommended I do so."

"Thank you," Geary said.

The next step involved calling a fleet meeting, taking care to schedule it an hour in advance so no one would get worked up thinking another crisis had erupted.

But that hour delay, combined with the unofficial communications that were interwoven with the official fleet net, meant that by the time the meeting took place, Geary's news was already widely known. "Is there anyone who hasn't heard that we'll be heading home?" he asked the commanding officers virtually seated at the virtually very long table. "All of us except *Boundless*, which is now officially not just a ship, but also an embassy of the Alliance, the first embassy of a human government to an alien species in all of history. And you all here helped make that happen, as well as establishing first contact with the Taon, and the Wooareek. Congratulations on earning yourselves another place in the history books."

"What did we give up to the Dancers to win their acceptance?" Commander Sasorith asked, her concerns reflected on the faces of most of the captains of the other new ships.

"Not a thing," Geary said. "They've agreed to keep talking, and they've agreed to the creation of a human border force that will control traffic between Dancer-controlled space and human-controlled space."

"They're not being given free access to human space?" Commander Hassan said anxiously.

"No," Geary said. "No giveaways. But we have ensured the Alliance will continue to have a strong voice in whatever happens in the future between the Dancers and humanity. We have done what we needed to do."

He paused, seeing the reassurance, but also the continued worries, on the faces of the captains of the new ships, and also some of those from the older ships in the fleet.

A lot had happened. The elephant that was Article 16 was still in the room, mentioned or not. He owed it to them to address that head-on.

"I believe I misspoke a moment ago," Geary said, looking along the lines of faces before him. "I said we did what we needed to do. That's an important thing, to identify what needs to be done. But it's not the only thing. Often, people of good intent can have different interpretations of what needs to be done, especially when the options we have are all challenging."

He took a deep breath, steadying himself and his voice. "But what we *need* to do is not the only question we should ask ourselves. We also have to ask ourselves what we *should* do. No matter how clear the need may seem, we also must examine whether our actions are right. Whether we are doing what we think we have to do, or doing that which will honor us and our ancestors.

"These aren't easy questions. I don't think they're meant to be in a universe that seems constructed to challenge us at every turn. But we have been given the will and the means to make our own decisions.

And I continue to believe that we are called on to make choices that reflect what is right, even if those choices bring us no personal benefit, even if those choices exact a price from us."

He paused again, wanting to get the next statement right. "I said at the time, and I say again now, that the responsibility for invoking Article 16 not long ago was mine. I have no doubt as to the rightness of that decision, and will bear whatever price it might demand. I firmly believe that the actions and decisions you all ultimately took were the right ones. And I will stand with you, to the end, if anyone should question your honor or your devotion to the Alliance.

"Thank you all. I often thank the living stars for having given me the opportunity to have commanded such individuals. It has honored me beyond measure. Now, let's get ready to go home."

The room was silent for several seconds, everyone gazing at him.

"Black Jack!" someone shouted.

Then everyone did.

Geary cast a despairing glance at Desjani, who shook her head at him. "Do not look at me. *You* keep doing these things."

But when she looked along the table at the cheering captains she smiled.

THE movements of hundreds of ships also came down to decisions about individuals.

The remaining "special security forces" on the new ships had been gradually replaced by Marine detachments drawn from the Marines aboard the assault transports. In turn, the special security personnel had been gradually transferred to the same transports. Not confined as those from *Implacable* still were on *Typhoon*, but in normal berthing aboard *Haboob* and *Tsunami*. Geary hadn't been able to determine that any from the other new ships had committed any crimes. They'd been overbearing at times, and weren't exactly liked by the crews of the ships they'd left, but that wasn't ground for charges. He intended getting them to the fleet's home base at Varandal Star System and dumping them on the nearest unsuspecting ground forces commander to deal with longer term.

There were other individuals he'd be sorry to see go, however.

Lieutenant Iger, Lieutenant Jamenson, and even General Charban had been taking breaks from long hours, now that most communications with the Dancers were through *Boundless*, but Geary found both John Senn and Dr. Cresida in the work space with the Dancer transmitter.

"We're used to being here," Senn explained.

"It's being here that I need to talk to you about," Geary said. "Citizen Senn, your commitment to participating in this mission expired when *Boundless* reached embassy status. The fleet is going to be heading home. Do you want to be transferred back to *Boundless*, or stay on *Dauntless* and come home with us? Before you answer, I should add that Ambassador Rycerz would love to have you. She's gained a new appreciation for what an historian can bring to the table."

Senn grinned. "Good. It's nice to be appreciated. But, uh, if it's okay," he said, obviously trying not to look at Dr. Cresida, "I'd like to stay on this ship and get back to our home. There are really old remains on worlds in the Alliance that I'd love to look at again, knowing what I now know about the Dancers and the Taon and the Wooareek. Maybe I can even get a doctorate now that I have to be taken as seriously as everyone else and not be dismissed as the weird guy yelling 'It was aliens!'"

"You'll never be like everyone else," Dr. Cresida murmured, her eyes on her calculations.

"All right," Geary told Senn. "How about you, Doctor? Do you want to return to *Boundless*? I'm told that Dr. Bron is staying, but Dr. Rajput wants to come back with us. I'm putting him on *Daring*, which has room for him."

Dr. Cresida looked at Geary, her expression unrevealing. "No. Thank you. I'd also prefer to stay on this ship. There are ideas I'd like to pursue using resources available in the Alliance. Although . . ." She glanced at Senn. "I think before I do that I've earned a break from research work. Maybe I'll go look over some ancient ruins. If there's someone qualified to show me around."

Senn smiled so broadly Geary was afraid his face would split. "That'd be great."

"And, Admiral," Cresida added, looking back at Geary, "since I do not know how much we'll have cause to interact in the future, I want to be sure that I tell you that you were not at all what I expected."

Somehow, that flat statement sounded like a very large compliment. Geary nodded to Cresida, keeping his expression solemn. "Thank you, Doctor. I try to always listen to good advice, even when it reminds me that sometimes even the best alternative isn't necessarily a welcome one."

"'It is my business to know what other people do not know,'" Cresida said.

Geary had recently sought distraction by rereading some very old stories. "'The Adventure of the Blue Carbuncle,' right?"

"Very good," Cresida said. "There may be hope for you yet, Admiral."

He also had to deal with the problem of Dr. Macadams. Ambassador Rycerz had informed Geary, with badly feigned regret, that somehow there weren't adequate quarters aboard *Boundless* for the former lead scientist dealing with contacts with the Dancers. That and complaints about working relationships had led her to "reluctantly" request that Geary take Macadams back to Alliance space. That had required a pair of no-nonsense guards to escort a loudly protesting Macadams off *Boundless* and to temporary quarters aboard *Typhoon*.

Geary made a note to himself that he owed the commanding officer and crew of *Typhoon* for making them put up with Macadams during the upcoming journey.

He also had to check in with Captain Matson. "If you need any-thing before we go, just ask."

"Thank you, Admiral," Matson said, still slightly stiff in his deal-ings with Geary after recent events. "Captain Smythe has been very generous. *Boundless* is straining at the seams to hold all of the supplies and fuel cells we have aboard, and the Dancers are now discussing sup-plying us with fresh vegetables and fruit to augment those we can grow in our hydroponic spaces. We'll be fine for a long time. That's not to say we won't be grateful whenever supply ships arrive with news from the Alliance."

IT was almost time. Geary sat in his stateroom, gazing at the display over his desk that showed a wide region of space, the stars themselves obliv-ious to the shadings that defined those vast expanses claimed and oc-cupied by various species. Most of what little was known about those other species was still due to the star chart provided by the Dancers. He looked at the stars controlled by the Taon, wishing he'd had another opportunity to speak with Lokaa. Far out beyond lay the stars where the Wooareek lived, likely able to conquer or wipe out humanity in short order, but apparently uninterested in anything but "peace to all" and eager to trade with humanity.

There were others out there, known only by the different colors shad-ing the star chart, their names, their appearance, and everything else about them mysteries yet to be solved.

Sometimes he felt tired, overburdened by responsibilities, weary of decisions upon which lives rested. But then he saw something like this, something that spoke of all there was yet to know and discover and explore, and something deep inside him stirred with eagerness and enthusiasm to learn just one more thing.

Maybe that was what it was to be human. Or maybe all intelligent species shared that urge in one way or another.

Another thing yet to be discovered.

He was about to head for the bridge when Desjani stopped by.

"I thought I'd escort you to the bridge, Admiral," she said, standing just inside the doorway.

"Thank you," Geary said. "I guess everyone is eager to get going."

"Get going, yes. It might not be so much fun when we get there. You do realize that when we reach home that whole *Fortuna* thing is going to hit the fan. Rich people aren't supposed to die when they do stupid things."

He shrugged. "We have records of everything. If anyone can figure out something we should have done better, should have done differently, they're welcome to try. I'm not looking forward to the fallout from that, but what's the worst that can happen? I've got a house on Glenlyon waiting for me if the Alliance decides I'm too much trouble."

"Waiting for us, you mean."

He studied her doubtfully. "You'd leave *Dauntless*?"

It was her turn to shrug it off. "It doesn't matter how good I am at this job. Sooner or later they're going to succeed in getting me replaced as commanding officer. I figure that will happen about three milliseconds after you retire."

"Probably," Geary agreed. "You didn't mention that the Syndics are likely raising hell about their flotilla being destroyed, despite the evidence showing we had no alternative, and the Syndics we managed to save."

"Many of whom, like the people from the *Fortuna*, are still temporarily insane," Desjani pointed out. "And then there's the big thing."

Geary nodded again, trying to look unconcerned. "The Article 16 thing."

"There's a chance those orders were legitimate."

"A very small chance," Geary said. "And, even if that proves to be true, I don't regret questioning them. I've said if we get back and the orders prove to be real, I'll resign, and I will."

She laughed. "After what you did here? After you stood against four battle cruisers, facing them down with nothing but your spirit and your stubbornness? When that gets around, Black Jack will be more untouchable than ever."

"I am *not* Black Jack," he said. How many times had he said that since being awakened from survival sleep?

"Yes and no," she replied, surprising him. "One time when Rione and I were exchanging words—and don't look at me like that, yes, sometimes we talked to each other—she said to me, 'No, he's not Black Jack, he's who Black Jack should have been.' I hated it when she said that because I always hated it when she said something I had to agree with. No, you're not that 'perfect hero' the Alliance dreamed up to inspire us all. I realize that guy would've destroyed this fleet and the Alliance a hundred times over by now. You're who he should have been. The living stars saved the Alliance by making you who we needed, not who we thought we needed. Argue that all you want. It won't change any minds."

He couldn't help laughing. "I think I've learned better than to try arguing with you. Though I . . . never mind. I'll never see him in the mirror."

"That's one reason why you're him."

"Fine."

"And," she added, "if you do resign, I'll be right behind you. I liked that house on Glenlyon."

"Yeah," Geary said, smiling at the memories of their brief time together there. "Maybe even if the Article 16 stuff, and the *Fortuna* stuff, and all the other stuff, pans out okay, the Alliance will still want to put me out to pasture. What else can they ask me to do?"

"Did you actually say that?" she demanded. "Tell me you didn't just wave a big red flag at fate that way."

"Sorry," Geary said.

"There are still those medal-happy, racial-purist jerks on the other side of Sol and Old Earth. What if the Alliance wants you to try to talk to them?" She paused, thinking. "Although there would be a simple solution to dealing with those guys."

Geary closed his eyes. "Please don't say we could just kill them all."

"All right, I won't say it. But it is the simple solution. And, quite frankly, the galaxy would be better off without people like that."

He decided it was time to change the subject. "Regardless of what happens when we get back, I'm sure you'll be happy to leave here."

"Yes and no. There's still so much we don't know about the Dancers," Desjani said. "One thing that I'd especially like to know is what those things were in the street."

"During the night?" Geary said. "One of the biologists on *Boundless* has a theory about that, linked to the fact that we never saw any young Dancers. She thinks the Dancer young might go through a larval stage that is significantly different than their adult form."

"Seriously? The Dancers warned us not to go out, meaning those were dangerous, whatever they are." Desjani shuddered. "I guess when it comes to things to complain about in kids, stuff like their music and disrespect come in well below a monstrous larval stage."

"It would help put young humans into perspective," Geary agreed, standing up. "Let's go to the bridge, Captain."

As they walked, Geary wondered what had been happening in the Alliance, and at Unity Star System, in his absence. How had the debates and investigations in the Senate gone? Could those orders General Julian had brought possibly have been real?

He took his fleet command seat on the bridge, gazing at his display where the ships of the fleet were spread out in the immense box formation. *Boundless* was still close but had already begun to move away into a far but still closer orbit of the Dancer-occupied planet.

"I just realized something," Desjani said.

"What's that, Captain?"

"Even though *Boundless* is staying and *Mistral* is already back home, this is still the first time we're coming back with more ships than we started out with. Congratulations, Admiral."

He laughed. "That is a nice thing."

"Admiral, you have an incoming call from Ambassador Rycerz."

He accepted the call, seeing Rycerz seated at her desk in her office aboard *Boundless*. The ambassador was still beaming, riding the high from the unexpected breakthrough. "I wanted to say a last goodbye, Admiral. I guess we showed them, didn't we?"

He knew she was referring to those who'd tried to set this mission up for failure. "We showed them. Good luck. I can't even imagine all you still have to work out with the Dancers."

"There's still a lot to determine," Rycerz said. "I didn't totally write off your speculations that knowledge about other species is a form of currency among aliens. We'll have to see about exploring that possibility now that our very basic goals have been achieved. The things we can learn! Our physical frontiers may be getting closed down by contacts with other species, but our frontiers of knowledge have grown enormously."

"I was just thinking the same thing a short time ago," Geary said. "A lot of people are particularly going to want some of the knowledge the Wooareek have."

"And I have no doubt the Wooareek are smart enough not to give it to us. Can you imagine what would happen if technology like that was dumped in our lap?"

"The enigmas have a habit of dropping disruptive, double-edged technology in our lap," Geary pointed out.

"If that isn't a cautionary example, I don't know what is." Rycerz paused, her eyes looking somewhere only she could see. "If the Wooareek are truly ethical aliens, maybe humanity will end up learning something from them that is far more important than whatever technological secrets the Wooareek have."

"That would be huge," Geary agreed.

"In addition to the proposal for the mosaic force for humanity to start debating, your ships are carrying my report to the government back to the Alliance. I wanted to be sure you knew it fully endorses your actions. And I wanted to be sure you knew I am grateful for all the times you could have used your power to run roughshod over me, and didn't. This really was a team effort. We're going to face immense challenges in the future with the aliens we've already met and those we've yet to meet, but I think we're off to a good start." Ambassador Rycerz waved. "May you have a safe journey home, Admiral. I hope we meet again someday."

"Thank you, Ambassador," Geary said, smiling and waving back. "May the light of the living stars shine on you and the tasks ahead of you."

The call ended, he looked around the bridge, seeing everyone watching him. Checking the display, he confirmed that the Dancer ships which would escort his fleet through the Dancer hypernet were waiting ahead of the fleet.

"All units in the Alliance fleet, this is Admiral Geary. Immediate execute, accelerate to point zero five light speed."

ACKNOWLEDGMENTS

I remain indebted to my agent, Joshua Bilmes, for his ever-inspired suggestions and assistance, and to my editor, Anne Sowards, for her support and editing. Thanks also to Robert Chase, Kelly Dwyer, Carolyn Ives Gilman, J. G. (Huck) Huckenpohler, Simcha Kuritzky, Michael LaViolette, the spirit of Aly Parsons, Bud Sparhawk, Mary Thompson, and Constance A. Warner for their suggestions, comments, and recommendations.